THE HOUSE AT SEA'S END

BOOKS BY ELLY GRIFFITHS

The Crossing Places
The Janus Stone
The House at Sea's End

THE HOUSE AT SEA'S END

A RUTH GALLOWAY MYSTERY

Elly Griffiths

MARINER BOOKS
HOUGHTON MIFFLIN HARCOURT
BOSTON • NEW YORK

First Mariner Books edition 2012

Copyright © 2011 by Elly Griffiths
Map copyright © Raymond Turvey

www.hmhco.com

First published in Great Britain in 2011 by Quercus

Library of Congress Cataloging-in-Publication Data
Griffiths, Elly.
The house at sea's end / Elly Griffiths.—1st U.S. ed.
p. cm.
"First published in Great Britain in 2011 by Quercus"—T.p. verso.
ISBN 978-0-547-50614-2 (hardback)   ISBN 978-0-547-84417-6 (pbk.)
1. Galloway, Ruth (Fictitious character)—Fiction. 2. Women forensic
anthropologists—Fiction. 3. Veterans—Crimes against—Fiction.
4. Norfolk (England)—Fiction. 5. Germans—Great Britain—Fiction. I. Title.
PR6107.R534H68 2012
823'.92—dc22
2011029652

Printed in the United States of America
DOC 10 9 8 7 6
4500740944

For Gabriella, who also avoided Halloween.

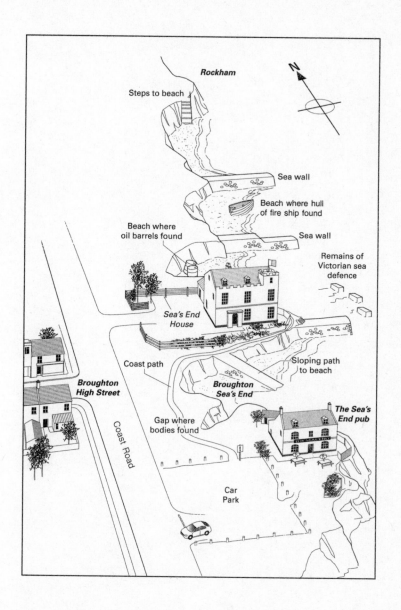

Rockham

Steps to beach

N

Sea wall

Beach where hull
of fire ship found

Beach where
oil barrels found

Sea wall

Remains of
Victorian sea
defence

Sea's End
House

Coast path

Sloping path
to beach

Broughton
High Street

Broughton
Sea's End

The Sea's
End pub

Gap where
bodies found

Coast Road

THE SEA'S END

Car
Park

PROLOGUE

November

Two people, a man and a woman, are walking along a hospital corridor. It is obvious that they have been here before. The woman's face is soft, remembering; the man looks wary, holding back slightly at the entrance to the ward. Indeed, the list of restrictions printed on the door looks enough to frighten anyone. No flowers, no phones, no children under eight, no coughers or sneezers. The woman points at the phone sign (a firmly crossed out silhouette of a rather dated-looking phone) but the man just shrugs. The woman smiles, as if she is used to getting this sort of response from him.

They press a buzzer and are admitted.

Three beds in, they stop. A brown-haired woman is sitting up in bed holding a baby. She is not feeding it, she is just looking at it, staring, as if she is trying to memorise every feature. The visiting woman, who is blonde and attractive, swoops down and kisses the new mother. Then she bends over the baby, brushing it with her hair. The baby opens opaque dark eyes but doesn't cry. The man hovers in the background and the blonde woman gestures for him to come closer. He doesn't kiss mother or baby but he says something which makes both women laugh indulgently.

The baby's sex is easy to guess: the bed is surrounded by pink cards and rosettes, even a slightly deflated balloon announcing 'It's a girl'. The baby herself, though, is dressed in navy blue as if the mother is taking an early stand against such stereotyping. The blonde woman holds the baby, who stares at her with those dark, solemn eyes. The brown-haired woman looks at the man, and looks away again quickly.

When visiting time is over, the blonde woman leaves presents and kisses and one last caress of the baby's head. The man stands at the foot of the bed, pawing the ground slightly as if impatient to be off. The mother smiles, cradling her baby in an ageless gesture of serene maternity.

At the door, the blonde woman turns and waves. The man has already left.

But five minutes later he is back, alone, walking fast, almost running. He comes to a halt by the bed. Wordlessly, the woman puts the baby into his arms. She is crying, though the baby is still silent.

'She looks like you,' she whispers.

1

March

The tide is out. In the early evening light, the sands stretch into the distance, bands of yellow and grey and gold. The water in the rock pools reflects a pale blue sky. Three men and a woman walk slowly over the beach, occasionally stooping and looking intently at the ground, taking samples and photographs. One of the men holds something that looks rather like a staff, which he plants into the sand at regular intervals. They pass a lighthouse marooned on a rock, its jaunty red and white paint peeling, and a beach where a recent rock fall means that they have to wade in the sea, splashing through the shallow water. Now the coastline has transformed into a series of little coves which appear to have been eaten out of the soft, sandstone cliff. Their progress slows when they have to clamber over rocks slippery with seaweed and the remains of old sea walls. One of the men falls into the water and the other men laugh, the sound echoing in the still evening air. The woman trudges on ahead, not looking back.

Eventually they reach a spot where the cliff juts out into the sea, forming a bleak headland. The land curves away sharply, leaving a v-shaped inlet where the tide seems to be moving particularly fast. White-topped waves race towards jagged rocks and the seagulls are calling wildly. High up, on the furthest point of the cliff, is a grey stone house, faintly gothic in style, with battlements and a curved tower facing out to sea. A Union Jack is flying from the tower.

'Sea's End House,' says one of the men, stopping to rest his back.

'Doesn't that MP live there?' asks another.

The woman has stopped at the far side of the bay and is looking across at the house. The battlements are dark grey, almost black, in the fading light.

'Jack Hastings,' she says. 'He's an MEP.'

Although the woman is the youngest of the four and has a distinctly alternative look – purple spiky hair, piercings and an army surplus jacket – the others seem to treat her with respect. Now one of the men says, almost pleadingly, 'Don't you think we should knock off, Trace?'

The man holding the staff, a bald giant known as Irish Ted, adds, 'There's a good pub here. The Sea's End.'

The other men stifle smiles. Ted is famous for knowing every pub in Norfolk, no mean feat in a county reputed to have a pub for every day of the year.

'Let's just walk this beach,' says Trace, getting out a camera. 'We can take some GPS readings.'

'Erosion's bad here,' says Ted. 'I've been reading about it. Sea's End House has been declared unsafe. Jack Hastings is in a right old two and eight. Keeps ranting on about an Englishman's home being his castle.'

They all look up at the grey house on the cliff. The curved wall of the tower is only two or three feet from the precipice. The remains of a fence hang crazily in midair.

'There was a whole garden at the back of the house once. Summer house, the lot,' says Craig, one of the men. 'My granddad used to do the gardening.'

'Beach has silted up too,' says Trace. 'That big storm in February has shifted a lot of stone.'

They all look towards the narrow beach. Below the cliffs, banks of pebbles form a shelf which then falls steeply into the sea. It's an inhospitable place, hard to imagine families picnicking here, children with buckets and spades, sunbathing adults.

'Looks like a cliff fall,' says Ted.

'Maybe,' says Trace. 'Let's get some readings anyway.'

She leads the way along the beach, keeping to the edge of the cliff. A sloping path leads from Sea's End House down to the sea and fishing boats are moored higher up, above the tide line, but the sea is coming in fast.

'There's no way off the beach this side,' says the man whose grandfather was a gardener. 'We don't want to get cut off.'

'It's shallow enough,' says Trace. 'We can wade.'

'The current's treacherous here,' warns Ted. 'We'd better head straight for the pub.'

Trace ignores him; she is photographing the cliff face, the lines of grey and black with the occasional shocking stripe of red. Ted plunges his staff into the ground and takes a GPS reading. The third man, whose name is Steve, wanders over to a point where a fissure in the cliff has created a deep ravine. The mouth of the ravine is filled up with stones, probably from a rock fall. Steve starts to climb over the rubble, his boots slipping on the loose stones.

'Careful,' says Trace, not looking round.

The sea is louder now, thundering in towards land, and the sea birds are returning to their nests, high up in the cliffs.

'We'd better head back,' says Ted again, but Steve calls from the cliff face.

'Hey, look at this!'

They walk over to him. Steve has made a gap in the pile of rubble and is crouching in the cave-like space behind. It's a deep recess, almost an alleyway, the cliffs looming above, dark and oppressive. Steve has shifted some of the larger stones and is leaning over something that lies half-exposed in the sandy soil.

'What is it?'

'Looks like a human arm,' says Ted matter-of-factly.

Detective Sergeant David Clough is eating. Nothing new in that. Clough eats almost constantly throughout the working day, starting with a McDonald's breakfast, moving on through several Mars Bars and a Pot Noodle for lunch, through a sustaining sandwich and cake at tea time before treating himself to a pint and a curry for supper. Despite this, Clough's waistline is admirably trim, a fact he attributes to 'football and shagging'. Recently, though, he has acquired a girlfriend, which has cut down on at least one of these activities.

Clough has had a trying day. His boss is on holiday and Clough was secretly hoping that this would be the week when a serial killer stalked Norfolk and was caught personally by super-policeman David, soon to be Sir, Clough. But, instead, he has had two break-ins, one taking and driving away and one old dear found dead on a stairlift. It's not exactly *Miami Vice*.

His phone rings, blasting out an irritating jingle from *The Simpsons*.

'Trace! Hi, babe.'

Detective Sergeant Judy Johnson, who is (under protest) sharing a desk with Clough, makes gagging motions. Clough ignores her, ingesting the last of his blueberry muffin.

'Dave, you'd better come,' says Trace. 'We've found some bones.'

Clough leaps into action, grabs his phone and dives for the door, yelling for Judy to follow him. The effect is slightly ruined by the fact that he has forgotten his car keys and has to come back for them. Judy is still sitting at the desk, stony faced.

'What do you mean "follow me"? You don't outrank me.'

Clough sighs. It's typical of Judy to raise objections and ruin their only chance of action this week. Ever since she was promoted last year she's been getting above herself, in Clough's opinion. Okay, she's a good enough cop but she's always picking him up on detail – a piece of paperwork left undone, a date missed, a phone call unrecorded – paperwork never solved a crime, Clough tells her in his head, though not in person; Judy is fairly formidable.

Now he tries to fix his face into an imitation of the boss at his most impatient.

'Human bones found at Broughton Sea's End. We'd better get going pronto.'

Still Judy doesn't move.

'Where were they found? Exactly?'

Clough doesn't know. He was too busy swinging into action to ask questions. He glowers.

'Was that Trace on the phone? Did she find them?'

'Yeah. She's doing some sort of survey of the cliffs and what have you.'

'An archaeological survey?'

'I don't know. All I know is they've found some bones, human remains. Are you coming or are you going to ask questions all day?'

Sure enough, by the time that they arrive at Broughton Sea's End, the tide is coming in and it's too dangerous to go down onto the beach. Clough shoots Judy a reproachful look which she ignores completely.

Trace and Steve are waiting for them at the top of the cliff, near the entrance to Sea's End House. The sea has reached the bottom of the sloping path, the waves breaking with a smack against the stone. On the far side of the cove, the cliffs rise up, dark and straight, cut off now by the tide.

'You were a long time,' Trace greets Clough. 'Ted and Craig have gone to the pub.'

'Irish Ted?' says Clough. 'He's always in the pub.'

Judy gets out her notebook and double checks the time before writing it down. Clough is finding her incredibly irritating.

'Where exactly did you find the bones?' she asks.

'There's a gap in the cliff,' says Steve. 'A sort of ravine.' He's a wiry weather-beaten man with grey hair in a pony-tail. Typical archaeologist, thinks Clough.

'How did you find them?' asks Judy.

'I was investigating a rock fall. I moved some of the bigger stones and there they were, underneath. The soil was prob-ably dislodged by the landslide.'

'Are they above the tide line?' asks Judy. Across the bay, the first waves are breaking against the foot of the cliffs.

'At present we think they're protected by the debris from the rock fall,' says Trace.

'Spring tide though,' says Steve. 'It'll be a high one.'

'If we clear away the rocks and dig a trench,' says Trace, 'the sea'll get them for sure.'

They watch as the water advances, incredibly quickly now, joining rock pools together, submerging the sea walls, turning the little bay into a churning pool of white.

Trace looks at her watch. She hasn't made eye-contact with Clough since he arrived; he doesn't know if she is pissed off with him for being late or just in professional, archaeologist mode. It's a new departure for him, going out with a career girl, much less a girl with punk hair and a pierced tongue who wears Doc Martens. They met when Trace was involved with another case involving archaeologists and buried bones. Clough remembers how strongly he felt drawn to Trace from the very first when he saw her digging, her thin arms quilted with muscles. Even now he still finds the muscles (and the piercing) incredibly sexy. For his part, he just hopes that the six-pack compensates for the fact that he hasn't read a book since he got stuck halfway through *Of Mice and Men* for O-Level English.

'Are you sure they were human bones?' Judy is asking.

'Pretty sure,' says Trace. She shivers slightly. The sun has gone in and the wind is rising.

'How old?'

'I don't know. We'd need Ruth Galloway to have a look.'

Trace, Clough and Judy exchange looks. They all have their own memories of Ruth Galloway. Only Steve does not react to the name. 'Isn't she the forensics girl? I thought she'd left.'

'She was on maternity leave,' says Judy. 'I think she's back at work now.'

'Should be at home looking after her kiddie,' says Clough, rather ill-advisedly.

'She's a single mother,' snaps Trace. 'Presumably she needs the money.'

'How did you come to be on the beach?' asks Judy hastily.

'We're doing a survey for the university on coastal erosion. We're surveying all the north-east Norfolk beaches. We've made some interesting finds as well. Palaeolithic hand axe at Titchwell, a Roman bracelet at Burgh Castle, lots of ship-wrecks. Steve was examining the cliffs here when he saw the rockfall. The bones were in the gap behind. It looks like they were buried fairly deeply but the earth got dislodged when the stones came down.'

'How come you're discovering these things?' asks Judy,

as they walk back along the cliff path. 'If the sea's advancing, wouldn't it cover everything up?'

Clough is glad she has asked this. He'd wanted to but was scared of looking stupid in front of Trace.

'Tides change,' says Trace shortly. 'Sand gets moved; parts get silted up, other parts uncovered. The pebbles get pushed further up the beach. Things that were buried become exposed.'

'Like our bones,' says Steve. 'They may have been buried well above the tidal line but the water's getting closer, it's wearing the earth away. Then part of the cliff came down on top of them.'

'Did you get a good look at them?' asks Clough.

'Not really,' says Steve. 'Tide was coming in too fast. We didn't want to get stranded on the wrong side of the beach. But, just at a glance, I'd say we were looking at more than one body.'

Clough and Judy exchange glances. 'Definitely human?'

'In my humble opinion, yes.'

'We found something else too,' says Trace, whose opinions are never humble.

They have reached the pub. Its sign, which, rather tactlessly, shows a man falling off a cliff, creaks in the gathering wind. They can see Ted through the window, raising a pint to his lips. In the yellow light from the window, Trace holds out something that looks a bit like loft insulation, a small ball of fluffy, yellowish fibres.

'What is it?' asks Judy.

'Cotton wool?' suggests Clough.

'Whiffs a bit,' says Steve. There is, indeed, a strong sulphuric smell coming from the material.

'Fantastic,' Clough rubs his hands together. 'The boss is going to love this.'

'Where is Nelson anyway?' says Trace.

'On holiday,' says Clough. 'Back on Monday. He'll be counting the days.'

Judy laughs. Nelson's dislike of holidays is a byword at the station.

2

Detective Chief Inspector Harry Nelson is sitting by a pool with a glass of beer in his hand, thinking dark thoughts. It is evening and fairy lights, strung in the trees, are twinkling manically in the still water. Nelson's wife Michelle is sitting beside him, but she is carrying on an intense discussion about highlights with the woman at the next table and has her back turned. Michelle is a hairdresser so this is her area of expertise, and Nelson knows better than to expect a pause in the monologue. His own area of expertise – murder – is less likely to prove a promising starting point for conversation.

When Nelson informed Michelle that he had a week's holiday still owing, she suggested that they go somewhere 'just the two of us'. At the time, he had quite liked the sound of this. Their eldest daughter, Laura, had left for university in September and their seventeen-year-old, Rebecca, was unlikely to want to spend an entire week with her parents. 'Besides,' said Michelle, 'she won't want to miss school.'

Nelson had grunted sceptically. Rebecca hardly ever

seemed to go to school, her life as a sixth-former apparently consisting entirely of mysterious 'free periods' and even more mysterious 'field trips'. Even her A-Level subjects are incomprehensible to Nelson. Psychology, Media Studies and Environmental Science. Psychology? He's seen enough of that at work. Every so often his boss, Gerry Whitcliffe, will wheel out some weedy psychologist to give him an 'offender profile'. The upshot of this always seems to be that they are looking for an inadequate loner who likes hurting people. Well, thanks and all that, but Nelson reckoned he could have worked that out for himself, with no qualifications except a lifetime in the police force and an O level in metalwork. Media Studies seemed to be another name for watching TV, and what the hell was Environmental Science when it was at home? It's about climate change, Michelle had said knowledgeably, but she couldn't fool him. They had both left school at sixteen; as far as higher education was concerned, their children had entered a different world.

Nelson had fancied Scotland, or even Norway, but he had to use up his week before the end of March and Michelle wanted sun. If you don't go for long haul, the only sun in March seemed to be in the Canary Islands, so Michelle had booked them a week's full board in a four star hotel in Lanzarote.

The hotel was nice enough and the island had a strange ash-grey charm of its own, but for Nelson the week was purgatory. On the first night, Michelle had struck up a conversation with another couple, Lisa and Ken from Farnborough. Within ten minutes, Nelson had learnt all he had ever wanted to know about Ken's job as an IT consultant or Lisa's as a beautician. He learnt that they had two children, teenagers, currently staying with Lisa's parents (Stan and Evelyn), that they preferred Chinese takeaways to Indian and considered George Michael to be a great all-round entertainer. He learnt that Lisa was allergic to avocados and that Ken had Irritable Bowel Syndrome. He learnt that Lisa went to Salsa on Wednesdays and that Ken had a golf handicap of thirteen.

'How many children do you have?' Lisa had asked Nelson, fixing him with an intense short-sighted stare.

'Three,' said Nelson shortly. 'Three daughters.'

'Harry!' Michelle leant forward, gold necklaces jangling. 'We've got *two* daughters, Lisa. He'll forget his own name next.'

'Sorry.' Nelson turned back to his prawn cocktail. 'Two girls, nineteen and seventeen.'

Only once, in the course of the evening, did the conversation falter and die.

'What do you do for a living, Harry?' asked Ken.

'I'm a policeman,' answered Nelson, stabbing ferociously at his steak.

'Thank God,' said Nelson to Michelle when they got back to their room. 'We'll never have to talk to those God-awful people again.'

'What do you mean?' asked Michelle, wrapping herself in a towel and heading for the shower.

Nelson hesitated before answering; he didn't want to piss her off too much as he was counting on first-night-of-the-holiday sex. 'Well, we haven't got a lot in common with them, have we?'

'I liked them,' said Michelle, turning on the water. 'I've asked them to join us for crazy golf tomorrow.'

And that was it. They played golf with Lisa and Ken, they went sightseeing together, in the evenings they ate at adjoining tables and once, in a night of unparalleled awfulness, they had visited a karaoke bar. Hell, muses Nelson as he sits listening to the relative merits of gold versus red with a hint of honey, can hold nothing worse than singing 'Wonderwall' in a duet with a computer programmer from Farnborough.

'We must get together another time,' Ken is saying now, leaning towards Nelson. 'Lees and I were thinking of Florida next year.'

'We've been to Disneyland Florida,' says Michelle, 'when the girls were younger. It was great, wasn't it Harry?'

'Grand.'

'Well, time to go again without the kids,' says Ken. 'Why should they have all the fun eh?'

Nelson regards him stonily. 'Harry's a real workaholic,' says Michelle. 'It's hard to get him to relax.'

'Must be a stressful job, being a policeman,' says Lisa. She'd said the same thing, with variations, whenever his job was mentioned.

'You could say that,' says Nelson.

'Harry's had a tough year,' says Michelle, in a sympathetic undertone.

You could say that, too, thinks Nelson, as they finally leave the poolside restaurant and repair to the lounge for coffee. Last year had produced two child-killers, at least three madmen and a curious relationship, the like of which he had never known before. Thinking about this relationship, Nelson stands up suddenly. 'Going to stretch my legs,' he explains. 'Might give Rebecca a quick call too.' Mobile phone reception is better in the open air.

Outside, Nelson walks around the pool twice, thinking of crimes with which he could charge Ken. Then he retreats into the darkness of the 'Italian Terrace', a rather desolate area full of empty urns and artistically broken columns.

He clicks onto Names and scrolls down the Rs.

'Hallo,' he says at last. 'How are you doing?'

Dr Ruth Galloway is, in fact, doing rather badly. Phil, her Head of Department at the University of North Norfolk (UNN), had insisted on holding a planning meeting at five o'clock. As a result, Ruth was late at the childminder's for the third time that week. As she screeches to a halt in front of the terraced house in King's Lynn, she can't help thinking that her name is now on some mysterious black-list of Bad Mothers. The childminder, a comfortable older woman called Sandra, found after much exhaustive inter-viewing and reference checking, is understanding. 'Doesn't matter, love. I know how it is when you're working,' but Ruth still feels guilty. She never knows quite how to talk to Sandra. She's not exactly a friend but she's not a student or another academic either. She once heard one of the other mothers (Sandra looks after two other children) having a chat with Sandra in her kitchen, all about her husband and his untidiness, about her other children refusing to do their homework or eat their greens. It sounded so friendly and comfortable, Ruth longed to join in. But she doesn't have a husband or any other children. And her job as a forensic archaeologist, specialising in long-dead bones, is hardly conducive to cosy kitchen chats.

As soon as four-month-old Kate sees Ruth, she starts to cry.

'That always happens,' says Sandra. 'It's relief at seeing Mum again.'

But as Ruth struggles to get Kate into her car seat, she can't detect any relief or even affection in her crying. If anything, she just sounds plain angry.

Kate was a big baby. Long rather than heavy. 'Is your partner tall?' one of the midwives had asked, putting the red-faced bundle into Ruth's arms. Ruth was saved from having to answer by the arrival of her parents, hot-foot from Eltham, bearing flowers and a copy of *Baby's First Bible Stories*. Her mother was meant to have been with her during the birth but contractions had started during a Halloween party hosted by Ruth's friend and sometime druid, Cathbad.

Cathbad, wearing white robes to honour the good spirits, had accompanied Ruth to hospital. 'First babies take ages,' he had assured her. 'How do you know?' Ruth had shouted, rent by pain which seemed both unbearable and continuous. 'I have had a daughter,' said Cathbad with dignity. 'You didn't have her,' Ruth yelled, 'your girlfriend did.' Cathbad had ignored Ruth's yelling, swearing, and assertions that she hated all men and him in particular. He had scattered herbs on her, walked around the bed muttering incantations, and finally had just held her hand.

'She'll be hours yet,' said the midwives cheerfully. But Kate had been born at ten minutes past midnight, thus avoiding Halloween and arriving in time for All Saints' Day.

'I don't hold with all that Catholic nonsense,' said her mother, when Ruth informed her of this fact. Ruth's parents were both Born Again Christians and considered that they alone of all denominations knew The Truth – a delusion which, as Ruth could have told them, they probably shared with every religious cult since the Assyrians first started burying bits of pottery alongside their ancestors, just to be on the safe side.

When Ruth had looked down at her daughter's furious little face, she had been surprised by a rush of recognition. Whatever she had expected, it wasn't this. The books had talked about Mother Love, about euphoria and joyfulness and feeding on demand. Ruth was too exhausted to feel euphoric. She wasn't even sure if, at that moment, what she felt was love. All she felt was that she knew her baby: she wasn't a stranger, she was Ruth's daughter. That feeling carried her through the agonies of breast-feeding (nothing like the bucolic descriptions in the book), through the loneliness that engulfed her as soon as her parents had left, through the sleepless nights and zombie-like days that followed. She knew her baby. They were in this thing together.

Her mother had been pleased with the choice of name. 'Short for Catherine, just like your Auntie Catherine in Thornton Heath'. 'It's not short for anything,' Ruth had retorted, but she found that, increasingly, when she spoke, people tended not to hear. This was a shock for Ruth, who has been a university lecturer for all her working life. People used to pay to listen to her. Now, unless she was talking specifically about the baby, her mouth simply opened and shut like one of those nodding dogs in cars.

Cathbad had also liked the name. 'After Hecate, the witch goddess. Very powerful magic.' Her friend Max, an expert in Roman History, had made the same point. 'Hecate was sometimes called the child nurse, you know.' Ruth did know, but Kate was not named after Hecate or Auntie Catherine or Santa Caterina of Siena (suggested by a Catholic priest of Ruth's acquaintance). She was simply Kate because Ruth liked the name. It was attractive without being twee, strong without being hard. You could hear it prefaced by Doctor or followed by MP. At the same time it was cute enough for a baby.

The future Dr Kate Galloway continues to yell in the back seat as Ruth makes for home. She lives outside King's Lynn, on the North Norfolk coast, not in one of the many picturesque seaside resorts but in an isolated cottage facing a desolate but beautiful stretch of land known as the Saltmarsh. 'You won't be staying in that awful house after you have the baby, will you?' her mother had asked. 'Why not?' Ruth had answered.

She loves the house, loves the view that stretches over the marshes into nothingness, loves the expanse of sky and the sound of the sea, loves the birds that darken the evening sky, their wings turned to pink by the setting sun. But she has to admit that the winter was hard. She spent Christmas with her parents in south London and was only too glad to leave, having had enough of praying before meals and listening to her sister-in-law talk about calories. But when she and Kate were finally home, alone in the little house with the wind roaring in from the sea, she had felt a slight but none the less real stab of fear. They were on their own; they truly were in this thing together. Ruth's cottage is one of three but one house is empty and the other is owned by weekenders who visit less and less often now that their children have grown up. Her nearest neighbours are in the village, a mile away along a dark, exposed road raised up over the flat marshland, and the houses were mostly boarded up for the winter.

Throughout the whole of that January, Ruth and Kate scarcely left the house. Ruth was sustained by Radio 4 (the two episodes of *The Archers* were oases of delight in her day) and by watching Kate. She hadn't realised that a baby would change day by day. One day Kate could smile – she mostly smiled at Ruth's cat, Flint – the next gurgle, and on one joyous occasion she slept through the night. Soon she was greeting her mother with a whole-body wriggle and delighted waving of the legs. This probably saved Ruth's sanity.

When, in February, Cathbad arrived to celebrate Imbolc, the coming of Spring (slightly premature as there was still snow on the ground), he astounded Ruth by asking her when she was going to return to work. Her hermit-like existence had become her only reality; her world had shrunk to four walls and a computer screen. But when Cathbad mentioned work she realised how much she missed it. She missed her students and her colleagues but most of all she missed the archaeology, the painstaking sifting of evidence, the age-old puzzles of bones and soil, the delight in discovery.

Leaving Kate with her friend Shona, who seemed to have bought the whole of Toys R Us for the occasion, she went to see Phil. Then she came home, ordered some work clothes on-line (her pre-baby clothes had become mysteriously tight) and set about weaning Kate onto a bottle. This last task proved so difficult and emotional that it severely tested Ruth's new-found resolve. But she persevered, and by early March she was back at work.

For years Ruth has been a fan of *Woman's Hour* but it is only now that she begins to see the point of all those features about 'juggling' and the impossibility of 'having it all'. With a little application, it was perfectly possible to put adequate childcare provisions in place. What she hadn't bargained for were the emotions. She felt terrible about leaving Kate, yet when she entered her office for the first time, her own office with her name on the door, she felt a relief so strong that she almost cried (and Ruth doesn't, on the whole, do tears). If she is late to pick up Kate, she feels guilty of almost every crime against humanity. She longs to be with her baby, but when she is she's assailed by a feeling almost of panic. Will she ever escape or will she be trapped in the mother world forever?

Now, she parks her rusty car outside her cottage. The security light comes on, illuminating the overgrown garden and the scrub bushes blown flat by the wind. Kate has fallen asleep and, though this means she probably now won't sleep again before midnight, Ruth is grateful. She carries the car seat into the house and places it in the middle of the sitting room. Flint comes up and sniffs Kate's face. Ruth carries him away. Her mother is full of stories about cats sitting on babies and suffocating them but Flint's attitude so far has been one of detached friendliness and Ruth relies too much on his companionship to suspect him of sinister motives. She feeds him, makes tea and toast for herself and prepares to enjoy an hour's peace.

The phone rings as soon as she has sat down. It is Nelson.

'Hallo. How are you doing?'

'I'm fine. Where are you ringing from? Are you back?'

A hollow laugh. 'No, I'm still here in bloody Lanzarote listening to the most boring man in the world talk about hard drives.'

'Sounds like fun.'

'You've no idea.'

There is an expensive international pause.

'How's Katie?'

'Kate.'

Impatient grunt. 'Is she okay?'

'She's fine. She's sleeping.' From where she is sitting Ruth can see Kate's little chest rising and falling. Though she no longer checks every ten minutes to see if her daughter is breathing, she still does it every hour.

'How's the childminder? Working out all right?'

'Jesus. You ran a police check on her. Twice.'

'Things can get past those checks.'

'She's fine. Not a murderer or a child molester. Fine.'

There is another silence while they both think of people who turned out to be not quite what they seemed. Ruth has assisted the police on two murder cases, both involving children.

'I'll be home tomorrow.'

But Ruth knows that home does not mean home to her.

'It's very cold in Norfolk,' she says, dampeningly.

'Christ Almighty. It's always cold in bloody Norfolk.'

He rings off and Ruth sits on the sofa thinking complicated and uncomfortable thoughts. When Trace rings and tell her that they have discovered a mass grave at Broughton Sea's End, it's a relief as much as anything.

3

The next day is Saturday, and at low tide Ruth, Ted and Trace walk along the beach to Broughton Sea's End. Kate has been left with Sandra for the morning. 'It's no trouble,' said Sandra but Ruth feels that it is. Weekdays are all right because that is the arrangement but weekends are an imposition. Ruth also has an absolute dread of asking for favours. She hates ringing up and saying, in that special wheedling voice, 'Can I ask . . . would you mind . . . you've saved my life . . . you're a star.' She'd rather cut the crap and do the thing herself but, as she's finding out, being a working mother means asking for favours. She stumps across the sand in a bad mood.

It is a grey morning. The mist still lingers inland, but at the edge of the sea the air is cold and clear. It's hard going, walking over pebbles and rocks encrusted with tiny, sharp mussel shells. Ted is almost unforgivably breezy for a man who hasn't had a drink yet. He exclaims at unusual rock formations, finds a piece of fool's gold and a coin, worn completely smooth by the sea. He throws floundering crabs back into the water and writes his name in the sand. Trace walks in silence, occasionally taking notes. Ruth finds this rather irritating but she is grateful not to have to make small talk.

As they round the headland, Sea's End House towers above them, grey against the grey sky. With the rest of the coastline hidden by fog, it seems to float out into the sea like a doomed ocean liner, lights blazing as it heads towards the ice-floe.

'Welcome to the end of the line,' says Ted, with undiminished good humour.

Ruth looks up at the cliffs. The stone is sandy, soft and crumbly at the edges where it has been eaten away in bite-sized chunks. 'Sandstone,' she says.

'Yeah,' Ted agrees. 'Sandstone all along this stretch. That's why erosion's so bad.'

'There was a sea wall,' says Trace, 'but it disappeared years ago. There are the remains, over there.'

They all look out to sea where, about a hundred yards away, two or three large boulders are sticking out of the water like giant stepping stones.

'Trouble is,' says Ted, 'most of the defences were built in Victorian times. The cliffs behind them were too steep. When the walls went, there were no banks or anything to slow the tide down.'

'Should have been fixed,' says Trace. 'Even fifty years ago there would still have been time.'

Ted shrugs. 'It's global warning, innit? Seas are rising and there's nothing we can do about it.' He grins happily as he says this.

Ruth walks towards the cliffs. She can see there has been

a recent rock fall, rubble and stone have spilled out onto the beach and the cliff face is streaked black and grey.

'Round here,' says Ted.

In the furthest, most inaccessible corner of the beach, there is a gap in the cliff, a narrow cleft running from the coarse grass at the top to the beach below. This has been partly filled with rubble from the cliff fall but Ruth can see where some of the debris has been cleared away. She approaches carefully. 'Look first,' her mentor, Erik Anderssen, used to say. 'Look, then plot, then dig. You will never get that first look again.' She takes pictures of the cliffs and the rock fall and draws a map in her notebook. Then with Ted's help she clears away some of the bigger stones. In the narrow space between the two cliff walls, the sand has been worn away, exposing something that looks at first like more stone, smooth and white.

Bones.

Ruth leans forward. She can see at once that there must be several bodies buried here. The bones are piled on top of each other but she can make out at least three thigh bones. Long, sturdy bones, which means the bodies may well be male. There is also a faint smell of rotten eggs. For a moment Ruth feels dizzy, remembering other mass graves, bones white in the sun. She takes a deep breath. She must plot this find, mark where the bodies are lying. 'Sometimes,' Erik used to say, 'the most important thing is the direction.'

'What do you think?' comes Ted's voice.

'There are several bodies here,' says Ruth. 'We need to tell the coroner.'

'Do you think they're recent then?' asks Ted.

'There's a good chance they're recent.'

Ruth thinks that she has seen hair and teeth – signs that the bodies could be fairly modern but, then again, only the year before last she found a perfectly preserved body buried in a peat bog, that turned out to be over two thousand years old. But peat is alkaline, which preserves bone; sand is acidic. Digging on sandy sites, you are unlikely to find human remains because the bones have been eaten away. If these bones, buried in sandy soil, are still in relatively good condition, they may well be modern.

'Dave said he'd tell the coroner on Monday,' says Trace in an off-hand voice.

Ruth looks at her curiously. So it's true that Trace is dating Dave Clough. Rather her than me, she thinks.

'We should do it today,' she argues.

'Isn't the boss man back on Monday?' says Ted. 'Maybe they're waiting for him.'

'He'll be jet-lagged,' says Trace. 'Probably won't be in until Tuesday.'

'He's only in Lanzarote,' says Ruth.

There is a short silence.

Ruth steps over the wall of rubble. The gap between the cliffs is only about a metre wide, getting narrower as it goes back. It is much colder here and the air smells dank. Ruth shivers, and not entirely from the cold. Who would bury bodies here, in this inaccessible spot? She is willing to bet that it wasn't for any good reason. She has her excavation kit with her but she doesn't want to do any digging yet. Just look, says the voice in her head. If Trace is right about the tides, when they clear away the rocks this grave site will be destroyed altogether. All the more reason to make proper notes now. The bodies are lying north to south. She thinks that they are in correct anatomical position, stretched out, back-to-back. Taking her trowel, she scrapes away a little of the sand. There are definitely two bodies below, maybe more.

'How many there?' asks Ted, peering in.

'Not sure. At least four.'

'Four dead bodies, buried fairly recently,' says Ted. 'You'd think somebody would have noticed.'

'Yes,' says Ruth. She has seen something else, though she doesn't want to mention it just yet. The bodies are bound, their hands tied behind their backs.

They can't get a signal from the beach so Ruth, Ted and Trace climb the slope by Sea's End House. Ruth is out of breath by the time they have reached the top. She has got her figure back after having the baby, which is a shame – she was rather hoping to get someone else's. Pre-pregnancy Ruth weighed twelve and a half stone, now she is almost thirteen. On the whole this doesn't bother her. She always wears loose dark clothing and doesn't look in mirrors much. What she doesn't like, though, is feeling so unfit, especially as Trace has bounded up the hill like a gazelle and is now punching numbers into her iPhone.

'Cool,' says Ted, indicating the phone.

'It's useful for work,' says Trace defensively.

Ruth, who has never felt the need to have anything more than the most basic mobile phone, looks at her sceptically.

Though you wouldn't know it to look at her, Trace comes from a very wealthy Norwich family. Most archaeologists' salaries don't run to iPhones.

However, it seems that even the newest technology is not proof against Broughton Sea's End.

'Not a flicker,' says Trace disgustedly.

'Someone's coming,' says Ruth. A man in a waxed jacket is walking purposefully towards them. Two depressed-looking spaniels run at his heels.

'Take cover,' mutters Ted.

But the natives, it seems, are friendly.

'Can I help?' says the man. 'It's impossible to get a signal here. It really is the land that time forgot.' He manages to say this as if he is rather proud of the fact.

'We're archaeologists,' says Trace importantly. 'We need to make an urgent phone call.'

Ruth can almost see the thought bubble rising from the man's head: how can anything to do with archaeology possibly be urgent? Aren't archaeologists to do with the past – long-dead bodies, ancient artefacts, dusty museums? How can they be standing on his driveway, sea-splattered and panting, talking about urgent phone calls? But whatever the thought bubble says, the speech bubble is polite to a fault. 'You're very welcome to use the phone in the house,' he says. 'Follow me.'

Silently they follow him towards the house. The spaniels trot obediently behind them. Close up, Sea's End House looks more gothic than ever, with grey stone walls, tiny mullioned windows, and a studded oak door more suited to a castle. When this last is pushed open, they enter a vast hall panelled in oak. A stained-glass window reflects pools of green and gold onto the parquet floor and a stag's head stares morosely down at them. Ruth is reminded of a public school (which is surprising as she went to a plate-glass comprehensive). She can almost smell the school lunch – cabbage and overcooked lamb.

'Some place you've got here,' says Ted.

The man smiles rather sardonically and leads them through a door hidden in the panelling, along a stone corridor and into a cavernous kitchen. The servants' quarters, thinks Ruth.

She also thinks that she should be the one to make the phone call but Trace grabs the receiver leaving her and Ted facing their new friend across a kitchen table that would comfortably seat twenty.

'Let me introduce myself. Jack Hastings.'

Jack Hastings? The name rattles around in Ruth's head as she shakes its owner's hand. She is sure she has seen him before. Is he an actor? Someone from the university? The man who does the weather reports on Look East?

Thank God for Ted who always says what he's thinking. 'You're the MP bloke aren't you?'

'MEP,' corrects Hastings smiling.

'I saw you on TV protesting about the French.'

Hastings smiles. He has a charming smile, which is presumably why he uses it so often. 'Well, the English have been protesting about the French for centuries. It's part of a grand tradition.'

Ruth suspects that Hastings enjoys being part of a grand tradition. He's a good-looking man of about sixty, sandy haired and slightly less than medium height. He compensates for his small stature by standing very straight; he is the most upright man she has ever seen, thinks Ruth, noting his chin tilted upwards, his weight on the balls of his toes. He bounces slightly as he faces them across the kitchen, eyebrows raised and even his hair seeming to stand slightly on end.

In the background, Ruth can hear Trace saying 'I'll ask her' and can't help feeling slightly smug. She takes the phone and tells the coroner that, in her opinion, the bones are probably less than a hundred years old. No, they're in no immediate danger from the tide; yes, the police have been informed. The coroner says that he will issue a permit and excavation work can start on Monday.

When she puts the phone down, Trace and Ted are sitting at the table and Hastings is making tea. Ted grins but Trace avoids meeting her eye.

'I didn't catch your name,' Hastings is saying pleasantly.

'Ruth. Dr Ruth Galloway.'

'Tea, Dr Galloway?'

'Thank you.'

'Milk and sugar?'

'Just milk.'

'Hope you don't mind tea bags. My old ma, she lives with us, insists on making the real thing in a pot with strainer and tea cosy and all that malarkey but I can't be doing with it.'

'I'm all for malarkey myself,' says Ted, in the Irish accent which he sometimes affects.

Hastings laughs heartily. 'Well,' he says, 'are you going to tell me what you've found on the beach?'

Ruth feels inclined to tell him to mind his own business but Trace, wanting to assert herself says, 'We're part of a team researching the effects of coastal erosion on the North Norfolk coast line.'

Jack Hastings' face darkens. 'Don't tell me about erosion.'

We weren't about to, thinks Ruth, but Hastings is off.

'My house is disappearing day by day. Fifty years' worth of erosion in three years. I've lost nearly a mile of land. Every morning I walk out to see how much of my garden has disappeared in the night. Three coastguards' cottages have fallen into the sea. The Martello Tower has gone. The lighthouse is in disrepair. We can't even launch the lifeboat because the ramp just isn't there any more. And what do the council do about it? Nothing. Bloody socialist government.'

From this Ruth deduces that Jack Hastings does not stand in the Labour interest.

'Would cost a ton of money to stop the sea,' says Ted reasonably.

'Yes, but where does it end?' says Hastings, making an obvious effort to speak in a more measured voice. 'Soon the Broads themselves will be flooded. Norfolk will disappear.'

Ruth thinks briefly how pleased Nelson would be to hear this news. Aloud she says, 'Have you lived here long, Mr Hastings?'

'All my life. My father built the house in the Thirties.'

'Thirties?' says Trace. 'It looks older.'

'No. Art Deco gothic, I'm afraid. Gingerbread? My wife made it, it's very good.' Ruth accepts a piece though Trace refuses with a shudder. It would probably double her calorie intake for the day.

Ruth hopes that the prospect of Norfolk disappearing from the map has taken Hastings' mind off their urgent phone call, but she underestimates the politician. He turns to Trace with another wide smile.

'So what have you found today? A dead body?'

'Four dead bodies actually,' snaps Trace.

There is a silence. Ted leans back in his chair, grinning broadly. Ruth looks daggers at Trace, who ignores her. And, for a second, Jack Hastings' face looks completely blank, wiped clean of all his urbane charm. Ruth notices how pale his eyes are, almost colourless beneath the sandy brows. Then the smile flashes on again and the warmth and animation flood back.

'Four bodies. How extraordinary! Where did you find them?'

'This is a police investigation now,' says Ruth. 'We're not at liberty to say.'

She thinks how like a police officer she sounds – at liberty to say! – she has noticed before how Nelson and co always fall back on these stock phrases. They sound wrong in her mouth somehow.

But Hastings nods understandingly. 'Of course. If I can be any help, though . . .'

'You've already been a great help,' says Ruth.

'I've lived here all my life, as I say. Not much about the village that I don't know.'

There is a silence while they all think about the fact that someone seems to have buried four bodies on

Hastings' doorstep without anyone apparently being any the wiser.

'Do you know how long they've been there, Ruth?' asks Hastings.

Ruth notes the use of her first name and the fact that Hastings is now deferring to her. She also notes that he has asked the most important question.

'We won't know until we've excavated the skeletons and run some tests,' she says.

Hastings jumps on this. 'So it's just bones then?'

'I can't say,' says Ruth. 'The police will be here soon to fence the area off. We'll excavate on Monday.'

'Well, feel free to use Sea's End House as your base,' says Hastings. 'Most of the time there's just me and Stella here now. And Ma, of course. We rattle around somewhat.'

Why don't you move then, thinks Ruth. Especially in view of the fact that your house is falling into the sea.

'Children have left home,' says Hastings, with a rueful smile. 'Just us oldies and the dogs left.' He pats one of the spaniels, who looks at him adoringly.

'How many children do you have?' asks Ted.

'Three. Alastair, Giles and Clara. The boys are both married now with their own children. Clara's the youngest. She's just finished university. Not quite sure what to do with herself.'

'Well, tell her there's no money in archaeology,' says Ted.

Hastings laughs. 'Oh, Clara wants to save the world. She's just been out in Africa digging latrines and what have you.'

'She sounds great,' says Ruth. 'We ought to be off now.'

'There's no hurry,' says Trace. 'The police haven't arrived yet.'

'I've got to collect my daughter from the childminder.'

She looks up just in time to catch Trace's expression of amused contempt.

4

'Four skeletons you say?'

'At least four, according to Ruth Galloway.'

It's Monday and Nelson is back. He has called a team meeting for nine but now his boss, Superintendent Gerald Whitcliffe, has forestalled this by strolling into his office, leaning all over Nelson's lovely clean 'to do' list and 'having a word'.

'Just thought you'd like a heads-up, Harry, that's all.'

Heads up? What the hell does that mean? Sometimes it seems as if he and his boss speak an entirely different language, and not just because Nelson was born in Blackpool and Whitcliffe in Norwich. Still, he's not going to give Whitcliffe the satisfaction of asking for a translation.

'Could be a delicate situation, you see.'

'Why?'

'Well, it's right on Jack Hastings' doorstep.'

Nelson feels he should know the name but he's not quite in work mode yet. Not that Lanzarote is exactly the other side of the world, even though it felt like it at times. Michelle and Lisa have exchanged addresses and the two families are planning to meet up in the Easter holidays.

'Who's Jack Hastings?'

Whitcliffe laughs indulgently. 'Where have you been hiding, Harry? He's the MEP who keeps ranting on about his house falling into the sea and the government doing nothing about it. Lives at Broughton Sea's End, that big castle-type place up on the cliff. Did you see his documentary, *An Englishman's Home*?'

'Must have missed it.'

'Anyway, turns out these bones have been found at the bottom of the cliffs. Just across the beach from Hastings' place.'

'What's the problem? Surely he wouldn't want to stop us investigating?'

This is said with a slight trace of irony, remembering other influential friends of Whitcliffe's who have not always been helpful to the police. Whitcliffe doesn't get it. He never thinks that Nelson is being funny; he just thinks he's being Northern.

'Of course not. Just that we have to make sure that we do it all by the book. Can't afford to cut any corners.'

'I never do,' says Nelson. And now he *is* being funny.

An hour later, Nelson and Clough are driving towards Broughton Sea's End. It is normally the junior officer who drives but Nelson hates being a passenger and Clough likes to leave his hands free for eating so they are in Nelson's dirty white Mercedes, doing seventy along the winding coastal roads.

'So, boss,' says Clough, as the North Norfolk coastline shoots past, blurry and indistinct, caravan parks, pubs, sand dunes, pitch and putt. 'Do you think we've got another serial killer on the loose?'

'I assume nothing,' says Nelson.

'Still,' says Clough hurriedly, fearing another variation on Nelson's 'never assume' lecture, 'seems funny, doesn't it? Four skeletons in one grave. It's an out-of-the-way place, too; cut off by the tide most of the time.'

'We don't know anything yet. Skeletons could be bloody Stone Age.' Nelson has never forgotten the first time that he met Ruth Galloway. He had called her in to investigate a body found at the edge of the Saltmarsh, which he had thought might be that of a child and, in a way, he was right. Except that this child had died over two thousand years before.

'Trace says that Ruth thinks they're comparatively recent,' says Clough.

'Ruth's not always right,' says Nelson.

And when they reach the beach at Sea's End the first person that Nelson sees is Ruth, with the entirely unwelcome addition of a child slung around her neck.

'Why the hell have you brought Katie?'

'Childminder's sick,' says Ruth.

'What were you thinking? It's way too cold for a baby.'

'She's well wrapped up.'

Katie looks like an Eskimo child, thinks Nelson. She is wearing an all-in-one thing with built-in feet and mittens. She is sound asleep.

'I hadn't got time to make other arrangements,' says Ruth.

'What about Shona?'

'She's teaching.'

Nelson knows he can't say any more. Not here. He glares at Ruth and crunches away across the shingle. He doesn't like this beach; it feels claustrophobic somehow, with the cliffs looming on one side and that monstrosity of a house on the other. He looks across at the turrets of Sea's End House. Presumably that's where Whitcliffe's mate lives. Never trust a man who flies the Union Jack. Everything is so bloody grey – grey stone, grey sea, grey sky. Nelson has a very clear idea of what the seaside should look like, a vision that stays remarkably true to his native Blackpool – sand, big dippers and donkeys. Not this God-forsaken pile of rubble in the middle of nowhere. There's not even a slot machine, for heaven's sake.

At the far side of the bay there is an opening in the cliff, a sort of cleft about a metre wide. The mad Irishman Ted is there, clearing stones away with a shovel. Trace is there too, talking into her phone. Nelson sees Clough give her a little wave. Pathetic.

'Top of the morning to you,' Ted greets him.

'Is this where the skeletons were found?'

'Yes, in this recess. The opening was blocked off by a rock fall. I've cleared most of it away now.'

'We've started on the trench.' Ruth appears next to him. 'It's difficult because there's not much space to dig.'

There is already a neat trench in the narrow gap between the tall cliffs. Nelson looks at it with pleasure. Annoying though archaeologists can be he admires their way with a trench. His scene-of-crime boys could never get the edges that straight. Then he looks closer. The trench appears to be full of bones.

'Jesus,' he says. 'How many in there?'

'Just the six, I think,' says Ruth. She leans over and Nelson looks anxiously at Kate, suspended in her baby sling. How safe were those things anyway . . . ?

'Any idea how old the bodies are?' he asks.

'I think they're fairly recent,' says Ruth. 'Bones buried in sand usually disappear after a few hundred years.'

Not for the first time, Nelson marvels at what archaeologists consider recent. 'So they could be a hundred years old?'

'I think it's likely they're more modern than that,' says Ruth cautiously. 'We'll do C14 dating. Also there's hair and teeth. We can run a number of different tests.'

Nelson knows from previous cases that C14, or carbon fourteen dating, measures the amount of carbon left within a body. When we die we stop taking in carbon 14 and it starts to break down so, by measuring the amount of C14 left in a bone, archaeologists can estimate its age. He also knows that dates can vary by as much as a hundred years. This may not seem much to Ruth but it's not very helpful when deciding whether or not you're dealing with a recent homicide.

'Anything else?' asks Nelson, straightening up.

'Bodies appear to be adult male, well-built . . .' She pauses. 'They're bound, back to back. One has what looks like a bullet wound in the thoracic vertebrae, another looks as if he was shot in the back of the head.'

'Natural causes then,' says Clough, who is hovering in the background

Trace laughs but Nelson glares furiously at his sergeant.

Murder is no laughing matter, whether it occurred twenty, seventy or two thousand years ago.

'What will you do now?'

'We'll expose all the skeletons, then we'll draw and photograph them in situ. Then we'll excavate, skeleton by skeleton. They should all be done on the same day.'

'You can't dig with a baby round your neck.'

'I can supervise.'

'Give her to me.'

'What?'

'Give the baby to me. Just for a bit. I'll sit in the car with her, it's too cold out here.'

The wind has picked up in the last few minutes. They can hear the waves crashing on the beach and sand blows around them. Kate stirs fretfully.

'She probably needs feeding,' says Ruth.

'Well feed her and then leave her with me. Just for a bit.'

'Jesus, boss,' says Clough. 'Are you setting up as a nanny now?'

'Just for ten minutes,' says Nelson. 'Then it's your turn.'

Ruth's first reaction is one of intense irritation, followed by an almost blissful sense of release. As Nelson carefully lifts Kate out of her sling, it is as if Ruth has her old body back, her old self back. She straightens up, feeling the gritty wind full on her face, her hair whipping back. She knows she is smiling.

Kate has had almost a full bottle of milk, her eyelids are drooping. Nelson sits with her in the front seat of the

Mercedes, Clough watching open-mouthed from the passenger side.

'She should go to sleep now,' says Ruth.

'If she doesn't, Cloughie'll sing her a lullaby,' promises Nelson.

Kate's head rests against Nelson's blue waxed jacket. Her fine dark hair, with its one whorl that never goes in the same direction as the rest, suddenly looks unbearably fragile.

'I'll get back to the excavation,' says Ruth, not moving.

'Don't hurry back on our account,' says Nelson, who is still looking down at Kate.

Ruth finds herself almost running back along the cliff path. She can't wait to get down to the beach and start work on the trench. She wants to assert her authority on the proceedings, to check that the skeleton sheets are properly filled in, that there is no mixing of bones, that everything is securely bagged and labelled. But, more than that, she wants to be involved. It is over six months since she did any practical archaeology. She knows that Trace thinks that she is using Kate as an excuse not to do her share of the hard work, to 'supervise' instead. Ruth is the expert here, she's entitled to sit back and delegate, but Trace will never know how much Ruth wants to dig, to forget everything in pure physical hard work. She would not have admitted it, but by the time she looks down at the bodies stretched out back-to-back in their sandy grave she has almost forgotten that she has a baby.

The trench is still fairly narrow and Ruth squeezes in with difficulty. Ideally, she'd like more time to look at the context but she knows that the sea is advancing. High tide is at six, and with the stones cleared away the sea will probably come all the way into this inlet. Time to excavate the bodies. First she takes photographs, using a measuring rod for scale. Then she draws the skeletons in plan. Finally, bone by bone, she starts on the first body. As she lifts each bone, Trace records it on the skeleton sheet and marks it with a tiny number in indelible ink. All the bones are present and, as Ruth had thought, there are teeth too; each tooth also has to be numbered and charted. When she comes to the skull, she sees that there is some hair still attached, ash-blond, almost the same colour as the sand.

There are fragments of rope around the wrists.

Ted whistles. 'Their hands were bound.'

'May be able to get DNA from the rope,' says Ruth. 'There could be blood or sweat on it.'

'Will we get DNA from the bones?' asks Ted.

'Maybe,' says Ruth. 'But DNA can be contaminated by burial.'

Trace says nothing. She is working efficiently but silently, placing each marked bone in a paper bag.

Ruth looks at the skeleton sheet. She is sure that the bodies are adult males. She can see the brow ridges on the skulls, the pronounced nuchal crest at the back of the head, the large mastoid bones. This first skeleton also has a particularly square jaw. Ruth wonders whether they will be able to get a facial reconstruction done but, as she looks at this skull lying on the tarpaulin with sand blowing around it, she has an uneasy feeling that she knows exactly what its living form would be. A tall man (the long bones show that), blond haired with a jutting chin. A Viking, she thinks, though she knows this is historically unlikely. She thinks again of her first mentor – Erik Anderssen, Erik the Viking.

'How are you doing?' She recognises Clough's voice but does not look up.

'Okay. First body's almost out.'

'Baby's asleep,' says Clough, sounding amused. 'Think the boss is about to drop off too.'

Ruth says nothing but Trace says, slightly bitchily, 'Never knew Nelson was so soft about babies.'

'Well, he's got kids of his own, hasn't he,' says Ted, carefully lifting out the second skull.

'They're grown up now,' says Clough. 'Turning into right stunners.'

Ruth wonders whether Ted has children. She knows very little about him beyond the fact that he went to school in Bolton and is famous for his prodigious drinking. She also thinks it is inappropriate for Clough to refer to Nelson's daughters, one still at school, as 'stunners'. She wonders what Trace thinks.

The second body is slightly shorter and the few tufts of hair are dark. When they reach the hands they see that an index finger is missing.

'Could be very useful, that,' says Ted.

Ruth agrees. She is almost sure these men were killed within living memory. If that is the case, a distinguishing mark will be very useful.

The next body is laid out in an identical position, hands behind the back. The only difference is that something is clasped in the right hand, its skeletal fingers still clenched.

'What's that?' Ted leans in.

Gently Ruth prises the fingers apart. Still they seem unwilling to give up the object they have grasped for so long. A flash of gold, white beads.

'Is it a bracelet?' asks Trace.

'It's a rosary,' says Ruth.

She has seen one before, of course. A picture comes into her mind of Father Hennessey, the Catholic priest she met while investigating another long-buried body. She has a vivid memory of a ruined house, a deserted garden, an archway silhouetted against the sky and Father Hennessey holding a rosary, passing it from one hand to the other, his lips moving. Father Hennessey's rosary was black and ornate. This is smaller and simpler, white beads on a gold chain, a cross at one end.

'May be able to trace that,' says Trace.

'Nah,' says Ted. 'Those things are ten a penny.'

Ruth puts the rosary into a separate bag.

'It's all evidence,' she says.

They can now see the lower bodies, which are lying on what looks like a white sheet. On the sheet are some tiny balls of fluff. Ted bends closer.

'Looks like the stuff we found the other day. Smells the same too.'

'We can try to identify the material,' says Ruth. 'It'll help with dating.' She stands up, easing her back. Her earlier euphoria is overtaken by a sudden wave of tiredness. She's out of practice at digging. Her neck and shoulders feel as if she is wearing an iron collar. Also the trench is starting to feel claustrophobic, the cliffs lowering over her with the triangle of sky above.

Ted is watching her. 'Why not let Trace take over for a bit?' He leans forward. 'It'd be good practice for her.'

She smiles at Ted, grateful for his tact. He grins back, showing two gold teeth. She climbs out of the trench, being careful not to damage the sides, and Trace takes her place.

Ruth walks back across the beach, noticing that white-flecked waves are starting to appear on the horizon. They *must* keep a watch on the tide. She climbs the slope and walks slowly along the cliff path to the car park. Nelson's filthy Mercedes is parked by an ominous-looking sign saying 'Beware! Danger of Land Slides'. The car window is half open and, through it, Ruth sees Nelson, head back, eyes shut, Kate nestling on his shoulder. For a moment, she just stands there. She has only once before seen Nelson asleep and she remembers how his face is completely changed, the fierce lines softened, the eyelashes surprisingly long, the mouth unguarded and vulnerable. Kate's head is pressed against Nelson's neck. From reflex more than anything, Ruth reaches in to see if Kate is breathing. Still asleep, the baby turns her head away. Nelson's eyes open immediately.

'Ruth. Bloody hell. You made me jump.'

'Sorry,' says Ruth.

Nelson winds down the window. 'I wasn't asleep,' he says defensively.

'It's okay,' says Ruth. 'I won't tell Clough.'

'How are you getting on?'

'Okay. Four bodies almost excavated.'

'Think you'll get done today?'

'I hope so.' She looks at the sky which is a pale, wintery blue, the sun high and hazy. 'It's only midday now. High tide should be at six, and we'll have to have it done by then otherwise the trench will flood. We've cleared away the rubble from the cliff fall, you see. Nothing to stop the sea getting in.'

'What are you going to do with Katie? She can't stay here all day and I've got to get on.'

'She can sleep in her car seat for a bit.'

'What if she wakes up?'

'I'll sit with her.'

Nelson looks at Ruth without saying anything. Kate stirs slightly and he readjusts his hold, his hand looking very large against her little back. Ruth finds herself staring at Nelson's wedding ring. Has he always worn one?

'Shall I take her?' she asks.

'Perhaps you'd better.'

Ruth opens the car door and Nelson climbs out. He places the sleeping baby in Ruth's arms and tucks her blanket carefully round her. Ruth looks at Kate to avoid looking at Nelson as he does this.

'She's beautiful,' says Nelson softly.

'Don't.'

'I can't help it, Ruth. I've hardly seen her before today.'

Whose fault is that, thinks Ruth. But she knows she isn't being entirely fair. Nelson has asked several times if he can see Kate, but so far Ruth has always made excuses. She's tired, she's got a cold, I'm tired, I'm working. Nelson has a right to see Kate but there is only so much she can take.

She keeps her eyes down, fiddling with Kate's blanket. 'Can I see her again?' asks Nelson. His voice seems to come from a long way away.

'Sure,' says Ruth. 'Cathbad's talking about having a naming ceremony. You and Michelle can both come.'

This time she looks up and meets Nelson's eyes. Dark eyes, more black than brown, eyes that he has passed on to Kate.

'Thanks,' says Nelson. Then he turns away and strides off along the cliff path, towards the excavation.

5

By sunset, all six skeletons have been excavated. The carefully logged bones, packed in boxes marked 'Pathology', are
waiting to be winched up the cliff by Ted and Craig. The
tide is almost upon them. Trace, standing higher up the
beach, is up to her ankles in water. Sly little waves are lapping
at the edges of the trench. The sea is blue in the setting sun
yet Sea's End House, high on the cliff, is already in darkness. Ruth is in the trench, getting a last look before the sea
destroys it. Examining the context in which a body is buried
– the earth filling a grave and any objects (glass, fibres,
animal bone, coins, pottery) found within that earth – is
central to a forensic archaeologist's work. In normal circumstances Ruth would spend days in the trench taking soil
samples, making detailed plans and drawings, but now she
knows that in five minutes the whole area will be full of
salty water and any remaining clues will be lost forever. She
remembers the dig ten years ago when Erik discovered the
wooden Bronze Age henge on the Saltmarsh beach. Every
day, Erik had had someone on 'tide watch'. Even so, Peter,
Ruth's ex-boyfriend, had nearly died when, with terrifying

swiftness, the sea had flooded the marshland, leaving him cut off from the others. Erik had saved him. One good deed to set against other, darker, actions. Ruth hopes that this was taken into account when Erik faced his maker. Not that she believes in any such thing, of course.

'Better hurry, Ruth,' shouts Trace, looking at the path where the waters are now swirling and foaming. 'We've got to wade across the beach before it gets too deep.'

'Okay.' Ruth takes a last photograph. 'A grave is a foot-print of disturbance,' she tells her pupils; the natural layers destroyed, soil and stones churned up together, vegetation growing differently. Someone dug this hole deliberately and, judging from its position, they hoped that it would never be found. If she had more time she might be able to tell exactly which digging implement was used, but now all she can do is note the way that the strata have been sliced through: the 'grave cut' it's called. She bags some soil and a few fragments of wood and glass, worn smooth by sand and sea. She has already removed what may prove to be their most significant find – a single bullet. Then she climbs, rather awkwardly, out of the trench.

The last box is being hauled up the cliff, swaying wildly in the wind as the two men pull on the ropes. Ruth squints up at the dark shape, strangely reluctant to leave until the last skeleton has left its resting place. 'Come on!' yells Trace. There is only a thin line of pebbles left, and in places the waves are already pounding against the rocks. Trace and Ruth run along the narrow strip of land, hugging the cliff, trying to dodge the waves. As they reach Sea's End House, they have to wade out to the stone jetty. Trace surges ahead, creating a wake in the churning water. 'Jesus,' she shouts, above the noise of the sea. 'It's deeper than it looks.'

They have an anxious few minutes, struggling against the surprisingly strong undertow. The wind sounds loud and angry and it is nearly dark. Twice Ruth almost loses her footing. She can feel water seeping unpleasantly over the tops of her wellingtons. She should have worn waterproof trousers. She tries not to think that the reason she didn't was because they make her look like a Michelin man and she knew that she would be seeing Nelson.

At three o'clock Ruth had rung Shona who had finished teaching for the day. Shona drove over and collected Kate, taking her back to her house in King's Lynn. Ruth trusts Shona (up to a point) but she also knows that the nearest her glamorous friend ever comes to motherhood is weekend visits from her married lover's children. She hopes she won't take Kate for a McDonald's.

Wiping the wet hair from her eyes, Ruth sees that Trace has reached the path. Without checking to see if Ruth is all right, she runs up the slope towards Sea's End House, slapping her pockets for her iPhone. Ruth climbs slowly out of the icy water, her trousers now drenched almost to her thighs. She looks back. Across the bay, in the car park, she can just make out Ted and Craig loading the boxes into a van. Clough is there too. She can see his reflective jacket. Nelson has not come back. On the beach, the sea has reached the inlet and waves rush joyfully into the narrow cleft between the rocks. The grave of the six men has been destroyed. Water covers the beach, the biggest waves breaking against the cliffs with a sound like smashed glass.

Ruth walks slowly up the slope. She is desperate to get back to Kate but she has to check that all the finds are accounted for. In the car park her Renault is beside the plain white police van. Ted and Craig are shutting the double doors. Clough is watching. A little way apart Trace is talking into her phone. Clough catches Ruth's eye. 'She loves that thing more than me.'

Ruth hasn't usually got much time for Clough, whom she regards as the worst sort of sexist, racist Neanderthal policeman, but something in his expression touches her. She is also surprised to hear him use the word 'love', even facetiously. Can the famously commitment-phobic Clough really have fallen at last?

Ruth smiles. 'I'm sure she doesn't.'

Clough shrugs, looking rather rueful. 'Bone boxes are in the van. Post-mortem's set for tomorrow, nine o'clock.'

'Does Nelson know?'

'He said to say he'd see you there.'

'Thanks.' Ruth has a last few words with Ted before heading back to her car. Clough calls after her. 'Look after that baby of yours. She's a little star.'

Wonders will never cease, thinks Ruth as she drives off into the night. Kate has turned her into a nervous wreck and Clough into a human being. Whatever will she accomplish in the next four months of her life?

The first thing that Ruth hears as she approaches Shona's house is the sound of crying. More than crying; this is screaming, wailing, the sound of a banshee in full-throated howl. The neat terraced house seems almost to be pulsating with the noise. Ruth runs up the path but Shona has opened the door before she reaches it. A scarlet-faced monster squirms in her arms.

'I'm sorry, Ruth. I've tried everything. Lullabies, classical music, ride-a-cock-horse. The lot. She's been at it for nearly an hour. I think she must be ill or something.'

Ruth reaches out her arms for Kate who takes a deep breath, leans into her mother's neck and instantly falls asleep. The silence feels immense, far more than mere absence of sound.

'My God.' Shona sounds both awed and rather resentful. 'All she wanted was her mum.'

'She's probably just cried herself to sleep,' says Ruth, speaking gruffly to hide how she feels. This has never happened before. Secretly she has never felt before that she is any better than anyone else with Kate. It is her mother, comfortably upholstered and full of maternal authority, or Sandra, who have seemed like the real experts. Ruth may feel that she knows Kate but she has never been sure that the compliment is returned. Until now.

Juggling Kate with what now seems to be practised ease, she follows Shona into the sitting room. The normally stylish room bears the signs of Shona's struggle to placate the baby. A half-full bottle of milk rolls on the polished wood floor and CDs of suitably soothing classics lie scattered over the sofas. The TV is showing some primary coloured children's programme and an open bottle of wine sits on the coffee table.

Shona follows Ruth's glance. 'Didn't even have time to get myself a glass.'

Ruth doesn't comment on the fact that Shona has been drinking while in charge of her baby. It's her fault, her lack of contingency planning, that has led to Shona having to cope with a screaming baby all afternoon and she's grateful – if slightly worried at the urgency with which Shona now grabs a glass and fills it to the brim.

'Do you want some?' asks Shona as an afterthought.

'No thanks. I've got to drive.'

'I'll make you a cup of tea,' says Shona, not moving.

'It's okay,' says Ruth. 'I ought to be going.' She starts to arrange Kate in her car seat, an unnecessarily complicated device bought for her by Cathbad.

'How was the dig? Things looked pretty busy when I left you. What did you find?'

Ruth looks over her shoulder at Shona, who is sitting cross-legged in an armchair, her bright red hair falling over her eyes. In the past she has had reason to distrust Shona's interest in her work but she feels that she, or Kate, owes her something, information at the very least.

'Six skeletons,' she says. 'They look comparatively recent.'

'Good God, Ruth,' says Shona, sounding almost amused. 'Are you going to be mixed up in another murder?'

'I wasn't exactly mixed up in the last one,' says Ruth with asperity. 'Unless you count a madman trying to kill me.'

'I would definitely count that.'

'Well, in this case, I've simply been called in to examine the bones. Look at how they've been buried and so on.'

'Mmm.' Shona looks unconvinced. 'I saw the mad Irishman there,' she says. 'And that purple-haired bitch. Anyone else from the university?'

Ruth looks curiously at Shona as she struggles with the last strap. Shona also works at the university, teaching English, but for the last year she has been having an affair with Ruth's boss, Phil. Just before Christmas, much to everyone's surprise, Phil left his wife for Shona. Ruth isn't sure if Shona herself wasn't rather shocked by this development. Certainly she hasn't rushed to move Phil into her house. He is renting a flat nearby 'while the kids get used to the situation'. Presumably Shona knows a good deal about the workings of the archaeology department. Ruth wonders why she dislikes Trace so much.

'Steve and Craig from the field team,' she says. 'I thought Phil might look in.'

'Oh, he had a meeting with some sponsors,' says Shona vaguely.

'How are things?' asks Ruth, not sure that she really wants to know. She gets on all right with Phil, he's a decent enough boss, but that's as far as it goes. He's very much the new style of archaeologist, obsessed with technology and appearing on television. Ruth has always got the impression that Phil regards her as a throwback, an expert in her own field but a grafter, a plodder, not someone suited to the centre stage. Which suits her fine. Their working relationship works. She just doesn't particularly want to get to know Phil in his new guise as her best friend's partner.

'Oh, all right,' says Shona, twisting a strand of hair between her fingers. 'His wife's being a cow.'

'Well, it must be difficult for her,' offers Ruth. 'They were married for ... how long?'

'Fifteen years. But it hadn't been working for the last five.'

Not for the first time, Ruth wonders how Shona, who is, after all, an astute literary critic, can be so gullible when it comes to men. Who says the marriage hadn't been working for the past five years? Phil, presumably. Ruth has met Phil's wife, Sue, at various department functions over the years and the couple always seemed perfectly comfortable together. They have two children, boys, who must be teenagers by now.

'Fourteen and twelve,' says Shona, in answer to Ruth's question. 'I get on brilliantly with them.'

Ruth can believe that this is true. She imagines Shona, with her beauty and vivacity, utterly charming the two boys. Whether the infatuation, on either side, will last, is another matter.

Ruth picks up Kate's bottle, blanket and the various stuffed toys that have become strewn around the room. Shona makes no move to help her, just stays curled up in her chair, sipping her wine. She obviously feels that her work is done and, really, Ruth agrees with her.

Ruth stuffs the last toy in the nappy bag and says, 'Thank you, Shona. I'm sorry you had such an awful time of it.'

'That's okay,' says Shona, not denying that it was awful. 'Any time.'

'I'm praying Sandra will be better tomorrow,' says Ruth.

Driving home across the Saltmarsh, she thinks about her friendship with Shona. They met when Ruth first started working at the University of North Norfolk, but they only really got to know each other on the henge dig. When Ruth looks back to that time – Erik's ghost stories around the camp fire, the smell of peat smoke in the morning, the wind whistling through the rushes at night, the unforgettable first sight of the henge, black against the blue-grey sand – she thinks of Shona, her red hair flying out behind her as she ran over the sand dunes like a sea sprite shouting 'It's here! The henge is here!' Shona had been Ruth's first real friend in Norfolk and Ruth values her friends highly. Ever since adolescence, when her parents retreated into the church, putting their relationship with God, it seemed, above their relationship with her, Ruth has relied on her friends for support. She has never been one for the gang. She is bemused by her students, with their hundreds of friends on Facebook or Bebo. Are these real friends, people who would look after your cat or drive you home from hospital, or are they just an amorphous mass, happy enough to leave cute messages (lol!) on your wall but completely removed from your everyday life? How can you have three hundred close friends?

Ruth has always preferred just two or three. Alison and Fatima at school, Caz, Roly and Val at university, Josephine Dumbili from that holiday in Crete. And now Shona. As, over the years, Fatima, Caz and Val acquired husbands and children (Roly is gay and Alison determinedly single in New York) they seemed to move, inexorably, further away from Ruth and she relied more and more on Shona, who sometimes seemed her only ally in a world of motherhood, family holidays and smug Round Robins at Christmas ('This year Ellie joined Sophie and Laura at the grammar school'). When she found out that Shona had been lying to her for years, ever since the henge dig in fact, the betrayal hit Ruth hard. But her need for Shona was too strong and their friendship mended itself, not quite as strong as before but pretty resilient all the same. Ruth hopes it can withstand Kate, who seems a force more powerful than ten hurricanes, and that scary two-headed beast called Shona-and-Phil.

She is nearly home. The road is raised up over the flat marshland; at night it seems as if you are driving into nothingness, isolated, vulnerable, a prey to the winds that thunder in from the sea, 'direct from Siberia,' as the locals always say with pride. Ruth turns on the radio and Mark Lawson's fruity voice fills the car, telling her about an experimental play that she has never heard of and will never see. Thank God for Radio 4. Ruth prays that Kate will stay asleep and maybe (wonderful thought) sleep all the way through the night. Surely she must be exhausted after all that screaming?

When she gets to her cottage, she carries Kate in, opening and shutting the door soundlessly. She knows from experience that, though Kate can sleep through any amount of radio programmes about experimental drama, the smallest unexpected sound will wake her up. She once cried for half an hour after Ruth sneezed. She lifts Kate out of the car seat and carries her carefully up the steep staircase. 'You can't have a baby in that house,' her mother had said, 'the stairs are a death trap.' But Ruth successfully negotiates the hazard and lays Kate down, still fast asleep, in her cot. There is a spare room but it is tiny and full of junk so, at present, she and Kate are roommates, a situation which she can see lasting until Kate is about eighteen.

The phone rings as Ruth is switching on the baby monitor. She races downstairs to stop the dreadful clamour. Her ears strain to hear if Kate has woken up but there is silence from the bedroom.

'Yes?' whispers Ruth into receiver.

'Ruth. It is I. Tatjana.'

Of all Ruth's friends, the very last one she expected.

July 1996. Bosnia. The hottest summer on record. Ruth flew to Srebrenica as part of a team from Southampton University, led by Erik. They stayed in what had once been a four-star hotel but had been bombed so badly that the top three storeys had been destroyed. The remaining rooms were a nightmarish mix of erstwhile luxury and recent necessity. Camp beds were ranged, four deep, in the ballroom, the chandeliers, miraculously undamaged, swayed crazily in the wind that blew through broken window panes and ripped-up floorboards. On the stairs the red carpet was ripped and, in some cases, charred and bloodied. The double doors in the lobby had been replaced with corrugated iron, most rooms had at least one window broken, and in the Grand Dining Room the Red Cross had set up a medical base where starving women and traumatised children waited on spindly gilt chairs and viewed their scared reflections in floor-length mirrors.

'The Shining,' said one of Ruth's colleagues, as soon as he saw the pock-marked corridors of The Excelsior, and the joke stuck. 'He-ere's Johnny,' the archaeologists would say, returning to the ballroom at night and making grotesque shadows in the light from the oil lamps (there was no electricity or hot water). One of the doctors, Hank from Louisiana, perfected a Jack Nicholson impression so lifelike that the Bosnian interpreter screamed whenever she saw him.

Thinking back, Ruth doesn't really remember feeling scared, though a lot of the time she was. She remembers more adolescent emotions: feeling left out (the other volunteers were all older than her and veterans of disaster scenes), feeling unsure, lonely and, above all, uncomfortable. She will never forget, though, her first sight of the graves in Srebrenica. So many bodies, contorted, grinning, arms and legs twisted over one another. The bodies on the surface decomposed quickly in the hot sun but lower down, below the water table, they found men, women and children miraculously preserved. The heat and the stench were almost unbearable. They spent days in those hellish pits, exposing body after body, using trowels, spoons and even chopsticks to pick up every minute fragment of bone. 'Lose one tooth or even a foot bone,' one of the anthropologists used to say, 'and you're an accomplice to the crime.'

There were tensions too. The authorities just wanted the graves exhumed as quickly as possible but the archaeologists wanted to identify as many of the dead as they could. 'To know our dead,' declared Erik, 'is a fundamental human right. It is why the Egyptians built pyramids and the Victorians built mausoleums, why even the most primitive man buried his ancestors in a sacred place alongside his pots and spears.' But the War Crimes Tribunal did not want to know about the Egyptians or the Victorians, they simply wanted the evidence recorded and the guilty brought to justice. 'But who is guilty?' Erik would say at night in the ballroom, the lamplight glinting on his long, silver-blond hair. 'In war it is the victor who writes the history.'

Tatjana had been one of the interpreters, but it soon emerged that she had a degree in archaeology from an American university so she joined the forensics team. Ruth was drawn to her from the first. Tatjana was quiet but composed. She wasn't scared to make her opinions known and Ruth admired that. She was attractive too, with straight dark hair cut in a fringe and large brown eyes. Ruth and Tatjana began spending time together, working side-by-side in the field by day, and at night, they moved their sleeping bags to a quieter corner of the ballroom, away from the American group with their guitars and games of spin the bottle.

Despite this, Ruth didn't know very much about Tatjana. She came from Trebinje, near the Adriatic coast. It was rumoured that she'd lost her husband in the siege of Mostar but, then, almost every Bosnian had lost someone. You stopped asking after a while and just assumed tragedy. Certainly, in repose, Tatjana's face sometimes looked unbearably sad but she had a reserve that prevented anyone from getting too close. Ruth didn't mind this. She was a private person herself and disliked it when people asked probing questions in the name of friendship.

So, she was surprised, and rather pleased, when Tatjana suggested one evening that they go for a picnic. She remembers that she had laughed. The word picnic conjured up images of cucumber sandwiches and grassy meadows, not this nightmare land where the rolling fields usually turned out to be full of human bones rather than checked tablecloths and cupcakes. But Tatjana had 'borrowed' a jeep from one of the militia (she could always get round the soldiers) and she had a bottle of wine. What could be nicer? There was a pine forest on the edge of the town. Ruth had never been there, it was on the Serbian border and there were bandits in the hills, as well as the more picturesque dangers of bears and wolves.

'It'll be fine,' Tatjana had said. 'Where's your sense of adventure?'

Where indeed? Ruth rather felt that she'd used up her quotient of adventure in volunteering for Bosnia in the first place. But the idea of being outdoors on a summer evening, of sitting on the grass and talking about Life, was too good to pass up. So Tatjana drove the jeep up to the forest and the two girls did indeed sit on the grass, drinking wine from the bottle, and talking about archaeology, Erik, careers, men, the state of the world. Ruth remembers that she was just feeling pleasantly sleepy and, for the first time that summer, almost relaxed, when Tatjana said, 'Ruth. Will you do me a favour?'

Ruth will never forget the way that Tatjana's face had become transformed, how it blazed with light. How she suddenly looked both incredibly beautiful and incredibly scary.

'Of course,' Ruth said nervously. 'What?'

'I want you to help me find my son.'

6

The coroner, a horrendously cheerful man called Chris
Stephenson, speculates that the bodies have been in the
ground no longer than a hundred years. Ruth makes no
comment on this. She has her own research to conduct on
the bones. She will measure and analyse, looking for
evidence of disease or trauma. She'll send samples for Carbon
14 and DNA testing. She will do isotopic tests on the bones
and teeth. Yet, even with all this technology, she still thinks
identification is unlikely. If the bodies have lain in the earth
all that time, why should anyone claim them now?

Stephenson agrees with Ruth that the bodies are male,
aged between twenty-one and fifty (no signs of arthritis or
typically ageing conditions, all adult teeth fully erupted)
and that cause of death was probably gun shot. On four
bodies there were entry and exit wounds which suggested
that the men had been shot in the back of the neck, 'execu-
tion style,' Chris Stephenson explained jovially. The bullet
found in the grave was from a .455 cartridge, the type used
in a Webley Service revolver, a gun used by British soldiers
in both the First and Second World Wars.

'Are we looking at something that happened in one of the wars?' asks Nelson as they leave the autopsy room, shaking off the smell of formaldehyde and the humour of Chris Stephenson.

'It's possible,' says Ruth. 'The dates could fit but . . . six bodies? How could six soldiers be killed and just buried under the cliff without anyone knowing about it? There'd be records, wouldn't there?'

'Maybe they weren't soldiers.'

'The bodies were military age.'

'Well, we need to find out,' says Nelson, heading across the car park to where his Mercedes is parked beside Ruth's little Renault. 'I'll set Judy Johnson on to it. Get her talking to the locals. Most of them look as if they were alive in the war. The First World War at that.'

'You should talk to Jack Hastings,' says Ruth. 'He says there's nothing about the village that he doesn't know.'

'Good idea,' says Nelson, to her surprise. 'Why don't you come with me? Seeing as you know him and all? Unless you've got to get back to the childminder?'

'I don't have to collect Kate until five,' says Ruth with dignity.

It is only when she is in the car, hurtling through the Norwich suburbs, that she realises she has walked into a trap.

Broughton Sea's End is a tiny village, getting smaller by the year. Of the houses on the seaward side of the road, only Sea's End House, the pub and two coastguards' cottages remain. In places the cliff has retreated to within yards of the road and only a rather inadequate barbed wire fence separates the driver from the sea below. Out to sea, the lighthouse is a sturdy landmark, waves crashing against its steps, but Ruth knows from the internet that the lighthouse has not been operable for over twenty years. Once or twice, a plume of spray breaks right over the cliff, drenching the car. Nelson swears and puts on the windscreen wipers.

'All this salt's murder on the bodywork.'

'That's not exactly what I was worrying about,' retorts Ruth.

'Oh, this road's safe enough,' says Nelson airily. 'It's been here a good few years.'

But so had the other coastguards' cottages, thinks Ruth. And the Martello Tower and the lifeboat ramp. The sea is winning this battle.

They pull up in the car park, near the 'Danger' sign and walk back across the coast road towards the village. It's a tiny place, just one street of houses, a convenience store-cum-post office and, behind them, a church – Norman by the look of its tower. There is not a living soul in sight. The wind whips in from the sea and seagulls call loudly overhead.

'Jesus,' says Nelson. 'Who in their right mind would live here?'

But Ruth rather likes the village. She has no idea why (she was brought up in South London after all) but she is drawn to lonely coastal landscapes. She loves the Saltmarsh with its miles of sand and bleak grassland. And she likes Broughton Sea's End. She likes the shuttered-looking houses, the shop selling fishing nets and home-made jam, the wind-flattened shrubs in the gardens. They walk back along the

High Street, cross the road again and set off towards Sea's End House. A solitary dog walker is struggling along the cliff path.

Something about the walker, or perhaps the dog, is familiar.

'I think that's him,' says Ruth to Nelson. 'Jack Hastings.'

Sure enough, the man and his dog turn into the drive that leads to Sea's End House. Nelson hurries to catch up with them.

'Mr Hastings?'

Jack Hastings turns in surprise. The wind seems to take Nelson's words and throw them into the air. Hastings puts his hand to his ear.

'DCI Harry Nelson,' Nelson shouts. 'Of the Norfolk police. Could I have a few words?'

Hastings now registers Ruth's presence. 'Ruth, isn't it? The archaeologist?'

Ruth supposes a politician has to have a good memory for names, but she is nevertheless impressed.

'Dr Galloway is assisting us with our investigations,' says Nelson, lapsing into police-speak.

'You'd better come in, then,' says Hastings politely.

Ruth is interested to note that this time Hastings leads them into a baronial sitting room where vast sofas lie marooned on acres of parquet. Presumably archaeologists deserve the kitchen, but the police count as guests.

'Can I get you a drink?' asks Hastings, shrugging off his coat. 'Tea? Coffee? Something stronger? Keep out the cold?'

'I'm driving,' says Nelson. 'Coffee would be grand.'

Ruth would love 'something stronger' but she feels sure

that Nelson would disapprove. Not only will she be driving later but she is also going to be operating a heavy baby. 'Coffee would be lovely,' she says.

She wonders if Hastings will ring a bell and summon discreetly uniformed staff but he trundles off by himself, accompanied by the spaniel. Ruth and Nelson sit alone, facing a monstrous fireplace built of stones so vast that they could be rejects from Stonehenge. The room has large sash windows which rattle in the wind and French doors opening onto a stone terrace. Beyond the terrace is the sea, iron grey, flecked with white. There's no fire lit in the massive iron grate and Ruth finds herself shivering.

'Upper class buggers don't feel the cold,' says Nelson, noticing.

'I must be distinctly lower class then,' says Ruth.

'No, you're middle,' says Nelson seriously. 'I'm lower.'

'How do you make that out?'

'You went to university.'

'That doesn't make you middle class.'

'It does in my book. My daughter, now, she's well on her way to being middle class.'

'Is she at university? What's she studying?'

'Marine biology. At Plymouth.'

Ruth does not quite know how to reply to this but luckily the door creaks open and Hastings enters, carrying a tray. He is accompanied, Ruth is surprised to see, by an elderly woman bearing a coffee pot.

'Let me introduce my mother, Irene,' says Hastings, putting the tray on a rather ugly brass trolley. 'She's in charge of all the tea- and coffee-making round here.'

Certainly Irene seems to take an immense proprietorial interest in making sure that they have all the coffee, milk, sugar, sweeteners that they require. Ruth is quite exhausted by the end of it. She expects Irene to fade away once the drinks are served but the old lady settles into a chair by the window and reaches for a sewing basket placed nearby.

'Mother loves her knitting' is Hastings' only explanation.

'Mr Hastings,' says Nelson. 'I believe you know about the discovery made under the cliffs here?'

'The four skeletons,' says Hastings, leaning forward in his chair. 'Yes.'

'Six skeletons, in point of fact.'

'Six?'

'In confidence,' says Nelson, noting how much Hastings seems to enjoy these words, 'the archaeologists think the bodies were probably buried between fifty and seventy years ago. I believe your family has lived in this area for many years. I wondered whether you could remember hearing of any incident in the war. You'd be too young yourself, of course,' he adds hastily.

Hastings smiles. 'I'm sixty-five. Born in 1944.'

'Ever hear of anything strange happening? Any disappearances? In the war perhaps.'

Hastings throws a quick glance at his mother, knitting by the window. A row of plants sits on the window ledge, some in pots, others in more eccentric containers – soup bowls, hats, what looks like a riding helmet.

'I was only one when the war ended, Detective Inspector,' says Hastings. 'My dad was the captain of the Home Guard.'

Ruth has an immediate picture of *Dad's Army*, of Captain

Mainwaring and the other one, the butcher, shouting, 'Don't panic!' She starts to smile but then, listening to the wind whistling through the windows, she thinks: I wouldn't have liked to live here in the war.

Nelson asks tactfully, 'Is your father ... still ...?'

'No. He died in 1989.'

'Is there anyone else still alive who remembers that time? Perhaps your mother?' Nelson looks over at the serenely knitting figure.

'Ma,' Hastings raises his voice. 'The detective is asking about the war.'

'I'm sure you would have been a youngster,' says Nelson gallantly.

Irene Hastings gives them a very sweet smile. She must have been pretty once, thinks Ruth. 'I was a good deal younger than my husband,' she says. 'We were married in 1937, I was only twenty, Buster was forty-four. I had my first child, Tony, when I was twenty-one. Barbara came along a year later. Jack was the baby.'

'Where is your oldest son now?' asks Nelson. He wonders why Jack, 'the baby', has inherited the house over his brother's head.

'He died when he was still in his thirties. Of cancer.'

'I'm sorry,' says Nelson.

'The inspector is asking about the Home Guard,' says Jack quickly, perhaps to deflect attention from the dead Tony. 'Are any of them still alive?'

'The Home Guard were mostly older than my husband. He was forty-six when the war started. He'd fought in the first, of course.'

'Got the MC,' chipped in Hastings. 'The Military Cross.'

'Yes, he got a medal, Jack,' says Irene in a faintly chiding tone, 'but he never forgot the horror of it all.'

'So are none of the Home Guard still alive?' pursues Nelson.

'Well, there were a few young boys. You could be in the Home Guard if you were too young or too old to fight. I'm not sure about Hugh or Danny. Archie's still alive, though. He sends us Christmas cards, doesn't he, Jack? He must have been about sixteen when war broke out. He joined up later, of course.'

'Archie?' says Nelson, getting out his notebook. He's prepared to like Archie; it was his dad's name.

'Archie Whitcliffe.'

'And the other two – Hugh and Danny?'

'I think Hugh still lives somewhere nearby. I saw him a few years ago, just after his wife died. I don't think he's dead though. I always read the *In Memoriam* column in the local paper.'

Cheerful, thinks Nelson. He supposes though, at Irene's age, the *In Memoriam* column is just a way of keeping up with your friends – Facebook for the over-eighties.

'Do you remember Hugh's surname?'

Irene's face crumples. 'I'm so sorry, I don't.'

'That's okay. And Danny?'

'I'm afraid I don't know anything about him.'

While Nelson is digesting all this, the door opens and a girl comes in, this time accompanied by two spaniels.

'Is Flo's paw better, Dad?' she asks and then stops, looking around in surprise.

Hastings is positively beaming. 'My daughter, Clara,' he says.

So this is the famous Clara. Ruth knows that Clara has finished her degree (she is the one who wants to change the world) but, otherwise, she would have taken her for a teenager. Clara Hastings is tall, taller than her father, and slim, with thick blonde hair cut in a shoulder-length bob. She is devastatingly attractive.

Hastings introduces Ruth and Nelson. Clara shakes hands politely with Nelson but her face brightens when she hears the word 'archaeologist'.

'That sounds fascinating. I'd love to do something like that.'

'I like it,' says Ruth guardedly.

'I'm out of work,' confides Clara. 'Dad despairs of me. I've got a degree in law but I just don't want to be a lawyer. All that making rich people richer. I want to do something useful with my life.'

'What about the police force?' suggests Nelson, deadpan.

The girl wrinkles her nose. 'Well . . .'

'Clara's a real Leftie,' says her father fondly. 'She's against all kinds of authority.'

Clara would get on well with Cathbad, thinks Ruth. Aloud, she says, 'Are you looking for work? We might have some casual work on one of our spring digs.'

'Oh that would be great,' says Clara. 'In the meantime, I'll do anything. Dog-walking, gardening, babysitting.'

'Babysitting . . .' repeats Ruth, thoughtfully.

As they leave Sea's End House, the rain starts. Within minutes they are drenched, buffeted by great wet winds from the sea. As they reach the car park, they see that the lights are already on inside the pub.

'Have you had lunch?' asks Nelson. He isn't wearing a coat and his shirt is sticking to his back but he doesn't seem cold. He always seems impervious to the elements.

'I don't want lunch,' says Ruth but she is shivering. Her hood has blown back and her wet hair is trickling down her neck.

'Come on,' says Nelson, sensing weakness. 'Just a sandwich.'

'Okay,' says Ruth.

The trap is set.

The Sea's End is a squat, pebble-dashed building. Presumably, on a summer's day, it's the perfect place for a glass of white wine or a jug of Pimms. There are tables outside (though the sun terrace has long since fallen into the sea) and there is a spectacular view across the bay. But on a wet March afternoon the place seems dour and charmless. Ruth gets the feeling that, as this is the only pub in the village, the landlord has not tried very hard to keep up with the times. The walls inside are pine-clad, the floor covered with rather dirty lino. The tables are pine too, and sport plastic menus and ketchup bottles. A group of men stand drinking at the bar, watching *Bargain Hunt* on television.

'Blimey,' says Ruth, tapping a grooved wall. 'It's like being in a sauna.'

'I'll take your word for it,' says Nelson. 'I've never been in a sauna.'

'I thought you went to the health club.'

'For a swim, yes, or to the gym. I don't go in the *sauna*.' He sounds horrified.

'You should try it. In Norway everyone goes in the sauna and then they run outside into the snow.' As she says this, she thinks of Erik, who had a sauna in the grounds of his Norwegian lake house. She remembers black sky, white snow, naked figures running laughing through the trees. It had been innocent, she tells herself rather defiantly, a Scandinavian Eden.

'Rather them than me,' says Nelson, looking at the menu. 'What'll you have?'

'Oh, just a ham sandwich and a Diet Coke. I'll buy it.'

'No, you're all right.' Nelson gets up and goes to the bar. Ruth watches him rather warily. The exchange has put her on her guard. The last thing she wants is another row with Nelson over money.

But when Nelson comes back to the table, he doesn't seem inclined to chat. He checks his phone and then places it carefully on the mat in front of him. Then he moves it to the left of the mat, then to the right, then on top of it, then below, then to the left again.

Ruth can't stand any more. 'What did you want to talk about?'

'Talk?' He says it like it's a foreign word.

'Yes, talk. That's why you got me here, isn't it? Why you suggested lunch.'

'I just thought you might be hungry . . .' Nelson begins, but he has the good grace not to go on. 'I don't know, Ruth,' he says, looking down into his (full fat) Coke. 'I'm so confused. I think about you and Katie all the time.'

Ruth finds herself breathing fast. 'Don't,' she says. 'Don't think about us.'

'You can't say that, Ruth. She's my daughter. I want to help. I want to be involved. I want to give you money, at least.'

There is a pause while the landlord slops their sandwiches down on the table. Ruth tries to speak calmly. 'I know you want to help but you can't, can you? If you start giving me money, Michelle will find out. I've got to do this thing on my own.'

'But she's my—'

'I know,' Ruth interrupts. 'But you've got your family. You don't want to break up your marriage. I respect that. But I'm afraid it means that I make the decisions about Kate.'

Nelson looks as if he is about to explode. The thought of anyone else making decisions is complete anathema to him. But, quite suddenly, all the fight seems to go out of him and he says, in a low voice, 'I just want to be involved.'

'You can see Kate any time.'

'Yes, for half an hour, sitting in my car.'

'And that's another thing,' says Ruth. 'If you keep offering to look after her, someone will suspect something.'

'Who?'

'Judy, maybe. Or even Clough.'

Nelson snorts.

'Clough's not stupid, you know. And she does look a little bit like you.'

The look of gratification on Nelson's face is almost ludicrous.

'Really? Do you think so?'

'Well, she's prettier than you.'

Nelson grins, reluctantly. 'That's true. Okay, I'll be more careful but I can't help how I feel. I feel protective about her. Like I do about my daughters . . . my other daughters. I can't change that.'

'You'll have to try and hide it. Especially when there are other people around. You should have seen Clough's face when you offered to hold her.'

'Do him good. He'll have his own some day. If he ever grows up, that is.'

'I really think he's in love with Trace.'

Nelson grunts. 'Don't talk to me about love. Even Judy's getting married. It's all the girls at the station ever talk about.'

Ruth wondered whether she should take Nelson to task for referring to fellow police professionals as 'girls', but she's far too interested in the news to attempt re-education. Also, she's glad of the change of subject. Nelson's probably a lost cause, anyway.

'Is she? She's been with her boyfriend a long time, hasn't she?'

'Since they were at school.'

'God, I can't imagine that.' Ruth thinks of the boy she was going out with at sixteen, a spotty youth called Daniel Harris. She thinks he became a plumber. He's probably loaded. Maybe she should have married him.

'Hen parties, wedding lists. That's all I ever hear. Even Whitcliffe—' He stops.

'What?'

Nelson is silent for a moment, chewing his sandwich.

Ruth takes an unenthusiastic bite of hers. It tastes of wet plastic.

Nelson pushes his plate away. 'Did you catch the name of the bloke in the Home Guard?' he says. 'The one who's still alive?'

'Archie something.'

'Archie Whitcliffe. I think he's my boss's grandfather. He talked about him once. Local hero. Fighting on the home front and all that.'

'Will that make things difficult for you?'

'Maybe. Whitcliffe's touchy about his family. He's Norfolk born and bred. Explains a lot, in my opinion. He won't want me bullying his war hero granddad.'

'But you're not going to bully him, are you?' asks Ruth sweetly. 'You're just going to ask him some questions.'

'Whitcliffe thinks I'm too forceful.'

'Why ever would he think that?'

This time Nelson gets it. 'I've no idea. I'm a real pussy cat.'

This makes Ruth think about Flint. She hasn't seen him today. She hopes he's all right and hasn't got shut in somewhere. Since she lost her other cat last year, she's become rather neurotic about Flint.

'Are you finished?' she says. 'I should be getting back to work.'

As they drive back through the squalling rain, Nelson asks, 'Do you think we'll get anywhere with identifying the bodies?'

'We might do,' says Ruth. 'I can do isotope analysis.'

'What's that when it's at home?'

'It tests the chemicals and minerals present in teeth and bone. Put simply, the teeth will tell us where someone grew up, the bone will tell us where they ended up.'

'Why's that?'

'Because bone keeps growing. It renews itself, from the inside out. The teeth provide a record of the time that they were formed, the bones will show the chemicals and minerals absorbed more recently.'

'That's good then, isn't it?'

'Yes . . .' Ruth hesitates. 'It's just . . . we can do the tests, but without the records to cross check it doesn't really help with identification. I suppose if we find out roughly where the men may have come from, we could make enquiries there. The trouble is it's so long ago.'

'People have got long memories,' says Nelson grimly. 'That's one thing I've learnt on this job.'

7

Nelson drops Ruth at the station and she drives straight back to the university where she has a tutorial at three. The Natural Sciences building is quiet. It's a grey afternoon and most of the students are probably in Halls or in the union bar. Ruth climbs the stairs to her office, thinking about Tatjana and Nelson and Kate and what Jack Hastings' mother meant by 'he never forgot the horror'.

Hearing Tatjana's voice had been a real shock. After Bosnia, Tatjana had moved back to the States and married an American. There had been a few Christmas cards. Tatjana and her husband (Rick? Rich? Rock?) were living in Cape Cod. Tatjana was doing some archaeological work and trying to write a book. Rick/Rich/Rock was a doctor, specialising in geriatrics. 'No shortage in Cape Cod,' Tatjana had written with typical terse humour. That had been almost ten years ago.

'Ruth.' Tatjana had sounded unnervingly the same. 'I had your number from the university. I hope it's okay?'

'It's fine.' The office was not meant to give out personal numbers, but in an age when tutors send their students text messages and communicate via Facebook (not that Ruth would ever do either of these things), nothing was really private any more.

'So you're still teaching?' Tatjana's accent had almost gone, replaced with a slight East Coast whine, but the inflection was still foreign, the ends of each word crisp and emphasised.

'Yes, I'm a lecturer in forensic archaeology. I teach postgraduates mostly.'

'Did you ever write the book?'

'No. Did you?'

'No.' Tatjana's laugh, that sudden staccato bark, brought back the past more vividly than anything else could. The ballroom, the oil lamps, Erik telling stories about vampires, Hank playing 'Smoke on the Water' on the guitar.

'And Erik,' said Tatjana. 'Do you still see Erik?'

'Erik's dead,' said Ruth. 'It's a long story.'

'Erik dead. Dear God.'

'Yes.'

'And you, Ruth: What's your news? Are you married? Children?'

Ruth took a deep breath, watching the flickering green light from the baby monitor. 'I'm not married but I have a child. A baby.'

Ruth remembers that there was a brief silence before Tatjana said, 'A baby, well that *is* news. Congratulations, Ruth. A boy or a girl?'

'A girl. Kate.'

'Kate.'

Another silence and Ruth could almost hear the years

rushing past, a whooshing sound like walking through falling leaves.

'I'm coming to England,' said Tatjana at last. 'I'm giving some lectures at the University of East Anglia. I wondered, could I stay with you? For a week or two?'

Ruth thought a lot of things in that moment: her cottage is a long way from UEA, two weeks is a long time, she would have to tidy the spare room. She thought so long that Tatjana said, 'Of course, if it's a problem . . .'

'No,' said Ruth. 'No problem. It'll be wonderful to see you again.'

But will it be wonderful, thinks Ruth, searching for the key card to open her office. Seeing Tatjana will bring back a whole slew of memories, not all of them pleasant. For many years afterwards she'd had nightmares about Bosnia. Bones gleaming in the sun, a hotel with endless corridors, door after identical door, grand staircases leading into nothingness, the flames of a bonfire, Tatjana's face in the darkness.

The last time she saw Tatjana it had been a harrowing occasion. She still thinks about it, wonders if she could have said or done anything differently, if, by some small change, she could have made events turn out another way. She doesn't know if, even fourteen years later, she's ready to revisit that scene. She feels too fragile – not enough sleep, too many confrontations with Nelson. But Tatjana is her friend, and over the last year, she's learnt a lot about friendship. Tatjana must want to see her badly if she's made so much effort to get in touch. She mustn't turn her away. She mustn't let Tatjana down again.

While she is scrabbling in her organiser bag – it has so many zips and pockets that it's almost impossible to find anything – she notices that the lights are on inside her office. She pushes open the door and finds Cathbad sitting at her desk, under the poster of Indiana Jones, reading *Alice in Wonderland.*

Although not entirely surprised – Cathbad makes rather a speciality of materialising in unexpected places – Ruth is taken aback to see him there, calm as a Buddha in his lab coat, his long hair in a ponytail, an expression of serene benevolence on his face. Although she sometimes sees Cathbad around the campus (he is a technician in the chemistry department), he rarely comes near the archaeology corridor. He once trained as an archaeologist under Erik and, perhaps for this reason, studiously avoids Phil, Ruth's boss. Certainly no two men could be less alike than Erik and Phil.

'Lewis Carroll,' says Cathbad dreamily, 'such a visionary.'

'I thought he was a paedophile.'

'He was a sad little man who liked the company of young girls. What's wrong with that?'

'Ask Nelson.'

Cathbad smiles. To everyone's surprise, including their own, Cathbad and Nelson get on rather well. Twice they have faced considerable danger together and Cathbad is convinced that Nelson saved his life on one of these occasions. They are bound together by this circumstance, he says, forever. Nelson grunts sceptically when he hears this, but despite a famed intolerance for anything even slightly fey or alternative Nelson finds Cathbad good company. Beneath the New Age trappings is a keen intelligence at work in Cathbad. Nelson sometimes thinks that he would have made a good detective.

'Nelson sees demons everywhere. How are you, Ruthie?'

Ruth is startled. For one thing, it seems like years since anyone has asked about her rather than Kate. For another – Ruthie? Only Erik ever called Ruth Ruthie.

'I'm fine. You look different. What is it?'

Cathbad raises a slightly self-conscious hand to his face and Ruth realises.

'You've shaved off your beard.'

For the past few years, Cathbad has sported a black beard, dramatically at odds with his greying hair. Without it he looks younger, more approachable and, to Ruth's surprise, rather good-looking.

'Maddy persuaded me.'

Maddy is Cathbad's teenage daughter. It's news to Ruth that they're in contact. 'Good for Maddy. It's a distinct improvement.'

Ruth puts her bag on the visitor's chair and waits for Cathbad to vacate hers. Instead, he smiles up at her, eyes very dark in his clean-shaven face.

'How's Hecate?'

'Kate,' snaps Ruth. Jesus, why can't anyone get her name right?

'I was thinking that it was about time for her naming ceremony.'

Cathbad has appointed himself Kate's godfather. Ruth

quite likes the idea of godparents (anyone turning up with presents is surely a Good Thing) but has refused to have Kate christened because of the little problem of not believing in God. Cathbad, who likes any opportunity to have a party, has suggested a pagan naming ceremony instead. Ruth doesn't believe in the pagan gods either but at least Cathbad's plans don't involve a church. A picnic on the beach was his last suggestion.

'Bit cold on the beach,' she says now.

'We could have a bonfire.' Cathbad loves bonfires. He says they are libations for the gods but Nelson is convinced that he is a closet arsonist.

'You're not going to start sacrificing goats, are you?'

Cathbad looks hurt. 'Of course not. It's a very simple ceremony. We're just going to show Kate to the gods, that's all.'

'Still sounds a bit Wicker Man.'

'Forget the gods. Just see it as a party to welcome Kate to the world.'

'That sounds okay, I suppose.'

'Great. I'll organise it. Shall we say Thursday week? Are you going to invite your parents?'

'I don't think a pagan naming ceremony will be quite their thing somehow.'

'Are you sure? What about Shona?'

'She'll come.' Shona loves a party almost as much as Cathbad does, and despite a Catholic upbringing she is definitely on the side of the pagans.

'You'll have to invite Phil too,' says Ruth mischievously. 'They're together now.'

'In that case I will invite him,' says Cathbad with dignity. 'Even though I find him a rather negative spiritual presence.'

It's mutual, Ruth wants to tell him. But she doesn't. Despite everything, she quite likes the idea of a party for Kate. She gives in and sits in the visitor's chair. Good old Cathbad. He's been a real support to her over the first few months of Kate's life. He deserves to be a godparent.

Cathbad's next words, though, wipe the indulgent smile from Ruth's face.

'We'll have to have Nelson.'

'Why?' asks Ruth warily.

Cathbad looks at her blandly. One of the most irritating things about him is that you never quite know what he's thinking.

'I see Nelson as a sort of spiritual father to Kate.'

'Do you?' Ruth's heart is beating fast but she keeps her face still.

'He can be a Guardian. Someone to watch over her.'

'Nelson's a Catholic. He wouldn't come to a pagan ceremony.'

'He's not hung up on ritual. He'd come. I'm sure of it.'

That's what Ruth's afraid of.

'We must invite his wife too,' she says.

'I've only met her once,' says Cathbad, 'but she seems a beautiful soul.'

'She's very pretty,' says Ruth drily.

'I meant spiritually beautiful,' says Cathbad. Ruth isn't convinced. For all his high-flown spirituality, Cathbad is susceptible to good-looking women.

'All right,' says Ruth. 'We'll have a party and a bonfire. Invite all the beautiful people.'

Cathbad smiles and, long after he has left and Ruth is preparing for her tutorial, she still seems to see the smile lingering in the air, like the grin on the face of Lewis Carroll's famous cat.

8

A week later Ruth gets the results of the isotope analysis. She rings Nelson immediately but is told, importantly, that he is out 'on police business'. His mobile phone is switched off so she leaves a message and waits impatiently, looking down at the data in front of her, tapping her phone against her teeth. When it rings, she jumps a mile.

'Ruth?' It's Ted.

'Hi, Ted. What's up?'

'We've found something on the beach.'

'What?'

'Some barrels.'

'Barrels?'

'Old oil barrels. They might be linked to the bodies we found. Do you want to come and have a look?'

Ruth hesitates. Nelson could be hours and she doesn't feel ready to settle down to any other work. She has no tutorials this afternoon and doesn't have to collect Kate until five. And she's intrigued; how could some old oil barrels be linked to the six skeletons?

'Okay,' she says. 'I'll come over.'

Ted is waiting for her by the cliff path. It's a beautiful afternoon; sunny but cold, with no wind. The tide is out and the shallow rock pools are a bright, unearthly blue. Ted is rubbing his hands together with what looks like glee but could just be an attempt to get the circulation back.

'This way.'

He leads the way past the jutting headland and onto the next beach. To get there they have to climb over the remains of the old sea wall and Ruth is soon out of breath. Ted rushes on ahead, bounding over the slippery rocks like a goat. Is there such a thing as a sea goat? Ruth pauses on the highest part of the wall, getting her breath back and enjoying the view. In front of her is a perfect picture-postcard bay – white sand, blue sky, seagulls calling – a desert island courtesy of Radio 4. Ted's footprints in the wet sand are like Man Friday's. Ruth could almost believe that no-one has ever been on this beach before. Although it is only a few miles from resorts like Cromer, this coastline is remote and hard to reach. The cliffs are high and there are no paths or steps. And there's always the danger of being cut off by the tide. The cliffs are dangerous too, full of caves and fissures, overhanging precariously in places. The only creatures at home here are the birds – hundreds of them – nesting on the sheer rock face. Despite living near a bird sanctuary, Ruth is not fond of birds.

A tiny figure on the deserted beach, Craig is clearing away sand with a shovel. He looks like an illustration of an impossible task, one of the labours of Hercules or a punishment in the Underworld.

Another, less classical, allusion comes into Ruth's head, inspired perhaps by Cathbad's championing of Lewis Carroll:

> The Walrus and the Carpenter
> Were walking close at hand.
> They wept like anything to see
> Such quantities of sand.
> 'If only this were cleared away,'
> They said, 'it would be grand.'

Ruth climbs down from the wall and walks carefully over the rock pools towards the beach. As she gets closer, she sees that, in fact, Craig is clearing the sand away from a large object – several large objects – that lie half-buried at the foot of the cliff. Closer still, she sees that they are oil barrels, orange with rust and studded with limpets.

Craig is red in the face from his exertions. He greets Ruth and Ted with 'Just the three of them, I think.'

'What are they doing here?' asks Ruth, bending close to examine the corroded metal. 'It's such an isolated place. Miles from anywhere.'

'I used to come birds-nesting here as a child,' says Craig. 'We actually used to climb up without ropes or anything. Madness really. The cliffs are eighty foot high in places.'

'I used to go in for extreme archaeology,' says Ted. 'Went into these caves once in the cliffs on the Firth of Clyde. Thirty metres down and full of giant spiders.'

'Fascinating,' says Ruth. She has no time for extreme archaeology, which seems to her to abandon the most sacred precepts of the subject – time, patience and care – in favour of laddish thrill seeking. 'Why do you think they could be linked to the bodies?

'Take a look inside,' says Ted.

The nearest barrel has a hole in its side, leaving a wickedly jagged edge. Peering gingerly inside, Ruth smells a heady mix of petrol and the sea. She gags. The barrel is half-full of stones which have either fallen from the cliffs or been swept in by the tide, but the smell is still all-pervasive. The second barrel is also open to the elements and inside, under the stones and beach debris, Ruth can see something whitish. The third barrel, as Ted says, is still sealed.

She puts on protective gloves and reaches inside the second barrel. The stones are tightly packed, a mixture of chalk and flint, with a stray crab leg or two thrown in for good measure (probably dropped there by seagulls). Ruth reaches down as far as she can and manages to get a hold of the something white. She pulls.

'Let me help,' says Ted.

Together, they drag out a wad of cotton fibres, once white but now stained grey and yellow, smelling strongly of rotten eggs.

Ruth almost chokes again. She takes a deep breath. 'It looks like—'

'The stuff we found buried with the bodies,' says Ted. 'That's what I thought.'

'The barrel's full of it,' says Craig. 'It stinks to high heaven.'

'Could be something dead in the bottom of the barrel,' says Ruth. 'A fish maybe?'

'Nah,' says Ted sniffing knowledgeably. 'That's sulphur, that is.'

Sulphur. The word has an ominous sound. Sulphur and brimstone. The devil dancing in front of a yellow fire. Ruth shakes her head irritably. Her parents are big experts on the devil but she doesn't expect him to come invading her thoughts like this. Especially as he is something else she doesn't believe in.

The third barrel is still sealed. Ruth pushes at it experimentally; it doesn't budge but there is a faint sloshing sound.

'Think it's full of petrol,' says Ted.

'Petrol?'

'Yeah, the beach stinks of petrol.'

Ruth realises that this is true. Petrol must have leaked copiously from the first barrel so that the whole area smells like a garage forecourt. Looking down she sees that the sand is black with oil.

'Well we'd better get the fire brigade to look at it,' says Ruth. 'Put some hazard signs up. All we need is some idiot with a cigarette . . .'

'Goodnight Vienna,' agrees Craig. He starts to pack up his equipment. Ruth likes him; he's the only archaeologist who doesn't argue with her.

'What about the stuff we found in the barrel?' asks Ted.

'I'll take a sample to the lab.'

'Rather you than me,' grins Ted.

Further inland, overlooking gently rolling hills and flat water meadows, Nelson and Judy are smelling a rather different smell. Antiseptic, lavender and cut flowers masking another, more elemental, odour.

'Christ, I hate these places,' says Nelson for the tenth time, shifting impatiently in his chintz armchair.

'I can't imagine anyone likes them much,' says Judy. She is finding her boss rather trying. It's not her favourite way to spend an afternoon – interviewing some gaga old bloke in an old people's home – but it's her job and she has to get on with it. She thinks that Nelson just resents the fact that Whitcliffe has insisted that he attend this rather routine interview. His attitude, as he shifts in the too-low chair, seems to suggest that, if it wasn't for this intrusion, he would be out catching criminals and righting wrongs. As it is, he'd probably only be in another of Whitcliffe's meetings.

As for her, she'd be catching up with paperwork and trying not to think about her hen night in two weeks' time. There's a notice on the staff room wall for people to sign on and she saw, to her horror, that there were at least thirty names on it. Surely there aren't thirty women at the station? 'Oh, people are bringing friends,' said Tanya, a friend and fellow WPC. 'The more the merrier.'

Judy is sure that it'll be very merry. They are starting off in a wine bar, then out for a meal then on to a club. She has asked for no fancy dress but she's sure there'll be an element of comedy headgear and novelty suspenders. Oh yes, everyone will have a whale of a time. Everyone except the bride herself, that is.

'Would you like to come this way?' a uniformed figure is smiling down at them. She is probably not a nurse but her manner – a crisp mix of kindness and professionalism – certainly suggests a hospital ward. But this isn't a hospital, Whitcliffe stressed that. 'Absolutely super place. Granddad loves it. They play bowls and do gardening. There's even an archery team. Real home from home.'

Greenfields Care Home, as they walk through its cream-painted corridors, is certainly clean and well-organised, but homely? Judy can't imagine anyone wanting to decorate their homes with prints of Norfolk Through the Ages or hand-sanitisers or stairlifts or notices on fire safety. And it doesn't seem terribly like home to have a room with a number, even if it does have your name on it, in cheerful lower case letters.

'Archie? Visitors for you.'

Archie Whitcliffe, who greets them at the door of his tiny room as if he were Jack Hastings himself, looks disconcertingly like his grandson. Superintendent Gerald Whitcliffe is tall and dark, vain about his hair and his suits. Archie Whitcliffe is also tall, though slightly stooped, with immaculate silver hair. He isn't wearing a suit but his cardigan and trousers are freshly pressed and he is wearing a tie, regimental by the look of it.

He shakes hands briskly. 'So you work for Gerald?'

That isn't quite how Nelson likes to look at it, but he nods. 'Yes. I'm Detective Chief Inspector Harry Nelson and this is Detective Sergeant Judy Johnson.'

Archie positively twinkles at Judy. 'What a mouthful. Do you mind if I call you Judy?'

Judy smiles back. 'Not at all.' There's no reason to antagonise the old boy, after all.

The room contains only a single bed, a desk with a television on it, an armchair and a bookcase. As well as the ubiquitous Norfolk print, there are several framed family portraits. Judy cranes her head to catch a glimpse of a teenage Whitcliffe.

'Here,' says Archie obligingly. 'Gerald at his passing out parade.'

Judy looks at the newly qualified policeman, saluting, his neck vulnerable under the new cap. He looks about twelve.

'He's done so well,' she says. 'You must be proud of him.'

'Course I am. Proud of all my grandchildren.'

'How many do you have?'

'Ten. Gerald's the oldest.'

Jesus wept, thinks Nelson. The Whitcliffes are breeding like rabbits. There truly is no help for Norfolk.

Archie sits on the desk chair, gesturing Nelson to the armchair. Judy perches on the bed.

'Mr Whitcliffe,' Nelson begins. 'Superintendent Whitcliffe, Gerald, may have told you about the skeletons found buried at Broughton Sea's End ...'

'He has.'

I bet he has, thinks Nelson. Despite the matter being strictly police business.

'We believe these skeletons are of a group of men who may have died anywhere from forty to seventy years ago. This obviously includes the war years. I wondered if, as a member of the Home Guard, you remember any sort of incident at Broughton Sea's End.'

Archie is silent for a long time. Along the corridor someone is playing the piano accompanied by some rather weedy singing. 'If You Were the Only Girl in the World'.

'You were in the Home Guard,' prompts Nelson.

'Yes.' Archie seems visibly to straighten in his chair. 'The

Local Defence Volunteers we were called at first. I was too young to join up at the start of the war. Did later, of course. Tank Corps.' He gestures to the tie.

'There were some other youngsters in the troop, weren't there?' Nelson glances at his notes. 'Hugh and ... er ... Danny.'

'Yes.'

Nelson wonders if it's his imagination or does Archie stiffen slightly? He looks at Nelson pleasantly, a calm smile on his face. The tension is in his body which is completely still. Too still, surely?

'Are you still, in touch with Hugh and Danny? Do you know if they're still alive?'

'I corresponded with Hugh a few years ago. I haven't heard from him since.'

'Do you have an address for him?'

'I'm sorry, no.' Archie does not bother to go and look. He just stares at Nelson out of bland blue eyes.

'A surname?'

'I don't think I can remember.'

Nelson looks at Judy who leans forward and asks, 'What about Danny?'

'I haven't seen him since the war, my dear. I'd clean forgotten him until you mentioned his name.'

Nelson tries another tack. 'Tell us about the captain of the Home Guard. I believe he was Jack Hastings' father?'

'Yes. Buster Hastings. Hell of a chap. A real old devil, one of the old school. He'd been in the trenches in the first lot, you know. Tough as old boots. Ran a tight ship too. We weren't just playing at soldiers. We did manoeuvres. Night manoeuvres. Patrolled the cliffs. On moonless nights, the *darks* we called them, we went out in the boat.'

'Why?' asks Judy.

Archie's eyes bulge. 'Looking for invaders, of course. We were sure, at the start of the war, we were sure the Nazis were going to come. And Norfolk was the obvious place. All those little coves. So easy to land a boat at night. Hence the manoeuvres.'

'And did you ever see anything?' asks Nelson lightly.

Archie Whitcliffe sits up even straighter. 'If I had, I wouldn't tell you. We took a blood oath, you see.'

Ruth, Craig and Ted are in the pub, The Sea's End. Ruth knows by now that any excavation involving Ted invariably ends in the pub. Ruth drinks Diet Coke and the men drink bitter. Everything is the same as on her visit with Nelson – the same men at the bar watching apparently the same TV programme, the same sticky floor, the same laminated menus. The only difference is that instead of feeling nervous and keyed-up she feels relaxed, enjoying the company of her colleagues. Since having Kate, opportunities for drinks with the boys (never her forte anyhow) have been few and far between.

'Have a real drink,' says Ted. 'They do a good bitter here.'

'I can't, I've got to drive.'

'One won't hurt.'

'And I've got to pick up Kate.'

'Is that your baby?' asks Craig. 'How old is she?'

'Nineteen weeks,' says Ruth. She wonders if she'll ever get used to giving Kate's age in months or even – incredible thought – in years.

'She's a darling,' says Ted, in his Irish voice. 'Even Nelson seemed taken with her. Not a man much given to senti-ment, our Nelson.'

Ruth keeps her face blank. Ted can't possibly know anything, she tells herself. Keep calm. Keep smiling.

'Do you know him well?' Craig is asking Ted.

'Not really,' says Ted. 'We worked with him on another case, didn't we, Ruth? Got a short fuse, Nelson, but he seems a good copper for all that.'

'What do you think about this case, Ruth?' asks Craig.

'Well,' says Ruth, not able to resist a tiny twinge of pleasure at having been asked her opinion, 'I'd say the bodies had been in the ground about seventy years, which brings us to the war years. I think the bones are of men aged between twenty-one and about forty, which makes them military age. I'd say they were soldiers.'

'We didn't find any uniform though,' says Craig.

'No clothes at all. Just the length of cotton. Maybe it was used to drag the bodies along the beach.'

'Something fishy definitely went on,' says Ted happily. 'Shot at close range, nothing to identify them. Are we thinking Germans or English?'

Ruth thinks she knows the answer to this but, for some reason, she wants Nelson to be the first to know. She stalls. 'I've sent off for isotopic analysis. That should tell us, broadly speaking, where the men were from.'

'Wonderful thing, science,' says Ted. Craig smiles. Archaeologists are divided into those, like Ruth's boss Phil, who adore science and technology and those who prefer the more traditional methods, digging, sifting, observation. Ted is definitely in the latter camp.

Despite the fact that it is three o'clock in the afternoon, Ted orders a steak and kidney pie.

'I love a good steak and kidney,' he says. 'No-one makes it any more.'

'I do,' says Craig. 'I was brought up by my grandparents so I can do all the old-fashioned stuff. I've got a mean way with a brisket of beef.'

'My mum used to cook oxtail,' says Ruth, remembering. 'I'm surprised it didn't turn me into a vegetarian.'

'A good oxtail soup is delicious,' says Craig. 'I'll make you some one day.'

There is a slightly awkward pause. Ted raises his eyebrows at Ruth over his (second) pint. Ruth is rather relieved when her phone rings. She goes outside to take the call.

It's Nelson. At last.

'You wanted to speak to me.' He sounds anxious.

'I've had the results of the isotopic analysis.'

'Is that all?'

'What do you mean "is that all?" It's important. The tests show where the men came from.'

'And where was that?'

'Germany.'

9

When Nelson gets home, he looks at the map emailed to him by Ruth and labelled, bafflingly, 'Oxygen Isotopes Values for Modern European Drinking Water.' When he has made sense of the key he realises that the area pinpointed by Ruth covers not only Germany but parts of Poland and Norway as well. However, most of the region is in Germany, which makes Ruth's a pretty safe bet. Which means that the six men found buried at Broughton Sea's End were in all likelihood German soldiers. Which means that someone shot them at close range and buried them in a place where, without coastal erosion, they would probably never have been found. Which means that Archie Whitcliffe and Dad's Army have a lot of explaining to do. He is definitely hiding something. A blood oath! Jesus wept.

He rings Whitcliffe who, typically, isn't answering his phone. It's six o'clock. Whitcliffe is probably out on the town somewhere. If you can go out on the town in Norwich, that is. Whitcliffe isn't married but Nelson has no idea if he is gay or what his mother would call a 'womaniser'. Tony and Juan, who own Michelle's hair salon, seem to know every gay person in Norfolk and Nelson has never seen Whitcliffe at one of their parties. Not that Nelson often goes to Tony and Juan's parties. It's not homophobia, he explains to Michelle, so much as plain old-fashioned misanthropy. But, gay or straight, Whitcliffe's life outside the force is a closely guarded secret. He's a career officer, a graduate, someone adept at saying the right thing in the right words at the right time. He has nothing in common with Nelson who joined the cadets at sixteen and thinks of himself as a grafter rather than a thinker. Whitcliffe may be a Norfolk boy but to Nelson he seems more of a Londoner – smooth and slightly shifty, the sort of person who wears red braces and drinks in City wine bars. But ambitious policeman Gerald Whitcliffe is also the grandson of a man who, in the war, took a blood oath to protect ... what? Who?

Nelson is still brooding on the Whitcliffe family when Michelle comes wafting in from work. She's the manageress of the salon now; it's the sort of place frequented by women who spend their mornings having coffee and their afternoons shopping. On the rare occasions when Nelson has visited his wife at work he has had to fight his way through shiny Land Rovers outside and designer carrier bags inside. Still, it pays well.

Michelle kicks off her shoes. She always wears high heels for work. Nelson approves. In Blackpool women still dress up for work and to go out in the evening. It's different down

south. His own daughters seem to spend all their time slop-
ping about in ridiculous puffy boots. As for Ruth, he can't
remember her shoes but he is sure that (unlike the Land
Rovers) they bear evidence of mud and hard work.

'Want a cup of tea?' Michelle asks, putting her head round
the door of the study (still called the playroom by Laura
and Rebecca).

'I should make you one,' says Nelson, not moving.

'Don't bother,' says Michelle, without rancour. 'I'll do it.'

He hears her moving about in the kitchen and is struck
by a sudden tenderness for her. They have made this home
together – the shaker-style kitchen, the sitting room with
its leather sofas and wide-screen TV, the four bedrooms
and two en-suite bathrooms. And soon, when Rebecca goes
to university, they will be on their own in it. Nelson and
Michelle married when he was twenty-three and she was
twenty-one. Michelle was pregnant with Laura within six
months of the wedding. They have hardly ever been on
their own. In Blackpool, when Nelson was working all hours
as a young policeman and Michelle was looking after the
children, her mother was in almost permanent residence.
Nelson hadn't minded. Against all tradition, he likes his
mother-in-law, an attractive sixty-year-old with a vibrant
taste in sequinned jackets, and he had realised that
Michelle needed company. When he was promoted and
they moved down to Norfolk (which was *Michelle's* idea, as
he is often reminding her) there were always the kids,
their friends, other mums, neighbours. The house has never
been empty. But now Nelson can hear the leaky tap drip-

ping upstairs and the clink of the cups as Michelle takes them out of the dishwasher. Soon it will be just the two of them.

Nelson follows Michelle into the kitchen, where she is sorting out the post.

'Why don't you ever open letters, Harry?' she asks mildly.

'They're always bills.'

'They still need opening. And paying.'

Nelson ignores this. Michelle always pays the bills from their joint account. 'Have you heard from Rebecca?' he asks.

'Yes. She's staying the night at Paige's.'

'She's never here, that girl. Is she going to do her homework at Paige's house?'

'Coursework,' corrects Michelle. 'I expect so. She's working very hard, you know.'

Nelson doesn't know. Rebecca seems to spend most of her time at home watching reality TV or doing something inexplicable called 'chatting on MSN'. He can't remember the last time he saw her read a book, but then, he's not exactly a reader himself.

Michelle has reached the last letter which is encased in a rather eye-catching purple envelope. She holds it up for Nelson's attention.

'This is a bit different.'

'Probably a nutter,' says Nelson, surveying it with a professional eye.

And, in a way, he's right.

You are invited, reads the black text on the pale mauve card, *to Kate's naming ceremony. Place: under the stars. No presents please, just your positive energy.*

'Kate,' says Michelle, 'it must be from Ruth.'

'Must be.'

'It doesn't sound like Ruth. Oh...' she turns the card over and laughs. 'It's from that mad warlock. Cathbad. He's the one that works at the university, isn't he?'

Nelson acknowledges that he is.

'Well, he's certainly taking an interest in Kate. Harry, you don't think...?'

'What?'

'You don't think he could be the baby's father?'

Nelson looks at his wife who is now pouring boiling water into the teapot. She always makes a proper pot, just like his mum does. In her bare feet, her black trousers sweeping the floor, her blonde hair loose, Michelle looks beautiful and rather touching, like a child dressed in her mother's clothes. But she's not a child; she's forty (something she is consciously trying to forget). Has she really never suspected about Ruth? But Nelson knows the answer to this. With an attractive woman's unconscious vanity, Michelle would never think of Ruth – overweight, untidy Ruth who thinks more about her career than her waistline – as a potential rival. Michelle likes Ruth but she really hardly thinks of her as a woman. She's one of Nelson's colleagues, like Clough or Judy, not a sexual threat at all.

Michelle hands Nelson a cup. 'Shall we go?'

'Where?'

'To the naming ceremony. Shall we go? Might be a giggle.'

'I don't know,' says Nelson, taking his tea and heading back to the study. 'I'm up to my neck in work at the moment.'

* * *

Despite repeated attempts, he doesn't get through to Whitcliffe until the morning. He tells his boss that he needs to speak to Archie again, new evidence has emerged which makes him a very important witness, related to the Superintendent or not. But Nelson is too late. His grandfather, Whitcliffe informs him stiffly, died last night, just before midnight.

10

'Was he ill?' asks Clough, rather indistinctly, through a mouthful of chocolate chip cookie.

'He seemed fine when Johnson and I saw him yesterday,' says Nelson, swerving to overtake a farm lorry.

'It's Johnson, that's what it is,' says Clough. 'She's a jinx. Remember last year?'

Nelson does, indeed, remember last year, when Judy interviewed a sick old woman with startling, and tragic, results.

'Maybe he had a heart condition, though,' says Clough, licking crumbs from his fingers. 'How old did you say he was?'

'Eighty-six,' says Nelson.

'There you go, then,' says Clough. 'Old age, that's what did it. Mystery solved.'

Was it really as simple as that, wonders Nelson, as he takes the turning for Greenfields Care Home. Old man dies. No mystery, just the expected end of a long life. But eighty-six is no great age these days. His own mother, Maureen, is more active at seventy-four than many people in their thirties. Every day you read about people living to a hundred, or even older. The Queen must be worn out writing all those telegrams. And Archie Whitcliffe, standing proudly in his neat cardigan and regimental tie, had certainly seemed the picture of elderly good health. No-one at the Home had mentioned a heart condition and Archie showed no tell-tale signs of heightened colour or shortened breath. He had been calm and measured, even intimidating. *If I had, I wouldn't tell you. We took a blood oath, you see.*

But only a few hours after saying those words Archie was dead. He died in his sleep, apparently of a massive stroke. That can happen at any age, Nelson knows, but nevertheless the sequence of events troubles him. That is why he is on his way to the Home, despite Whitcliffe's thinly veiled discouragement. 'Might be more respectful to wait a few days.' Well, Nelson will be respectful, but he knows from experience the value of getting immediate statements. He wants to speak to the last people who saw Archie Whitcliffe alive.

He would have preferred to take Judy rather than Clough but Judy, much to his disgust, has the day off. 'It was booked ages ago,' says Nelson's PA, Leah. 'I think she's having a wedding dress fitting.' Jesus wept. The station is becoming more like an episode of *Friends* every day (he knows about *Friends* from his daughters). So, as two officers are required and it is imperative to stick to the rules, he has to take Clough and pray that he doesn't give vent to his much-aired views on euthanasia ('after seventy it's kinder').

Clough, however, seems subdued by the surroundings, though when the last person to have seen Archie alive turns out to be an extremely pretty Filipino carer, he cheers up considerably.

The carer is called Maria and her eyes are red from crying. Nelson doesn't know why but he is relieved to see this evidence of human emotion. The owner of the Home, a formidable woman called Dorothy, said all the right things earlier but he had got the impression that Archie's death was primarily an inconvenience to be dealt with as speedily and efficiently as possible. She hadn't been too pleased to see two policemen littering up her entrance hall, either.

'Everything's quite above board,' she said. 'The doctor's signed the certificate.'

'There's no suggestion of foul play,' said Nelson in his policeman voice. 'But Mr Whitcliffe was an important witness in another enquiry. I need to know if he said anything before he died.'

'I'll get Maria. She did Archie's bed call. She was the last person to see him before he passed away.' She gave the impression that it had been in bad taste for Nelson to use the 'd' word.

The bed call turns out to involve helping Archie get into bed. 'Sometimes people need help with toilet,' explains Maria. 'But not Archie. He did everything by himself.'

'In good shape, was he?' asks Nelson. 'For a man his age?'

'He was one of our fittest clients.' Maria's eyes brim with tears. 'That's what makes it so sad.'

Clough pats her arm sympathetically. Nelson gives him a look.

'Miss – er – Maria,' he says. 'If it doesn't distress you too much, I'd like you to go over everything that happened with Archie yesterday. Don't leave anything out, even if you think it's not important. I want to get a complete picture.'

Maria dabs her eyes with a tissue. 'I see him in the morning, just a check call. He is reading.'

'Reading? A book?'

'No. I think it was a letter.'

'Did you have any visitors that day? Apart from DS Johnson and myself.'

'I don't think so. I can check the book.'

'Did he have regular visitors?'

'His grandchildren come sometimes with their families. Some very sweet little children. They like playing in the garden, feeding the fish. There's a friend who comes too, an old lady.'

'Did you ever see the grandson who's in the police?'

'No.'

So much for Whitcliffe's claim that he visits all the time.

'So, yesterday, you saw Archie in the morning. What time approximately?'

'About eleven.'

'When did you see him next?'

'Not until the bed call. I have some hours off so I can pick up my little boy from school.'

'What time was the bed call?'

'Nine.'

'Bit early for bed isn't it?' says Clough.

'We have so many clients,' says Maria. 'We have to start early. Archie was one of the latest because he likes to watch *Panorama*.'

'Please go on,' says Nelson, shooting Clough another look.

'I go in. He is in his pyjamas watching telly. I put his teeth in a glass. Tidy away his clothes, turn down bed.'

'How did he seem?' asks Nelson. 'In good spirits?'

Maria pauses for what seems like a long time. 'No,' she says at last. 'He seem . . .' She stops, searching for the word. 'Thoughtful. Yes, he seemed thoughtful. Usually we chat, about the telly, about my little boy. He's five. Archie always remembers him. At Christmas he gives me money to buy him a present.' She presses the tissue into her eyes.

'But yesterday he seemed thoughtful . . .' Nelson prompts gently.

'Yes. I was a bit worried about him so I went back, about half an hour later. His light was still on but he wasn't reading. He likes to read. Murder mysteries mostly. I buy them for him from the charity shop. But yesterday he was just lying in bed. I thought he was asleep but when I lean over him he grabs my arm. I don't think he knows who I am. He says a name, sounds something like Lucy.'

'Something like Lucy?'

'Yes. All morning I'm trying to think.' Her smooth brow furrows. 'I am trying to think of the name.'

'Lucy-Ann?' suggests Clough. 'Lucille?'

'Maybe it wasn't a name,' says Nelson. 'Maybe it was something else, like "lucky".'

Maria shakes her head. 'No, it was a name. I've heard it before.'

'Lucia? Luke?'

'No.' Maria's brow clears and she almost smiles. 'I remember now. Lucifer. He said Lucifer.'

'Lucifer,' says Clough. 'Bloody hell.'

They are in Archie Whitcliffe's bedroom, which already

has an abandoned feel. The bed is stripped, the pillow grave-stone-smooth. On the bedside table, Archie's teeth are still in their glass, next to a copy of *The Nine Tailors*. The family photos still smile down from the walls, but now even the cheerily grouped children seem oddly sad. There is no-one left to look at their forced jollity, no-one except Dorothy and her staff when they clear the room, ready for their next 'client'. Nelson looks out of the window. The grounds are immaculate but empty. A gardener is cutting the grass but, although it is a fine spring day, no-one is sitting in the basket chairs carefully arranged on the patio. Nelson turns back and, as he does so, he notices a yellowing photograph pushed to the back of the desk. Several middle-aged men sit in a row outside a house, a house which looks vaguely familiar. Three much younger men crouch in front of them. At the bottom, in spidery handwriting, is written: 'Broughton Sea's End Home Guard 1940.'

Which was Archie? The gangly boy in front, trying not to smile but obviously delighted to find himself alongside these hardened veterans? The one with his hat at a jaunty angle, gas-mask in hand? Perhaps the serious one with glasses. Which of the older men was Buster Hastings? The scary-looking fellow with the walrus moustache or the fat one with buttons straining? Maybe the one looking vaguely in the wrong direction ... Of course, that must be Sea's End house in the background. He recognises the grey stone but realises that the picture must have been taken at the back of the house, in the garden that has since fallen into the sea.

Archie's newspaper is still folded back at yesterday's TV.

He has ringed the programmes he wanted to watch. *Countdown, Coronation Street, Panorama*, an afternoon film matinee of *Went the Day Well?* The shaky blue pen makes Nelson feel suddenly very sad.

'Come on,' he says. 'There's nothing here. Let's go and see the doctor.'

'No signs of satanic ritual then, boss?'

'Show some respect,' growls Nelson. Even as he says it, though, he remembers how Archie described Buster Hastings yesterday. 'Hell of a chap,' he had said.

A real old devil.

Ruth, like Judy, has taken the day off. Tatjana is arriving tomorrow and the spare room is still full of old boxes so she has dropped Kate at Sandra's. She stopped off for strengthening croissants, has made a pot of coffee and is now preparing to transform the room into a bijou boudoir, suitable for someone with American standards of hygiene and comfort. The trouble is, for the last twenty minutes she has been sitting on the floor reading an article about Ian Rankin from a two-year-old copy of the *Guardian* (found at the bottom of one of the boxes). It is only the arrival of Flint, purring and standing on Ian's face, that brings her back to the job in hand. Jesus, how do people ever tidy anything? She moves stuff from one box to another but it is still *there*, in the way. How do people like her sister-in-law ever manage to have houses where everything is shut away in cupboards and all the storage jars actually contain the thing they say they do? Ruth's sugar jar contains small flint flakes, evidence of prehistoric tool-making. Coffee is full of miscellaneous pens and Tea is a strange herbal mix of Cathbad's, almost definitely hallucinogenic.

That's another worry. Cathbad's ridiculous naming-day party. It's tomorrow night and Cathbad seems to have invited half the university. And now Tatjana will be there too. What will she think about a crowd of pagans dancing around the inevitable bonfire? Ruth has never discussed religion with Tatjana. She knows that Tatjana, like Nelson, was brought up as a Catholic, but living through a civil war tends to change people's perceptions of good and evil. Ruth shivers; she hopes that they can get through these few weeks without ever discussing life or death or any of the points in between. They will have nice, civilised chats about archaeology, admire Kate, drink white wine and visit Norwich Castle. The past does not need to intrude at all.

What the hell is in this box? Old sample bags full of dust and pieces of flint, lecture notes, a model of a Stone Age causewayed enclosure made for the university open day, complete with plastic sheep, a theatre programme (*A Little Night Music* – when had she ever gone to see that?) and, oh my God, a picture of Ruth, Peter and Erik standing by the henge, as triumphant as if they had made it themselves.

She peers more closely at the photo. Christ, she is wearing a bikini top. She must have been at least three stone lighter then. Erik is in a billowing white shirt that has a faintly druidical feel. Peter is wearing a Chelsea football vest; his face red and sweaty. It had been a hot summer, she remembers. Working in the sun all day had been hard; they all wore hats, Ruth's a wide-brimmed straw number, Peter's one of those legionnaire's caps with a flap at the back,

Erik's a jaunty panama. In the photo Erik is waving his hat, very white against the improbably blue sky. Now Erik is dead and the henge has disappeared, its timbers taken to a nearby museum to be preserved. Cathbad and the other druids had protested violently. 'They belong to the wind and the sky,' Ruth remembers Cathbad shouting, his purple cloak flying out behind him as he took his position in the centre of the sacred circle. 'They are not yours to take, to bury in some soulless museum.' Erik had sympathised but the university, who was funding the dig, had insisted. And now the timbers lie in an artificially controlled climate behind smoked glass, no longer a henge, just some oddly shaped pieces of wood.

Ruth thinks about Broughton Sea's End, about the sea advancing, eating away at the cliffs, destroying brick and stone, uncovering secrets. Was there a link between the bodies and the oil drums? The strange-smelling material had certainly looked the same. She has taken it to the lab (her car still reeks) and will run tests on it. Six German soldiers, shot and buried under a remote cliff, buried in sand so their bones will disintegrate, oil drums containing petrol and diesel fuel. Ruth is reminded of a film that she saw years ago with her father. Nazis marching through an English village. What was its name?

She has got precisely nowhere with the tidying. The bed is still buried under boxes, although Flint has found a pillow and is kneading it busily. She will have to be ruthless. Erik sometimes used to call her Ruth the Ruthless. Time to live up to her name. She'll get some black plastic bags and chuck the lot away.

As she crosses the sitting room she sees, with a shock, that there is somebody at the front door. Her bell hasn't worked for years but her few visitors know this and usually hammer and yell. God knows how long this polite person has been standing there. She opens the door, prepared to apologise.

A man is standing on the doorstep, smiling. Blond and good-looking, there is something unmistakably foreign about him. Maybe it's the green coat or the backpack – or the smile, which shows extremely white teeth.

'Dr Ruth Galloway?'

'Yes.' She likes it when people use her correct title. She doesn't see why strangers should call her Ruth and she despises 'Miss'.

'My name is Dieter Eckhart. I wish to talk to you about some dead German soldiers.'

11

'You'd better come in,' says Ruth.

Dieter Eckhart steps politely over the piles of books and folders in the sitting room (part of the tidying process) and perches on the edge of the sofa. Ruth offers him tea which he accepts but disconcerts her by asking for lemon instead of milk. She hasn't got any lemon but finds a wizened lime at the back of the fridge (from Shona's tequila phase). It'll have to do.

'I am sorry to trouble you at home,' says Eckhart, accepting the unpleasant-looking drink with every appearance of pleasure. 'But I ask at the university who is the forensic archaeologist in charge of the case.'

Ruth is gratified that someone has identified her as being in charge but rather mystified as to how Dieter Eckhart has managed to find out about the bodies so quickly. Thanks to Whitcliffe, there has been nothing in the British press.

The mystery is soon explained. From his backpack Eckhart pulls a map of Norfolk, a book about the D-Day landings and a crumpled letter written in thin black ink.

'I'm a military historian,' he says. 'I have written several articles about the rumoured German invasion of Norfolk in the Second World War. One day last month I received this letter.'

He hands it to Ruth:

Dear Mr Eckhart
Please excuse my presumption in writing to you. I read your recent article in History Today *entitled 'The Great Invasion Mystery' and it awoke some very vivid memories, memories that I have, for many years, been trying to suppress. I was a member of the Broughton Sea's End Home Guard from 1940 to 1941. I was one of the three younger members of the platoon which was captained by one Buster Hastings. I am now 86 and in poor health, yet a memory of a particular event in 1940 has haunted me all my life. I feel I must discuss it with you. You, sir, are a young man, an academic and a German. It is for these reasons that I feel compelled to contact you. A great wrong was done many years ago, Herr Eckhart, and, unless we tell the truth to the generations that follow, the evil will lie waiting beneath the earth.*
I am, sir, your honourable former enemy,
Hugh P. Anselm.

Ruth looks across at Dieter Eckhart, who is calmly sipping his tea. Her mind is racing. The rumoured German invasion of Norfolk. Nazi officers patrolling the streets. Six bodies found buried under the cliff. *The evil will lie waiting beneath the earth.*

'I made enquiries,' says Eckhart. 'There was indeed a Home Guard platoon captained by a man of that name. I decided to come to England. For many years I have been planning to write a book about the invasion.'

'But they didn't really invade, did they?' responds Ruth. 'I mean, I know there were rumours, and there was a film. I saw it with my father. But there was never any evidence.'

'I believe there was,' says Eckhart, putting down his cup. 'But I believe that the evidence was deliberately destroyed.'

'So you think the Germans came here? To Norfolk?'

Eckhart looks at her. He has very blue eyes, which reminds Ruth of Erik. He says, as if reading from a script: 'In September 1940, in the village of Crostwick, Norfolk, villagers reported seeing a convoy of army trucks carrying dead German soldiers. Later that same month two bodies were found on the Kent coast between Hythe and St Mary's Bay. They were identified as German soldiers by their uniforms. The bodies were burned from the waist down.'

'Burned?'

Eckhart continues as if she hadn't spoken. 'On October the twenty-first the corpse of a German anti-tank gunner, Heinrich Poncke, was recovered from the beach at Littlestone-on-Sea. The discovery was openly reported in the press at the time.'

'But I thought all these stories had been disproved,' says Ruth, impressed, despite herself, by this recital. 'The invasion was one of the myths of the Second World War. Like nuns parachuting or Hitler having a double.'

'The parachuting nuns may well have been a myth,' says Eckhart with the ghost of a smile, 'but the invasion definitely happened. It was not the full-scale exercise that had been planned, the so-called Operation Sealion, but I believe that small reconnaissance groups did land on the Norfolk and Kent coasts in September 1940. The story has been denied and the solders involved vanished into thin air.'

'How could they just vanish?' says Ruth, but she has an uneasy memory of the bodies at Broughton Sea's End, bodies buried in sand, sand which destroys bone. 'Why would anyone want to deny that an invasion happened, if it did happen?'

'Because,' says Eckhart, 'what we are looking at is a British war crime.'

Ruth is silent, thinking of Bosnia and the war crimes tribunal, thinking of Hugh P. Anselm's letter. *A great wrong was done many years ago.*

Eckhart looks at her for a moment and then continues. 'I arrived in England yesterday and I went at once to Broughton Sea's End. I learnt that the son of Buster Hastings still lived in the same house and I asked for an interview. He refused. He did not want, and I quote, to speak about his father, who was a war hero. *Especially not to a German.* I accepted this. I wandered around the village. It is very small, very picturesque. I went to the local pub. And there I had a stroke of luck.' He pauses.

'What?' prompts Ruth.

'I met Jack Hastings' daughter Clara. She told me about the bodies found on the beach. Then I knew. I knew I had uncovered the truth.'

I uncovered it, you mean, thinks Ruth. Or, rather, Ted, Trace, Steve and Craig did. She is beginning to find Eckhart's manner rather irritating.

'I don't understand,' she says. 'Why didn't you just go to see this Hugh Anselm, the one who wrote the letter?'

'That was, of course, my first plan,' says Eckhart unperturbed. 'But when I arrived at his home, a settlement called, I believe, sheltered housing, I discovered that he was dead.'

'Dead?'

'Yes. A week before the warden had discovered him, sitting in his stair-climbing device.'

'A stairlift?'

'Yes. A heart attack I am told.'

Ruth shivers. She knows that there can be nothing sinister about Hugh Anselm's death, he was eighty-six after all and had described his health as 'poor'. All the same, the letter, with its references to evil and wrong-doing, had spooked her. It reminded her too vividly of other letters, letters about death, ritual and sacrifice, the letters which were her first introduction to Nelson and the Serious Crimes Unit. And, now, to think that its author was dead . . .

'There's another survivor from that time,' she says, thinking that this information can't possibly be classified. 'Archie Whitcliffe. He lives in a nursing home somewhere near Broughton.'

Dieter leans back, compressing his lips into a thin smile. 'Archie Whitcliffe too is dead. He died yesterday.'

'Are you sure?'

'Perfectly. I have just come from the nursing home. Apparently the police are investigating.'

The police. That meant Nelson. Ruth feels obscurely hurt

that Nelson hasn't told her about Archie Whitcliffe's death. But, then, it only happened yesterday. When she told him about the bodies being German he had just left the Home after interviewing Archie. That reminds her.

'How did you know the bodies were German?' she asks.

For the first time, Eckhart looks disconcerted. 'It was an assumption,' he says at last, rather stiffly. 'An informed guess.' He looks at Ruth, the blue gaze very intense. 'But you know, don't you? You know that they are German.'

Ruth sighs. Eckhart knows so much she doesn't see any point in stalling. 'Yes,' she says. 'Mineral tests on the bones show that the bodies probably come from Germany.'

'So,' says Eckhart softly. Then he smiles at Ruth. He really is very good-looking. 'In that case, Dr Galloway, I know who your soldiers are.'

12

'*The Eagle Has Landed*,' says Nelson. 'That was the film. Michael Caine was in it. Not a lot of people know that.'

'Michael Caine wasn't in the film I mean,' says Ruth. 'It was a much older film. Black and white. I went to see it with my dad when it was part of some film festival.'

Nelson shrugs. 'I don't go much on films myself. I like Michael Caine though. He's a real actor.'

As opposed to what, thinks Ruth. But she doesn't see any point in pursuing the matter. Besides, she almost knows what Nelson means. Nelson, meanwhile, shows distinct signs of impatience. He's not one for small talk and Ruth is sure he has only come to her house, in response to her phone call, because he hoped to see Kate.

'So what did this journalist bloke have to say?' he says now, pushing his coffee cup away and getting out a notebook.

'He was a military historian,' says Ruth. 'As I say, he'd been researching the rumoured German invasion of Norfolk. Apparently six commandos from the Brandenburger Regiment went missing in September 1940. The story is that they were part of a team based in Norway, whose job was to infiltrate the British mainland, do reconnaissance and sabotage, that sort of thing. He has their names and everything.' She hands Nelson a sheet of paper.

'"Major Karl von Kronig,"' he reads. '"Oberstleutnant Stefan Fenstermacher, Obergefreiter Lutz Gerber, Gefreiter Manfred Hahn, Gefreiter Reiner Brauer, Panzerfunker Gerhard Meister . . ."' Bloody hell. No wonder they didn't win the war with names like that. Take them a year and a half to do the roll call. What the hell's "panzerfunker" when it's at home?'

'Radioman,' says Ruth knowledgeably, though she only learnt the word a few hours ago. 'And here's something you should know. Stefan Fenstermacher was missing a finger.'

'It's them then,' says Nelson. 'Don't you think?'

'I think so, yes,' says Ruth. 'All the men were from a region near Brandenburg, which fits with the isotope analysis. One of the bodies was missing a finger. The ages seem right.'

'So the only question is how did a group of six German commandos end up buried under a cliff in Broughton Sea's End?'

'Do you think Archie Whitcliffe knew anything about it?'

'I think he did,' says Nelson slowly, 'but he died before we could find out more.'

Ruth looks at him curiously. 'Do you really think his death could be suspicious?'

Nelson sighs. 'I don't know, Ruth. Old man dies, no suspicious circumstances, doctor signs the death certificate right off. But, I don't know . . . The day before he'd more or less admitted he knew something about the deaths. Said he couldn't tell me because he'd taken a "blood oath". Next day, he dies. You don't have to be Poirot to think that's a bit suspicious.'

'You might think it's more suspicious when you hear this,' says Ruth. And she tells him about Hugh P. Anselm.

'Hugh,' says Nelson slowly. 'He was one of the men that Mrs Hastings mentioned. One of the three youngsters in the troop. Hang on . . . found dead on the stairlift . . .' He is silent for a minute, thinking.

'What is it?' asks Ruth.

'I don't know. It just rings a bell somewhere. I think I ought to go to this sheltered accommodation place, talk to the warden. And I'll ask for an autopsy on Archie Whitcliffe. There'll be a battle royal with Whitcliffe, mind.'

'Why? Doesn't he want to know if his grandfather was murdered?'

It is the first time either of them has used the word 'murdered'. It doesn't seem to go with the world of care homes and stairlifts, but Nelson thinks of Archie Whitcliffe's face when he talked about the blood oath, of Maria's words: 'Lucifer. He said Lucifer.' Then, for no reason at all, he thinks of Jack Hastings standing proudly in front of his fireplace whilst his mother knitted placidly in the background. 'He never forgot the horror.'

He turns to Ruth. 'Whitcliffe's funny about his family. You know what it's like in Norfolk. His family have lived in their little village for donkey's years. Probably intermarried with donkeys by the look of 'em. Whitcliffe's proud of his grandfather, thinks of him as a war hero. He was touchy enough about us interviewing him so he won't want an inquest. He'll want to bury him properly, coffin, flowers, black horses, the lot. He won't want me holding things up, suggesting that the old man was done away with.'

'Is Whitcliffe the only relative?' asks Ruth, who has never met Nelson's boss.

'No. There's a whole bunch of grandchildren, according to Archie.'

'Well, some of them might support you.'

'It's possible. Whitcliffe's talked about a sister. There's a brother too, I think.'

Nelson frowns at the floor, which is still covered with books and packing cases. Ruth wonders when he's going to leave. She'd like another few hours of tidying before she has to collect Kate. She suspects Nelson of holding out for a sight of Kate. He'd been most put out to hear that she was at the childminder's.

Sure enough, when there is a sudden knock on the door, Nelson's first words are, 'Is that Katie?'

'No, she's still slightly too young to drive herself home,' says Ruth, getting up. Who can it be? Dieter Eckhart, back with some more Eagle Has Landed stuff? Shona stopping by for a gossip? Cathbad?

But when she opens the door, she is greeted by an elegant woman with short, streaky hair, carrying a suitcase.

'Ruth!'

'Tatjana . . .' Ruth stammers. 'I wasn't expecting you till tomorrow.'

'You didn't get my text?'

Ruth shakes her head. Her phone is upstairs, buried under a pile of rubbish.

'I'm sorry,' says Tatjana, looking back at the taxi, already performing a clumsy U-turn in the narrow road.

'It doesn't matter. Come in.'

Ruth is aware of a dark figure looming in the background. 'Tatjana,' she says. 'This is Detective Chief Inspector Harry Nelson.' She doesn't know why she gave him his full title but she is surprised at the sudden interest on Tatjana's face.

'Pleased to meet you, Detective Chief Inspector,' she says.

'. . . it's a deeply stratified alluvial site in the Paleocoastal tradition, so of *course* we were surprised.'

'Of course.' Ruth can't remember exactly which site they're talking about. Is this still Arlington Springs Woman? Over the past few hours Tatjana has ranged from the European Palaeolithic to the Beaker people and Civil War sites in Dorset. Ruth thinks they are now on New World archaeology, a subject on which Tatjana turns out to be rather an expert, but Ruth is finding it hard to keep up. She knows she is rather insular about archaeology, preferring British or European sites (Britain was, of course, part of the European landmass only ten thousand years ago) to those in the Americas or the Antipodes.

She is also distracted because she has collected Kate from Sandra's and the baby, not content to remain snoozing picturesquely in the background, is making a bid for centre stage, cooing and emitting high-pitched yelps like a miniature cheerleader. Ruth thinks she is being rather sweet but she is scared to take her attention off Tatjana for too long. So she sits on the floor with Kate, who is propped up by cushions, occasionally handing her a brightly coloured toy which

Kate ignores in favour of chewing the TV remote control. Tatjana has, so far, not looked in Kate's direction once.

Nelson had stayed only a few minutes, long enough for Tatjana to pronounce him 'interesting' which, Ruth discovers, is her highest term of praise.

'How come you are entertaining a policeman in the afternoon?' she asked, raising her eyebrows slightly. Ruth hoped she wasn't blushing.

'I'm seconded to the Serious Crimes Unit,' she said, trying to adopt a Serious Crimes face. 'I help with their investigations sometimes. Forensics, bones, dating, you know.'

'And is there much serious crime in Norfolk?' Tatjana still looked amused.

'You'd be surprised,' Ruth says. She needs to leave Kate and start supper. As all she has in the fridge are two chicken breasts and a very old tomato (she had planned to go shopping tomorrow), the options are limited. She is going to call it chicken cacciatore and hope for the best. At least Tatjana has brought some Duty Free wine. The problem is that she can't leave Kate on her own and she doesn't like to ask Tatjana to keep an eye on her. Eventually she puts Kate into her baby seat and carries the seat into the kitchen. Jesus, there was a time when she could go out of the house any time she wanted; now even a trip to the next room is complicated.

Tatjana follows her, continuing the story of Arlington Springs Woman. Ruth tries to listen, cook, and respond to Kate at the same time. But before long Kate feels ignored and her cheerleader yelps dissolve into full-scale crying. Ruth picks her up and jiggles her up and down, whilst heating a bottle of milk in a saucepan. Tatjana watches from the doorway, glass of wine in hand.

When Ruth is sitting down with Kate (plus bottle) on her lap, Tatjana asks, in a tone of academic enquiry, 'So, what about Kate's father? Is he involved?'

'He's married,' says Ruth shortly.

'That must be tough.'

'It's okay,' says Ruth, settling Kate more comfortably into the crook of her arm. 'I wouldn't want to be married. I like living here on my own.'

'With Kate.'

'Yes. With Kate. And Flint.'

Flint had received a much better welcome than Kate. Tatjana had bent down, tickled his chin and told him that he had very fine whiskers. Flint, as was his wont with people who fancied themselves cat lovers, ignored her completely. Perversely, with Nelson, who prefers dogs, Flint is positively skittish, jumping on his lap at every opportunity and shedding hairs over his trousers.

'It must be lonely here sometimes,' says Tatjana. 'Do you have neighbours?'

'The house next door is empty. The other side are holiday people. They usually come down for a week or two in summer.'

'And your work at the university. Is it good?' Perhaps Tatjana is realising that Ruth has contributed very little to the archaeology stories.

'It's okay. I like my students. I like teaching. I haven't done any interesting digs for a while. The last one was a year ago, on the Saltmarsh, with Erik.'

'I can't believe that Erik is dead,' says Tatjana. 'How did it happen? I always thought he'd live forever.'

'He died here on the marshes,' says Ruth. 'It was dark, the tide was coming in. He drowned.' She hopes that Tatjana won't want to hear the details; she never wants to think about that night again.

'Dear God.' Tatjana is silent for a minute. Kate's eyelids droop, the bottle lolls out of her mouth and a fine stream of milk pours onto Ruth's arm.

'Ruth.' Tatjana sounds pained. 'Your sleeve.'

'It doesn't matter,' says Ruth. 'She's nearly asleep. I'll put her down in a minute.' She can feel Kate getting heavier and heavier in her arms. It is six o'clock, with any luck she'll sleep now for a good part of the night.

Tatjana sits opposite, looking at Ruth so intently that she is embarrassed, conscious of the contrast between Tatjana's sleek clothes and salon-perfect hair and her own crumbled, milk-stained appearance.

'I look a mess,' she says, meeting Tatjana's gaze.

'You look great,' says Tatjana. 'You haven't changed at all.'

Ruth knows that she has. She is older, fatter and sadder. But she has noticed before that if you don't do anything to yourself people will assume that you haven't changed. Also, that you don't care.

'I'm forty,' she says.

Tatjana grimaces. 'Me too.' Unexpectedly, she reaches out and touches Kate's hair. 'It seems a long time ago, doesn't it? Bosnia?'

It did, but it also seemed like yesterday. Ruth only has to close her eyes and she sees the hotel, Erik telling stories by candlelight, Tatjana standing in the dark holding a gun. Whatever else, they mustn't talk about Bosnia.

So she tells Tatjana about the bodies at Broughton Sea's End.

Tatjana's son, Jacob, was dead. Ruth was grateful that Tatjana told her this straight out, saving her from making any crass comments like, 'I didn't know you had a son, how old is he?' making things worse and worse, as if they could possibly be worse. In that summer of 1995 Ruth did not know what it was to have a child, and to lose a child . . . well, that is still unimaginable. She remembers that she sat there, in the shadow of the pine trees, literally stiff with shock. She simply did not know what to say; her life's experience so far had not prepared her for that moment. Her parents were experts on death and the afterlife, of course. They would have known what to say. 'We're praying for you.' 'I'm sure he's in heaven with all the other little angels.' But Ruth could say none of this. She didn't believe in God, especially not in a God who could take a child just so that he could have another little angel. What can you say to a girl your own age who has lost her child?

Perhaps fortunately, Tatjana did not seem to expect Ruth to speak. Calmly, almost coldly, she told the story. Tatjana had married young, her husband was another academic and, unusually for a Yugoslavian man of that time, he supported her career. Even now, Ruth remembers the expression on Tatjana's face when she said the word 'career'. When Jacob was born, Tatjana continued with her studies, teaching part time at the university. Then, when Jacob was two, she got the chance to study for a PhD at Johns Hopkins

University. Encouraged by her husband, Tatjana left Jacob with her parents and went to America. While she was away, all hell broke loose.

'My husband died very early on. He was in a convoy of trucks taking the injured out of Mostar. His truck was hit by a grenade. I was trying to arrange for Jacob and my parents to fly out to the US when I heard that their village had been attacked. I couldn't get news, I was going mad. Eventually I travelled there overland, a nightmare journey. The village was destroyed. As if it had never been.'

'But do you know for sure that Jacob—'

Tatjana had laughed. A sound that Ruth hopes never to hear again.

'I tracked down one of the only survivors. She told me that she had seen Jacob and his grandparents shot. The only question remaining is: where is his body?'

She had looked at Ruth in the dappled light from the trees.

'I must find his body, Ruth. You know what Erik says about needing to find a grave. It's true. You need to see the dead, to bury them, to mourn them. Otherwise . . .' Her voice dropped away. 'Otherwise you cannot continue to live.'

'But how can . . .' Ruth was miserably aware of how inadequate she sounded. What a poor confidante she was proving. She too lapsed into silence.

'I don't know,' said Tatjana briskly. 'You know they are moving bodies all the time to try to hide their crimes.' This was true and it made the archaeologists' job much more difficult. On some sites it was clear that they were dealing with secondary, sometimes even tertiary, burials, bodies that had been moved several times to avoid detection. Sometimes they could use 3-D imaging to gauge the depth of a grave but often they had to rely on their knowledge of strata and earth movement to tell how many times and how recently a body had been buried. At other times they just had to guess, to use their 'archaeologist's sense' as Erik put it.

'I need to make enquiries,' Tatjana was saying. 'I can ask everyone we meet about the village and what happened to the bodies. That's where you can help me, Ruth.'

'Of course I will.'

'And,' Tatjana had said, almost as an afterthought, 'I know the name of the man who did this. That will be helpful.'

Ruth did not know why but Tatjana told her anyway. 'So I can kill him.'

13

The sheltered housing looks rather pleasant in the spring sunshine. The grounds are immaculate, the grass cut in neat deckchair stripes, the beds full of daffodils. The buildings too are attractive, low and red brick, doors and windows freshly painted. Not bad, thinks Nelson approvingly, one day he might have to fix his mum up with something like this. Not yet, though. Maureen Nelson goes mad if anyone mentions the words 'pensioner' or 'sheltered' or, especially, 'warden'. Besides, when the time comes, Nelson has two older sisters who will manage the whole thing, complaining all the time about the extra work but scorning any offers of help, especially from him. It's handy being the youngest sometimes.

Now, Nelson presses the bell marked with the dreaded word 'warden', but surely even Maureen wouldn't disapprove of the charming, soft-spoken man (possibly Irish, like Maureen herself) who ushers him through the double doors and into a ground floor flat.

'Do you live on site?' asks Nelson.

'Yes,' says the warden, whose name is Kevin Fitzherbert.

'Lots of places, they say "warden" but it's just a voice on the end of the phone, not someone living downstairs who'll come and unblock your sink for you.'

'Is that what you do? Unblock sinks?'

'That, and find lost glasses, help people up if they take a tumble, change the channel on the TV – there's hell to pay if they can't get *Countdown* – undo jars, post their pools coupons.'

Nelson looks round the room. It is comfortable and extremely neat with a single armchair pushed close to the TV, remote control and folded *Radio Times* on the arm.

'Are you married, Mr Fitzherbert?' he asks, accepting an invitation to sit down.

Kevin Fitzherbert looks slightly discomforted. 'Divorced. My wife and I . . . we had our problems . . . but I'm off the drink now, been off it for five years. I'm in AA. Made a completely new start.'

Not for the first time Nelson wonders at the things people will disclose to the police without being asked. The fact that Kevin Fitzherbert used to have a drink problem might be relevant or it might not. Either way, Nelson stores the information away and smiles non-committally.

'Tell me about Hugh Anselm,' he says.

'Ah . . .' Fitzherbert looks genuinely sad now, the Irish lilt well to the fore. 'That was a tragedy, so it was. A fine gentleman. A true gentle man, if you get my meaning. One of the old school.'

Nelson wonders where else he heard this phrase recently. 'How did he die?' he asks.

'Heart attack,' says Fitzherbert. 'He had a heart problem.

Angina. It was very serious, the slightest exertion could trigger an episode. He knew he could go any time. I try to call on the older residents once a day, check they're all right. Most people like a regular time. I used to see Hugh at nine o'clock, he was an early riser. We'd have a cup of tea, have a go at the *Telegraph* crossword together. He was a whizz at crosswords, Hughie. Anyway, I called on him as usual and there was no answer. I thought it was odd so I used my master key and went in. He was sitting in his stair-lift, seatbelt on, stone dead.'

'Why did he have a stairlift?' asks Nelson, suddenly thinking. 'Aren't these all flats?'

'No, some are maisonettes. They're the nicest units really. Hugh had some stairs and climbing made him breathless, so he used the lift.'

'How long did they think he'd been there?'

'Almost twenty-four hours the coroner thought. He must have got into the lift just after I'd left him the day before.'

'The coroner. Did the police investigate? One of my team?' The incident must have happened when he was on his holiday, thinks Nelson. It still rang a faint bell though.

'Yes, a nice fellow called Clough. I remember the name because I used to be a big Forest fan.'

Clough! That's why the story seemed familiar; Nelson must have read it in the weekly report. Although Clough isn't really to blame – the death appeared to be natural causes and he did write it up – Nelson still feels slightly irritated with his sergeant.

'Mr Fitzherbert,' he says, leaning forward, 'as I said on the phone, I'm interested in anything Hugh Anselm may have told you about the war. Especially his years in the Home Guard.'

'I know you mentioned it and I've been wracking my brains so. But the truth is he never talked about the war. I think he'd been in the RAF but he never spoke about it. He was all for peace, Hugh. Wouldn't even wear a poppy. Said Remembrance Day should be as much about the German war dead as the British. He said there was no good side and no bad side, only winners and losers. He was a bit of a Leftie really. Used to write all these letters to the papers about Iraq and so on.'

'But he read the *Telegraph*?'

'Ah, that was just for the crossword. He took the *Guardian* too and the *New Statesman*. History magazines as well. He was a fine, well-educated man.'

'Mr Fitzherbert, I know it sounds odd but did Hugh Anselm ever mention . . . Lucifer?'

'Lucifer? Dear God, no.' In an instinctive gesture, Fitzherbert's hand hovers over his forehead. A Catholic then.

There's nothing else here, thinks Nelson. Hugh was a fine, well-educated man who died, aged eighty-six, of a heart attack. No close family, Nelson has already asked. His wife died eight years ago. No children. Nobody to mourn him except Kevin Fitzherbert, who missed his company over the crossword.

But, at the door, Nelson has a Columboesque last thought.

'The stairlift. Was it up or down?'

Fitzherbert's brow creases. 'That's the funny thing. It was halfway up.'

'Halfway up? Had it broken?'

'Must have done, but it's an odd thing. They're serviced regularly, and when I saw Hugh sitting there I pressed the button. It was an instinctive thing really. And the lift moved instantly.'

'So why would it stop halfway up?'

'Something must have interfered with the current. Or Hugh pressed the button by accident.'

'Or someone could have stopped it,' says Nelson.

Nelson drives back to the station, thinking hard. On the face of it, the deaths of the two old men could be from natural causes. But there are enough questions now to add up to a suspicion. How did the stairlift stop in mid air? What did Archie mean by the word 'Lucifer' and what was the blood oath sworn by the two men when they were still teenagers? There's something else too that's nagging at him. Something to do with an armchair, a *Radio Times* and Ruth Galloway. He frowns, taking the corner by the Campbell's Soup factory on two wheels.

When he gets in, he asks Leah for black coffee and fills in a form requesting an autopsy on Archie Whitcliffe. His boss will see it, no question, but it makes sense to get the wheels in motion. 'Just following procedure,' he'd say, when challenged. Whitcliffe is a great one for procedure.

As he is laboriously filling in the boxes, Clough appears in the doorway.

'You wanted me, boss?' Nelson had sent him a text.

'Yes, sit down a minute.'

Clough sits down, his jaws still working on some item of food lodged in his back teeth.

'It's about Hugh Anselm.'

Clough looks blank.

'The old man found dead in the stairlift.'

'Oh, yes. It was while you were on holiday. Poor old bloke got in his stairlift, had a heart attack, found the next morning. I filed a report.' Slightly defensively.

'The stairlift stopped halfway up. You didn't think that was odd?'

'The warden thought it must have malfunctioned. Or the old boy pressed the wrong button by mistake. There were no suspicious circumstances.' Definitely defensive.

'What happened to Hugh Anselm's stuff? His belongings?'

'I don't know. I presumed next-of-kin took them.' Clough looks curious now. 'What's this all about, boss?'

'Probably nothing.'

'Is there a link to old man Whitcliffe?'

That's the trouble with Clough. He's not as thick as he looks.

'Possibly. They were both in the Home Guard, and before he died Hugh Anselm wrote a letter to a German military historian. He said something had happened in 1940 that had haunted him all his life. A "great wrong" he called it.'

'Do you think it was the murder of our six chums?' The team now know that the dead men were almost certainly German. Nelson has heard Clough calling them 'the Nazi boy band'.

'I don't know and now there's no-one left to ask.'

'Suspicious,' says Clough happily.

'Yes.'

Clough is on his way out when Nelson calls him back. 'Cloughie, what do you know about *Countdown*?'

'*Countdown*, boss? It's a quiz programme. Teatime TV. For the oldies. It's a word game. Dictionary corner and all that.'

'The sort of thing someone who liked crosswords would enjoy?'

'I suppose so.'

Because Nelson had identified the thought that was nagging at him. Archie's newspaper, folded back at his day's viewing. *Countdown, Coronation Street, Panorama*, an afternoon film matinee of *Went the Day Well?*

When Clough has gone, he googles *Went the Day Well?*

'Chilling classic,' he reads, 'imagining the brutal Nazi invasion of a sleepy English village.'

14

'We gather today to bless a child.
A new life that has become part of our world.
We gather today to name this child.
To call a thing by name is to give it power,
and so today we shall give this child a gift.
We will welcome her into our hearts and lives
and bless her with a name of her own.'

Cathbad is in full swing. He made a bonfire in the back garden and placed a trestle table in front of it. He then put a goblet of wine and a bowl of olive oil on the table and has invited the guests to form a ring around the fire.

Ruth, carrying Kate in her blue snow suit, follows him rather reluctantly. She had been surprised to see how many people turned up for the naming day party. Tatjana, of course, was already in residence and was quickly chatting to Phil about Arlington Springs Woman. As well as Phil there was Shona, Cathbad's friend Freya from the modern languages department, Trace and Clough, Ted, Judy and, surprisingly, Dieter Eckhart and Clara Hastings.

'I met Cathbad at the university,' explained Dieter. 'He invited me. I hope you don't mind.'

'Why should I mind?' said Ruth, rather sulkily. Cathbad can hardly know Dieter, who is doing some research in the history department, very well. Ruth suspects him of extending the invitation to annoy Phil, who might be jealous of Dieter's academic reputation (and his good looks). What is more surprising is how close Dieter and Clara seem, arm-in-arm, laughing warmly over shared jokes, speaking in German together. He has only been here a few days after all.

'Clara's been a great help to me,' Dieter explained. 'Telling me many stories of local history.' He gave Ruth a rather meaningful look.

Clara laughed. 'And I've been practising my German. I spent a year in Germany before going to uni but I'm awfully rusty. I wish I'd worked harder at school now.'

'I bet you were the model pupil,' said Dieter with a smouldering look.

'Oh, I was useless,' said Clara carelessly. 'I was expelled from two schools.'

Well, Dieter was certainly making every effort to help Clara catch up, retiring with her into a corner of Ruth's sitting room and managing, with clever body language, to block out the rest of the company altogether.

To her surprise, Ruth found that she was enjoying the party. It's been a long time since she had so many people in her house and, since Cathbad and Freya provided the food and drink, it's hardly a strain on her as hostess, though she had trouble finding enough plates and glasses (Clough is drinking from a Winnie the Pooh mug and Phil is eating from one of Kate's moulded plastic bowls). Ruth was just settling down to a good chat with Judy when there was a thunderous knock at the door.

'That'll be the boss,' said Clough. 'Trying to force entry.'

Oh please God, no.

But Clough was right. Standing framed in the doorway were Nelson, unsmiling in jeans and a leather jacket, and Michelle, carrying a huge, beribboned parcel.

'I know we weren't supposed to bring presents,' said Michelle. 'But I think this'll be useful.'

Ruth accepted the present with thanks, her heart sinking. Despite Cathbad's directive, Kate was actually doing quite well for gifts but the Nelson offering dwarfed the rest.

'Do open it, Ruth,' said Michelle, accepting a glass of punch from a suddenly attentive Cathbad. Where the hell had he found a clean glass?

Ruth hates opening presents with other people watching (memories of grisly Christmas mornings pretending to be grateful for a Bible) but there was no refusing without looking churlish. Gingerly, she tore the pink flowered paper.

'Wow! It's a . . . it's wonderful . . . what is it?'

It was a pink gingham chair attached to a wide base on wheels. The chair had a tray in front bristling with things to touch and press and crinkle. It looked faintly alarming, like a power base for a pink-checked alien. Ruth had a sudden flashback to Doctor Who and the Daleks. Exterminate, exterminate.

'It's a baby walker,' laughed Michelle. 'You put her in the

chair and she can walk around. Well, she won't be able to do it yet, but in a few months she'll be whizzing about.'

Ruth found the idea of Kate on wheels rather frightening. At least, like the Daleks, she won't be able to go upstairs.

'Wow. It's fantastic. Thanks.'

'Where's Kate? I haven't seen her for ages.'

In the first months of Kate's life, Michelle had put herself out to be kind to Ruth. She came all the way to the Saltmarsh to coo and offer advice. She suggested meeting in town, she volunteered to drive Ruth and Kate to the park, she even offered to take Kate swimming 'at my club'. Ruth was touched, and she yearned for female friendship, especially from someone who had been through the whole baby thing herself, but however much she tried to pretend that Kate had no father, that she had sprung fully formed from Ruth's brain like a modern-day Athena, she couldn't quite face the prospect of playing happy families with Nelson's wife. So she wriggled out of the invitations, pleading work and tiredness, and when Michelle eventually stopped ringing, she felt both relieved and disappointed.

But this evening Michelle was all friendliness, and admiration for Kate.

'Oh, isn't she gorgeous? Can I hold her?'

Ruth is always surprised how maternal Michelle is. For someone so glamorous, she doesn't give a thought to sick on her shoulder or a baby grabbing handfuls of her hair. She held Kate expertly (not even relinquishing her glass) and nuzzled her head.

'Oh, she's lovely. I'd forgotten how they smell. Look, Harry. Do you want a hold?'

'I'm fine, thanks,' said Nelson.

Now, as the guests traipse out into the garden, Ruth looks back and sees Nelson helping Michelle on with her swishy red coat. She smiles and leans back against him. Behind them, Dieter and Clara are still whispering together. Love is in the air, thinks Ruth sourly, it must be the effects of Cathbad's home-made punch.

'This ceremony is called a wiccaning or a saining,' Cathbad explained earlier. 'It's to introduce Kate to the Gods.'

'Or, if you don't believe any of that tosh,' put in Ruth, 'it's just a party.'

But, now, in the dark, with the fire leaping upwards, it does feel more like a ceremony than a party.

'The Guardians, that's Shona and I,' says Cathbad modestly, 'should stand either side of the table. Ruth, you hold Kate in the middle.'

Ruth obeys. She's willing to go along with Cathbad only so far. At the first sign of human sacrifice, she'll be straight back indoors.

'What is the baby's full name?' he asks in his Druid voice, echoey and impressive.

'Kate,' says Ruth. 'Kate Scarlet.'

She looks at Nelson and finds, to her horror, that she can't look away. Only the two of them know the significance of the name though, to judge by Judy's sudden start, some of the others might guess. Scarlet Henderson, the little girl involved in the abduction case that first drew Ruth and Nelson together.

For a full minute, Ruth and Nelson stare at each other across the flames. Then, to Ruth's relief, Cathbad starts speaking again.

'May the gods keep this child pure and perfect, and let anything that is negative stay far beyond her world.'

He puts his finger in the olive oil and gently touches Kate's forehead. Ruth watches him closely to check that he doesn't trace any sinister symbol on her, but no, it's just a touch. Then, he puts his finger in the wine and places a drop on Kate's lips. She smiles. Her mother's daughter.

'May you always have good fortune,' intones Cathbad, 'may you always have good health, may you always be joyful, and may you always have love in your heart.'

Once again, Ruth looks at Nelson. He is staring into the fire.

'You are known to the gods and to us as Kate Scarlet. This is your name, and it is powerful. Bear your name with honour, and may the gods bless you on this and every day.' He passes the wine to Ruth. 'Drink and pass on.'

He then addresses the wider circle. 'As you drink, say aloud: "I honour you, Kate Scarlet."'

Ruth takes a sip. The wine rushes to her head like whisky. 'I honour you, Kate Scarlet,' she croaks. She passes the cup to Shona who takes an enthusiastic gulp. 'I honour you, Kate Scarlet,' she says, her voice loud and clear. She passes the cup on to Dieter.

'I honour you, Kate Scarlet,' he bows slightly.

'I honour you, Kate Scarlet,' echoes Clara.

'I honour you, Kate Scarlet.' Clough sounds as if he is laughing.

'I honour you, Kate Scarlet.' Trace is expressionless.

'I honour you, Kate Scarlet.' Tatjana, putting the stress on the 'you'.

'I honour you, Kate Scarlet,' Ted booms as loudly as Cathbad himself.

'I honour you, Kate Scarlet.' Judy's voice is soft.

'I honour you, Kate Scarlet.' Phil's self-conscious mumble.

'I honour you, Kate Scarlet.' Freya's fervent whisper.

Michelle takes the cup with complete self-possession. 'I honour you, Kate Scarlet.' Nelson takes the wine. His lips move but no-one hears any words. The flames have risen so that Ruth cannot see his face.

Cathbad replaces the cup on the table. 'Can I have her?' he asks Ruth. Rather reluctantly Ruth hands over the bundle in the blue snow suit. Cathbad holds the baby up to the night sky. 'Welcome, Kate Scarlet. We ask the gods to watch over you and over your father and mother.' He turns to Ruth, smiling. 'That's it.'

Numbly, Ruth follows Cathbad back into the house. Why did he say that about father and mother? Does he suspect something or did he just download the whole thing from paganceremonies.co.uk? That's the trouble with Cathbad, you never know how much is airy-fairy spiritual stuff and how much is good old-fashioned stirring. Did the other guests suspect anything? She doesn't think any of them were listening very hard – they all had the slightly glazed expression of people in church. Nelson will have noticed though, she's sure of that.

Kate has fallen asleep and Ruth is glad to escape upstairs and put her to bed. She takes off Kate's snow suit and puts her, still dressed in her babygro, into her cot, under the blanket knitted by Ruth's mother. What would Ruth's parents make of the ceremony around the fire? In all probability, they'd be searching for their bell, book and candle at the first sight of the fire or the oil or the cup of wine.

But when Ruth goes downstairs and starts talking to Judy over the remains of the punch, Judy says, 'It reminded me of the Catholic mass. You know, sharing the wine and all that.'

Ruth wonders if the analogy also occurred to Nelson who, like Judy, was brought up a Catholic.

'Are you getting married in a Catholic church?' she asks.

Judy grimaces. 'Yes. The full nuptial mass. Darren's a Catholic too. We met at school.'

'It must be nice,' says Ruth, 'knowing someone that well.'

Judy fishes a slice of orange out of the punch and eats it meditatively. 'It is nice. I mean, we've got the same memories, the same friends. Our families all know each other.' She laughs. 'I can't help wondering what it would be like to go to bed with someone you hardly know. God, I must be drunk.'

Ruth thinks of a dark night, a terrible discovery, an unknown body moving against hers.

'It may be exciting,' she says, 'but I think the best thing must be to go to bed with someone who knows every inch of your body.'

'Sounds fun.'

Ruth whirls round to find Nelson standing behind her. She knows she is blushing like a bonfire.

'This is women's talk,' says Judy.

'So I gathered. We're off, Ruth. Thanks for a . . . well, thanks.'

'Have you spoken to Dieter? About the bodies?'

'We had a quick chat. He seems a bit preoccupied now.'

Ruth glances over to the sofa where Dieter and Clara are still nose to nose, his hand brushing the back of her neck.

'Is that Jack Hastings' daughter?' asks Nelson.

Ruth nods.

'Wonder what he'll think about her snogging a German?'

'Don't mention the war,' warns Ruth.

'Right. Well, goodbye.' He leans towards her as if he is about to kiss her cheek but, at the last minute, veers away again. Michelle swoops over and enfolds Ruth in a scented embrace.

'We must meet up very soon,' she says.

'What on earth does she see in him?' says Judy, as the door closes behind the Nelsons.

'His sparkling personality?'

'Hardly.'

Now Tatjana is ladling away at the punch.

'That man, Nelson,' she says, 'he is very attractive.'

Judy snorts and turns away to talk to Cathbad.

'Do you think so?' says Ruth.

'Yes,' says Tatjana dreamily. 'He is very powerful, very dark. I think he has a secret.'

Ruth looks at her sharply but Tatjana is staring into the punchbowl. In the kitchen Ted and Clough have started singing. 'I wanna be near you. You're the one, the one for me.'

Tatjana shoots a sidelong glance at Ruth. 'I think I felt a spark though.'

'What?'

'I think he was attracted to me,' says Tatjana. 'I felt it.'

Ruth says nothing. She doesn't quite know what to make of the new, sexually confident Tatjana. She prefers the quiet girl sitting in the pine forest, drinking wine in defiance of the wolves.

'He's married,' she says at last.

'And his wife is very beautiful,' says Tatjana, 'but not clever enough for him, I think.'

'I wanna be near you,' bellow Ted and Clough from the kitchen. 'You're the one for me.'

Ruth suddenly feels very tired. She wants to lie down and sleep for a week. Would it be very rude to go to bed and ask the last one out to turn off the lights?

Judy appears at her shoulder. 'Bye, Ruth. Thanks for a lovely evening.'

'You're not driving are you?' Ruth doesn't know what was in the punch but she's betting it was ninety per cent proof.

'No, Trace is giving me a lift. As soon as she can stop Cloughie singing, that is.'

In the other room, the concert ends abruptly. Not for the first time, Ruth envies Trace's natural authority.

'You must come on my hen night,' says Judy. 'It's a week on Saturday. I'm dreading it.'

'Why do you want me to come then?' laughs Ruth. 'So I can dread it too?'

'I need someone on my side.' Judy turns politely to Tatjana who is still standing by the punch. 'You must come too. A fine English tradition for you.'

'I'd love to,' says Tatjana, much to Ruth's surprise.

Ted also cadges a lift with Trace, leaving Cathbad, Ruth, Freya and Tatjana to start to clear away plates and eat the last of the crisps. Phil and Shona left shortly after the ceremony and Dieter and Clara seem to have disappeared.

'That was an interesting experience,' Tatjana is saying to Cathbad.

'It's important,' says Cathbad, 'to introduce the baby to the household guardians.'

Tatjana stacks glasses neatly in the sink.

'So, Cathbad,' she says, 'how long have you been a devil worshipper?'

15

The next morning Nelson drives to work in a sombre frame of mind. Last night felt like one of those weirdly scientific Japanese tortures designed to discover how much one person could stand in a short space of time. He prides himself on his self control but there are easier things in life than watching your wife hold your illegitimate baby. And what was Cathbad playing at around the fire? Nelson is sure that when he said the words, 'we ask the gods to watch over you and over your father and mother', Cathbad looked straight at him. Does Cathbad know that Nelson is Kate's father? Before she was born Cathbad overheard something which may have given him a clue and Nelson has no doubt at all that he has remembered, word for word. Cathbad is also well in with all the university lot – maybe Ruth has confided in Shona or even that slimy Phil. Christ, probably everyone at UNN knows by now – Nelson's hands are wet on the steering wheel. If so, it's only a matter of time before Michelle finds out.

Michelle likes Ruth. She wants to help her. 'She doesn't know the first thing about looking after a baby' she told a decidedly twitchy Nelson on her return from a visit to Ruth and the new-born Kate. 'I caught her reading today.' '*Reading?*' echoed Nelson, rather wildly. 'Yes, she was feeding Kate and reading some old archaeology book.' 'What's wrong with that?' Michelle had laughed. 'When you have a baby you don't have time for reading. Not if you're doing it properly.' Was Ruth doing it properly? She doesn't quite look comfortable with a baby, the way Michelle does. Ruth still holds Kate slightly warily, as if she might explode, but she seems to do all the right things and, sometimes, she looks at Kate with an expression that makes Nelson's heart ache. And she talks to the baby all the time, even if she does address the five-month-old like one of her postgraduates. 'We're going outside now, Kate. You might find it a bit cold at first but that's just the contrast with inside . . .'

No, to Nelson's anxious eye, Ruth seems to be doing just fine. He'd worried about her going back to work but the childminder seems competent (unknown to Ruth, Nelson has run a third check on Sandra) and he knows that, as he's hardly in a position to help her openly, Ruth needs the money. He has offered to give her some money every month (he'd tell Michelle it was a retirement scheme or something) but Ruth refused. 'I want to do this on my own,' she said. A statement which, though courageous and admirable in many ways, nevertheless fills Nelson with dread.

When it comes down to it, does he have any rights at all where Kate is concerned? None at all, says a lawyer whom he has secretly consulted. 'If your name isn't on the birth certificate, you're no-one.' Nelson has never seen Kate's birth certificate but he's betting it's 'father unknown'. Ruth could do anything – emigrate, join a commune, refuse to send Kate to school – and he couldn't do a thing about it. Jesus, she's already had a pagan christening service. His mother would turn in her grave (the shock of Kate's parentage would have killed her). When Cathbad put the oil on Kate's forehead Nelson had surprised himself by how strongly he wanted Cathbad, anyone, to trace the sign of the cross there. *I baptise you in the name of the Father, and of the Son and of the Holy Spirit.* Once a Catholic, as they say. And Kate Scarlet! Why had Ruth done that? Even today, when he thinks of the name Scarlet, he feels as if his heart will break.

By the time he reaches the station he is sunk in gloom and the sight of Whitcliffe waiting for him in his office does nothing to cheer him up. He knows that Whitcliffe won't have dropped in for a cosy chat about his promotion prospects.

Whitcliffe is holding a piece of paper. When he sees Nelson he strides forward and thrusts the paper into his face.

'What is the meaning of this?'

Nelson has never known his boss so angry. Normally Whitcliffe keeps his distance and speaks in a light monotone. Now he is eyeball to eyeball with Nelson, his face red, his voice, in which the Norfolk accent has suddenly come to the fore, choked with fury. In an odd way, for the first time, Nelson almost likes the man. But he knows he must be careful, very careful.

'What do you mean, sir?' He throws in the 'sir' to appease Whitcliffe.

'Mean? I mean this!' Whitcliffe waves the paper again. Nelson backs away slightly.

'What is it?' Though he knows very well.

'How dare you ... how *dare* you ask for an autopsy on my grandfather.'

'I had good reasons, sir,' says Nelson stolidly.

They glare at each other. Whitcliffe is still breathing heavily but his colour has faded and, when he speaks, his voice is almost back to RP.

'Perhaps you'd be good enough to share your *reasoning* with me.'

'Why don't we sit down?' Nelson attempts a soothing tone and feels as if he has scored a point, especially when Whitcliffe takes the subordinate's chair and allows him to take his place behind his own desk. But, as soon as they are seated, Whitcliffe returns to the attack.

'How dare you do this, Harry. Behind my back.'

'I'm the officer in charge of the investigation,' says Nelson. 'I followed procedure. I contacted the coroner's office and copied you in. Otherwise you wouldn't have known,' he adds.

'I know everything that goes on round here,' spits Whitcliffe. Nelson hopes this isn't true.

'Look – er – sir ... I know this is difficult for you–'

'Difficult!' Whitcliffe looks ready to explode.

'Your grandfather is dead and, naturally, you're upset. But I have reasons to suspect that death was not by natural causes.'

'I'll be fascinated to hear them,' says Whitcliffe nastily.

'The day before your grandfather died,' says Nelson, 'Detective Sergeant Johnson and I interviewed him about the bodies found at Broughton Sea's End. I asked him if he remembered anything from his time with the Home Guard. His words were: "If I knew anything I wouldn't tell you. I took a blood oath."'

'Is that your only—'

'I didn't think much of it,' says Nelson smoothly, 'though I thought he was concealing something. That night he died.'

'He was an old man. He had a stroke.'

'Two weeks ago,' Nelson goes on, 'another old man died. His name was Hugh Anselm and he served with your grand-father in the Home Guard. Shortly before he died he wrote to a German historian telling him that something terrible had happened at Broughton during the war. Two weeks later he was dead. He died in his stairlift. It had stopped halfway up the stairs. It's possible that it was stopped deliberately.'

There is a silence. Gerry Whitcliffe stares at Nelson as if he is trying to read his mind. Nelson keeps his face bland. In the background he can hear Clough and Tanya arguing about whose turn it is to go out for chocolate.

'Are you suggesting—' begins Whitcliffe.

'I'm not suggesting anything, sir,' says Nelson. 'But there are just too many coincidences for my liking. Both Mr Whitcliffe and Mr Anselm died before they could tell their stories. I don't like that. I don't like that at all.'

'But who could possibly have killed them?'

'I do have a name,' admits Nelson.

'What name?'

'Lucifer.'

Ruth and Tatjana are walking up a hill. After two weeks of mostly fine weather, it is cold with a biting east wind.

Forecasters are talking happily about possible snow showers and the sky is a heavy, leaden grey. Not really the day for a pleasant country walk but Tatjana has expressed interest in a Roman site near Norwich and Ruth, who has no lectures this morning, is determined to entertain her guest. Besides, she knows the site well. She was called in last year when human bones were discovered in one of the trenches. The archaeologist who organised the dig is a Roman expert called Max Grey. He is an intelligent, attractive man and Ruth has sometimes allowed herself to think about him in a singularly unprofessional way. But the site also holds darker memories – a wolf circling in the night, letters written in blood, a dead baby. Ruth shivers and pulls her anorak tighter. Tatjana, dressed in a trendy suede jacket, looks half frozen.

'I'd forgotten how cold it is in England.'

'It must get cold in Cape Cod.'

'Yes, but we have warmer houses.'

Tatjana hasn't spoken much about her life in America. She and Rick seem to spend most of their time sailing and cooking gourmet meals. Ruth has seen photos of a low white house, shiny cars, shiny people, a vast gleaming boat. She thinks of her tiny cottage, the spare room still half full of boxes, her battered Renault 5. 'You've done so well, Tatjana,' she said once. 'Two incomes, no kids,' replied Tatjana, her face closing.

At the top of the hill, the ground drops away again. To the untrained eye, there is little to see, some grassy ridges and hollows, a trench running southwards and a rather forlorn-looking sign. But Tatjana draws in her breath. 'It's quite a big settlement.'

'Yes, Max thinks it was a vicus, a garrison town. The road,' she gestures to the trench, 'leads to the sea.'

Tatjana strides over to the sign, which is the only evidence of the lottery money which funded the dig. Max is hoping for a further grant next year. He says that half the town is still underground.

'It says here that bodies were found buried under the walls.'

'Yes. Max thought they may be foundation sacrifices. You know, offerings to Janus.'

'The God of Doorways?'

'Yes, and of beginnings and endings.'

Tatjana looks thoughtful. 'I would have thought that human sacrifice was more Celtic than Roman.'

'Well, the Romans often adopted Celtic Gods and traditions. They were pragmatists in that way.'

Tatjana turns away. 'I'm sure the Celts were pragmatists too. When your land is invaded, you tend to be.'

Ruth curses herself. How the hell have they got back to Bosnia? But when Tatjana turns back she is smiling. 'It's beautiful up here,' she says. 'You can see for miles.'

'Yes,' says Ruth. 'In the summer it's lovely. There's a great pub here too.'

'A pub,' says Tatjana. 'Does it do beer and ploughman's lunches?'

'You read my mind,' says Ruth.

Judy, too, is feeling the cold. Nelson has dispatched her to Broughton with a brusque instruction to 'talk to the locals about the war'. Great idea, thinks Judy, except that on a

day like today the locals are very sensibly inside watching
TV. So far she has spoken to a surly teenager and a lost
tourist looking for Great Yarmouth. She has already walked
through the village twice, not that this has taken very long.
It's really just the one street – a Victorian terrace – and,
behind it, a few newer-looking houses. There is only one
shop, but by the looks of it, some of the other houses used
to be shops. They have large bow windows, now swathed in
net curtains, and in some cases the shop names remain,
written or engraved under the eaves. 'S. Austin and son,
Fishmonger'. 'T. Burgess, Butcher'. 'Ronald Caffrey, Grocer'.

The one remaining shop occupies the end of the row. Is
this why it has survived when S. Austin, T. Burgess and
Ronald Caffrey were all forced to hang up their aprons? It
certainly doesn't have a very prepossessing window display
– a few shrimping nets and a dusty bucket arranged around
a collection of ancient-looking magazines: *Knitting World,*
Horse and Hound, The Coarse Fisherman. What would happen,
Judy thinks, if she asked for a copy of *Cosmopolitan* or, worse,
the *Guardian*?

A bell clangs loudly behind her and a bespectacled man
appears from behind a bead curtain.

'Yes?' His eyebrows are raised. The shop clearly does not
encourage passing trade. It is an odd mix of supermarket,
newsagent and post office. Tins of tomatoes share shelf space
with string, sellotape and lurid pink Mother's Day cards (though
Mothering Sunday was three weeks ago). The post office counter
bears a large handwritten sign saying 'Closed'. Another sign
gives parcel weights in pounds and ounces. Evidently the metric
system has yet to reach Broughton Sea's End.

Judy shows her warrant card which causes the shop-keeper's eyebrows to disappear further into his sandy hair.

'Police?' he echoes faintly.

'Just a few routine enquiries,' says Judy, putting on a reassuring voice. 'In fact, we're interested in something which may have happened fifty or sixty years ago.'

'I'd hardly remember it then, would I?' says the man huffily, though, to Judy, he could be any age.

'I just wondered if there were any residents who *could* remember those days,' says Judy soothingly. 'People older than yourself. After all, in a shop like this you must get to know everyone in the community.'

Her flattery is not entirely wasted. The eyebrows come down slightly.

'We try. We're a valuable local resource. You must sign our petition to save the post office.'

'I will.'

'In a few years' time shops like this will vanish completely. It'll be all supermarkets and chain stores.'

Good thing too, thinks Judy. But then she thinks: if I were an old person and I wanted a copy of *Knitting World*, I wouldn't want to have to catch a bus to the next village. Mind you, didn't Nelson say that the whole of Broughton was slowly falling into the sea?

'I think it's dreadful,' she says. 'I hate supermarkets myself. I never go in them.' This is true; she buys all her groceries on-line.

The man leans on the counter, eyebrows back in place, friendliness itself.

'You're so right. Supermarkets are all very well but where's the personal touch?' He leers at her.

'I'm sure you're always delivering groceries to the old folk.'

'Well, I can't lift much because of my back but I've always got a cheery word for them when they collect their pensions.'

'Speaking of older people . . . ?'

'Yes.' He straightens up, looking slightly suspicious once more. 'Well, there was Mr Whitcliffe, a fine old gentleman. But he went into a home a good few years ago.'

'I've met Mr Whitcliffe.' Judy does not feel inclined to go into details.

'His grandson's in the police force, I believe.'

'He's my boss. My ultimate boss.'

'Really?' This has the effect of banishing some of the suspicion. The Whitcliffes, a local family, are obviously to be trusted.

'Anyone else from that era?'

'Mr Drummond died a couple of years ago. There's Mrs West. She lives at number two Cliff Road. One of the new houses.'

'Thank you,' says Judy. She gives him her card. 'Could you ring me if you think of anyone else?'

The man nods. He is squinting at the card.

'Johnson. Are you one of the Cromer Johnsons?'

'No,' says Judy. 'I'm not from round here.'

She walks to Cliff Road. There are only four houses, modern versions of fishermen's cottages with exposed brick and fake weatherboarding. There is no answer at number two. Number one is also empty, but at number three she is told that Mrs West ('a lovely old lady') died last year. So much for local knowledge.

Disconsolately she wanders on to the end of the road. The church, squat and imposing, lies on her left, raised on a slight hill surrounded by gravestones. Judy climbs the short flight of steps and reads that the church of St Barnabas dates from the tenth century. It was built in Saxon times, burnt down and rebuilt in the Norman era, became derelict in the Middle Ages and was rebuilt (again) by a Victorian philanthropist. The notice board proclaims the church as Anglican but, as Judy's Irish Catholic father would say, 'It was ours once.' She tries the door; it's locked.

It is starting to rain. Judy puts up her hood and decides to call it a day. She has done her best but everyone in Broughton Sea's End is either dead, or in an old people's home or inside reading fishing magazines. It's an odd place, pretty but rather sad. Maybe it's just the weather but everything looks grey and washed out and somehow defeated. 'Fight coastal erosion' said a sign in the shop window, but Judy can't imagine the residents doing anything so energetic. No, the sea will get them; the houses, the shop, even the church. The sea will win in the end.

As she turns back to the steps, a name on one of the gravestones catches her eye. She goes back to have a look. 'Keaton "Buster" Hastings MC. Born: 1893. Died: 1989. He fought the good fight.' This must be Jack Hastings' father. Someone who clearly did relish a fight. What had Archie said about him? *Hell of a chap... Tough as old boots. Ran a tight ship too. We weren't just playing at soldiers.* There is none of the usual stuff about Buster being a loving husband and father but lying in front of the headstone is a fresh bunch of red roses.

Walking back through the graves, some lovingly tended, some overgrown with ivy and softened by moss, Judy finds: 'Sydney Austin, born 1880, died 1961'. 'Thomas William Burgess, born 1890, died 1971'. 'Ronald Caffrey, born 1901, died 1996'. The boss was right; they're all here. They're just all dead.

Might as well be hung for a sheep as for a lamb, thinks Nelson as he dials the number for Wentworth and Thenet, Solicitors. Whitcliffe has grudgingly agreed to the autopsy, saying that he'll speak to other family members. He then stalked out of the station, speaking to no-one. Nelson takes advantage of his absence to find out about Archie's will. Wentworth, when Nelson finally gets hold of him, is wary. Only when Nelson points out that the will's contents will be in the public domain once it has cleared probate, does the lawyer relent.

The will is simple. Archie's money is divided equally between his grandchildren, including Whitcliffe. It's not much but Nelson assumes that, whatever money Archie once had, it has long since disappeared to pay the bills at the Greenfields Care Home. The only other bequests are a writing case to Hugh Anselm and a hundred pounds and some detective books to Maria.

There is also a rather unexpected message for Whitcliffe: 'Gerald, I'm so proud of you and I know you'll do the right thing. Please take care of Maria and George.' George? This must be Maria's son, the one Archie used to buy presents for. But why didn't Archie take care of George himself, instead of asking his grandson to do it? Nelson can't exactly imagine Whitcliffe in the role of caring uncle to George. And why did Archie care so much in the first place? Maybe he saw Maria as a surrogate granddaughter but, then again, he was hardly short of grandchildren.

When was the will written? Two years ago, says Wentworth. Archie was not to know that Hugh would predecease him by a matter of weeks. Archie mentioned corresponding with Hugh some years ago – was this correspondence more significant than it seemed, important enough to be marked by a memento? Nelson has made an appointment to see Hugh Anselm's niece, his closest relative. He doesn't expect much. According to Kevin Fitzherbert, the niece, Joyce Reynolds, visited maybe twice in ten years. Nevertheless, she has inherited all of her uncle's effects (including, presumably, the writing case) and so it may be worth talking to her. There's always a chance that an avid letter writer like Hugh Anselm may have a journal or an unpublished novel somewhere.

He is thinking about letter writing and *Countdown* and crossword puzzles when his phone rings.

'Nelson,' he barks.

'Jack Hastings here,' answers another, equally authoritative voice. 'Are you aware that there's a Kraut journalist hanging round my daughter?'

Nelson wonders whether to affect surprise and force Hastings to tell him about Dieter Eckhart and his suspicions, but in the end he settles for faint distaste at such shockingly un-PC language. 'I've spoken to a *German* military historian called Dieter Eckhart,' he says.

'That's the fellow. Turned up at my house, if you please. An Englishman's home is his castle, I told him.'

Nelson ponders how much Hastings loves this phrase. He uses it in almost every TV interview (Nelson has looked them up) and it is, presumably, why he still insists on living in the fortress-like house on the cliff. Delusions of grandeur.

'I sent him away with a flea in his ear,' Hastings continues. 'Then I find out he's been pestering Clara.'

'Pestering' is not how Nelson would describe the distinctly mutual snuggling on Ruth's sofa, but it's hardly worth mentioning this now. Instead, he says, 'Why did Eckhart want to speak to you?'

For the first time, Hastings sounds discomfited. 'He had some ridiculous theory about those bodies found under the cliff. Thought they were German, or some such nonsense.'

Time to stir Hastings up a little, thinks Nelson. 'Our forensic tests show that the bodies were very possibly of German origin,' he says.

There is a silence. 'What?' says Hastings.

'Mineral analysis shows that the six bodies found in Broughton were of possible German origin,' repeats Nelson patiently. 'And we believe we know their identities.'

'You do?'

'Dieter Eckhart has been researching the disappearance of six German commandos in September 1940. I assume that's why he came to you.'

'What the hell's it got to do with me?'

'Your father was in charge of the Home Guard at that time.'

There is another silence and then Hastings says, in a more conciliatory tone. 'Look, I'm more than happy to help with any police enquiry but my mother's old and she's not very strong. Something like this could upset her, make her ill. And Clara, well, she's sensitive . . .'

Nelson remembers the blonde girl bouncing into the sitting room at Sea's End House. Sensitive is not the word he'd use.

'We'll be very low key,' he assures Hastings. 'But I'll need to speak to you again.'

'Understood,' says Hastings, sounding subdued.

'One more thing, Mr Hastings. Does the name Hugh Anselm mean anything to you?'

'Hugh Anselm? No I don't think so.'

'Your mother mentioned a Hugh, one of the other young men in the troop. That was Hugh Anselm.'

'Very possibly, but what's he got to do with anything?'

'I think he may have been murdered,' says Nelson.

16

'I did my best,' says Joyce Reynolds, 'but I've got my own family, you see.'

'It must be difficult,' says Judy sympathetically, 'looking after an elderly relative.'

Joyce Reynolds relaxes and looks saintly, though, as Judy and Nelson both know, her only contact with Hugh Anselm, her elderly uncle, was a yearly Christmas card and those two visits to the sheltered housing estate. Two in more than ten years.

'Was he lonely?' Nelson had asked Kevin Fitzherbert.

'Lonely?' Fitzgerald smiled, rather sadly. 'Sure and we're all lonely here. Hughie coped with it better than most. He had his books, his crossword, his letters. He hadn't shut the world out.'

'Your uncle sounds an interesting man,' says Nelson, accepting a second biscuit. Joyce Reynolds had not wanted the police to visit but, now they're here, she's determined to put on a good show. She is a stout woman in her late fifties, wearing a ruffled blouse over black velvet trousers. She has obviously dressed up for them, thinks Judy, though she's sure it's lost on Nelson. Joyce Reynolds is the daughter of Stephen Anselm, Hugh's elder brother, who died in 1984. Joyce herself has three children and two grandchildren. She shows them the photos.

Judy looks at the pictures with interest. All those brides with frothing dresses and trailing veils. All those hats, all those smiles. She tries, and fails, to imagine her own wedding photos. The dress, tried on last week, is undeniably lovely, the problem is the person inside the dress. Judy doesn't suffer from unduly low self esteem; she's certain that, with the help of hairdressers and a vat of make-up, she'll look pretty enough, it's just . . . the *expression*. How on earth is she going to manage that dewy smile, that look of mingled sentiment and rapture, when all the time she's just counting the minutes until it's all over and she can put on her old jeans and watch *Top Gear*? Still, she mustn't think about that now. She's a police officer, conducting an investigation. Clough would love to be here, putting his oar in, being all boys together with the boss, but it's her call because she's good at interviews. She'd better get on with it.

'Sergeant Johnson's getting married soon,' says Nelson suddenly.

Judy glares at him. She knows what he's doing, of course. Softening a potentially hostile witness with some personal details, the human touch, trying to *empathise* (a word Nelson usually hates). It's probably a good move but it doesn't stop Judy wishing Nelson would fall into a fiery hell-hole and be tortured by sadistic demons.

The witness, though, is definitely softened. 'Are you?' Joyce turns to Judy with what appears to be genuine interest. 'When?'

'In May. At St Joseph's.'

'The Catholic church?'

'Yes.'

'I was brought up a Catholic,' says Joyce, 'but my husband didn't hold with it so I became a Unitarian.'

'Was Hugh a Catholic?' asks Nelson.

'Yes,' says Joyce. 'Dad used to say he was quite religious as a boy but I never remember him going to church.'

'Have you got any pictures of your dad and Hugh?' asks Nelson cosily. He tries to smile apologetically at Judy. She ignores him.

In a drawer, far below the fat satin wedding books, Joyce has a brown envelope containing some sepia photographs. Two boys, both wearing glasses, gaze up at them. The elder is in school uniform, the younger in a white suit with sash.

'First Communion?' asks Judy.

Joyce shrugs. 'I suppose so. Here's Hugh in RAF uniform. He couldn't fly planes because of his eyes but he did navigation, I think.'

The same intense, short-sighted stare. The same slightly stiff pose. Hugh Anselm was one of those men who don't look quite right in uniform. He seems nervous, unsmiling, hands clenched at his sides. He must have joined the RAF after the Home Guard, thinks Judy.

'What did your uncle do after the war?' asks Nelson.

'Went to university. The only person in the family to go. Dad always said that Hugh was the clever one.'

'And after university?'

'I'm not sure. He did lots of jobs. He was a teacher, worked in a bank, even ran his own restaurant for a while. As I say, we weren't exactly close.'

'What's this picture?' asks Judy, pulling out a photo of a group of men standing proudly beside a boat. Hugh is older here but the glasses and the anxious expression are the same.

'Oh that must be the lifeboat. He was a keen lifeboatman.'

'At Broughton Sea's End?' asks Nelson.

'I suppose so.'

'There isn't a lifeboat any more, is there? I think someone told me that they can't use the ramp these days.'

Joyce Reynolds shrugs. 'I don't know. It's a weird out-of-the-way place, Broughton. When they were little we used to take the children on the beach there sometimes but I haven't been for years. Uncle Hugh didn't like the beach at Broughton. He said it had an unwholesome atmosphere. That was the way he used to talk.'

Nelson examines the photograph. 'Did your uncle ever talk about Jack Hastings?' he asks. 'Or his father, Buster?'

'Is he the man who lives in the big house on the cliff? The one that's meant to be falling into the sea? No, I can't remember Uncle Hugh ever mentioning him.'

'Buster Hastings was the captain of the Home Guard.'

'Hugh didn't talk about the war. He was a bit of a communist, if you want the truth. It was one reason why we didn't see so much of him. My husband doesn't stand for that sort of thing.'

Like Catholicism, thinks Judy. Mr Reynolds' prejudices are clearly wide ranging.

'Mr Anselm had a fascinating life,' says Nelson. 'I'm surprised he didn't write a book.'

'Oh, he was always writing,' says Joyce. 'I've got a pile of the stuff somewhere.' And she disappears, returning with a bulging cardboard box which she puts into Nelson's arms.

Nelson looks inside. The box is full of files, exercise books and letters. He opens a book at random. *5th January 1963*, he reads. *I'm no longer entirely convinced about Kennedy*. The words are small and neat, written in a thin italic hand. He finds a blurred copy of a letter to Nestlé complaining about their business practices in the Third World. *Yours sincerely, Hugh P. Anselm*.

'What did the P stand for?' he asks.

'The what? Oh, in Uncle Hugh's name? Patrick, I believe.'

'Can I borrow these?' he asks, indicating the box of papers.

'Keep them,' says Joyce carelessly. 'I haven't got the time for reading.'

Nor, it seems, has Maria. Archie Whitcliffe's favourite carer looks rather bewildered as she shows them the list of books left to her in the old man's will.

'It was very kind of him but' – she spreads her arms out wide – 'I'm afraid my English isn't good enough. And these, they sound difficult. '

Maria doesn't have the actual books yet (or the money also left to her) but the solicitors have forwarded a list of titles.

They are sitting in Maria's cramped Norwich bedsit. The

place is scrupulously tidy but extremely bare – just a double bed, a table and two chairs. She must share the bed with her little boy, thinks Judy. The only evidence of the child is a plastic box of toys and a teddy bear on the bed. Maria's bedside table is an old black trunk on which are displayed pictures of a smiling elderly couple and a large statue of the Virgin Mary. No television, no radio. How does she entertain the kid? wonders Judy. With the toys neatly stacked away in the box? With the statue of the universal mother? Maria says that Archie gave her money to buy him toys. What did she buy?

'Books,' is the surprising answer. Maria opens the trunk and brings out pristine editions of Winnie-the-Pooh, Peter Rabbit and Babar the elephant.

'We read them at night,' says Maria. 'I want him to have a proper start in life. George is very smart, very good at reading.'

'Did Archie leave you all his books?' asks Judy. She imagines the old man and the pretty young mother sitting together, talking about Agatha Christie and Babar and the future mapped out for the surprisingly named George. Maybe Archie wanted George to have his library.

'No,' says Maria, looking worried again. 'Just a few.'

'Particular favourites?'

'No. I never heard of most of them.'

'Why do you think he left them to you?' asks Judy.

'I don't know. I used to buy books for him, from charity shops. Maybe this is to say thank you.'

Shrugging, she hands Judy the list. Nelson reads over her shoulder.

The Third Truth by Kurt Aust
Love Lies Bleeding by Edmund Crispin
Evil Under the Sun by Agatha Christie
The Fourth Assassin by Omar Yussef
One Step Behind by Henning Mankell
The Hound of the Baskervilles by Sherlock Holmes
Sea Change by Robert B. Parker
Lost Light by Michael Connelly

'And these titles don't mean anything to you?' asks Nelson.
He only recognises one of the books, the Agatha Christie.
He thinks he's seen it on telly. Oh, and *The Hound of the
Baskervilles*. He knew a dog handler once with a German
Shepherd called Baskerville.

'No,' says Maria, her eyes filling. 'It was kind of him
though. He was always very kind.'

It was kind, thinks Nelson as they descend the gloomy
staircase, smelling of cabbage and worse. But more money
would have been more useful. Enough to buy a proper bed
for the boy and maybe a TV. Well, perhaps they're first
editions and will be worth millions. Maria deserves a break.
The exorbitant fees at Greenfields obviously don't go towards
the carers' wages.

Outside he takes a deep breath and sees Judy is doing
the same.

'Not much of a life is it?' he says.

'No.' Judy chews her lip. 'When I think of all the things
my sister's kids have.'

'Most kids today have too many things,' says Nelson
opening the car door. He thinks of the hundreds of toys he

has thrown out or recycled over the years: games lacking half the pieces, Barbies with missing limbs, electrical gadgets ignored after the first thrill of acquisition, the unread books.

'I wonder about George's father,' says Judy. 'He obviously doesn't help much.'

Nelson starts the car, forgets that he has left it in gear and curses as the Mercedes jerks forwards. Christ, why are people always talking about fathers? Johnson's been funny all day, come to think of it. The way she kept looking at the wedding photos at Joyce Reynolds' house and now getting all misty eyed about the little boy. He knows she's getting married and all that but she's got to learn to keep emotion out of policing.

'Where are we going now?' asks Judy, bracing herself as he takes a corner.

'Sea's End House,' says Nelson. 'I think it's time we asked Mr Hastings a few more questions.'

'Bone has both a mineral and an organic content in the ratio of two to one.'

Ruth is addressing a motley group of students in the university's smaller lecture theatre. It's a stuffy room and one or two of her audience look almost asleep. She must make more of an effort to engage them but the subject, The Dating and Treatment of Bones, is not exactly an exhilarating one, even to her. The trouble with the MA course is that a lot of the students come from overseas, mostly Asia, and English isn't their first language. By the time that she gets onto decalcification and fossilisation, she senses that she will have left most of them behind.

She presses a key on her PowerPoint. Like most academics, Ruth is secretly happier with handwritten slides.

'This is an example from the *Mary Rose*. Anaerobic silt is excellent for preservation of bones.'

Unlike the bodies at Broughton Sea's End, buried in sand. Did whoever buried them know that, over time, their bones would crumble into nothingness? Yet, in Ruth's experience, evil has a habit of finding its way to the surface. *The evil will lie waiting beneath the earth.*

The last slide. 'Cremation destroys the organic content of bone. Prehistoric cremations weren't hot enough to destroy the bone altogether. Flesh was burnt away but the bone remained – becoming white and fragile but mostly retaining its shape. These bone fragments provide valuable evidence for forensic archaeologists. Any questions?'

One interesting question about mummification and Ruth is heading back to her office, just time for a quick sandwich before her two o'clock tutorial. Having Tatjana in the house has cut down on the amount of time that she can spend working at home. It also means that she has to do some proper food shopping. She'll go to the supermarket after she's collected Kate. It's a hassle but Kate loves sitting in the baby seat of the trolley, smiling at the other shoppers and trying to eat cereal boxes.

It has been a strain, in some ways, having Tatjana to stay. The cottage is really too small for two adults. Ruth remembers how when she and Peter split up, amidst all the feelings of sadness, loss and guilt, there was also a distinct relief that she could now spread her books all over the sitting room floor and go to the loo with the door open.

She and Tatjana seem to spend a lot of their time apologising to each other and waiting for the other one to go first down the stairs. Whenever Kate wakes in the night Ruth is full of guilt that Tatjana's sleep has been disturbed and when, after a hard day's work, she would really like to slob out and watch *Coronation Street*, she has to pretend to be interested in reruns of *Time Team* on Channel 4. Still, Tatjana has started her teaching which means she is out all day. And some things have been nice – having someone to talk to about work, cooking proper meals, having an excuse to open a bottle of wine with supper, having someone to laugh with when Flint gets stuck in the cat flap.

Ruth grabs a sandwich from the canteen and rushes back to her office before she can become trapped in a long discussion with one of her colleagues about exam grades or Prehistoric burial practices. She also keeps a weather eye out for Cathbad. She's fond of Cathbad and she appreciates the interest he takes in Kate, but recently he has made one too many references to Nelson being Kate's spiritual father. She knows Cathbad suspects something but he'll never know the truth unless she tells him and, if she's honest, sometimes the urge to tell someone is very strong. When she was first pregnant, she quite liked the idea of hugging a secret to herself, like the baby growing inside her. But now, sometimes she wonders how she ever thought she'd have the strength to get through Kate's whole babyhood, her whole *life*, without ever telling anyone who her father is.

Of course, one day she'll have to tell Kate herself, but by then who knows what will have happened? Nelson's daughters will have left home, it'll no longer be so important to

protect them, perhaps Nelson himself will have left Michelle
... But she stamps firmly on that thought, seeing Nelson at
the naming day party helping his wife on with her coat,
Michelle laughing against him. Nelson has never in his life
looked at her like that. She just has to face it; he loves
Michelle, he doesn't love her. And, she tells herself, she
wouldn't want to live with Nelson anyway. He's too sexist,
too Neanderthal, way too bossy. Good in bed though, she's
shocked to find herself adding.

She hurries across the courtyard to the Natural Sciences
Department. It's a bitterly cold day, icy winds and the occasional eddy of snow. She's amazed that, even in these conditions, a couple has still found time to linger under the
covered walkway that leads to the main building, kissing
and wrapping their arms around each other. As she gets
nearer, she recognises Dieter Eckhart in his green Germanic
coat and Clara Hastings, slim and girlish in jeans, with her
hair in a ponytail. They are so engrossed that they don't
notice Ruth and she hardly wants to engage them in conversation. When she is safely inside, she looks back from a first
floor window. They are still standing there, with the snow
whirling around them, locked in a passionate embrace. But,
as Ruth watches, Dieter Eckhart raises his head and looks
straight at her. His eyes are as pale and cold as the snow.

The wind is even wilder at Broughton Sea's End. As Nelson
and Judy cross the bridge, they have to bend double to avoid
being blown over. The snow has turned into stinging sleet,
causing Judy to pull her woolly cap down over her eyes
(Nelson never wears a hat). Below them the sea thunders

against the rocks. How can Sea's End House withstand many more poundings like this, thinks Judy. The furthest turret seems almost at the edge of the cliff, the Union Jack whipping furiously to and fro. I wouldn't like to sleep in this house, she decides. The wind and waves are so loud that she wonders whether anyone will hear their knock on the door, although Nelson leaves the brass lion's head positively vibrating.

But, after a few minutes, the door is opened and a dark-haired woman is smiling at them.

'DCI Nelson.' Nelson doesn't smile back. 'I rang to say I was on my way.'

'Oh yes, hallo,' says the woman. 'I'm Stella, Jack's wife.'

She is charming, thinks Judy. Or maybe she'd be predisposed in anyone's favour after they'd ushered her in from the freezing cliff top and installed her in a kitchen with an open fire and twinkling pots and pans. There's even a sweet old lady knitting by the fire to complete the picture.

'My mother-in-law, Irene,' says Stella. 'Mother,' she raises her voice slightly. 'It's the policeman come back to talk to us.'

Judy suppresses a smile at the thought of Nelson being reduced to 'the policeman', like a character in an Agatha Christie play. Irene smiles sweetly at Judy.

'You're not the same girl that came before.'

'No,' says Nelson, rather quickly. 'That was Dr Galloway, the forensic archaeologist. This is Detective Sergeant Johnson.'

Judy says hallo and accepts an offer of tea. So the boss came here with Ruth, did he?

'Shall we stay in the kitchen?' Stella Hastings is saying. 'It's much warmer than the drawing room. Jack won't be long. He's taken the dogs out.'

Drawing room, thinks Judy. She doesn't know if she's ever heard anyone calling it that in real life. She shoots a glance at Nelson who raises his eyebrows.

Stella puts the kettle on and Irene starts arranging cups and saucers. The fire hisses and the sleet hammers against the windows. Judy takes a proffered shortbread and hopes that the interview takes a nice long time. She has no desire to be out on the road again with an increasingly grumpy Nelson. She hopes that Jack Hastings doesn't come back too soon. She can't imagine anyone taking a walk in this weather but she supposes that, if you have dogs, you have to take them out. A good reason for not having dogs.

She is halfway through her second cup when Jack Hastings appears, accompanied by what seems to be a sea of dogs, but soon resolves itself into two hysterically wagging spaniels.

'Detective Chief Inspector. What a pleasant surprise.'

The irony, if it is irony, doesn't register on Nelson's stony face.

'I did say that I'd like another chat.'

'A chat? Yes, fine. Fine. Chat away.'

Hastings stands in front of the fire and rubs his hands together. It's a remarkably defensive pose, thinks Judy, like a stag at bay or, perhaps, a politician facing questions across the floor of the house.

'Mr Hastings,' begins Nelson, 'last time I was here we talked about the Home Guard, about any members that might still be alive. Your mother mentioned Archie Whitcliffe. He used to send you Christmas cards, apparently.'

Hastings looks over at his mother, who is making another pot of tea, deep in concentration.

'I remember . . .' he says hesitantly.

'Mr Whitcliffe was living at the Greenfields Care Home. Did you ever visit him there?'

'No.' Hastings looks bemused now.

'What about Hugh Anselm? We spoke about him on the phone.'

Suddenly Irene Hastings puts down the teapot and bustles purposefully from the room. Nelson wonders if he ought to call her back. She's the one who remembers the war years, after all. Jack Hastings does not seem to have noticed his mother's departure.

'Hugh Anselm,' he says. 'I don't remember the name.'

'You mother mentioned him. He was one of the younger members of the Home Guard. Archie Whitcliffe was another.'

'She has wonderful recall of those years,' says Stella, who has briskly taken over the tea-making. 'But thinking about it can make her upset. They were desperate times here in Broughton, I think.'

Nelson continues to address Jack Hastings. 'So you've never met Archie Whitcliffe or Hugh Anselm?'

'I don't think so, no. What's all this about?'

'Archie Whitcliffe died last week. Hugh Anselm a few weeks earlier.'

'But you can't think there's anything suspicious about their deaths, surely? I mean they must have been old men.

On the phone you said that you thought this Hugh chap
had been murdered.'

Judy looks at Nelson. It's unlike the boss to say something like this to an outsider. Never assume, that was Nelson's
mantra. Why would he suddenly start sharing his assump-
tions with a member of the public, especially someone who
appears almost to be a suspect? She remembers the initial
investigation into Hugh Anselm's death. At the time Clough
had described it as a tragic accident, there was even a sort
of black humour about the situation. 'Old dear dead in a
stairlift.' Now the everyday deaths of these two old men are
taking on a very different aspect and there is something
sinister at work in the cosy room, even if Judy can't work
out exactly what it is.

'We're following several lines of enquiry,' Nelson replies
now, perhaps regretting saying so much in the first place.

Jack Hastings looks at his wife and it appears as if she is
about to speak when Irene comes back into the room. She
walks up to Nelson and places a photograph on the table
in front of him.

'That's Archie,' she says quietly, 'with his hat at an angle.
My Buster used to have a go at him about that. That's Hugh,
with the glasses.'

Judy peers over Nelson's shoulder. The picture is in black
and white and shows a group of men standing in front of
a grey-walled house. This house, she realises. At first glance
they look identical, homogenised by baggy, ill-fitting
uniforms and by a sort of sepia-tinted nostalgia. But, looking
closer, Judy sees that the three men in front are a lot younger
than the others. Even in sepia, they look full of life.

'I've seen this picture before,' says Nelson. 'There was a copy in Archie Whitcliffe's bedroom.' He looks at Irene. 'Which was Buster?'

Judy is betting on the walrus moustache, who looks like a old-style army major, the sort of man who could be described as a 'real old devil'. But Irene points to a small, insignificant-looking chap at the far right of the picture.

'That's Buster. Jack looks very like him, doesn't he?'

'Very,' says Nelson.

'That's Edwin Butler next to him, he'd been badly shell-shocked in the first lot. That's Syd Austin, he had the fish shop in the village. His son was killed at Dunkirk. That's Donald Drummond, he was the gardener here. That's Ernst Hoffman, the one with the moustache. He was German by birth but his family lived in Broughton for years. He was interned at the start of the war and sent to the Isle of Man. Buster kicked up such a fuss that he was released. Ernst was a scientist, a very clever one.'

Stella wasn't wrong about the old lady's memory, thinks Judy. She looks back at the photograph. It's hard to connect these faded figures, like something from a history book, with the stories of life and death. But to Irene the photo isn't a historical curio, it's a memento of her husband, of his friends.

Hugh is unsmiling, as awkward and intense as in his First Communion picture. He looks like the sort of boy who might grow up to do the *Telegraph* crossword. Archie looks far more cheerful, grinning away as if the whole thing is a game of cowboys and Indians. He looks like his grandson, Judy realises. The same good looks and proud bearing, but where

Gerry Whitcliffe seems afraid of showing his true feelings, Archie looks afraid of nothing.

'Mrs Hastings,' Nelson addresses Irene who is still looking at the photo, smoothing its edges lovingly. 'Do you remember any talk of a German invasion in 1940?'

Jack Hastings laughs but Irene says serenely, 'There was always talk but it never came to anything, did it?'

'Was invasion a big fear in these parts?'

'Yes,' says Irene, carefully covering the teapot with a knitted cosy. 'We were sure they would come. Buster was sure. He insisted on nightly patrols. They had a boat too. I think it was Syd's. They'd go out on the moonless nights, sailing along the coves. Buster thought it would happen on a moonless night.'

Judy hears Archie's voice: *On moonless nights, the darks we called them, we went out in the boat.* What happened on that dark night, nearly seventy years ago?

'He set up defences along the beach,' Irene was saying. 'Ernst helped him. He knew all about explosives, you see. "They won't take us by surprise," Buster used to say. "They won't find Broughton undefended."'

'What happened to the defences after the war?' asks Judy.

'I don't know', says Irene. 'Later on, the invasion didn't seem likely any more. We never spoke about it again.'

'What about you?' asks Nelson. 'Were you part of this defence scheme?'

'Oh yes,' says Irene proudly. 'I was on the listening post.'

'Listening post?' repeats Judy. It sounds made-up, almost childish. Stella takes up the story, smiling at her mother-in-law.

'During the war, Detective Sergeant, there was a military listening post at Sheringham, a few miles from here. It was literally a building, a tower really, where people listened for Nazi ships out to sea. It was manned by women. Irene was one of them.'

Womanned, thinks Judy. She knows better than to say it aloud though.

'What do you mean, they listened for ships?' asks Nelson.

'Just that. There were German E-boats out at sea. They could listen in on their Morse code. How do you think the code-breakers at Bletchley Park got the codes in the first place? From the listening posts. It was really important war work.'

'The E-boats didn't use Morse code,' cuts in Irene. 'We could hear them talking to each other in German. Where are you, Siegfried? I'm here, Hans.'

Nelson and Judy exchange glances. Now it seems more like a children's game than ever. *Where are you, Siegfried?* Nelson turns to Irene. 'Did your husband ever discuss with you what you'd do if the invasion actually happened?'

'Oh yes,' says Irene. 'My job was to shoot the children and shoot myself. Buster didn't want us taken prisoner, you see.'

'He was mad,' says Judy. 'Buster Hastings was mad.'

They are sitting in Nelson's car. Nelson has turned on the engine to demist the windows. Outside it is still raining, the windscreen wipers struggling under the weight of water. Occasionally a gust of wind rocks the car.

'Kill the children and kill yourself,' says Judy. 'Didn't some Nazi do that?'

'Frau Goebbels, yes. She killed her six children rather than have them live in a world where Germany had lost the war.'

'It doesn't make sense,' says Judy. 'Even if the Germans had invaded, women and children would have been okay. They wouldn't have come to a crazy little place like this anyhow.'

'But they did come,' Nelson reminds her. 'Six Germans arrived and six Germans were killed.'

'Do you think Buster Hastings did it?'

'It's possible. He certainly seems a determined character.'

'He was mad.'

'Maybe.' Nelson is thinking of a world where a man would tell his wife to kill their children, rather than have them fall into enemy hands. A world where fishmongers, gardeners and clever scientists were prepared to kill to defend their little piece of land. Desperate times, Stella Hastings had said.

'Do you really think Archie and Hugh were murdered to stop them telling the truth about it?'

'I don't know,' says Nelson wearily. 'I feel like I don't know anything.'

But before they are halfway back to the station a message comes through on Judy's phone. Clough has just come back from the autopsy. Archie Whitcliffe was killed, not by a stroke but by asphyxiation.

17

The noise, thinks Ruth, is indescribable. In fact, it has gone beyond noise and has become simply a white sheet of pain, against which everything else appears in harsh silhouette, like the strobe light that turns Judy's white shirt into pure migraine. There's no music as far as she can tell, just thumps and crashes and the occasional ear-splitting screech. Her head has become a mere amplifier for the noise. She can't think, she can't feel, she can't speak. She wonders if she's about to pass out.

'It's great isn't it?'

A young policewoman, a friend of Judy's, bobs in front of her. She is dancing wildly, her head thrown back in ecstasy, arms flailing.

'Great,' yells back Ruth but the girl has danced away again, back into the whirling throng. Ruth looks at her watch. One o'clock. Surely, surely she can go home soon.

Lights, red and green this time, criss-cross the walls like snakes. Was this what the Inca sacrifice ritual was like, the *capacocha*? Deafening noise, incomprehensible sounds, adherents dancing in a drug-crazed frenzy, the victim garlanded and clothed in gold (she is wearing her best trousers), the tribal drumming, the sacred knife raised on high, the blessed moment of blackness, of death, of unbeing. The longer Ruth stays in the Zanzibar nightclub, the more she longs to be put out of her misery. Maybe she just needs some mind-altering drugs, but when she reaches for her glass it's empty. Oh God, this means she has to fight her way to the bar and be ignored by the pierced and tattooed barman (the High Priest). Maybe there's drink in someone else's glass. But all the other women in the hen party are drinking lurid cocktails with blue curaçao or advocaat. Ruth is the only one on white wine. Yawning, she reaches under the table for her shoes (they are so uncomfortable that she has taken them off) and sets out on her quest. Maybe after one more drink she can go home.

The evening started in a wine bar. That was quite pleasant – lots of talk about sex and wedding dresses, lots of plays on the theme of arresting, handcuffs and full body searches, some talk of software and hardware (Darren is in computers). But at least there had been real wine and Ruth had liked Judy's colleagues, with the exception of Tanya, whom she finds slightly scary. After the wine bar they had had a meal and things started to blur somewhat. Ruth tried to stay soberish; she doesn't get out much and she wanted to do justice to her seafood risotto. But the wine kept flowing and soon she was discussing star signs with a policewoman called Mindy (Pisces) and singing along to *Mamma Mia*. Judy unwrapped some presents, all of which seemed to be furry handcuffs, and after much badinage with the gamely smiling waiters the party moved on to the Zanzibar.

Here things started to go downhill. As soon as she entered the club with its zebra-striped walls, leopard-spotted chairs and tiger-skin tables, Ruth was struck by a wave of tiredness so acute that she could have lain down and slept on the snakeskin floor. Despite the skull-crunching noise, she had difficulty keeping her eyes open. Judy, on the other hand, who earlier on had confessed to Ruth that she 'never wanted to get bloody married anyway', suddenly had a second wind and dragged the others out onto the dance floor where they scandalised the cooler clubbers by dancing round their handbags and demanding Abba songs.

Tatjana is in the middle of them, her hips, in skin-tight jeans, gyrating like a teenager. 'Tatjana's *fab*,' pronounced Judy. Ruth, sitting alone at the tiger-skin table, knows that *she* isn't fab, that she's forty, that she has a five-month old baby who'll be awake in four hours, that her shoes hurt and the waistband of her best trousers is digging into her skin. She's too old for all this and she's just remembered that she never liked clubbing anyway.

Should she ring Shona again? She decides against it. She has already rung four times, and the last time Kate had finally gone to sleep and Shona said that she was about to follow. Shona has kindly offered to stay the night (she will sleep in Ruth's bed and Ruth will have the sofa) so that Ruth and Tatjana can 'let their hair down'. Ruth's hair, unpleasantly sticky from Tatjana's application of hairspray, feels as if, metaphorically, it is in a tight little bun. She doesn't want to let her hair down and do wild things: she wants to be in bed with her baby beside her and Flint purring on the duvet. Still it was kind of Shona to offer. She had originally asked Clara but she said apologetically that she couldn't do Saturday. Probably out with Dieter, thinks Ruth, remembering the embracing figures in the snow.

She seeks out Judy and asks if she wants another drink. Judy appears to be in a trance, her hair across her face, her limbs twitching randomly. Glancing around, Ruth sees that everyone else is in the same state. Except Tatjana, who is dancing abandonedly with an exceptionally handsome black man.

'What?' says Judy.

Ruth repeats her question.

'No,' says Judy vaguely. 'You're all right.'

Ruth approaches Tatjana, who is now draped around the man's neck. His hands are firmly clenched on her bottom.

'I might go soon,' says Ruth, trying not to look.

'Go?' repeats Tatjana, eyes shut.

'Home. Check on Kate.'

'Kate?'

Ruth gives up. She decides against another drink. Instead, she takes her gold lottery ticket and goes to retrieve her coat. She'll send Tatjana a text to say that she's left.

Outside, it is freezing. There is already frost on the ground and on the nearby parked cars, none of which seem to be taxis. Ruth decides to walk to the station, to see if there are any cabs there. Her feet are blocks of ice in her unaccustomed high heels and she finds it impossible to walk fast. Some passing youths shout at her but she ignores them, head down. She wishes she'd brought a woolly hat, gloves, her trusty wellingtons . . .

'You want a lift?'

A car has come to a halt beside her and she looks down at a smiling, toothy face. The car is a dark saloon, slightly battered.

'Are you a taxi?' she asks.

'Sure. Minicab.'

For a moment she is tempted to get in beside the sinister smiling man. At least she'd be warm in his car. Before he murders her, that is.

'It's okay,' says Ruth, trying to walk faster. 'I'm meeting someone.'

The car glides along beside her for a few minutes then, to Ruth's relief, it veers away. She has reached the reassuring lights of the station. Here, thank God, are other people – a few disconsolate football fans clutching lager bottles, a bemused-looking man with a briefcase and a mother holding a baby. What can she be doing at King's Lynn station at two in the morning? Ruth tries to give the woman a reassuring mother-to-mother smile but she looks away, clasping the sleeping child against her shoulder. Should Ruth offer them a room for the night?

The taxi drivers do not want to go as far as the Saltmarsh.

'New Road? That's miles.'

'No can do, love. It's out of my zone.'

Ruth is desperate. She almost considers going back to look for the smiling man in the minicab. But, eventually, someone takes pity on her.

'All right,' says a fat man in a Ford Cavalier. 'Sunday rates, mind.'

It is Sunday, thinks Ruth as the taxi shoots through the deserted streets. In a few hours, people will be getting up, going to church, buying the papers. For the first time in a

while, she thinks of her parents. Sunday is the most impor-
tant day of the week for them; church, elders' meetings,
Bible classes, a roast meal with all the trimmings. She
pictures her mother and father walking down Avery Hill
Road, dressed in their best clothes, thinking of Salvation.
She really must take Kate down to see them soon.

In a remarkably short time they are on New Road,
crossing the marshes, blackness around them, the sea somewhere close, whispering in the dark.

'Bloody hell,' says the driver. 'What do you want to live
here for? Gives me the creeps.'

'I like it,' says Ruth. Stop talking, she adds silently, and
just get me home.

'Isn't this the place where they found that little girl?
About a year ago?'

'I think so.'

'Rather you than me, love. I'd be scared of the ghoulies
and ghosties, living out here.'

But Ruth isn't scared of ghosts. She pays the driver his
Sunday rates and lets herself into the cottage. Creeping
upstairs, she looks at the sleeping Kate. Her little face looks
stern and thoughtful through the bars of the cot. Beside
her Shona sleeps peacefully, her long hair spread out on
Ruth's pillow. Ruth takes a pile of bedding and heads down
to the sitting room. She isn't scared of ghosts. She is scared
of nightclubs, of having to enjoy herself, of something
happening to Kate, of waking up one morning and realising
that she is in love with Nelson.

Sighing, she curls up on the sofa, listening to the sea.

* * *

At Sea's End House, a single light shines from the turret. Like the beam from the deserted lighthouse, it illuminates the black waves as they thunder in towards land. They break against the walls of the house as if demanding entrance, turning the narrow inlet into a torrent, rising and falling as the moon waxes and wanes. Then, as the tide starts to turn, they retreat, sucking the stones from the beach where the six Germans soldiers lay buried, leaving the cliff path wet and gleaming. And leaving a body floating gently in the shallows, its blond hair streaming out in the dark water.

18

Ruth's first thought is that Kate is crying. Then she realises that the insistent noise is in fact her phone, ringing on the table next to her ear. Typical. The one morning that Kate doesn't wake at the crack of dawn someone decides to make an early morning phone call. Who the hell can it be?

'It's me,' says a brusque voice, though the screen is already flashing 'Nelson'.

'What is it?' asks Ruth blurrily. She has just realised that she is on the sofa, that her neck aches and that she has a splitting headache.

'Dieter Eckhart's dead. Fisherman found his body this morning. Washed up by Sea's End House.'

'*What?*'

'Eckhart's dead. Cloughie and I are at Broughton now.'

'What's the time?'

'Nine o'clock. I didn't think it was much use trying to get Johnson out of bed. Have a good time last night, did you?'

Nine o'clock! Why hasn't Kate woken up yet? Ruth is just about to rush upstairs in a panic when she sees Shona descending the stairs, carrying Kate in her arms. Kate looks smug; Shona triumphant.

Ruth wrenches her attention back to Nelson.

'Was it an accident?' she asks. 'Did he drown?'

Nelson gives a humourless laugh. 'Pathologist's here now. Cause of death – a knife wound to the heart. It wasn't an accident.'

'Does Clara know?'

'Yes. She identified the body.'

So many thoughts are swirling around in Ruth's head that she feels sick. Clara, Dieter, a knife wound to the heart, Tatjana, Judy, fisherman found his body this morning. Then Kate holds out her arms and everything else is forgotten.

Kate coos loudly into the phone.

'Is that Katie?' Nelson's voice softens. 'I'll call you later.'

The phone clicks off. Ruth looks at Shona, who is still holding Kate and looking pleased with herself.

'We've been up for ages,' she says. 'I got Kate dressed and gave her a bottle. We've been playing.'

Of the two, Kate looks the best for the experience. She is bright-eyed and bursting with energy. Shona has, in fact, dressed her in pyjamas and a jumper that is two sizes too big but she is overcoming these sartorial disadvantages with aplomb. She takes Ruth's phone and bites it, experimentally. Shona, on the other hand, looks pale and bleary-eyed, her hair is unbrushed and her shirt is on inside-out. But she is obviously so pleased with herself for having survived the night and the morning that Ruth feels a rush of affection for her.

'You've done brilliantly,' she says, taking Kate and putting her on the floor where she immediately rolls over on the rug – her favourite trick. 'Did you hear me come in last night?'

'No. Was it late? Did you have a good time?'

'So-so. I think I'm too old for clubs.'

'Rubbish. You just need the right company. Where's Tatjana?'

Shona has a distinctly ambivalent attitude towards Tatjana. Before she arrived, she was full of curiosity. 'I remember you talking about your time in Bosnia. I can't wait to meet her.' But when the two finally met at the naming day party, Shona had been decidedly cool. Maybe she hadn't expected Tatjana to be so attractive, maybe she resented the way that she had annexed Phil, maybe she was just jealous of Tatjana's relationship with Ruth but Shona, after exchanging a few cool pleasantries, announced to Ruth that she thought Tatjana was 'shallow'. 'What does your Bosnian friend think of me?' she asked, a few days later. 'She hasn't mentioned you,' Ruth had replied truthfully.

'I'm not sure where she is,' she says now. 'I suppose she went home with Judy or one of the others.'

'Maybe she met a man.'

Ruth thinks of the man Tatjana was dancing with. He was certainly gorgeous but would Tatjana really cheat on Rick?

'She's married,' she says.

Shona shrugs. 'When has that ever stopped any one? Who was that on the phone?'

'Nelson.'

'What did he want?'

'A new development in the case.'

'Jesus, Ruth. You're even starting to talk like a policeman. I'll get us a coffee, shall I?'

Nelson walks slowly back along the cliff path. The scene-of-crime boys are loading Dieter Eckhart's body into the white mortuary van. Clara and Jack Hastings stand watching. She had screamed when she first saw the body but now she is silent, her head on her father's shoulder. Although he is smaller than her, there is something infinitely protective about the way he is stroking her hair. Nelson, thinking of his own daughters, feels moved.

Clough is still talking to the fisherman, who gave his statement with the stolid air of one who regularly finds dead bodies tangled up in his nets. A duty policeman had answered the first 999 call but, as soon as it was clear that a body was involved, Nelson was on his way. Jack Hastings was already there when he arrived, his dogs barking excitedly as the fisherman and the PC hauled the corpse above the tide line. Nelson was wondering whether to summon Clara when she appeared, wearing a coat over her pyjamas. Clough had attempted CPR but soon gave up. As he turned the body onto its side, water spouted from the mouth and the head flopped backwards, eyes rolling. It was then that Clara screamed.

The deputy pathologist, whom Nelson much prefers to Chris Stephenson, estimated that the body had only been in the water for a couple of hours, but that was time enough for Eckhart's handsome face to become bloated and obscene. He is dressed in a white shirt and dark trousers and the knife wound, bloodless after immersion in the salty water, is almost directly over the heart. Nelson summons reinforcements to search for the murder weapon but he doubts that it will be found. Eckhart's body had become wedged between rocks; otherwise it would have been carried away by the tide. The knife could be halfway to Norway by now.

'Come on,' he says now to Clara and her father. 'It's perishing here. Let's go up to the house.'

Stella Hastings meets them at the door and guides Clara inside. 'Come on, darling. We'll get you dressed and you can have some hot chocolate to warm you up.'

Nelson stays in the doorway, feeling in the way but knowing that he must come in and, if possible, talk to Clara. Also, he'd rather like some hot chocolate. Jack Hastings takes pity on him.

'Come into the kitchen and we'll have something to drink,' he says. 'I'm sure you need to speak to Clara. She must have been the last person to see the poor fellow alive.'

Apart from the murderer, that is, thinks Nelson, following Hastings along the stone-flagged corridor. He notes also that the 'Kraut journalist' has become 'the poor fellow'.

Hastings' mother, Irene, is, as usual, knitting by the fire. Nelson wonders if she has been told of the morning's events, but as he sits at the scrubbed oak table she turns to him and says, 'Was it him? The German boy?'

'Yes.'

'Poor soul,' says Irene, knitting steadily without looking down. 'That path is wickedly slippery. Easy to lose your footing, especially if you've had a drop to drink.'

Nelson hesitates. He knows he must tell the Hastings family

how Dieter Eckhart was killed but he wants to choose his moment for doing so. At some point he'll have to take formal statements, from Clara at least. He thinks it's interesting, though, that Irene assumes that Dieter may have been drunk.

'We don't know what happened yet,' he says. 'There'll have to be a post mortem.'

Hastings puts a mug of tea in front of Nelson. Irene looks disapproving.

'Sorry, Ma,' he says. 'I couldn't find the cups.'

'Tea tastes better out of a cup and saucer,' says Irene. 'Don't you think so, Sergeant?'

'There's something in that,' agrees Nelson, accepting, with an effort, being addressed as sergeant.

'Will you be able to trace the next of kin?' asks Hastings, sitting opposite Nelson.

'I think so. He was affiliated to the university or we can contact his publisher. Shouldn't be difficult. My sergeant's on to that now.' He has sent Clough back to the station with specific instructions. He can't help emphasising the word 'sergeant'.

'Clara might know,' says Hastings. 'But she's terribly cut up. It was an awful shock.'

'She was very sweet on him,' cuts in Irene.

'Oh, I don't know,' Hastings looks annoyed now. 'She barely knew him.'

At that moment, Clara comes into the room. She is wearing jeans and a heavy jumper and looks pale but composed. She doesn't appear to have heard her father's words.

'Miss Hastings,' says Nelson gently, 'is it all right if I ask you a few questions?'

Clara looks round at her mother. 'Can I stay with her?' asks Stella.

'Of course. It's just a few informal questions. She can come into the station later to make a proper statement. You can all stay,' he adds, as Hastings and his mother show no signs of moving.

Clara sits down opposite Nelson and next to her father. Her mother puts a mug in front of her and she wraps her hands tightly round it.

'Miss Hastings . . . Clara . . . were you with Mr Eckhart last night?'

'Yes,' says Clara, her voice low but clear. 'We went to the pictures and then had a meal.'

'Did you come back to Sea's End House together?'

'Yes. He drove me. We got back at about eleven.'

'Did he come in? To say goodnight?' Nelson wonders if they were sleeping together. He imagines so, thinking of the entwined couple on Ruth's sofa but, at all events, they do not seem to have shared a room at Clara's parents' house.

'Just quickly. We had a cup of tea.'

'Was anyone else up?'

'Dad was in his study watching TV. I put my head round the door to say hallo.'

'I was dozing really,' says Jack Hastings. 'Can't stay awake after ten these days.'

'But you remember Clara coming in. Did you see Mr Eckhart?'

'I remember seeing Clara, she said something about what I was watching. It was football, I think. I didn't see Eckhart.'

'What time did Mr Eckhart leave the house?' Nelson asks Clara.

'About half eleven, I think.'

'Did you watch him drive off?' Nelson asks. 'Wave him goodbye?'

'No,' says Clara. 'He told me to go inside because it was so cold. I waved from the door, his car was still parked outside but he was texting and didn't see me. So I went upstairs, had a bath and got into bed.'

'What time was that?'

'Midnight. I remember looking at the time before I got into bed. You know how spooky it is when the clock says 00.00.'

'The witching hour,' says Irene. Clara shivers.

'When you drove up to the house,' says Nelson, 'did you see anyone hanging around? Notice anything suspicious?'

'No.' A smile fleetingly curves her pale lips. 'We were too busy to notice anything.'

'Too busy spooning,' explains Irene helpfully.

'What about you, Mr Hastings?' asks Nelson. 'Did you notice anyone hanging about outside the house?'

'No. I took the dogs out for their last run at ten-ish. They would have barked if there was anyone they didn't know.'

'Do you suspect that he was ... murdered?' asks Stella, almost in a whisper.

'I'm keeping an open mind,' says Nelson. 'Now I'll leave you in peace. I'll have a WPC contact you about making a statement, Miss Hastings. Take care of yourself now.'

Before he goes back to the station, Nelson asks Hastings to show him round the back of the house. Beyond the French windows and the terrace there are just a few metres of land before the broken fence and the sheer drop to the sea. Nelson goes as close as he dares and peers down. Far below, the sea is breaking against the rocks, jagged murderous-looking debris left by numerous cliff falls. For the first time, Nelson realises how close to destruction the house actually is.

'Is this where you walked the dogs?' he asks.

'No. Too dangerous for them here. They can easily go over the edge of the cliff, I've seen it happen. Dog chases a seagull and – wham. No, I always take them to the front garden at night.'

Nelson looks back at the house. There is really nowhere for a potential assassin to hide, no bushes, no trees, no outhouses. Just sheer grey walls and shuttered windows. He walks back around the side of the house, where the steep path leads down to the beach. He stops in front of a small green door.

'What's in there?'

'Gardening room. It's where we kept all our patio stuff, when we had a patio.'

Nelson tries the door; it's locked.

'Is it always kept locked?' he asks.

'Yes. No-one really uses it now.'

The front garden has some trees, though they are bent double by the constant wind that comes from the sea. It would be just possible, though, for a man to hide behind them in the dark.

'And you saw nothing when you went out last night?'

'No. As I say, the dogs would have barked if there'd been anyone lurking around.'

'Anyone they didn't know, that is.'

Hastings looks at him sharply but says nothing. As Nelson drives away, he sees Jack Hastings still standing in the front garden, frowning up at the house.

Nelson drives quickly, overtaking the myriad Sunday drivers out for a toddle along the coast. Dieter Eckhart was murdered, no doubt about that. Whether the killer was someone he knew remained to be seen. It usually is, Nelson knows that. Nine murders out of ten are committed by someone close to the victim. The dogs that didn't bark: isn't that a Sherlock Holmes story? Archie Whitcliffe would have known. Was there someone hiding in the garden that night? Or did the killer come from inside the house? Nelson would give a lot to know who Dieter Eckhart had been texting as he sat in his car outside Sea's End House.

Does Nelson really suspect Jack Hastings, a highly respectable politician, of killing three people just to preserve his father's reputation? On the face of it the thing is unlikely, but Nelson knows to look beyond the face of things. Buster Hastings is certainly revered in Sea's End House and Dieter Eckhart would have had no compunction in denouncing him as a war criminal if he could find the evidence. In Hastings' eyes, Eckhart had even corrupted his daughter. Nelson had noticed his face when Irene mentioned 'spooning'. Jack Hastings had not been happy that his daughter was dating a German, not happy at all.

Back at the station, a grey-faced Judy is sitting at her desk. All officers have been called in to work. Whitcliffe, horrified at the autopsy report on Archie, is throwing everything at the case.

'How are you feeling?' asks Nelson.

'Like death.'

'Well, there's a lot of it about. Good night last night?''

'Brilliant. I can't remember anything after midnight.'

'Did Ruth enjoy herself?'

'Ruth? I think she left early. Tatjana stayed the night at my place though. She was up at eight for a run. The woman's a marvel.'

'Any luck on Dieter Eckhart's next of kin?' says Nelson.

'Yes.' Judy looks at him sideways. 'I rang his university. Apparently he's got a wife and two children.'

19

'So he was married all along?' says Ruth.

'Apparently so,' says Nelson, who is finding it hard to drag his eyes away from Kate. 'His wife's due in England tomorrow. She's going to fly his body back home.'

'Did Clara know? That he was married, I mean?'

'I don't know,' says Nelson, who is building a tower of red and yellow bricks. Kate watches him narrowly.

Clara Hastings had been in that morning to make her statement. Nelson had asked Judy to drop Eckhart's wife casually into the conversation. Clara hadn't flickered. Towards the end of the session, though, she had grown tearful.

'It must be so hard for you,' Judy had said sympathetically. She is good at this sort of thing.

'I'm just thinking about his kids,' Clara had sniffed.

So she had known about the children.

Nelson adds another brick and then knocks over the tower. Kate laughs delightedly. She loves destruction. Ruth is beginning to regret letting Nelson come at a time when Kate would be in the house. It makes her uneasy to see them together. Whilst, on one hand, she wants Nelson to love his daughter (and, by extension, her?), she knows that the more attached Nelson gets, the more complicated their situation becomes.

'What did the post mortem say?' she asks, to bring him back to earth.

'Eckhart was stabbed with a sharp metal object. They think it was scissors.'

'Scissors?'

'Heavy-duty scissors. The sort used for dressmaking or cutting back plants. They were honed to a point apparently.'

'Honed. So someone had planned this? It wasn't spur of the moment?'

'No,' says Nelson soberly. 'Someone sharpened those scissors and waited.'

'Have you any idea who?'

'I've got lots of ideas,' says Nelson. 'Each more ridiculous than the last.'

'Do you think the same person killed Archie Whitcliffe and Dieter Eckhart?' Nelson has told her about the autopsy report on Archie. Death by asphyxiation was the verdict, probably with a pillow.

'Yes I do,' says Nelson, still looking at Kate as she thoughtfully sucks the building bricks. 'The method was different but I'm convinced the link was the murder of the six Germans. Someone is prepared to kill to stop that story getting out. There's Hugh Anselm too, the old chap in the stairlift. I'm sure he was murdered too.'

'It's so far-fetched though,' complains Ruth. 'Like something out a murder mystery.'

'Archie Whitcliffe was a big fan of murder mysteries,' says Nelson. 'Left a pile of them to his carer.'

'Really?' Ruth looks interested. 'What sort of books?'

'Nothing special. I hoped they might be worth something. She hasn't got two pennies to rub together, the carer, but they were just a load of old paperbacks. Second hand, most of them.'

'Do you have the list of the titles?'

'Somewhere. Why are you interested?'

'I don't know. Just an idea.'

Nelson gets Judy to fax through the list of titles (Ruth is almost the last person in the world still to have a fax machine). Ruth reads through the names while Nelson plays peek-a-boo with Kate. Ruth wishes Clough could see him.

The Third Truth by Kurt Aust
Love Lies Bleeding by Edmund Crispin
Evil Under the Sun by Agatha Christie
The Fourth Assassin by Omar Yussef
One Step Behind by Henning Mankell
The Hound of the Baskervilles by Sherlock Holmes
Sea Change by Robert B Parker
Lost Light by Michael Connelly

'Was there anything else?' she asks. 'Just the list?'

'Oh, there was some nonsense about which order to read them in. I can't remember it now. Ask Judy.' And he disappears behind the cushion again.

'This is it,' says Judy. Ruth can hear her rustling paper. 'He says, read them in this order: 3,2,2,2,2,3,1,2. Crazy, isn't it?'

'Maybe,' says Ruth, sitting down to look at the list again. Nelson, who is crouching on the floor beside Kate, looks up at her.

'What is it, Ruth?'

'I don't know. I just thought . . . wasn't this the bloke who liked crosswords?'

'That was Hugh Anselm.'

'But maybe Archie did too.'

'Maybe. He did watch that programme, *Countdown*,' says Nelson, remembering. 'Mind you, Cloughie says all old people watch *Countdown*.'

'Mmm.' Ruth occasionally watches it herself but she's not going to let Nelson know that.

'Do you think he's left us a clue then?' says Nelson smiling.

'It's possible,' says Ruth, turning back to the fax paper to avoid looking at Nelson pretending to be a bear.

Ruth always over-complicates everything, thinks Nelson, as he drives back towards King's Lynn and home. It comes of being an academic. Mind you, when he first met her, he had needed her professional expertise. He'd called her in to look at the Iron Age body but he'd also asked her about some weird letters that had been sent to him, letters full of allusions to mythology, ritual and sacrifice. Ruth had done great work, looking up all the references and working out what the nutter was trying to say. But maybe that has left her unable to take anything at face value. Sometimes a list of books is just a list of books. That's what he says to his team. 'Don't make things too complicated. Nine times out of ten police work is about simple stuff. It was a car number-plate that caught the Yorkshire Ripper, tax evasion that caught Al Capone. Never skimp on routine procedure.' Mind you, he can't see Cloughie and co being tempted to be too intellectual.

Katie's a grand little kid though. He'd forgotten how much fun they are at that age. Michelle always used to tell him off for making the girls too excited at bedtime. He'd done the bear routine with them too, the old ones are the best. He remembers Laura, hysterical with laughter, falling off the bed and crying; Rebecca screaming when he'd jumped out at her wearing a gorilla mask. Maybe Michelle had a point. He could see that it must have been irritating, stuck at home with young children, having to do all the discipline and boring bits, then having someone come home at bedtime pretending to be a bear. But, then again, he had to have *some* fun with them. In the early years he'd hardly seen his daughters during daylight hours. It'll be no different with Katie, he thinks. Worse because she won't even know who he is. He'll just be some lunatic stranger with funny voices and ingratiating presents. Cathbad will be more of a presence in her life than him. He grinds the gears furiously.

Michelle isn't home but, amazingly, Rebecca is. Even more amazingly, she's doing her homework. Admittedly, she's listening to her iPod, texting her friends and eating a cheese sandwich but she's also writing an essay entitled 'Coastal Erosion and its impact on Rural Communities'.

'What's this about, love?' he asks, dropping a kiss on her head.

'It's for environmental science. It's about all these people who're, like, getting really pissed off because their villages are disappearing.'

Nelson thinks of Jack Hastings who, by all accounts, is getting more than pissed off because Sea's End House is disappearing. Whitcliffe has shown him a surveyor's report condemning the house. Nelson thinks of the back garden, those few yards and then that vertiginous drop onto the rocks below. He tries to imagine how it would have been – a lawn, mown in those fancy stripes, roses, a sundial, Buster and Irene lounging in their deckchairs, drinking dry martinis, looking out over the cove. Will Jack be forced to leave the house his father built? He'll be pissed off then, all right. Could the strain of losing his house be enough to turn Jack Hastings into a killer?

As usual, Rebecca is flipping between several internet sites, looking for material. She's expert at cutting and pasting. Nelson hopes this will be enough for the A-Level examiners. She's too quick for him though, scanning to and fro, highlighting, dropping in text files, finding clip art—

'Hang on a second!'

'What?' She pauses in mid click.

'That last site. Something about the war.'

'Oh . . . do you mean ilovehistory.com?'

'Possibly. Can you go back?'

Obligingly, Rebecca finds the page and makes it large enough to be seen by his decrepit eyes.

The coastal defence, he reads, *was to include fifty tons of fuel, to be blown up in the shallow waters of the North Sea. This operation drew on fire ships used by Drake against the Armada . . .*

He goes into the kitchen to ring Ruth, switching on the kettle as he does so. She takes a while to answer and sounds hassled. He can hear Katie crying in the background.

'Ruth. Did you get the results back from the material? That you found in the barrel.'

'Yes. I sent you a report.'

'Tell me again.'

'It was gun cotton. Cotton dowsed in nitric and sulphuric acid. The material's immersed in the acid and then dried. Makes it extremely flammable.'

'I bet.'

'Apparently when it's lit it produces an almighty blast. Jules Verne uses it in one of his books to power a space rocket.'

'And what was in the other barrels?'

'A mix of adhesive tar, lime and petrol.'

The beach at Broughton Sea's End, thinks Nelson, as he drinks his tea, was one massive depth charge. The Home Guard had prepared a welcome for possible German invaders that would have blasted them into space. Was that the work of Ernst, the clever scientist? A German who had lived most of his life in Broughton Sea's End. A German determined to do all he could to defeat the Nazis. Maybe he was a German Jew . . . Nelson knows that all sorts of people were interned at the start of the war – old people, youngsters, Jews, communists – people who had no reason on earth to side with the Nazis. Why was Ernst living in Broughton in the first place? And why did he have such a close bond with Buster Hastings? *Buster kicked up such a fuss that he was released.* Why was Buster so determined to have Ernst on his side?

And why hadn't the defences been set off when the six Germans actually landed? The men had been shot from a few feet away, there was no sign of a struggle. Somehow Buster and his mostly ageing troops had been able to overcome six soldiers in their physical prime. But, having done that, why kill them? Surely they could just have taken the men prisoner? He's no military expert but isn't it important to take prisoners so you can interrogate them? The German commandos never gave up their invasion plans. Their secret died with them, buried under the cliffs until the sea itself exposed it.

Nelson is still sitting in the kitchen when Michelle comes home, tired from working late and distinctly put out to find that no-one has started supper.

After supper, Michelle and Rebecca settle down to watch *CSI Miami* – female bonding over mutilated body parts – and Nelson escapes back to the study. He types *Second World War Invasion* into the search engine and soon the screen is full of lurid stories: beaches black with bodies, the seas aflame, U-boats full of severed limbs, secret German bases off the Irish coast, 30,000 bodies burned beyond recognition washed up on the South Coast. Nelson enjoys a conspiracy theory as much as the next man (once, Cathbad almost convinced him that the Americans had never landed on the moon), but as a policeman he does require just a trace of evidence. It's all very well saying that the authorities have covered everything up but could an invasion on this scale really have been hushed up? In a place like Broughton this would, effectively, have meant buying the silence of everyone in the village.

But what if this is exactly what happened? What if, amidst all the hysteria, the Germans did land one small expeditionary party in an isolated Norfolk cove? There they met, not sleepy villagers and bemused fishermen, but a tightly controlled army unit prepared to kill.

He is about to call it a night when, scrolling down a site called 'Flame Over Britain', he comes across this paragraph:

The plan was simple. Under cover of darkness several aged tankers, their holds full of combustible fuel, would head across the channel to the enemy invasion ports of Dunkirk, Calais and Boulogne. At the entrance to these ports, the tankers would be abandoned by their skeleton crews and detonated. The subsequent blast would turn the sea into a burning sheet of flame. This operation, which became known as Operation Lucid, actually started life with a more sinister moniker – Operation Lucifer.

Lucifer.

20

'Remind me what we're doing here again, boss?'

Nelson and Judy are climbing the steps to the church of St Barnabas at Broughton Sea's End. It's a bitterly cold morning and the gravestones are covered with a fine layer of frost. The weather forecasters are talking about snow. In late March! What a county, thinks Nelson, forgetting that Blackpool hardly enjoys a Caribbean climate. He thinks of Norfolk as existing in a vacuum, entirely separate from the rest of England. Come to think of it, that's how most of the locals see it too.

Judy is standing looking up at a huge evergreen tree whose branches cover almost the entire graveyard. In its shade the frost is even thicker.

'We're here,' says Nelson, rubbing his hands together, 'because the vicar has copies of the parish magazine going back to the year dot.'

'Sounds wild.'

'Wild or not, I want to find out what was happening in this village during the war. I'm convinced that Operation Lucifer is the key to this whole case.'

'Don't say that name out loud,' hisses Judy.

Nelson laughs. 'Not getting superstitious in your old age are you?'

But there is, nevertheless, something spooky about the silent graveyard. The way the stones stick up as if something below the earth is stirring, the way the dark tree spreads its branches, the way the church door is bolted shut.

A figure appears from behind one of the largest stones. Judy screams.

'Forgive me if I startled you.' The figure resolves itself into a tall, white-haired man wearing clerical clothes. Nelson gives Judy a disgusted look.

'Father Tom Weston.' The man extends his hand.

'DCI Nelson.' Nelson shakes hands briskly. 'This is Detective Sergeant Johnson. It's good of you to meet us.'

'Not at all. I'm delighted that someone wants to look in the archives. There's not enough interest in local history.'

He takes out a medieval-looking key.

'Do you always keep the church locked?' asks Judy.

'Have to, I'm afraid. We've got some very valuable things in here – candlesticks, brasses, and so on – and I don't live on site. I've got three other parishes to look after.'

It is almost as cold inside the church as out. Judy blows on her hands to warm them and her breath billows like incense. The air smells of stone and damp and flower stalks. Someone has evidently been arranging the flowers because a magnificent display of lilies and ferns stands at the altar steps. Judy thinks of the red roses on Buster Hastings' grave. She must remember to see if they're still there.

As they cross the church, their feet echo on the stone flags. Passing the altar, Judy bobs instinctively. Nelson gives her a sardonic glance, correctly identifying Catholic Genuflecting Syndrome. Judy scowls.

Tom Weston leads them past wooden pews with embroidered kneelers, past a garish collage of Noah's Ark (the work of the Sunday School apparently) and through a door at the back of the church. This is obviously behind-the-scenes. There are piles of hymn books, a broken lectern, mops, buckets and one of those vacuum cleaners with a smiley face. 'Henry,' says Father Tom. 'I couldn't live without Henry.'

'Do you do the cleaning yourself?' asks Nelson.

'I have to sometimes. Good cleaners are hard to find.'

He does everything himself, they find out. He cleans, polishes, makes cakes for the Women's Institute, even runs the mother-and-baby group. There's a man who cuts the grass in the graveyard but that's it.

'Are you married?' asks Nelson. He assumed that vicars have wives that run their parishes for them. It's one of the advantages of being a protestant.

'I'm a widower,' says Tom Weston, opening a cupboard at the back of the room. 'Daphne died five years ago.'

'I'm sorry.'

'It's all right. It gets easier. At least I know she's in a better place.'

Faith must be handy sometimes, thinks Nelson, bending over the box of dusty magazines. His own vague Catholicism would never survive a real test – like something happening to Michelle or one of his daughters. He resists a temptation to cross himself to ward off this dreadful thought. Reflex action, like Johnson curtseying at the altar. How cross she'd been when he noticed.

The magazines are actually quite well-ordered, arranged in boxes according to year. Nelson starts on 1940, while Judy looks at 1939. Nelson is convinced that the Germans must have come ashore in the early years of the war, when the invasion scare was at its height.

'I'll go and make some coffee,' says Father Tom. 'There's a gas ring at the back here.'

Nelson watches the vicar blow dust from an ancient jar of instant coffee. There's instant milk too. Ruth would have a fit. She only likes poncy coffee in tiny cups.

Judy settles down on the floor to leaf through copies of the *Broughton and Rockham Parish News.*

'There's a recipe here for squirrel pie.'

'Very popular during the war,' says the vicar from the back of the room. 'Some of the old country folk still cook squirrel.'

'How long have you been in this parish?' asks Nelson.

'Since 1952. The year before the great flood.' He makes it sound like Noah's flood. Perhaps the Sunday School will make a collage of it.

'Flood?' echoes Nelson.

'Yes. Terrible affair. Constant rain, the seas rose, rivers burst their banks. We had boats sailing down the High Street at Broughton. Five people died.'

'I've heard about the flood,' says Judy. 'It was supposed to happen again wasn't it?'

'In 2006,' agrees Father Tom. 'I remember them testing

out the sirens. It brought it all back. We had a prayer cycle in all the Norfolk churches. And the flood never came.'

'I thought that was because 2006 was a particularly hot summer,' says Judy. Father Tom appears not to hear this.

'I should be retired by now,' he says, placing two steaming mugs on a packing case marked 'Palms'. 'But vicars are thin on the ground these days.'

'Do you remember hearing stories about the war years in Broughton?' asks Nelson, putting aside a magazine that seems to consist only of recipes for powdered egg.

'Some stories,' says the vicar carefully. 'They're close around these parts, don't talk much to outsiders.' He laughs. 'And after fifty odd years I'm still an outsider.'

'"Sea's End House commandeered by the army,"' reads Nelson. '"Buster Hastings, Captain of the Local Defence Volunteers, confirmed that his house was to be used for secret war work." Do you know what all that was about? The Local Defence Volunteers, they became the Home Guard, right?'

'That's right. Buster Hastings was in charge of the Home Guard. A bit of a martinet by all accounts. I'm not sure about the secret war work but I think I remember hearing that the house was used for surveillance, watching the sea. The lighthouse was in use then, of course, and they had a system of warning lights. And, of course, there was the listening post at Beeston Bump.'

'Beeston Bump?' Judy tries, not very successfully, to stifle a giggle.

'Great name, isn't it?' Father Tom smiles, showing long yellow teeth. 'It's a hill outside Sheringham. It's where the

Y station was, the listening post. Beautiful spot. We have open air church services there at Easter.'

'Sounds lovely,' says Nelson. 'How well do you know the Hastings family?'

'Quite well,' says Tom Weston, taking a sip of coffee. Nelson tries his; it's quite disgusting. 'Buster wasn't much of a churchgoer but his wife Irene was a stalwart of the parish for years. She still does the flowers.' Judy stores this nugget away.

'What about Jack Hastings?' asks Nelson.

'He always supports our fundraisers. We need a new roof for the tower. It leaks dreadfully. We've been collecting for years but we're no nearer to reaching our total. Oh well, God doesn't give up easily. Jack doesn't come to services much, but his wife Stella is a regular communicant. She's a good woman.'

Nelson senses that this is high praise from Father Tom. It seems that Hastings men delegated churchgoing to their wives.

'What about Archie Whitcliffe?' he asks. 'Did you know him?'

'Archie?' Father Tom's face softens. 'A grand old chap. He used to be one of the bellringers here. When we could still use the belfry, that is. I was sad to hear that he'd been taken.'

Been taken. It seems an odd phrase to use, even for a vicar.

'How did you know?' asked Nelson.

'His grandson rang me. Wanted me to conduct the funeral, but I understand that there's been some sort of delay.'

His eyes move from Nelson to Judy, who is still reading about wartime dances and keeping a pig in your back garden. Despite his years, and Father Tom must be at least eighty, his gaze is remarkably shrewd.

'Yes,' says Nelson straightening up. 'Can we take the rest of these magazines away with us?'

In the churchyard, Judy remembers to check Buster Hastings' grave. The roses have gone but now there is a bunch of spring flowers, tied in a straw bow. Clearly someone in the village still remembers the martinet with affection. Nelson and Father Tom have stopped in front of the war memorial. Nelson scans the names; many from the First World War, fewer from the second. One of the latter names, Geoffrey Austin, rings a slight bell. Didn't one of the Home Guard have a son who was killed at Dunkirk?

'I'm campaigning to have a new name added,' says Father Tom. 'One of the local boys who died in Afghanistan. The War Graves Commission isn't keen but I think we'll win through in the end.'

Nelson does not doubt Father Tom's ability to defeat the War Graves Commission. He has a feeling that Father Tom, like God, does not give up easily.

Judy comments on the tree, whose dark branches still make her feel slightly uneasy.

'It's a yew,' says Father Tom. 'They're traditionally found in graveyards. This one has been here for hundreds of years, since medieval times.'

'Why are they found in graveyards?' asks Judy, wrapping her coat around her. The sun is higher now but it's still very cold.

'They're evergreens, linked to immortality. There's an old superstition that at midnight, the witching hour you know, the yew provides a kind of conduit for the dead to rise.'

Complete bollocks, thinks Nelson. But where has he heard that phrase recently? *The witching hour?*

'The yew's a sacred tree for druids,' Father Tom is saying. 'If you know of any druids, that is.' He laughs heartily.

'We know one,' says Nelson.

They walk back to the car park in silence, each carrying a box of magazines. Nelson is thinking of Operation Lucifer, the sea in flames. There is nothing in the dull parish newsletters to suggest anything so terrifying or so memorable. According to the *Broughton and Rockham Parish News* the war years had been one long round of dances and rabbit shows (Flesh and Fur Fancy: Beat the Nazis by eating coney pie). But something had happened in this quiet village and Archie's last word had been 'Lucifer'. He really must have a good look through Hugh Anselm's papers.

Judy, for no reason at all, is thinking about Cathbad and yew trees.

They have come in Judy's car because Nelson's is in for its MOT. Judy, in the face of much teasing, drives a four-by-four, a flashy jeep with wheels like a tractor. As Nelson climbs into the passenger seat, he says, 'This car's too big for you.'

'It suits me fine.'

'What does Darren drive?'

'A Ford Ka.'

Nelson grunts as if his worst fears have been confirmed.

They drive along the coast road, Nelson trying not to tell Judy when to change gear (in fact, she's a far better driver than he is).

'Johnson!'

'What?' Judy brakes.

'Let's go to Sheringham. Have a look at this listening post thing.'

'Why?'

'I don't know. I just want to have a look at it.'

As Judy does a U-turn she considers that the boss is getting really hung up on this war business. It's true that whoever killed Archie Whitcliffe and Hugh Anselm (not to mention Dieter Eckhart) probably knew about Operation Lucifer but, in Judy's personal opinion, the truth must lie closer to home and to the present day. Don't overcomplicate; that's what Nelson himself usually says.

Beeston Bump turns out to be a long walk. A stunning one too, if you like that sort of thing, which Nelson doesn't. But Judy enjoys striding over the short, aromatic grass, the wide blue sky above and the sea thundering away below. It's a long haul, though, and they're both panting by the time they reach the top. The view, as Father Tom promised, is spectacular. The flat plains of Norfolk lie behind them, they can even see the church tower at Broughton and Sea's End House perched on the end of its promontory. In front of them is the sea, calm and clear.

All that remains of the listening post is an octagonal concrete base. Hard to imagine a building here, on this exposed point. A tower, Stella Hastings had said. Nelson looks out over the sea, sparkling innocently in the sun. How crowded it must have been seventy years ago – German E-boats, tankers stuffed full of petrol ready to ignite, Captain Hastings and his crew patrolling in their little dinghy. And, of course, the six Germans who died at Broughton Sea's End. What happened to their boat, he wonders. Father Tom had shown them a map of the East Norfolk coast. It was studded with little crosses. 'What are these?' Nelson had asked. 'Shipwrecks,' answered Father Tom. 'The coast is full of them. It's treacherous, this coastline, lots of dangerous rocks, shallow sandbanks. That's why we had the sea light at Broughton. You can't land a boat on some beaches because of all the submerged wrecks.' So, even under the sea, it's crowded.

His phone rings. Ruth.

'What is it?'

'I think I've come up with something.' She sounds excited. 'Can you come over?'

Nelson glances at Judy who is gazing rather dreamily out to sea. Probably thinking about her fiancé.

'Okay. I've got Johnson with me. We'll be over in half an hour.'

Ruth meets them at the door. To Nelson's secret delight, she's holding Kate.

'Hi, baby,' says Judy. 'Hey, she smiled at me!'

That was at me, thinks Nelson.

Ruth takes them into her sitting room which is as untidy as ever and where, now, Kate's toys and blankets and baby gym jostle for space with Ruth's books and papers and old coffee cups. Spread out on the table are a selection of murder mysteries. Skulls, daggers and spectral hounds grin up at them.

'I bought them from Amazon,' says Ruth. 'They're the books on Archie's list. The ones he left to Maria.'

'Why did you buy them?' asks Nelson, watching surreptitiously as Kate rolls on the floor under her baby gym. Shouldn't she be crawling by now? He can't remember any of the milestones though Michelle has them all recorded in albums, complete with first teeth and locks of baby hair.

'I wanted to see if I could crack the code. I thought it would be easier if I had the actual books.'

'What code?' asks Judy.

'Well, you remember the order Archie told Maria to read the books in? I think it was a code. I think he was trying to send her a message.'

'Have you worked it out?' asks Judy, her eyes round.

'I think so.' Ruth arranged the books on the table as if she is laying out Patience – or a magic trick. Judy leans forward, interested. Nelson wrenches his eyes away from Kate.

'Look. First I tried putting the books in the order Archie said. That puts *Evil Under the Sun* first. But then there are four twos in a row. It doesn't make sense. So then I thought: what if it's the third *word*?'

'What do you mean?' asks Judy.

'Well, the third word of the first title is Truth.' Ruth shuffles the books. 'The second word of the second title is Lies.'

'Truth and Lies,' says Nelson. 'That's deep.'

Ruth glares at him. 'The second word of the third title is Under.'

'I get it!' says Judy. 'Truth Lies Under.'

'Yes! The second word of the fourth title is Fourth.'

'Truth Lies Under Fourth,' says Nelson. 'What the hell does that mean?'

'The second word of the fifth title is Step. The third word of the sixth is Of. The first word of the seventh is Sea. The second of the eighth title is Light. Truth Lies Under Fourth Step Of Sea Light.'

There is a silence. Under the baby gym, Kate coos and chortles. Flint climbs onto the table and sits on the Sherlock Holmes book, purring loudly.

'What's a sea light?' asks Judy

Nelson hears Father Tom's voice, echoing in the dusty back room. *It's treacherous, this coastline, lots of dangerous rocks, shallow sandbanks. That's why we had the sea light at Broughton.*

'The lighthouse,' he says. 'It means the lighthouse. Under the fourth step of the lighthouse.'

21

April

The lighthouse. Ruth stares out of her office window, across the courtyard towards the artificial lake, and thinks about the impending trip to the sea light. It has already been put off twice because of bad weather and is now set for Saturday.

'Why don't you come?' Nelson had said on the phone. 'It's the weekend, after all.' How can he say that so casually? Doesn't he know that, *because* it's the weekend, Ruth is kept a prisoner by Kate? Of course he doesn't. Michelle has always done all the childcare and Nelson is as free as he ever was. Ruth imagines him at weekends, playing football or golf, going to the pub, with never a thought as to who is looking after his children. Of course, his daughters (his *other* daughters) are grown up now. He and Michelle can even go away on holiday together, not that Nelson seems to enjoy holidays but whose fault is that? The point is, he has escaped from the parenting years and Ruth is just beginning. In only eighteen years' time, she tells herself hollowly, I can go out on a Saturday.

The thing is she *wants* to go to the lighthouse. It was her idea, after all. She cracked the code and now she has to sit at home while Judy or Clough goes out on the police launch, climbs the precarious steps and finds . . . what? Does she really believe that there's something hidden below the fourth step of the Broughton Sea's End lighthouse? What could it possibly be? The truth, according to the code, but as an archaeologist Ruth knows that truth can prove remarkably elusive as the years go by. Is it a confession? A photograph? Another cryptic clue? Maybe Archie has set up a whole series of clues that will have them running all over the country, untangling acronyms and decoding acrostics, while the real murderer slips silently out of sight.

She pictures the lighthouse. It's a real landmark on the North East Norfolk coast, commemorated in countless post-cards and souvenirs. The tall red-and-white tower perched on a rock, seeming sometimes to rise straight out of the sea. Photos show it shrouded by mist on autumn mornings, almost hidden by crashing waves during winter storms and mirrored on a flat sea at the height of summer. The light-house is only a few hundred metres from the land but it is surrounded by rocks, making it almost impossible to reach except in calm weather. This is one of the reasons why the light is no longer in use. The main reason is that most ships nowadays are equipped with satellite navigation and have no need of picturesque lighthouses.

Ruth sighs and tries to get back to marking essays. She knows that she is behaving like a spoilt child, sulking because she's missing a day out. The trouble is that knowing doesn't make it easier to bear. She wants to go to the lighthouse, but Sandra is away for the weekend and Shona is spending Saturday with Phil and his sons and there is no-one to look after Kate. Tatjana is out on Saturday with the people from UEA but Ruth would never dream of asking her to babysit. No, Ruth will just have to stay at home like a good mother. Maybe she can bake a cake or something.

She looks out of the window again, remembering the day that she saw Clara and Dieter embracing in the snow. Then, as if summoned by the earlier memory, she sees a blonde woman walking across the courtyard, her arms full of books. Clara. Without thinking about it, Ruth taps on the window. Clara looks up, smiles. Ruth beckons. She could do with a break, some company, a cup of coffee. It'll stop her thinking about the lighthouse, unbreakable codes, Saturday morning telly.

Clara looks cold and rather forlorn, wearing a scruffy waxed jacket that has clearly seen many years of dog walking. Her hair is lank and rather greasy and her face is pale. Ruth feels a sudden stab of sympathy. She hasn't given much thought to what Clara must be feeling, losing her lover, realising that, in fact, she never had him. At least Dieter's wife will have a funeral to attend, a grave to visit, all the status and sympathy accorded to a widow. Clara is left with nothing.

'Do you fancy a coffee?' Ruth asks as Clara appears in the doorway. 'We can go to the canteen or there's a machine that's not too bad.'

'Machine will be fine,' says Clara. 'I'm just returning some of Dieter's books to the library.' She puts the pile of books on Ruth's desk. Ruth can't resist looking at the titles – Second World War history mostly, one treatise on the dating of bodies. Was Dieter doing his own forensic research then?

'How are you?' Ruth asks. 'This must be an awful time for you.'

Clara shrugs. 'I've been better. I know it's stupid because I'd only known him a few weeks but I really loved him, and to think that someone would kill him . . . like that . . .' She puts her hand over her mouth.

'It must be awful,' repeats Ruth inadequately. Clara burrows in her bag for a tissue and Ruth takes the opportunity to escape to the coffee machine. Clara probably wants a few minutes on her own, she tells herself.

When she returns with two steamy cups of coffee substitute, Clara seems a lot more composed. She tells Ruth quite calmly that Dieter's wife has flown his body back to Germany. 'I didn't see her,' she says. 'I don't think she knows anything about me.'

Did you know about her? wonders Ruth. But she doesn't say anything.

'The hardest thing,' Clara goes on, 'is not having anything to do. I haven't got a job. I'm not studying. All my friends have moved away. All I can do is take the dogs for walks, chat to Grandma, get in Mum's way in the kitchen. It's like being a teenager again.'

Maybe it's the word teenager that gives Ruth the idea. What do teenagers do to fill in the time? They take odd jobs, don't they? Washing cars, delivering papers . . . didn't Clara once say something about babysitting?

'I'd love to,' says Clara, looking cheerful for the first time. 'I'm not doing anything on Saturday afternoon. I'd love to look after Kate.'

'I shouldn't be long,' says Ruth. 'Nelson says the boat's leaving at two-thirty. I should be home by five at the latest.'

'Boat?'

'Yes, we're going out to the lighthouse. It's hard to explain but it's all linked to the bodies that we found in the cliffs.'

'The lighthouse?' says Clara. 'Dad owns it, I think.'

When Saturday comes, Ruth almost changes her mind. The sea is calm but the skies are heavy and overcast. Snow is forecast and there is an ominous yellow line on the horizon. But Clara appears promptly at one-thirty, full of plans for a fun afternoon with Kate, so Ruth has no choice but to put on her anorak and head out to the car. Clara stands at the window, waving, with Kate in her arms. For a moment, Ruth feels an almost overwhelming urge to rush back into the house, grab her baby and never let her go again. But, she reasons, she experiences a modified version of this urge every time she leaves Kate with Sandra. If she obeyed every irrational maternal impulse she'd never leave the house.

Ruth drives slowly along the coast road. Sometimes, in spring, you see groups of birdwatchers, binoculars in hand, trekking over the windblown grass in the hope of seeing a greenshank or a bar-tailed godwit. But, today, the Saltmarsh is deserted. There is a feeling of tension, almost expectancy, in the air. The grey-green reeds are sharply defined against the pale sky, a flock of snipe zigzags low over the road, water gleams between the ditches, dark and forbidding. Ruth turns on her car radio. Nothing like *Any Questions?* for driving away feelings of impending doom.

She is due to meet Nelson at Wyncham, along the coast

from Broughton. There is a jetty there and steps leading down to the beach. The police launch will come from Yarmouth and take them on the ten-minute trip to the lighthouse. As Ruth rounds the last bend, she sees the lighthouse rising starkly out of the grey sea. As she looks across the water, it seems to her that there is a flash of light from its high windows. Impossible; the light was taken away years ago, it is probably just a chance reflection. But Ruth feels uneasy. Why on earth did she ever want to go on this trip?

Nelson is waiting for her by the steps, accompanied by a man carrying what looks like a pneumatic drill. There is a third man too, someone short but very upright, bouncing on his toes as he looks out across the water. Can it really be . . .? Yes it can. Ruth parks her car on the grass at the top of the cliff next to Nelson's Mercedes and an old-style Jaguar that looks as if it has been preserved in aspic. Trust Jack Hastings to buy British.

'Ruth! You made it.' Nelson manages to give the impression that she's late though it is still only twenty past.

'Hallo, Nelson, Mr Hastings.'

'Jack, please.' Hastings is wearing a yellow sou'wester and seems full of bonhomie. 'Fine day for a cruise,' he says as he leads the way down the wooden steps. The launch is waiting by the jetty. It's a lot smaller than Ruth expected.

'Turns out Mr Hastings owns the lighthouse,' says Nelson. 'Lock, stock and barrel.'

'Only way to stop it being demolished,' says Hastings. 'I couldn't let that happen. Valuable part of our maritime heritage. Not that the government cares, of course.'

'What are you going to do with it?' asks Ruth. She is sure

she read somewhere about decommissioned lighthouses being turned into museums or even bed-and-breakfasts.

'Do?' Hastings turns to look at her. 'I'm not going to do anything. It's perfect as it is.'

Ruth looks across at the sleek stone tower that seems almost part of the rocks around it. She thinks she knows what Jack Hastings means. As she watches, the sun is once more reflected from the top windows – two flashes, like a signal.

Ruth wonders how much Nelson has told Jack Hastings about today's expedition. She is considering how to find out when Nelson says, rather repressively, 'I've told Mr Hastings about your theory concerning the lighthouse.'

Ruth notes 'your theory'. In other words, if the whole thing is a waste of time, it'll be Ruth's fault.

'Jolly good fun,' Hastings says, over his shoulder. 'Like something from an Arthur Ransome book.'

'Let's get on with it,' says Nelson. 'The tide'll turn in a minute.' They have had to wait until high tide so that most of the rocks will be under water. Nelson hates waiting for anything though time and tide, as Ruth could have told him, wait for no man.

A boatman in an RNLI jersey holds the craft steady as they clamber on board. It pitches alarmingly and, too late, Ruth remembers that, while she loves the sea, she hates boats.

From the shore the sea had looked completely flat, but as soon as they are away from the jetty, waves appear from nowhere and the little boat struggles against them. Ruth's stomach lurches in sympathy. Oh God, what if she's sick all over Nelson? Hastings, clinging to the rail with one hand, seems to be enjoying himself.

'Great fun!' he shouts, above the noise of the engine.

A wave crashes over the prow. Ruth cowers inside the little glass cabin. What will happen to Kate if she is drowned? She really must make a will.

The lighthouse is getting nearer. Close up it looks more derelict, rusty tears running down its sides. The rocks make it difficult to land. The launch pitches to and fro as the waves wash up over its sides. Ruth clamps her teeth together. Eventually, though, the skipper manages to get them close enough for his mate to jump ashore. He ties the boat onto the little landing jetty and stretches out a hand to help Ruth. Praying that she doesn't slip, she puts one foot on the side of the wildly rocking boat. Thank God she wore trainers. She manages an ungainly leap onto the rocks. It feels wonderful to be on solid ground.

Nelson jumps easily, he's surprisingly nimble for such a big man, but Hastings stumbles and nearly falls.

'Careful,' says the crewman cheerfully. 'If you fell in, we probably wouldn't be able to get you out again.'

An iron ladder leads from the jetty up to the lighthouse. Are these the steps referred to in the code? Ruth looks doubtfully at the rusty metal. How could anything be buried under here?

Nelson doesn't waste any time. He climbs the ladder, hand over hand, and disappears from view. Ruth follows, more slowly. She can hear Hastings behind her, breathing hard. The third man brings up the rear, struggling with the heavy drill.

Now they are standing looking up at the lighthouse

itself and Ruth sees that there are more steps, concrete
slabs leading up to the heavily barred door. They all stand
there in silence for a minute. Seagulls call plaintively from
the surrounding rocks. Ruth thinks of stories of lighthouse keepers sent mad by loneliness and wild weather.
Though they are not far from land, the shore is misty and
uncertain. Easy to imagine yourself miles from the world.

There are nine steps. 'Any idea if it's fourth step from the
top or fourth step from the bottom?' asks Nelson, rather
sardonically.

Ruth shakes her head, pulling her anorak tighter. It is
colder than ever.

'Let's try fourth from bottom,' says Nelson. 'We need to
get going before the weather gets any worse. Take it away,
Charlie.'

The man puts on ear-muffs and points the drill at the
fourth step. There is an explosion of noise. Dust fills the air
and the seagulls fly away, cawing angrily.

The concrete breaks easily. Nelson doesn't wait for more.
He kneels down and starts pulling away the rubble with his
bare hands.

'Is there anything there?' shouts Ruth.

'I think . . . yes, there's a box.' He leans into the hole.

'Hang on,' says Ruth, her forensic instincts outraged. 'You
can't do that. You have to plot the find, note exactly where
it is.'

Nelson ignores her. He reaches and straightens up, holding
something that looks like a steel container, about the size
of a shoe box. It seems unaffected by its sojourn underground; the metal gleams dully in the muted sunshine.

'What is it?' asks Ruth.

'It looks like a radio case,' says Hastings. 'I've seen one like it before. Survival radios, they were called. The boxes were stainless steel. My father had one in the war.'

Nelson shakes the box. Ruth winces.

'There's something inside,' he says.

'Is there a key?' asks Hastings.

'I'm not buggering about looking for a key,' says Nelson. He drops the box onto the ground, grabs the drill and aims it at the lid.

'Stop!' yells Ruth. 'You might damage whatever's inside. And you should be wearing gloves.'

Nelson looks at her darkly but he puts down the drill and asks Charlie if he can borrow his protective gloves. Then he tries the lid. It opens.

'Well, I'm blowed,' says Hastings. 'It wasn't even locked.'

Ruth leans forward as Nelson lifts something from the box. It is black and round, rather like a miniature steering wheel.

'What is it?' asks Ruth.

Again, it is Hastings who answers.

'It's a ciné film.'

Jack Hastings invites them back to his house to screen the film. It turns out he has an old-fashioned projector. 'I like old sixteen-millimetre films, it's a hobby of mine. Of course, you could have it converted to DVD but that would take time.'

Nelson hesitates. He knows he should take the film back to the station and have it converted but the excitement of finding it has made him reckless. He can't bear to wait another second without knowing what is on the film so carefully hidden and so cunningly traced. It's almost as if Archie Whitcliffe is urging him on, congratulating him (okay, Ruth) for having cracked the code, for following the clues all the way from the dusty paperbacks to the steps of the lighthouse. Who hid the film, he wonders. Archie? Or Hugh, the lifeboatman?

'The film might be damaged,' he says, 'but I suppose we could try.'

'That's the spirit,' applauds Hastings.

They are standing on the cliff top beside their cars. The launch has chugged off back to Yarmouth. The sky is still the same yellowy-white. It is four o'clock.

'Will you be joining us, Dr Galloway?' asks Hastings politely.

Ruth hesitates. 'I should get back.'

'Oh, Clara won't mind hanging on a bit longer,' says Hastings. 'Ring her.'

Ruth rings Clara who says she's happy to stay for another hour or two. 'We're having a lovely time. We've built lots of towers, listened to music and done some finger painting.' Ruth feels inadequate. She's never painted with Kate. And she notes that Clara's played Kate music instead of plonking her in front of the telly to watch *In the Night Garden*. Clara is obviously far better at the baby stuff than she is.

They drive in convoy back to Sea's End House. As they reach the gates the snow starts to fall.

'I should go back,' says Ruth.

'Oh, it won't settle,' says Hastings airily. 'I'm always right about the weather.'

22

The projector is in Hastings' study, a book-lined room with cracked leather sofas and two large dog beds. There is a fire and it is altogether cosier than the glacial drawing room. Ruth stands by the fireplace trying to warm her hands. The smell of dog and wood-smoke fills the air. Hastings draws the red velvet curtains and starts to fiddle with the projector, the sort seen in old films, two wheels with tape running between them. A huge screen is pulled down in front of the books and Stella Hastings comes in with tea and biscuits.

'Did you ever see such weather for April?' she says.

'Do you think it will get worse?' asks Ruth anxiously. The room is too warm and womb-like. She can see herself settling down on one on the sofas and never getting up again. She must get home to Kate.

'No, it won't last,' says Stella soothingly.

Stella backs out. The projector starts to whirr, circles with numbers inside appear on the screen. 8,7,6,5,4,3,2. Then, with what feels like shocking suddenness, a face appears. A dark-haired young man with little round glasses.

'What I am about to say,' he intones, 'is the truth, the whole truth and nothing but the truth.'

The man is dressed in uniform. Ruth isn't good at uniforms but she thinks that she sees wings above his pocket. RAF? The man sits close to the camera and looks nervous. Occasionally he glances anxiously at the operator, who is unseen. At one point the camera pans slowly round the room, showing a blacked-out window, a notice board, a furled Union Jack.

'Do you recognise the room?' Nelson asks Hastings.

'I'm not sure. It could be the old scout hut. The Home Guard used to meet there.'

'My name is Hugh P. Anselm,' the man is saying, pushing his glasses closer to his eyes. 'I'm a pilot officer in the RAF. Until recently, I was a member of the Home Guard at Broughton Sea's End.' He licks his lips and looks at the camera operator. 'What I am about to tell you occurred in the early hours of September the eighth, 1940. My colleagues and I took a blood oath never to divulge the events of that night. Accordingly, this message is only to be made public after my death and the death of my comrade Archibald Whitcliffe.'

'Archibald!' says an amused off-screen voice. Archie Whitcliffe is clearly the man behind the camera. Hugh Anselm ignores the interruption. He is speaking more fluently now, leaning in urgently.

'We will hide this message where it will not be found. When the time comes we will leave coded instructions as to its whereabouts. The story I have to tell is an unedifying one. Perhaps it will seem incomprehensible to the generations that come after us. I can only ask that you remember three things: it was war, we were scared and we were led by a very singular man.'

Ruth glances at Jack Hastings who is sitting behind the projector. He is leaning forward, his hand covering his mouth.

'On September the seventh, 1940,' says Hugh Anselm, glancing down briefly at his notes, 'the GHQ Home Forces received the codeword "Cromwell". This meant that an invasion was probable within the next twelve hours. Captain Hastings put our platoon on full alert. We had already placed the defences along the coastal strip; we had a fire ship moored off the beach, ready to ignite. At eleven p.m. three of us, under the command of Sergeant Austin, went out in the patrol boat. At midnight, we returned. At two a.m., just as we were preparing for another recce, our lookout in the tower signalled "enemy approaching", three long flashes of the torch, two short. Captain Hastings and Sergeant Austin went down to the beach.

'The rest of the platoon waited at the top of the cliff path. We saw a boat approaching, a small craft with an outboard motor, though that was silent. It was being rowed. We saw at once that it was moving slowly, only one man was rowing. The boat made its landing. Its occupants got out and we saw that two of the men were carrying a body. There were six men in total. Captain Hastings went down to the water's edge, raised his gun and ordered them to stop in the name of the King. They obeyed at once, putting up their hands. The leader spoke, in accented English. He gave his name as Karl von Kronig, a captain in the German army. He and his men were commandos on a reconnaissance mission. They had been hit by coastal artillery. One of his men was seriously injured. Captain Hastings signalled to us to put the men under arrest. We had been issued with ropes though we had hardly thought that they would submit so easily. We tied the men's hands and led them up the ramp and into the summer house, at the very end of the garden at Sea's End House. Donald had the key. Private Whitcliffe and I carried the injured man. He was groaning and we saw that he had been shot.

'In the summer house, there was a difference of opinion. Sergeant Austin, who had recently lost his son, wanted to shoot all six men. He had an old service revolver and I remember him brandishing it as he spoke. I spoke up, although as a private I hardly had the right. I said the men were prisoners of war and that it was our duty to take them into custody and find help for the injured man. I'm sure I spoke pompously and Captain Hastings was angry. He told me to hold my tongue. He pointed his gun at Von Kronig and asked if there were any other Germans in the vicinity. No, said Von Kronig, who was tall and blond with an air of command. They were simply a reconnaissance party. Captain Hastings told the man that Germany would never win the war. Von Kronig smiled and said that he thought they had won it already. Then Sergeant Austin shot him.

'He died immediately. Sergeant Austin was a crack shot. The other Germans shouted out but Captain Hastings pointed his gun at them and told them to be quiet. Captain Hastings gave his gun to Corporal Hoffman and told him to cover the men and let us know what they were saying (Corporal Hoffman was born in Germany). He led the rest

of us outside and told us that we would have to kill the rest
of the men. They would tell the authorities about the killing
of their captain and we had to protect Sergeant Austin.
Besides, we were at war and they were the enemy. We had
to shoot them and bury their bodies. I protested but Captain
Hastings told me to be quiet. Danny tried to back me up
but Donald said they were only filthy Jerries and would do
the same to us. Eventually, to my everlasting shame, I acquiesced.

'We led out the four men who could stand. Four of us
held them, their hands still tied behind their backs. They
did not know what was happening, mercifully for them.
Then Captain Hastings went behind them and shot each
one in the back of the neck and went inside to shoot the
sick man. None of us spoke. The wind was high and I don't
believe that anyone heard the shots. Sea's End House is very
isolated. One of the men called on God before he died. I
remembered that and, afterwards, I put my rosary into his
hands.

'Captain Hastings told us to take the men down to the
beach and bury them. There is a cleft in the cliffs, inaccessible except at low tide. Archie, Danny and I each carried
one of the bodies. The others were dragged on a length of
canvas, we'd used it earlier to make gun cotton. We burnt
the boat on the shore. By now it was dawn and I will never
forget seeing the sun rise on that morning and realising
that I was a murderer. Archie and I had the job of filling
in the grave and that is when I put my rosary into the
German soldier's hands. God forgive me, I have not said the
rosary since.

'At about six a.m. we went back to the summer house. Captain Hastings took out his knife and made a cut on each of our hands. One by one, we pressed our hands together so that the blood mingled and we swore never to divulge what had happened to a living soul. Then we went back to the house and Mrs Hastings made us breakfast.'

Hugh Anselm takes a deep breath and pushes at his glasses again. He looks so young, thinks Ruth. Eighteen? Nineteen?

'Private Whitcliffe and I will honour the oath we made,' he says, 'but we both feel that, one day, the truth should be known. We have only told one other person that this film exists. The last of the three of us left alive will leave instructions as to where to find this evidence. That is all I have to say. God have mercy on us all.'

The film stops abruptly.

Jack Hastings is the first to speak. 'My brother, Tony, heard the shots,' he says. 'He told me about it. He says he heard shooting and saw black shapes in the garden. People carrying bodies. I didn't believe him. He can only have been about three at the time.'

Ruth imagines the little boy at the nursery window, the figures moving in the dark, the sound of heavy boots on the path, the muffled oaths, the flames from the burning boat.

'We always thought that the summer house was haunted,' Hastings continues. 'Mother wouldn't let us go in there because it was so near to the cliff edge.'

'Are you going to tell your mother about this?' asks Nelson, jerking his head towards the blank screen.

Hastings looks troubled. 'I don't know. She has a right to

know, I suppose, but my mother worshipped my father. This could kill her. She has no idea about any of this.'

Ruth thinks of Hugh Anselm saying 'Mrs Hastings made us breakfast'. Did Irene Hastings really not know that she was feeding men who had just committed murder? Did her husband never tell her what happened that night?

'I never imagined . . .' Jack Hastings looks genuinely shocked, his hands shaking as he turns off the projector. 'I never imagined anything like this. I knew there was something. My dad sometimes talked about the Home Guard and it was never cosy stuff, never anything like the TV programme. He always said that they were ready for an invasion, that they would have fought to the death. But I never thought . . .'

'Did you ever suspect that this evidence existed?'

Hastings shakes his head. 'No, never.' He sits down, looking as if he'll never move again.

'I've got to go,' says Ruth. The ugly Thirties clock on the mantelpiece says six o'clock.

Through the stained glass in the front door, Ruth sees a strange blueish light. When she opens the door, she realises what it is. The world has changed. The long drive is covered with a heavy layer of snow, the trees are white with it, and Ruth's car is barely visible. The surface is virgin and unspoiled, until one of Hastings' dogs breaks free and starts running round in mad circles, barking hysterically.

'Jesus,' says Nelson. 'That's come down fast.'

'Oh my God.' Ruth feels sick. 'How am I going to get home?'

'We'll go in my car,' says Nelson. 'It's bigger and heavier. And it's got a wider wheelbase.'

Words like 'wider wheelbase' mean nothing to Ruth, but she takes in the fact that Nelson is offering to drive her home. Back to Kate. With only the briefest of farewells to Jack Hastings, they run across the white lawn to Nelson's Mercedes. The snow seeps into Ruth's trainers and, within seconds, she is freezing. Nelson sweeps the snow off the windscreen and gets in to start the engine. Thank God for German cars. Maybe the ill-fated captain was right and they did win the war.

Ruth leans forward in her seat, willing the car to negotiate the snowy drive. The wheels spin and Nelson swears but they move forward slowly, the soft snow hissing under the wheels.

'Should have chains on really,' says Nelson. 'But at least it's not icy yet.'

When they reach the road Ruth starts to breathe more easily, but as they near the main road they see that something is wrong. There are flashing lights, a man in a reflective jacket barring the way.

'Police,' says Nelson. He gets out of the car. After a brief discussion in which Ruth can see the reflective jacket shrugging obsequiously, Nelson comes back to the window.

'Road's blocked,' he says. 'Lorry's jack-knifed.'

'Oh no.' Ruth is rigid with horror. 'What shall we do?'

'There's no route cross-country,' he says. 'We'll have to go back to Sea's End House.'

'What about Kate?' Ruth's voice wobbles.

'She'll be fine, love. Clara's with her. And I'll get you home if I can. I'll phone for reinforcements. Get a chopper if necessary. Okay?'

'Okay.' Ruth manages a watery smile.

Jack and Stella are all concern. They usher Ruth into the kitchen while Nelson makes his phone calls. Irene, of course, makes them tea with bone china cups and saucers. At Stella's suggestion, Ruth rings Clara. The girl's cheerful voice is a distinct comfort.

'What a pain. That road is a nightmare. But don't worry, Ruth. I can kip down on your sofa. I've made up Kate's milk and she looks a bit sleepy.'

'Is Tatjana back yet?'

'No. But it's pretty wild outside, maybe she's stuck in town.'

'Maybe. I'll get home as soon as I can.'

'Okay. But don't worry. Really.'

Ruth clicks off the phone feeling better but still hyperventilating slightly. It's as if there's still an umbilical cord attaching her to Kate. She can go away from her baby for short stretches of time, but after a few hours she starts to panic. It's bad enough at the end of a working day, racing through the King's Lynn streets, desperate to press her face against Kate's and inhale her lovely baby smell. But now, stuck miles away from her, Ruth feels as if she will snap clean in two, so strong is the invisible pull of her daughter.

Nelson returns. 'Snow's started again. We can't get the chopper out in conditions like this.' Ruth thought he'd been joking about the helicopter. 'We'll have to sit it out for a bit, love.'

Love. It's the second time he's called her that.

'You must be our guests,' says Stella Hastings. 'We'll have

a nice supper and I'll make up the spare room for you, Inspector. Ruth, you won't mind having Clara's room?'

'No,' says Ruth. 'But the snow might stop soon.'

Hastings comes back into the room with snow on his peaked cap. 'Not much chance of that, I'm afraid. It's pretty heavy now. I walked up to the coast road and the lorry's stuck fast. I knew something like this would happen one day. I've warned the council time and time again.'

It's a strange, surreal evening. Despite further assurances from Clara (Kate is sleeping, she's fine, they're both fine), Ruth still feels tense and twitchy. She also can't forget the events of the day – the boat trip, the discovery of the buried box and, finally, the film itself. All through dinner – polished dining table, flickering candles, acres of silver and china – she keeps seeing Hugh Anselm's face, hearing his voice, the voice of a precocious teenager. *The story I have to tell is an unedifying one . . . there was a difference of opinion . . . to my everlasting shame, I acquiesced.* But his story was not a teenager's story. This was a man who had to face a terrible choice and bear an intolerable burden of guilt – all before he was twenty. What had the rest of Hugh Anselm's life been like, she wonders? Why did he decide, in the end, to break the oath? Why had he written to Dieter Eckhart? Dieter, who is now dead.

Yet Jack Hastings, who has just heard that his father murdered five men in cold blood, seems unaffected. Earlier, in the study, he had looked a broken man. Now he is every inch the genial host, pouring wine, telling amusing anecdotes about his family. His mother, Irene, smiles vaguely in the shadows. What does she know? What does she suspect?

Yet despite all these cross-currents of emotion, there is something almost magical about the evening. The formal dining room, the candlelight, the knowledge that outside it is still snowing, all conspire to make the little group around the table seem somehow removed from the rest of the world. It's as if, thinks Ruth, they have travelled in time. When they finally get up from the table and open the doors to the white expanse outside, will it be 2009 or 1940? Or will it be 1840, with carriage wheels whirling through the snow? Will the warning light shine in the tower, three short flashes, two long? Will Buster Hastings be walking down the cliff path towards the sea, gun in hand?

And, if she's honest, she likes the fact that she is there with Nelson. The configuration around the table, Jack and Stella, Ruth and Nelson, makes it almost seem as if they are a couple. She has never been out to dinner with Nelson and it is unlikely that she ever will again. So she enjoys looking at him across the table, she likes the fact that she and Nelson have some shared history to relate (they tell the story of the Iron Age body on the Saltmarsh, the discovery that first drew them together), she relishes the moment when, after repairing to the drawing room, they sit together on the sofa drinking brandy.

Irene has gone to bed. 'She sleeps downstairs; it's easier for her these days.' Stella, after checking on her mother-in-law, comes into the room with coffee in little gold cups, chocolates, coloured sugar.

'Blimey,' says Ruth, who has had rather a lot to drink, 'do you eat like this every night?'

She sees Nelson smiling into his brandy.

'We try to eat in the dining room at least once a week,' says Hastings. 'It's a shame to let standards drop entirely.'

'But most of the time we huddle round the kitchen table,' says Stella. 'Jack reads the paper and I listen to the radio. That's why it's nice to have guests.'

'Do you entertain a lot?' asks Nelson. He says 'entertain' like it's a foreign word.

'Not really.' There's a twinkle in Stella's eye as she passes round the cups. 'Jack's fallen out with most of the neighbours, you see.'

'Really, Stella! That's not true.'

'I can't stand most of my neighbours,' says Nelson. 'But the wife still insists on asking them round.'

It's the first time he has mentioned Michelle. At least he didn't say her name, thinks Ruth.

'You should be master in your own home, my dear fellow,' says Hastings.

'That's easier said than done,' says Nelson. 'I'm outnumbered. I've got two daughters, you see.' He looks at Ruth and away again. 'They gang up on me.'

'Clara could always twist Jack round her little finger,' says Stella. 'You've got all this to come, Ruth.'

Ruth smiles stiffly.

'I don't mind being outnumbered,' says Nelson. 'I haven't been first in the bathroom for over fifteen years. It's hard, though, when they grow up.'

Stella nods, her blue eyes warm. 'You're so right, Harry.'

I remember when Alastair left home I was bereft. I kept wandering into his room and crying. It was the same with Giles and Clara. That's why I'm glad that Clara's come back to us for a bit.'

'She'll soon be off again,' says Hastings. 'She's thinking seriously about the TEFL course.'

'You must be proud of her,' says Ruth. She thinks it's about time she said something.

'Oh we are,' says Stella. 'She hasn't had it easy. School was difficult. I was so pleased that she made it to university and got a good degree. I just hope that this latest thing . . .' Her voice trails off. The logs hiss in the fire. In the hall, a clock strikes.

'Midnight,' says Nelson. 'I must be for my bed.'

'Me too,' says Ruth and blushes. Nelson grins at her.

'Don't mind us, ha ha,' Jack Hastings is quick to enlarge on the joke.

'Really, Jack,' says Stella mildly. 'I'll show you to your room, Ruth. It's in the tower. Yours is the one above, Harry. It's got its own bathroom so you can make up for all those years of missing out.'

Clara's room is comfortable and untidy. Because it's in the tower it has curved walls and nothing quite fits. The bed juts out into the middle of the room, cupboards and book-cases stand awkwardly against the rounded walls. It was obviously once Clara's childhood bedroom – there is a rocking horse grinning in the corner and a pile of teddy bears on the widow seat. Equally obviously, it has been recently decorated, with blameless sprigged wallpaper and curtains held back with little bows. Ruth goes to the window and looks out. Far below is the sea. It looks wrong to see snow on the beach, like a negative, the black waves breaking on the white shore. Far off, she can see a flashing light. It's probably on the coast road but it makes her think of the lighthouse and the days when its beam would have shone out, warning sailors off the jagged rocks. At the foot of the tower there is a narrow line of snow before the land drops away. The garden and the summer house have disappeared forever. Ruth thinks of the night when the Germans landed, the shots in the dark, the little boy watching from the window. Perhaps this same window? She shivers.

She washes in the bathroom, a thin slice taken out of the room. Stella has lent her a nightdress but it's floor-length and frilly and she doesn't want to wear it. ('Why?' she asks herself sternly. 'Who will see it?') Instead, she keeps on her T-shirt and knickers. She is appalled to find herself stealing some of Clara's perfume. She doesn't know what she is thinking of. She and Nelson said a very brief good-night in the hall. She won't see him again until morning. She puts her phone on the bedside table, wishing she could ring home again. But Clara will be asleep. Funny to think of her sleeping in Ruth's bed and Ruth in hers (though Clara insisted that she would be comfortable on the sofa). When she last spoke to Clara, Tatjana wasn't home. She has obviously decided to stay the night in Norwich.

Ruth sighs. She feels twitchier than ever, every nerve strung up to snapping point. How is she ever going to get to sleep? She fetches a glass of water from the bathroom. Perhaps she's just a bit drunk. But slow sipping doesn't help. She goes to the bookcase. She'll read until she drops off. Clara is nothing if not eclectic in her tastes: law textbooks, Dickens, Jilly Cooper, Agatha Christie. Ruth thinks of Archie and his crime novels. What made him think of that elaborate code? And why leave it to Maria, whose English, according to Nelson, isn't that good? Perhaps that was a way to ensure that the film would never be found – a way of honouring his promise to Hugh but protecting the memory of the troop. And who, she wonders suddenly, was the third person who knew the secret? The person Hugh mentioned in the film. Presumably he too is dead by now.

Ruth takes out a copy of *Riders*; she loves books about horses. But as she does so she dislodges a small, leatherbound book that has been lying on top of Jilly Cooper's epic. It is a diary.

She knows she shouldn't open it. She knows that. She has no right to read Clara's private diary. It would be the worst possible invasion of privacy. She should just put it back on the shelf.

Ruth opens the diary.

I hate his wife, she reads. *I want to kill him for deceiving me.*

Ruth stops reading. Clutching the book, she goes to the window. The snow has stopped. Sea's End House lies under a cloak of silence; everything is muffled, enclosed, secret. The roads will be treacherous. Ruth is miles away from home. Clara is looking after her baby. She hears Clara's voice, on the night of the naming day party. *I was expelled from two schools.*

Why was she expelled?

She hears Stella. *She hasn't had it easy. School was difficult.* Why was school difficult?

On an impulse, Ruth goes to the bedside table and starts looking through the drawers. In the third drawer, she finds what she is looking for.

A pair of dress-making scissors.

23

'Nelson!'

The hall is dark. A winding staircase leads up to Nelson's room but the door is shut. Ruth starts up the stairs, but before she has reached the top the door opens.

'Ruth! What is it?'

Nelson descends the stairs. He is wearing a T-shirt and boxer shorts. Even in the state she is in, Ruth notices.

'Nelson!' She grabs his arm. 'I've got to talk to you.'

She turns and screams. A little figure is standing in front of her, wearing a long white robe.

'Ruth, for God's sake.' This is Nelson.

Ruth takes a deep breath and realises that the sinister figure is Irene and the robe is a candlewick dressing gown. She clasps the old lady's arm.

'Irene! Why was Clara expelled from school?'

Behind her, Nelson expostulates but Irene does not seem put out by the question. She blinks calmly once or twice.

'Such a silly fuss. I'm sure it was as much the other girl's fault as Clara's.'

'But what did she do?'

'They said she ... hurt someone.'

'Hurt? How?'

'Stabbed them. With some scissors.'

Ruth lets out a low moan and drags Nelson into her room. Unperturbed, Irene patters back downstairs.

'What's all this about?' protests Nelson.

'Didn't you hear? Clara stabbed someone when she was at school. She was expelled.'

'That was years ago.'

'And I found these in her bedside cabinet.'

Nelson takes the scissors and turns them over in his hand.

'Nelson!' Ruth almost screams. 'She's looking after our baby.'

Nelson looks at Ruth, dawning horror in his eyes. 'We've got to get to her,' he says.

'We can't. The coast road is blocked.'

'I'll get one of my team. I need my phone.'

He runs back upstairs. Ruth thinks she should get dressed but Nelson is back before she has had time to move.

'I'll call Judy. She lives near you.'

'But how will she get there?' wails Ruth.

'She's got a four-by-four. We tease her about it.'

There is an agonising wait before Judy answers the phone. Ruth hears Nelson's voice, barking orders as he paces round the room.

'. . . Ruth's place ... yes ... quick as you can, force entry if necessary ... you can phone for back-up but I'm not sure a squad car'll get through ... yes ... call me.'

'Does she think she can make it?' asks Ruth. She holds onto her arms to stop herself shaking.

'Yes. The roads are bad but she's got a pretty tough vehicle. She thinks it'll take about an hour.'

'An hour!'

'Snow's very deep in places.'

'Oh, Nelson.' Ruth collapses onto the bed. 'Do you think she'll be okay? Kate?'

Nelson sits next to her. 'I'm sure she will.' But his voice sounds shaky.

'What will I do if anything happens to her?'

'Nothing will happen to her. She'll be okay.'

Ruth starts to cry and, after a moment, Nelson takes her in his arms.

Judy almost misses the turning to New Road. The snow makes everything look strange and unfamiliar. She finds herself leaning forward, like an old lady in a Morris Minor. Her headlights make dingy yellow circles in the darkness; twice she's had to check that they're actually working. The snow has stopped but the roads are icing over. As she takes the corner, she feels the ground sliding away from her. If she's killed, it'll be Nelson's fault.

But the car's solid tractor-like wheels hold up well. Judy feels a surge of satisfaction. They'd all laughed at her for buying this car. 'Go off-road much, do you?' Clough had scoffed. Clough has been even more obnoxious than usual recently, calling her 'Bridezilla' and implying that the wedding plans are taking her mind off the job. Bastard. She wishes she hadn't invited him now. Besides, he's totally wrong. She is throwing herself into work to take her mind off the nightmare of dressing in white and saying 'I do' in front of hundreds of gawping spectators. Why didn't she insist on a registry office? Or the Caribbean. The Caribbean would be good.

Anyway, tonight she's one up on Clough. The boss called her, not him. It's because of the car, she knows, but that just shows she was right to buy a four-by-four. Sucks to Clough and his flashy Saab. The boss asked her for help and he'll be eternally grateful for . . . what exactly? Up to this point, the idea of being the heroine of the hour has taken her mind off the fact that she has no idea what this crisis is all about. Why is it so urgent that she has to drive to Ruth's house across icy roads, forcing entry if necessary? Is Ruth's baby in danger? But there's someone babysitting isn't there? 'A girl called Clara,' Nelson had said tersely. 'If she gives you any trouble, arrest her.' 'What?' 'Just do it, Judy, please.'

Please. He'd actually said please. And he'd called her Judy. Usually it's 'Johnson' or 'you'. A suspicion, which has been fluttering around in Judy's brain since the naming day cere- mony, now flaps its wings once again. Why is Nelson so concerned about Ruth's baby? Clough told her about the incident at Broughton. The boss falling asleep with the baby in his arms. What if . . . no, it's impossible.

New Road is a nightmare. One slip, Judy knows, and she'll plunge the car down the bank and will probably never be seen again. She grips the steering wheel. She's a good driver (much to her satisfaction she beat Clough on the police advanced driving course) but this is something else. She crawls forward, listening to the snow crunching beneath her wheels. One lapse of concentration, that's all it will take.

When she sees it, she thinks at first that she is halluci- nating. A dark hooded figure, trudging along at the side of the road. Who on earth would be walking along New Road through foot-high snow? Then she starts to panic. Her head spins with images of mysterious figures that appear beside unwary travellers, of car-crash victims who suddenly materialise on your back seat, grinning through their mangled faces, the third man – the hooded man – Christ on the road to Emmaus. She hears her breath, loud and uneven, filling the car. She checks her driving mirror. Pull yourself together, she tells herself. But the ragged breathing continues.

She is almost level now. What if the vision vanishes into the snow? What if it turns, brandishing an axe?

The figure turns, pulling the hood away from its face. It is Cathbad.

'I love her so much. I never thought I would love a baby this much.'

'I know.' Nelson strokes her hair.

'What if something happens to her?'

'It won't.'

'How do you know?'

Nelson says nothing. She can feel his heart beating through the thin T-shirt. She shivers.

'You're freezing. Get into bed.'

'Don't leave me,' says Ruth.

'I won't.'

'Cathbad!' Judy winds down the window, with difficulty because it is covered with snow. 'What the hell are you doing here?'

'Don't switch off the engine,' says Cathbad. With a deft

movement he opens the door and jumps nimbly into the high vehicle.

'Are you going to Ruth's?' asks Judy, closing the window and edging forward once more.

'Where else?' Cathbad is shivering even though, under his cloak, he is sensibly dressed in a parka and combat trousers.

'She's not there.'

'I know.'

'Then why?'

Cathbad calmly adjusts the seat so he can stretch his legs. 'I don't know. I just had this feeling. I rang earlier and I got a bad feeling about the girl who answered the phone.'

'A bad feeling? Jesus, Cathbad.'

'Why are *you* here?'

'Nelson had a bad feeling about her too.'

'Ah.' Cathbad sounds satisfied. 'So Nelson's starting to trust his instincts. That's good.'

'Is it?'

'For him, anyway. Careful.' The car begins to slide.

'It's icy here.'

'The temperature's dropping.'

No second sight needed there. Judy's dashboard says minus five degrees. The windscreen wipers scrape against ice. Judy can see only a few yards in front of her face.

'You were mad to try to walk it,' she says.

'There's a pleasure sure in being mad,' says Cathbad, 'that none but madmen know.'

It's a typical Cathbad answer. Judy decides to ignore it, she needs all her concentration for driving. Cathbad seems perfectly relaxed, humming under his breath. Last year, he was involved in a car chase with the boss. If he can survive that, nothing will faze him. Despite everything, though, Judy is glad to have company. The Saltmarsh, featureless in the dark, is a spooky place. The presence of another human, even one prone to irritatingly gnomic utterances, is indescribably comforting.

Ruth's cottage seems to come from nowhere. One minute they are crawling along through the unchanging white nothingness, the next, the blue gate is beside them and they can see the three houses, their roofs rounded with snow. The security light comes on as they park outside. Everything else is in complete darkness. It is two a.m.

'The houses either side are empty,' says Cathbad.

'I know.' Judy switches off the engine. 'I wouldn't live here in a million years.'

Outside it is so cold that Judy feels her heart clench with shock. Cathbad, though, seems fully recovered. He jumps down and makes for the front door. The wind is stronger here and the snow has formed fantastically shaped drifts, almost as high as the windows.

'Shall I knock? The bell's not working.'

'Cathbad?' Judy hates herself for this but she's scared. Suddenly too scared to move another step. 'What if—' She stops.

Cathbad takes her hands. Despite the cold, his hands are very warm. 'Judy,' he says. 'You are strong. You are a wonderful, strong human being.'

And the weird thing is, she does feel strong. Strong enough

to wrench herself free from Cathbad and hammer on the door. 'Open up!'

The sound echoes inside the house. Then silence. Judy and Cathbad look at each other.

'We'll have to force the door,' says Judy. 'I've got a crowbar in the jeep.'

Cathbad holds up his hand. 'Shh.'

Very slowly, the door opens. The chain is still on and a small voice calls, 'Who is it?'

'Police.' With shaking hands, Judy pushes her warrant card through the gap in the door.

There is a rattle as the chain comes off and they see a blonde girl, very young and scared, a blanket wrapped round her shoulders.

'I'm Sergeant Judy Johnson. DCI Nelson sent me.'

'I know you, don't I?' says Clara. 'You were at the party the other night.'

'Where's the baby?'

'Upstairs.'

Judy bounds up the narrow stairs. She isn't scared now, adrenaline rushes though her. Whatever she is about to see – and during the drive she has imagined every horror possible – she can cope with it. She flings open the door to Ruth's bedroom and can just make out the cot by the bed. She switches on the overhead light and strides across the room. Kate is lying on her side, a pink blanket pulled up to her chin. She is breathing steadily. Judy takes off her glove and touches the baby's cheek. It is warm. Kate whimpers.

'What's going on?' Clara is standing behind her. She still sounds scared.

'You didn't answer your phone. DCI Nelson was worried.' Judy is already punching in his number.

'I was asleep.'

'Boss? . . . Yes, she's fine, I'm looking at her now . . . of course I'm sure . . . yes, I'll tell her . . . okay.'

Clara is looking at her, almost in awe. 'How did you get here?'

'I've got a four-by-four.'

'Why is that druid with you?'

'I'll explain in a minute. Any chance of some tea?'

But when they get downstairs the druid has already made tea. The sofa is covered with bedclothes so they sit at the table by the window. There is an odd intimacy between the three of them, sitting at Ruth's table, in Ruth's house, drinking Ruth's tea. Looking after Ruth's baby. Clara cradles her mug in both hands, staring dreamily into space. Cathbad puts two sugars in Judy's cup, which is odd because he hasn't asked whether she takes sugar. She does.

'Did you tell Nelson?' he says.

'Yes.'

'Did he say thank you?'

'No.'

'Was Ruth with him?'

Judy catches Cathbad's eye. 'Yes.'

'The boss wants me to stay the night,' Judy says to Clara. 'Is that okay with you?'

Clara shrugs. 'Suit yourself. There are two beds upstairs. A single and a double.' She looks curiously from Judy to Cathbad.

'I'll take the double,' says Judy.

* * *

Ruth is leaning forward, her head between her knees. Nelson's voice seems to come from a long way off.

'Are you feeling any better?'

'Yes.' With an effort, Ruth straightens up. 'It's just the relief. Knowing that she's safe.'

'I know.' Nelson runs his hand though his hair until it stands up like a crest. He's quite grey now, Ruth notices. His chin is dark with stubble. It must be nearly morning, she thinks.

'What did Judy say again?'

'She'd seen Kate. She was sleeping peacefully.'

'And Clara?'

'She'd been asleep on the sofa.'

'Do you think she might have killed Dieter Eckhart?'

'It's possible.' Nelson rubs his face. 'Stabbing is usually a crime of passion. You say she'd written in her diary that she wanted to kill him?'

'Yes. I didn't read any more.' Ruth points at the little book on the bedside table.

'I'll take that with me tomorrow. The scissors too, though they'll have our prints all over them.'

Ruth shudders. 'I still don't like to think of her in the house with Kate.'

'I told Judy that she or Cathbad had to sleep in the room with her.'

'What on earth was Cathbad doing there?'

Nelson shrugs. 'You know Cathbad. He always turns up when you least expect him.'

They both think of other occasions when Cathbad has turned up, just in time to save or be saved. Cathbad is magic,

Erik used to say. He certainly seems able to materialise at will.

'I should go back to my room,' says Nelson. He picks up Ruth's watch from the bedside table. Half past two.

'Yes,' she says. But neither of them moves.

Ruth thinks that Nelson says something under his breath, but she doesn't hear. She shuts her eyes, moving towards Nelson as his lips close upon hers.

24

In the end, Judy opts for the single bed. She just doesn't like the idea of sharing a room with a baby. What if Kate wakes up crying? That, to Judy, is more terrifying than the hooded figure on the road.

'It's all right,' says Cathbad. 'I'll sleep in there.'

'I'm sorry,' says Judy. 'I'm just not very maternal.'

Cathbad looks at her. 'I wouldn't say that.'

'Do you have children?' asks Judy.

'A daughter.' Cathbad's voice drops. 'I didn't see much of her when she was growing up. I'm trying to make up for it now.'

They are standing, whispering, on the landing. This, like the snow and the tea earlier, makes them seem ridiculously intimate, as if they're flatmates or having what Judy's nieces would call a 'sleepover'.

'I'm not sure I want children,' she says. 'It's such a responsibility.'

'What does your fiancé think?'

Judy hesitates. How does Cathbad know she's getting

married? Has he noticed her engagement ring? There's something nasty about the way he says 'fiancé'.

'We've never discussed it,' she says, with dignity.

Cathbad grins. 'I'd start discussing it, if I were you.' And he disappears into Ruth's room.

Judy washes in the bathroom, noticing that Ruth uses surprisingly expensive soap. What is it about Cathbad that always makes her feel slightly uneasy? She first met him over a year ago. Nelson had needed to get across the Saltmarsh at night, in a storm, and Cathbad had been the only person to know the mysterious hidden pathway. Judy had been impressed with him then. She did not, like the rest of the team, see him as a nutcase, one of the weirdos that often hang around police stations offering unsolicited help and advice. There is a stillness about Cathbad that attracts Judy. He is contained within himself; he doesn't see the need to seek approval from anyone else. Darren is like a big golden retriever, rushing round and licking everyone. Like me, love me, pat me. And, yes, he wants ten children.

The next time Judy met Cathbad had been at a summer solstice party at the Roman dig at Swaffham. It had been a fairly wild night, she remembers. She had danced with Cathbad but then she had danced with Dave and Irish Ted too. She has an image of Cathbad lighting a fire, high up on a hill. The flames in the darkness, the druids chanting, the scent of burning herbs. Ruth had been there with her archaeologist friend, Max. What had happened to him?

It was only at the naming day party that she had really spoken to Cathbad. They had talked about Catholicism and paganism and the role of godparents. Judy tries to remember whether she told him that she was getting married. She does remember that she'd found him quite attractive at the naming day, which she hadn't before. What was different?

The spare room is tiny, just a single bed, a chest of drawers and a wardrobe. The rest of the space is taken up with cardboard boxes, stacked one on top of each other. It's not exactly cosy. The top of the chest is crowded with creams and make-up. Jesus, no wonder Tatjana looks so good. There is also a book written in some incomprehensible language and a picture of a beautiful, dark-eyed child. Judy picks up this last and examines it. She spent a long time chatting to Tatjana after her hen party and she never mentioned that she had a child. She turns the photo over. On the back, in a flowing hand, is written 'Jacob 1995'.

Judy gets into the narrow bed and determinedly turns out the light. She'd better get some sleep or she'll be useless tomorrow. The roads will still be bad after all that snow so getting home will be no joke. She supposes that she'll have to stay here until Ruth or Nelson gets back. She sits up.

'Cathbad?'

He appears in the doorway, still wearing combats and a black T-shirt.

'Cathbad, do you think Nelson is Kate's father?'

Cathbad sits heavily on the foot of the bed. 'Yes,' he says. 'Yes, I do.'

'Jesus.' Judy considers this. It feels wrong, sitting here

in the dark with Cathbad. It feels wrong because it feels right.

'Does anyone else know?'

Cathbad shakes his head. 'I don't think so. They're both very private people.'

'But the boss is married.'

'I'm sure he loves his wife.'

'But what about Ruth?'

Cathbad sighs. 'She loves him, I think. But him? He loves the baby, the idea of being a father again. But I don't think he'll ever leave Michelle.'

'Cathbad?'

'What?'

'Are you really a wizard?'

Cathbad grins, his teeth very white in the darkness.

'What do you think?'

'I don't know what I think.'

'I'm not a wizard,' says Cathbad. 'I'm just someone who tries to live a certain way. In harmony with nature, in harmony with the old traditions. My mother though . . .' He laughs softly. 'A few hundred years ago she would have been burnt at the stake. She knew a spell to make your hens lay, to charm back an unfaithful husband, to make a man irresistible to women. She was a witch, all right, even though she went to mass every Sunday. This was rural Ireland. Everyone went to mass even if they were queuing up in Mammy's back yard the next day.'

Judy tries to imagine Cathbad as a child. He seems ageless somehow. 'My dad's Irish,' she says. 'He's a bookie.'

'That accounts for the bond between us.'

'Is there a bond between us?'

'I think so, don't you?'

Judy moves her legs, trying not to touch Cathbad. The trouble is, the room's too small. It's getting smaller by the second.

'Do you want to go to sleep?' asks Cathbad.

It's as if he's asking a different question altogether. Judy struggles with her answer.

'Yes,' she says at last.

Much later, Judy wakes from a confused dream about ice floes, hooded figures, sacred fires. Groping on the floor, she finds her watch. Five o'clock in the morning.

The landing is silent. No sound from Clara downstairs. Suddenly a soft footfall makes her jump and something rubs against her legs. She stifles a scream and, looking down, meets luminous green eyes. Jesus, she'd forgotten Ruth had a cat. Shakily she strokes Flint's gently butting head. Where has he been hiding all this time?

In the bedroom, Kate is still sleeping, making little snuffling noises. Cathbad is lying across the double bed. Asleep he looks much younger.

'Cathbad?'

He is awake in an instant.

'You've shaved off your beard.'

Cathbad reaches for her, pulling her down on the bed next to him. He is strong, much stronger than he looks. He smells of wood smoke and expensive soap.

'We can't,' says Judy. 'I'm getting married in two weeks.'

'It was meant to be,' says Cathbad, kissing her neck.

I don't believe in any of that, Judy wants to say. I'm a rationalist, a policewoman and I've only ever slept with one man. But, instead, she is kissing him back, greedily, urgently, moving her body against his.

25

It is nearly nine o'clock when Ruth wakes up. The curtains are open and the room is full of light. There's no sign of Nelson. She goes to the window, wearing the duvet over her shoulders. Outside the sky is bright blue and the snow blindingly white. There are no footsteps on the path down to the beach, where the sea is breaking gently against the frosted pebbles. Still draped in the duvet, Ruth pads into the bathroom. From the bathroom window, which faces the side of the house, she sees Nelson, in his shirtsleeves, clearing the snow from around his car. She watches him dreamily, not thinking of anything very much. He is working hard, his breath billowing around him, but he's doing it all wrong, bending his back rather than his knees. Ruth noticed this once before. When was it?

How could she have gone to bed with him again? After trying so hard to keep her distance, to be independent, not to jeopardise his marriage. Perhaps she's pregnant. Maybe they'll continue to have sex once a year and, in a few years' time, they'll have a family of five. Don't be silly, she tells herself. It's highly unlikely that she's pregnant again and last night was a one off. *Another* one off. It was the snow, the house, the relief of discovering that Kate was all right. A combination of circumstances that will never occur again. Ruth is free to get on with her life. She leans against the window, her breath misting the glass.

As she watches, another figure comes out of the house. Jack Hastings. He is warmly dressed in a heavy coat and peaked cap with the inevitable dogs running around him. He says something to Nelson and Nelson laughs, the sound echoing up to Ruth's turret window. She retreats. She doesn't want them seeing her there, like some overweight Lady of Shalott. Time to get on with things.

She rings Judy. There's a long wait before she answers and Judy sounds distinctly odd, flustered, unlike herself. Is Kate all right, Ruth asks anxiously. Yes fine, says Judy, Cathbad's giving her some breakfast now. Is Cathbad still there then? Yes, the snow's still pretty bad on the Saltmarsh. What's Clara doing? She's making some tea. Please stay with Kate until I get there, says Ruth. I'll be as quick as I can.

She showers standing up in the bath, washing her hair with some violently scented gel. It's horrible, putting on the same clothes from last night. What was it that Nelson had said to her? 'I can't get you out of my head, Ruth. I try but you're there all the time.' She doesn't know how she feels about Nelson; it's all so complicated, so angst-ridden. But she knows one thing: when he said those words, a shock of pure pleasure had run through her. Nelson doesn't love her, she knows that, but at least he can't forget her. That's something.

Breakfast is awkward. Nelson doesn't meet her eye. Stella cooks them bacon and eggs, maintaining a steady flow of hostess chatter. Jack is silent, feeding bacon rinds to the dogs. Irene doesn't put in an appearance. 'Mother had a bad night,' explains Stella.

'Jack's found me some chains for the car,' says Nelson, still not looking at Ruth. 'The coast road is clear. We should be able to get through.'

'What about my car?'

'Better leave it here. I'll have someone pick it up for you. The important thing is to get you home.'

'Yes,' agrees Ruth.

'We ought to start as soon as possible.'

'Have some coffee first,' says Stella, taking the pot from the Aga.

And Ruth feels a curious reluctance to leave. She wants to see Kate, of course she does, but she also wants to stay here, having someone cook for her and make her coffee. She wants to sit by the fire and read the paper. She wants to huddle up on the sofa and look at the snow outside. She wants to be Stella's daughter. She wants to stay here with Nelson.

But as soon as Nelson has drunk his coffee he is standing up. 'Thank you for your hospitality,' he says formally.

'My dear fellow, don't mention it,' says Jack.

Now that Nelson has become 'my dear fellow', thinks Ruth, will it be difficult for him to raise the little fact of Jack's father being a murderer? She knows that Nelson has the film in his car, along with the diary and the scissors. His next visit to Sea's End House may turn out to be a very different affair. But Hastings, who yesterday had seemed so shaken by Hugh Anselm's film, is all charm and smiles. He shakes Ruth's hand warmly, brushing off her thanks. 'Any time, my dear. Glad we could help.'

Ruth turns to Stella. 'You've been so kind.'

Stella enfolds her in a hug. 'Come again. Bring your little girl.'

'I will.'

'Come on, Ruth,' says Nelson, impatient as ever. 'We'd better get going.'

The drive to the Saltmarsh is beautiful. The fields are white, glittering in the sun, the trees like a Christmas card. Everything ugly or utilitarian – the municipal dump, the holiday flats, the caravan selling hamburgers – has been covered with this kindly layer of magic. It's hard to believe that last night the snow had seemed terrifying, a malign force. Now it's sleigh rides and Santa and Holiday on Ice. They pass some teenagers sledging down a hill on bin liners, children building a snowman in their front garden, a family on their way to church, ears aglow with virtue. Ruth had forgotten that it was Sunday. They do see a few abandoned cars, an upturned bicycle, its wheels still spinning, but otherwise the snow seems delightful, designed purely for fun. The main roads have been gritted and, as they get nearer to King's Lynn, they see cars and buses. The world is getting back to normal.

'Thaw's setting in,' says Nelson. It seems like the first thing he's said for hours.

'It's incredible,' says Ruth. 'All this snow in April.' Her

mouth feels dry; she doesn't think she's ever uttered a more boring sentence.

They drive in silence across the Saltmarsh. The bleak landscape of stunted trees and wind-blown grass has been transformed and a smooth white terrain unfolds in front of them, like the surface of the moon. The birds are flying lower than usual, desperate for food; occasionally a sandpiper makes a kamikaze dive down into the reed beds and the ducks walk, bemused, on iced-over marsh pools.

'Ruth—' says Nelson.

'I can't wait to see Kate,' gabbles Ruth. 'It feels like years since I've seen her. It was so kind of Judy to drive all this way . . .' Her voice fades away.

'Ruth.' Nelson is stopping the car. Keep driving, Ruth urges him silently. I don't want to have this conversation now. Ever.

'We've got to talk.'

'What about?' says Ruth.

'Jesus! What about? About everything.'

'There's nothing to say.' Ruth fiddles with her seatbelt. Suddenly the car feels far too small. She knows that Nelson is looking at her but, for many reasons, she does not want to meet his eyes.

'Look, Ruth . . .' Ruth hears Nelson's voice gearing down to his persuasive tone. 'Last night was . . . well, it shouldn't have happened.'

'I know,' says Ruth, looking out of the window. In the far distance, she can see the sea.

'I mean it was . . . great, but—'

'What do you mean "great"?'

'You know what I mean. If I was single, it would be a different matter. But I'm not. We both know that.'

Would it be different? Ruth doubts it somehow. A single Nelson would never have looked twice at her; he would be off searching for a blonde Michelle clone. It was only circumstance, proximity and a host of other words meaning the same thing; meaning that she and Nelson were never really meant to be together.

'I know you're married,' says Ruth, trying to keep her voice calm. 'I've always respected that. I've never made any demands on you, even with Kate. Have I?'

'No.'

'Well, then. It'll never happen again. I'll make sure of it.'

Nelson sighs. Ruth doesn't know if it is with relief or regret. They both sit in silence for a moment, looking out across the endless white marshes. Then Nelson starts the engine.

Judy's jeep is parked outside the house, next to Clara's snow-covered Mini. Ruth leaps out of the car as soon as it stops. She doesn't look back to see if Nelson is following.

She opens the door to a bizarre domestic scene. Clara is sitting at the table, earphones in, reading. Judy is in the kitchen and Cathbad is lying on the floor playing with Kate.

Ruth rushes over and grabs Kate, holding her so tightly that she squawks. 'Hallo, sweetheart,' she whispers.

'Hallo,' answers Cathbad, still lying on the rug.

'Cathbad! How come you're here?'

'Ask Judy.'

Still carrying Kate, Ruth hurries over to Judy and hugs her awkwardly, the baby between them.

'Thank you so much for coming over.'

'It's okay. All part of the service. I was just making toast. I hope you don't mind.'

'Of course not. Have anything.'

'Well, there wasn't really anything else. Just cat food and baby food.'

'Where's Flint?'

'Asleep on your bed. He gave me the fright of my life last night.'

Nelson has come in and is talking in a low voice to Cathbad. Ruth walks over to Clara who is watching her rather quizzically.

'Thanks so much for staying last night, Clara.'

Clara takes out her headphones. 'That's okay. You didn't really need to send the cavalry over. I was quite capable of looking after Kate for one night, you know.'

Ruth smiles, slightly embarrassed. In the light of the day, her fears seem rather stupid. But then she remembers the diary. *I hate his wife. I want to kill him.* No, she's still glad that Judy was here last night. And Cathbad too. But why *is* he here?

Before she can ask him, Nelson cuts in. With his height, dark clothes and unsmiling face, he is incongruous in the small, cosy room. He seems determined to add to this impression, speaking in a brisk, businesslike tone, not making eye-contact with anyone.

'I'll drive you home, Clara,' he says. 'You still wouldn't want to risk the roads round here.'

'You can give me a lift too,' says Cathbad, who has taken a piece of toast from Judy.

'No,' answers Nelson brusquely. 'You go with Johnson.'

I'm Johnson again, am I, thinks Judy. But the boss had thanked her when he rang earlier. There's no doubt she's one up on Clough.

'I'll take you home, Cathbad,' she says, not looking at him.

Nelson and Clara head for the door. Ruth thanks Clara profusely, trying to make up for last night's lack of trust. Nelson says nothing.

Judy gathers up her phone and bag. 'Coming, Cathbad?'

'There's no need to rush off,' says Ruth. She rather likes the idea of sitting here with Judy and Cathbad, eating toast and talking about the marvels of Kate.

'We'd better be off,' says Judy. 'I've got lots to do.'

'Yes, the wedding's in a couple of weeks, isn't it?' says Ruth, wanting to seem friendly. 'You must be so excited.'

'If you say so,' says Judy. Rather rudely, Ruth thinks.

As soon as the door shuts behind Cathbad and Judy, Kate starts to cry. Having been angelic all night ('She only woke up once,' said Cathbad, 'but I sang to her and she went back to sleep') she now transforms into Damien from *The Omen*. Ruth tries milk, food, dancing round the room, singing. But obviously her singing isn't a patch on Cathbad's because, after the first few bars of 'The Wheels on the Bus', Kate howls louder than ever. In desperation, Ruth switches on the TV, jiggling Kate up and down as she fumbles with the remote. She flicks between sonorous church services and black-and-white films, trying to find something child-friendly. Eventually Kate stops sobbing and stares entranced at the screen which is bright green with little figures running around madly. She might have guessed. Kate has obviously inherited the football gene from her father. Another thing to hold against him. But Ruth is too grateful for the peace to feel too aggrieved. She settles down on the sofa, with Kate against her shoulder, to watch Manchester United versus Chelsea.

This is how, ten minutes later, Tatjana finds her.

'I didn't know you were a football fan, Ruth.'

'Tatjana!'

Tatjana looks flushed and rather excited, she is still wearing her work clothes (a beautifully tailored suit and long black coat) and carrying her briefcase.

'What happened to you last night?' asks Ruth. 'You didn't answer any of my texts.'

'I couldn't get a signal.' Tatjana puts down her case and strokes Kate's cheek with a casual finger. Kate doesn't move her eyes from the football.

'Where did you stay?' asks Ruth.

'With some friends from the university. The snow came down so quickly and I was told the roads here were impossible.'

'They were. I was snowed in at Sea's End House.'

'Really? Who looked after the little one?'

'Clara. Do you remember her from the naming day party?'

Tatjana opens her eyes wide. 'The blonde girl who came with the German fellow? But you hardly know her.'

Ruth bristles. She is always on the alert for criticism of her mothering. In any case her sensitivity is heightened because she feels guilty at how quickly she jumped at the chance to leave Kate with a comparative stranger.

'She's a very nice girl.'

'She's the one whose boyfriend was killed, right?'

'I hope you're not suggesting—' begins Ruth huffily.

'I'm not suggesting anything,' says Tatjana. 'Coffee?'

There is a rather uncomfortable silence while Tatjana makes coffee. Kate still watches the football, entranced. She gurgles delightedly when Chelsea scores. Ruth isn't sure whether Nelson would approve. Should she get up and help Tatjana with the coffee? In two weeks, this is the first time that Tatjana has offered to do anything in the kitchen. What did Tatjana mean about Clara? It's one thing for Ruth to suspect her in the dark of Sea's End House, quite another for Tatjana to imply that she had anything to do with Dieter's murder. Oh well, maybe Ruth asked too many questions about last night. Tatjana's a free agent after all.

When Tatjana puts a mug of coffee in front of her, she says, in a conciliatory tone, 'Thanks, Tatjana. It's been lovely having you here.' Tatjana is due to go home in two days' time.

'I've enjoyed it very much,' says Tatjana politely. 'It's been good to get to know you again. And to meet Kate.'

They both look at Kate, who has fallen asleep in Ruth's arms. The football plays on, unnoticed. Ruth sips her coffee, careful to avoid the baby's head. Suddenly Tatjana leans forward, her face urgent.

'Make the most of her, Ruth,' she says. 'Enjoy her. It doesn't last long.'

'I will.' Ruth's throat contracts.

'I only had Jacob for those few years,' Tatjana is saying softly. 'Now I wish I had spent every second of that time with him.'

Ruth eyes fill with tears. 'You couldn't have known.'

'No,' says Tatjana. She is tearless; her face has something of that blazing intensity that Ruth remembers from the evening in the pine forest. 'None of us can know. None of us can ever know what is going to happen. So take care of your baby, Ruth. She is all that matters.'

All that summer, Tatjana and Ruth had asked everyone they met about the little boy, his grandparents, the devastated village. When they met people from the south, near Trebinje, Tatjana became almost hysterical, thrusting her picture of Jacob into the faces of complete strangers, crying, begging them to help her. At other times, she was calm, almost clinical. She would tell Ruth again and again the story that had been told to her – the burning houses, the old people and children lined up, thinking they were going to be spared, the shots, the screams, the bodies flung into shallow graves only to be dug up again and buried who knew where. Ruth was Tatjana's only confidante, and at times she felt that the weight of all this grief was more than she could bear.

Once, she even tried to talk to Erik about it. She didn't want to betray Tatjana's secret, she just felt that she badly needed advice and who better to turn to than Erik, her mentor and friend?

It was hard to get hold of him. As the weeks went by, Erik seemed to spend more and more of his time fighting the authorities, mostly in the company of a Bosnian politician called Dragana (Ruth was to wonder about this relationship later). It was the old story. The various governments just wanted the graves exhumed; Erik wanted to spend time on forensic testing, cross-checking databases, trying to identify as many of the victims as possible. He began to take on a rather messianic appearance, wild-eyed, wildhaired, raving about the importance of knowing and naming the dead.

Then, one evening, she met him quite by chance. There was no running water at the hotel so they had a rota for carrying buckets up from the stream that ran through the town. The water was very pure, it came directly from the mountain, the locals said, but the archaeologists didn't take any risks; every drop had to be boiled and reboiled. Ruth was filling her buckets, standing knee deep in the water and enjoying the sensation of the cold on her tired legs, when she saw Erik sitting on the bank, throwing stones into the fast-flowing stream.

'Like Poohsticks,' she had said.

Erik had smiled uncomprehendingly. He often didn't get things like that.

'How are you, Ruthie?' He had got up to give her a hug. And, despite everything, Ruth remembers enjoying the moment, enjoying being alone with Erik in the cool, fernscented evening.

At a closer glance, Erik looked tired, his skin had a slightly stretched look and his famous blue eyes were ringed with red.

'Are you okay?' she had asked.

'Are any of us okay?' he had answered. Come to think of

it, Erik was probably the person who taught Cathbad his conversational gambits.

'I'm worried about Tatjana.'

And Erik had said, 'Poor Tatjana, she will never find rest until she can bury his body.'

She hadn't told him; but he had known anyway.

26

Nelson and Clara drive in silence over the snowy marshes. Once or twice, Nelson's radio crackles into action but he ignores it. Clara stares out of the window, treating him as if he is a taxi driver – or her dad. When they reach the road to Broughton Sea's End, Nelson pulls into a lay-by.

Clara looks up. 'What—'

Nelson pulls the small leather book out of his pocket.

'Is this yours?'

Clara's face changes so quickly it is almost comical. 'That's mine!' she spits. 'You had no right to take it.'

'Listen, Clara,' says Nelson. 'I could get a search warrant and come back and turn your room over. Is that what you want?'

'You wouldn't dare,' says Clara. But her face has changed again, become watchful.

'Of course I dare,' says Nelson. 'This is a murder investigation, not some bloody silly kids' game.'

Clara makes another grab for the diary but Nelson holds it out of reach.

'In this diary you say you hate Dieter Eckhart and want
to kill him.'

'I never said that!'

'Do you want me to read it to you?'

Clara puts her hand over her mouth as if to stop herself
speaking. Nelson notices that the nails are bitten to the
quick.

'When did you find out that Dieter was married?'

Clara says nothing.

'Must have been hard, to find out that your boyfriend
was married with children.'

Silence.

'What would your parents say?'

That does the trick. Clara's under-lip wobbles. 'Don't tell
them.'

'Clara.' Nelson attempts a gentle Judy-like tone. 'Did you
kill Dieter?'

'No!' Clara sits up, suddenly fierce again.

Nelson takes a plastic bag from the back seat. In it is a
see-through freezer bag (from Ruth's archaeology kit)
containing the scissors.

'Are these yours?'

Clara stares at the bag as if she can't believe her eyes.

'Clara.' More gently still. 'Are these yours?'

Clara shakes her head. Her voice is child-like. 'I borrowed
them from Grandma. She uses them for gardening.'

'When did you borrow them?'

'I don't remember. A few weeks ago.'

'Why did you want them?'

'I was cutting out a dress pattern. Dieter had invited me

to a ball at the university. I wanted to make myself something nice.' Her eyes fill with tears.

'Do lots of dress-making do you?'

'Yes, I do, as a matter of fact.' They are angry tears now. She brushes them away with the back of her hand.

'Clara . . .' He knows he can't go too far just now. Plenty of time to speak to her later if the scissors offer any clues. If he questions her too hard now, alone without a colleague, there's always the danger that she could lodge a complaint against him and jeopardise the whole investigation.

'If you want to talk to me,' he says, 'you know where I am.'

Clara flashes him a contemptuous look. 'Yeah. Right. Can you take me home now, please?'

After dropping Clara at Sea's End House, Nelson drives straight home. Michelle had been fine about him not coming back last night (she could see what the weather was like, after all), but she might be less than happy about him going in to work, especially on a Sunday. Besides, he could do with a shower and a sleep.

More than anything, Nelson wants to go home and sleep for a week. He wants to hold his wife in his arms and drift into blameless unconsciousness. But, unfortunately, he is wracked with guilt so acute that he wonders if he will ever be able to close his eyes again. As if it's not bad enough that he has betrayed his wife and slept with another woman, and that this other woman has given birth to his child, now he has to do it again. And what's more, he would do it again if he could. He knows that now. Ruth has a hold over him, not just as the mother of his child either. Last night, he had wanted to make love to her. As they sat at Jack Hastings' table in the candlelight, he had even fantasised that he was married to her. Married to a woman as bright and remarkable as Ruth, someone who would work side-by-side with him, someone who understands him, complements him, completes him. Whenever he thinks about Michelle, the first thing that comes to mind is her beauty. Nineteen years of marriage have not made him immune to the way she looks. The sight of her face can still make him catch his breath and, if he is honest, he enjoys having such a glamorous wife. If he was married to Ruth, people would no longer refer to his 'trophy wife' in half-admiring, half-resentful tones. No-one would say, 'what *does* she see in him', a comment that never fails to make him feel obscurely pleased with himself. But Nelson is attracted to Ruth, there's no denying it. And, last night, when he looked at her across the table, he had thought that she was beautiful, her full lips curving in a smile, her hair soft and untidy. He had wanted her, and although he might blame the snow, the isolation, the worry about Kate, that was the reason why he had taken her in his arms on Clara's bed. It was all his fault.

'It'll never happen again,' Ruth had said. Does that mean she doesn't want it to happen again? Nelson, even in his single days, was not a man much given to wondering if women fancied him or not. If he saw a woman he liked, he'd ask her out. If they said yes, he assumed that meant they liked him. If not; their loss. With Michelle, there had been no ambiguity. He had fallen in love with her the moment he saw her, in the Blackpool Rock Shop. Michelle had been with her little sister, buying brightly coloured sweets for party bags. Nelson had gone in with a friend to buy a joke present for a stag do. They had got chatting. Nelson, oblivious of his friend's rolling eyes and the little sister's giggles, had asked for Michelle's phone number. 'She's out of your league, mate,' his friend had said as they left the shop clutching a disgustingly phallic stick of rock. But Nelson had never thought so. She'd given him her number, hadn't she? And he was right. They were married six months later.

So he is not really equipped to work out whether Ruth is in love with him or not. The sex, he has to admit, is fantastic. They are bound together forever because of Kate, but love? He doesn't say the word, even to himself. He does know that sometimes he fantasises that he could have them both, the beautiful wife and the brilliant mistress, that he could enjoy both his teenage daughters and his miraculous baby. But he knows that life isn't like that. Nelson was brought up a Catholic. He knows that he is overdue some gigantic, cosmic retribution. The best he can hope for, he thinks, as he turns wearily into his drive, is that it holds off long enough for him to solve this case.

Entering the house, he is met by the most wonderful smell, the smell of childhood, evocative enough to make his mouth water and his eyes prickle. Michelle comes into the hall, wearing an apron over a designer tracksuit.

'I thought I'd do a roast for a change,' she says. 'It's such a cold day.'

Nelson kisses his wife's scented cheek. Over her shoulder

he can see Rebecca actually laying the table. Light shines on the glasses, cutlery and matching place mats (Lancashire scenes). Radio 2 is playing in the kitchen and the aroma of roast beef fills the air.

Nelson buries his face in Michelle's neck to hide his guilt.

After lunch, Nelson dozes in front of the football. Michelle and Rebecca have gone to Michelle's health club for a swim. Nelson knows he would sleep better upstairs but it's unthinkable for a healthy man to take to his bed in the middle of the afternoon. Besides, Man U are playing. So he drifts between sleeping and waking: Michelle, Ruth, a boat drifting in the dark harbour, the snow falling on the beach, the sound of shots in the night, Clara's face when he showed her the diary, a stooped figure standing on the landing.

Suddenly, he sits bolt upright.

What was Irene, who slept downstairs because it was 'easier', doing on the tower landing at midnight?

Clara said that the scissors belonged to her grandmother.

Nelson goes into the study where he has stored the boxes of parish magazines plus another box marked 'Sea's End'. In it are Hugh Anselm's papers and the ciné film, as well as some photos given to him by Stella Hastings. He takes out one photo and puts it in his wallet. Then he writes a brief note to Michelle and leaves the house.

At first there's no answer from Maria's bedsit then, just as he is turning away, a slightly scared voice says, 'Who is it?'

'It's DCI Nelson, Maria. Can I come up for a minute?'

The entry phone buzzes and Nelson takes the steps three at a time.

The room is scrupulously clean as ever. No smell of Sunday roast and no TV blaring in the background. Maria and her little boy are obviously in the middle of some board game. George is sitting on the floor, rolling a dice with great concentration.

'Snakes and ladders,' explains Maria.

'Grand,' says Nelson. 'My favourite game, though there's always a great big snake right at the end.'

'Would you like a cup of tea?' Maria is still looking worried.

'No thanks, love. I just wanted to show you a photo if that's all right.'

'A photo?'

'Yes.' Nelson pulls the picture from his wallet.

'You remember you said that Archie used to have a visitor, an old lady. Was this her, by any chance?'

Maria looks at the photo of Irene sitting outside Sea's End House. It was taken about a year ago, Stella had said.

'Yes,' says Maria slowly. 'That is the lady. Mrs Hastings.'

27

After George has gone to sleep, Maria always likes to look out of the window for a while. Not that the view's anything much – a garage forecourt, the houses across the street – once the sort of places where she could imagine a family living, now mostly bedsits like hers – the side of a giant billboard advertising a car, shiny red against a shiny blue background. But she likes sitting there in the darkened room (she doesn't want to put the overhead light on because of George), watching the world outside: the cars drawing into the garage, sales reps in suits impatiently tapping their feet as they wait for the tank to fill, harassed parents, young men with tattoos and cars with extra bits stuck to them; people hurrying past under the streetlights, lights going on in the bedsits, one after the other. She is hundreds of miles away from her family but, somehow, these faceless, anonymous strangers have become her family. And sitting there in the dark listening to George's noisy breathing (she must see the doctor about his sinuses again), she feels a curious affection, almost love, for the people outside. They all have their own lives, their little circles of light, but she, from her vantage point, can watch over them all. Sometimes she'll pick on one person, a woman labouring with heavy shopping or a pale-faced man jingling his loose change at the petrol pump, and say a decade of the rosary, especially for them. They'll never know, of course, but it makes her feel happy to do it.

Tonight, though, she doesn't feel cosy and secure. She feels jolted, uneasy. She knows why. It was that policeman, Nelson, coming here and asking questions. She doesn't like the police. She always suspects that when people see how she lives, how little money she has, they'll try to take George away from her. When he left, Nelson had tried to give her five pounds, 'to buy George a present'. She'd refused, almost angrily. She may only be an ignorant girl from the Philippines but she knew that you should never take money from a man, especially a policeman. She'd made her mistake once, with George's father, just a few months after she'd arrived in England, but she's not going to be caught again.

Archie had been different. Of course, he'd been an old man, old enough to be her grandfather, as he'd often said. But sometimes he didn't seem like an old man at all. His voice, for one thing, was still strong and echoing, not thin and apologetic like the old people at home. Archie still sounded like a soldier. Some of the other carers didn't like it; they thought he was too bossy, too full of himself. But Maria liked a man to be a man. She didn't mind Archie telling her what to do; he was her elder, after all. They had nice conversations, sitting in his little room in the evenings; they talked about George, about Maria's plans for him. He would grow up to be an important man, just like his father, and do great things in the world. Archie was an important man, Maria was sure of that. That was why it was wrong that he had been taken, suddenly in the night like that. Dorothy said they weren't to talk about it but Maria knew what she thought. It wasn't right. It wasn't what God intended.

Even the garage isn't the same tonight. Usually it is a great comfort to her because it is open for twenty-four hours, its little kiosk a beacon of hope through the night. But, tonight, there don't seem to be any cars, just one figure, in a long, black coat, standing beside the tyre gauge. Maria doesn't like the figure. She knows that people without cars shouldn't hang around garages but this person has been there for twenty minutes at least, just standing, not going into the shop or anything, just waiting, out of view of everyone except her. Maria goes away to check on George. When she comes back, the figure is still there. Is it a man or a woman? She can't tell. The person has a long coat and a woolly hat, its hair is hidden and she can't see its shape. Maria watches for another five minutes before she realises the awful truth. She isn't watching the figure. The figure is watching her.

Tired as he is, Nelson can't sleep. Michelle has gone to bed and Rebecca is watching some music programme in the sitting room. Nelson sits in the study, going through Hugh Anselm's papers. He doesn't know why he is doing this or what he expects to find. He just knows that he needs a breakthrough. Could Irene, over ninety at his guess, really have killed three people to protect her husband's name? It's unlikely, to say the least. Perhaps she could have stopped Hugh's stairlift, maybe even smothered Archie, but kill Dieter Eckhart, a fit young man in the prime of life? Surely not. Could someone have done it for her? Jack, for instance, or even Clara?

He should watch the film again but he just can't face it tonight. He can't face seeing Hugh Anselm, so earnest, so tormented, so *young*. Nelson isn't given to flights of fancy, but when he was watching the film he had the curious sensation that Hugh was speaking directly to him. Tell people about this, he was saying. Don't let this happen again. Find the person who killed me.

Hugh Anselm's papers date from about 1960. There is nothing about the murders and, as far as he can see, very little about the Home Guard. From 1960 onwards Hugh Anselm had kept a diary, which takes up about twenty exercise books. He didn't write every day and what he did write was mostly about politics. Hugh had high hopes of J.F. Kennedy and of Harold Wilson and, in both cases, disillusionment set in fairly quickly. He lost faith in Kennedy over the Bay of Pigs and, to Hugh Anselm, Kennedy's assassination was 'a tragedy but perhaps better to remember him this way? Otherwise his presidency would surely have dissolved in a haze of scandal and broken promises.' He admired Wilson for standing up to America over Vietnam and, especially, for setting up the Open University (Anselm was a great fan of further education, always going on courses) but he felt that, ultimately, Wilson had 'betrayed the workers'. Anselm's greatest loathing, though, is reserved for Margaret Thatcher. Page after page is devoted to her iniquities, her jingoism, her lack of compassion, even her hair ('dreadful helmet-like arrangement') and her voice ('reeking of insincerity'). Was this because Margaret Thatcher was Conservative or because she was a woman, wonders Nelson. He begins to detect, under Anselm's fervent socialism, a thin vein of snobbishness and sexism which made him deplore Shirley Williams' dress sense and wish that Tony Benn had retained his title.

There is very little about Anselm's personal life. His wife Anne is referred to mainly in terms of her political opinions. 'Anne has a fatal weakness for David Owen.' 'Anne thinks that Thatcher possesses normal maternal feelings – I disagree.' There are a few mentions of his brother Stephen ('Steve is one of nature's Tories.') and one reference to his niece Joyce ('a dreadful girl'). The only items of real interest are two letters, obviously in draft form, stuck in the back of one of the files.

The first is to Archie Whitcliffe:

Dear Archie (I am tempted to call you Archibald just to see you wince!)

You will wonder at hearing from me after all these years. I hope those years have been kind to you as, in part, they have been to me. I was prompted to write after reading of the promotion to Police Superintendent of one Gerald Whitcliffe. A brief check on the internet (a wonderful invention – are you 'on-line'?) revealed that this high-flyer was, in fact, your grandson. How proud you must be, dear Archie, and how wonderful to have grandchildren. My wife and I were never blessed with children and my dear Anne passed away last year.

Maybe it was this sad event which led to increasing thoughts of the past. Indeed, I find that, these days, I dwell more in the past than in the present. And this has led to a great desire to see you again, my old comrade. Not to discuss [this next word is heavily crossed out] *but merely to reminisce, two old friends together. Is it not about time? Maybe you too have had a letter from Daniel? It brought back so many* [. . .]

Here the letter ends, obviously unfinished. Was a finished version ever sent? Did the two old friends ever meet? There is nothing in the files to suggest that they did.

The second letter is to Irene Hastings:

Dear Irene,

What a pleasure to see you again after all these years. I did enjoy our morning together. Thank you for your condolences on the death of my dear Anne. You, of all people, will know what it is like to lose your helpmate of so many years. With reference to our discussion [. . .]

Here this letter, too, tails off.

So it seems that Irene Hastings had visited Hugh Anselm as well as Archie Whitcliffe. There is no date on either letter but Kevin Fitzgerald had said that Anne Anselm died eight years ago. In the letter to Archie, Hugh mentions his wife dying 'last year'. The letter to Irene may have been sent just after Anne's death, as Irene had been offering her condolences. What did Hugh discuss with Irene? Why was neither letter finished?

It occurs to Nelson that he never found that other letter,

the letter that Archie was reading on the morning that he died. He peers at the crossed-out word in Hugh Anselm's letter to Archie Whitcliffe. He thinks it is 'Lucifer'.

Maria stands in the shadows, watching the figure. Her heart is beating so loudly that it seems as if the whole building must echo with it. When she turns and sees George sleeping peacefully, it's as if she has ventured into another world: the night light, the statue of Our Lady, her work clothes hanging on the door. Then, looking back to the window, He is still there. She has started to think of the figure as He. Only a man could be that threatening, she is sure of this. He is now standing almost directly under her window, staring up. Sometimes He seems to disappear into the darkness, then a car passes and, briefly, she sees him. Still there, still waiting. Light, dark, light, dark.

Maria herself is now in darkness. She wishes she could draw the blinds but she's scared to show herself, even for a second. Flattened against the wall, she hopes that she can see him without him seeing her. What does he want with her? She says a few hurried Hail Marys but that doesn't shift him. She wracks her brain for a suitable saint. St Jude of Hopeless Causes? St Agnes who grew a beard to scare off a persistent suitor? Is this man a suitor? It's possible. A few men have pursued her, sometimes persistently. There was the cleaner at work who left a huge bunch of flowers outside her door. That had scared her. He knew where she lived. How had he got through the security door? For weeks she'd slept with a knife by her bed but then the cleaner had got another job and moved away and she had been safe once more.

But this man isn't a suitor, she is sure. He doesn't love her. There is nothing hopeful or expectant in the way he is standing. He is watching, as if they are playing a board game and he is waiting for her next move. When she moves, he will strike. He doesn't want to marry her; he wants to kill her.

Nelson yawns and rubs his eyes. He's exhausted but he doesn't want to go to bed just yet. If he leaves it a bit longer Michelle will be asleep. If she is awake, she might be in the mood for sex and, for the first time in his married life, Nelson doesn't want to sleep with his wife. He doesn't think he could stand the guilt.

He sits at the desk, listening to the TV in the next room. Hugh Anselm's words – pedantic, intelligent, sometimes sad – run on a constant loop through his head. Who had visited Hugh in February, switched off his stairlift and left him to die, struggling with the seatbelt, trying to reach the controls? Who had come to Archie's room in the night, smothered him and departed without a sound? Who had stabbed Dieter Eckhart and thrown his body into the sea? Was it the same person or three different people?

We have only told one other person that this film exists. The last of the three of us left alive will leave instructions as to where to find this evidence.

The last of the three . . .

Nelson goes back to Hugh Anselm's unfinished letters. *Maybe you too have had a letter from Daniel?*

He hears Irene Hastings' voice, the first time he met her. *Well, there were a few young boys. You could be in the Home Guard*

*if you were too young or too old to fight. I'm not sure about Hugh
or Danny. Archie's still alive, though...*

Danny. Daniel. The mysterious third man. The man whose
surname no-one remembers. The man who has vanished.
But Hugh had a letter from him and, knowing Hugh, he
will have kept the letter.

He goes back through the file, his eyes trained for any name
beginning with D. Daniel Abse, the MP. Danny de Vito, the
actor (Hugh was an unexpected fan of the American sitcom
Taxi). Daniel Barenboim (admired for his work in the Middle
East). But no letters from an ex-comrade called Daniel or Danny.

Eventually, in desperation, he goes back to the *Broughton
and Rockham Parish News*. There, between a recipe for snoek
casserole and an exhortation to Dig for Victory, he finds it.
December 1940.

TRAGIC DEATH OF BROUGHTON LAD

The body washed ashore on the beach at Broughton was
yesterday identified as being that of Daniel West, 18, son
of Marjorie and the late Lawrence West of the High Street,
Broughton. Daniel was an apprentice fitter at Jensen's
Garage and a keen member of the Home Guard. He was
hoping to be called up in the New Year. Mr Stephen Jensen,
50, described the boy as 'a real hard worker' and offered
his condolences to his mother.

So Daniel West had died, only a few months after the six
Germans were murdered. It seems inconceivable that neither
Irene nor Archie would remember this fact. But not as incon-
ceivable as the fact that Hugh Anselm apparently had a

letter from Daniel some seventy years after he died. It can't be the same Daniel. Surely?

He jumps because his phone is ringing. He can't find it at first because it has fallen into the box of papers. He gets it on the last note of the ring tone.

Clough.

'You'd better get down here, boss. It's that girl, Maria. She reckons someone's trying to kill her.'

28

It is past midnight when Nelson arrives at Maria's bedsit. Maria is sitting at the table with Clough beside her. A uniformed PC is checking the area around the house. George is asleep in the double bed. The whole thing feels slightly surreal, not least because their conversation has to be conducted in whispers. The room is dark apart from George's nightlight, which projects blue stars and moons onto the ceiling. Maria is clearly very upset – she has a mug in front of her and when she raises it to drink, her hand shakes.

'I made her tea,' says Clough. Rather defensively, Nelson thinks.

'Wonderful. I'll put you in for a medal.'

'She was hysterical.'

Maria raises huge, tear-washed eyes to his face. 'Someone is waiting outside my house. Someone is trying to kill me.'

'All right, Maria. Let's start at the beginning.'

Nelson tries to speak softly but George stirs in his sleep. Maria's face crumples. 'He must get his sleep! He's got school tomorrow.'

'Okay, okay.' Nelson lowers his voice another notch. 'Tell me about this mysterious person outside your house.'

'It was about nine o'clock. I was looking out of my window and I saw him. Looking at me.'

'Where was he standing, exactly?'

Maria takes Nelson to the window and points. The garage forecourt is deserted, the only light comes from the kiosk and from a huge illuminated advert for a Volkswagen Golf. As Nelson watches, a policeman comes slowly into view, shining his torch in wide, careful arcs. Nelson recognises him as Roy 'Rocky' Taylor, a local boy. Definitely not the brightest bulb in the box.

'He was standing there,' says Maria. 'Looking up. I see him at nine, ten, again at eleven.'

'Did he just stand there all the time?'

'Yes. But, at ten past eleven, there is a ring at my bell. I know it is him.'

'Did you answer?'

'No. I ring this number. It is the lady policeman, Judy, who came with you.' She shows him Judy's card. 'I ring Judy because I think she is kind.'

'Sergeant Johnson wasn't on duty,' puts in Clough. 'So I answered the call.'

Maria looks at him doubtfully.

PC Taylor appears at the door and Nelson goes to speak to him. There is no sign of any man hanging around. The people in the garage haven't seen anything. Their CCTV cameras don't cover the area near Maria's block of flats. Nelson wonders if the mysterious lurker knew this. He asks if Taylor has spoken to any of the other residents in the building. No, says the policeman stolidly, no-one asked him to.

Nelson sighs. 'All right, Taylor. Wait for us in the car.'

He turns back to Maria who is sitting back at the table. Clough is beside her, just far enough away to be professional.

'Maria, did you get a good look at this man?'

'No. It is dark. He is wearing dark clothes and a hat.'

'What sort of hat?'

'A knitted one. Like the hat George wears for football.'

'What colour?'

'Black.'

'Did you see his face? When he was looking up?'

'Not really.'

'Was he pale skinned? Dark?' Nelson treads warily in the PC minefield.

'Pale. Like you.'

'What was he wearing?'

'A long dark coat. Trousers.'

'Are you sure it was a man?' asks Clough.

Maria looks at him, her lip quivering. 'No.'

Clough and Nelson exchange glances. Nelson feels so tired that he can barely speak. There doesn't seem to be any evidence of Maria's mystery prowler but, then again, she was the person who was given Archie's cryptic clue, the unwitting recipient of a seventy-year-old secret. Could someone be trying to scare her? Could someone be trying to find the code for themselves?

'Maria,' he says. His soothing whisper comes out more like a sinister croak. 'You remember that Archie left you some books in his will?'

'Yes.' Maria looks up, surprised.

'Can I see them? The actual books.'

Maria goes to the black trunk beside the bed. She lifts the lid with difficulty (Clough rushes to help) and pulls out the eight battered paperbacks. Avoiding Clough's eye, Nelson carefully fans through the pages. In *Evil Under the Sun* he finds what he is looking for. A letter.

'Did you know this was here?' he asks Maria.

Maria looks bemused. 'No.'

'Do you mind if I borrow this for a bit?'

'No.'

Nelson folds the letter and puts it in his pocket. He is sure Ruth would have told him to wear gloves.

At the door, he asks, 'Maria, did you tell anyone that Archie left you the books?'

'Everyone at the home knew. Dorothy said it was a tribute to us all. That he left me something.'

Nelson isn't so sure about this. If Archie had wanted to pay tribute to Greenfields Care Home, he could easily have done it openly. No, the books were for Maria alone.

'Anyone else?' he asks.

'My mother. I phone her every Sunday. I told her.'

Nelson looks around the room, at the sleeping child under the blue light, the statue of Mary, the bare walls, the uniform hanging on the door, the breakfast plates already laid out next to the sink. He thinks of the letter in his pocket. Did anyone else know it was there?

'Try not to worry, Maria,' he says. 'I'm sure it was just some down-and-out looking for somewhere to kip. But I'll have a patrol car come past every half hour or so, just to make sure he doesn't come back. If you're scared for any reason, just ring me.'

'Or me,' says Clough.

'You're very kind,' says Maria. 'You'd better go now. George needs his sleep.'

Driving home, windows open to keep him awake, Nelson thinks about Maria and her delicate, compassionate relationship with Archie Whitcliffe. Why had the old man left her his books? Why did he make her the guardian of this secret, protected so long and with such ingenuity? Had Archie discussed his will with Hugh Anselm? Is this what was agreed at their last meeting, if it ever took place? *The last of the three of us left alive will leave instructions as to where to find this evidence.* Archie had been the last of the three. Why had he decided to pass on his secret in this way?

The house is dark. Michelle and Rebecca must both be in bed, but when Nelson goes into the study he sees that the computer is still on. By the blue light of the computer screen, he takes the letter from his pocket and reads:

Dear Archie and Hugh,

By the time you get this I will be long dead. I have asked my younger sister to post this on her eightieth birthday which will be in the year 2001. Can you imagine that date? I can't. What I think is that the world will have ended by then. Maybe some asteroid will have hit us just like Hugh is always saying.

I'm sorry but I just can't live with it. Knowing what we did to those poor fellows that night. I keep dreaming about it, and in my dreams they are coming for me because they

*know it was my fault. I should have stopped them. I know
you tried, Hugh, but it wasn't enough. I know we have made
the film so that one day everyone will know what happened
but I can't help thinking that we need some sort of <u>sacrifice.</u>
A life for a life. So that is what I am going to do. Tomorrow
morning, before it is light, I am going down to the beach at
Broughton. I am going to swim out beyond Sea's End Point.
I am going to swim and swim until I can swim no more and
then I am going to let the sea take me. It sounds beautiful
put like that, doesn't it? I don't think it will be beautiful but
it will be right. Then maybe the rest of you can live your lives
in peace.*

*I hope so much that you will be reading this at the end of
long, happy lives.*

Your friend,
Danny

Nelson sits there for a long time in the dark, the letter in
his hand. He is sure, beyond any doubt, that this is the letter
that Archie was reading on the night that he died. The letter
that he had hidden for so many years inside the Agatha
Christie classic. Was the title somehow significant? *Evil Under
the Sun*? But these murders were committed by the light of
the moon, witnessed only by Jack Hastings' wakeful little
brother, himself now dead.

Archie's memories must have been stirred by Nelson's
visit, which is why he went to sleep that night with the
word 'Lucifer' on his lips. Lucifer – the plan to turn the seas
into fire. Or maybe even a reference to Buster Hastings, the
'old devil' himself, the man who had murdered five people

in cold blood (not forgetting the man killed by his loyal sergeant) and forced his troop to take a blood oath, promising to keep his secret forever. Archie had kept his promise but, while he slept that night, someone had come into his room and suffocated him. Who is still alive who would kill to protect the Hastings name?

And who else might they kill?

29

All in all, Ruth is relieved to go to work on Monday morning. A policeman returned her car late on Sunday night and, by then, a lot of the snow had melted. During Sunday evening, as she and Tatjana watched TV, huge chunks of snow kept falling off her roof. When she went to bed, early because she was exhausted, she could see dark patches appearing in the Saltmarsh and the tops of the reeds emerging from the blanket of whiteness.

Monday morning is bright, almost spring-like. As she drives to work, the roads are clear, the snow remaining only as dirty sludge in the gutters. The university grounds are still white though. A huge snowman draped in a UNN scarf stands at the entrance to the Natural Sciences block but, as Ruth passes, its head falls forward, like a deposed tyrant. Soon all the snow will disappear, like a dream of winter. That's what Saturday night must be, Ruth tells herself sternly, a dream. Now she must get on with real life. She sighs, climbing the stairs to the archaeology corridor.

She has a meeting with the Field Team at ten. Trace isn't there but Ted, Craig and Steve squash into Ruth's tiny office and Ruth tells them briefly about the discovery of the film. The team are still employed by the university on their erosion survey but Ruth feels she needs to keep them updated as they were the ones that found the bodies in the first place. She has agreed with Nelson that she won't go into any detail, will just say that new evidence has emerged. She can't say how the film was found, either, though naturally the archaeologists are intrigued. Ted, in particular, keeps asking very awkward questions. 'How come this film has turned up after seventy-odd years? Who were the men anyway? That Dieter bloke said they were German. Have you any idea who killed them?'

'I can't tell you any more,' Ruth keeps saying. 'It's confidential. The police are still investigating.'

'Are they investigating Dieter's death?' asks Ted. 'Looks pretty suspicious to me.'

'I really can't say.'

Craig comes to her rescue by asking about Operation Lucifer. With relief, Ruth describes the explosive trail laid along the North Norfolk coast, the fire ships, the barrels of gun cotton.

'We'll get down there this morning and have another look around,' says Ted. 'We've still got a few miles of coast to go.'

'Well, be careful,' says Ruth. 'Some of the explosives may still be primed.'

Her whole life, she thinks, as the door closes behind the three men, seems suddenly to be full of unexploded bombs. Sure enough, before the Field Team have clumped to the end of the corridor, Phil appears, smiling engagingly.

'Can I have a word, Ruth?'

'I've got a tutorial in an hour.'

'It'll only take a minute.'

Phil sits opposite, crinkling his eyes in what Shona probably tells him is an attractive way.

'What about that snow, eh? Shona and I took the boys sledging. Great fun.'

'It must have been.'

'What was New Road like? Must have been hellish, out there in the back of beyond.'

'The snow was fairly deep on Saturday. It had cleared by this morning.'

'Shona tells me you've been making some exciting discoveries.'

Ruth curses herself for telling Shona about the lighthouse trip. She'd only done it because she wanted Shona to babysit.

'Yes. We've found some new evidence about the bodies found at Broughton Sea's End.'

Phil cocks his head on one side, inviting her to say more.

'I'm not sure how much I can tell you,' says Ruth awkwardly. 'It's a police matter.'

'Oh, come on, Ruth. I'm your head of department.'

This is true. But it's also true that Ruth is now seconded to the Serious Crimes Unit, part of the police team. She has a foot in both camps and the ground between has suddenly become a minefield.

'Dieter Eckhart, poor chap.' Phil ducks his head piously. 'He said the bodies were German.'

'Yes, we're pretty sure that they were German soldiers. The oxygen isotope analysis points that way.'

'Do you know how they were killed?'

'They were shot.'

Phil's eyes widen. 'By the British?'

'We have a statement to that effect.'

'A statement? From whom?'

'I don't think I can say.'

Phil changes tack. 'What about Eckhart's death? There are a lot of rumours floating around.'

'The police are investigating.'

'Do they think it was murder?'

'I can't say.'

'They do then.'

Ruth says nothing, and after loitering maddeningly for a few minutes Phil drifts away.

Monday is a busy teaching day for Ruth. She has another tutorial at two. She has a quick sandwich in the canteen and escapes to her office to prepare, treading warily as she passes Phil's open door. She doesn't want to get trapped into giving anything else away.

She is just finishing her sandwich and reading about bone disease in preparation for her students, when the phone rings. It's Craig. He and Ted have found a boat on the beach just beyond Broughton. It looks old. Could it be one of the fire ships she was mentioning? Does she want to come and have a look?

Ruth does want to, very much. She longs to escape from the university and do some real archaeology, examine a piece of evidence, feel the sun and wind on her face. But even if she leaves straight after her tutorial she still won't be back in time to pick up Kate at five. Sandra probably wouldn't mind keeping her an hour longer, or maybe Tatjana would go and pick her up? Tatjana's conference has finished and she was just saying that morning that she hadn't anything to do today. She leaves tomorrow, her bags are packed and she's done all the touristy things in King's Lynn and Norwich. Ruth has avoided asking Tatjana to have anything to do with Kate but surely she won't mind this one little favour. After all, Ruth has had her to stay for nearly three weeks.

She rings Tatjana on her mobile. She hadn't expected it to be difficult, had even expected Tatjana to interrupt and offer to get Kate, but Tatjana hears her out in silence. Ruth stammers and repeats herself. She remembers how much she hates asking for favours. When she has talked herself to a standstill, Tatjana says, 'Let me get this straight. You want me to pick up your daughter?'

Ruth does not like the way she says 'your daughter'.

'Yes,' she mutters.

'Just because you can't be bothered?'

'No! It's not that. It's just that Craig has found something which might be interesting . . .'

'Interesting but not vital. There's no necessity for you to go today is there?'

'No but . . .'

'You expect us all to run round after you, don't you?' Tatjana is laughing but her voice does not sound amused. 'Shona, me, Judy. We all have to look after your baby because you're too busy swanning around with Detective Inspector Nelson, pretending to solve crimes. That's not your job, Ruth. Your job is being a mother.'

'My job is being an archaeologist.'

'Yes, right.' Tatjana laughs again. 'How is that going, Ruth? How many papers have you written? Where's that book you were always going to write? It didn't happen, did it?'

'I've been—'

'Busy? Yes, busy having a baby without a father.'

Ruth is speechless. This is the sort of thing her mother says. Not Tatjana, who is meant to be her friend.

'I'm sorry you feel like this,' she says at last.

'Yes.' Suddenly Tatjana sounds very tired. 'I'm sorry too. Sorry for all of us. Especially Kate.' And she rings off.

Ruth is shaking. She looks at her phone as if it holds the key to Tatjana's outburst. She had known that Tatjana disapproved of her asking Clara to babysit, she had known and she had understood. Who knows better than she how Tatjana feels about putting career before children? Why had she ever thought that Tatjana would be on her side? Tatjana despises her for leaving her daughter in other people's care while she 'swans around' with Nelson. But she had never expected so much vitriol, so much . . . *hatred* was the only word. There was such a depth of contempt in Tatjana's voice that Ruth feels as if she has been physically attacked. And she feels humiliated too. She had thought she was doing quite well, trying to do the famous juggling thing, trying to be a good mother and keep her job, trying not to rely on other people. But it turns out that Tatjana thinks she *is* relying on other people. Is that what everyone thinks about her? Shona, Judy, Cathbad, Phil? Look at Ruth pretending to be a policeman. She can't even be bothered to look after her own baby, just dumps the poor thing with a childminder. She's not fit to have a child.

And maybe it's true. Hadn't she summoned Shona to take charge of Kate while they were excavating the bodies on the beach? This, despite the fact that Shona obviously couldn't cope and had let Kate scream herself almost sick. And even though Shona was clueless about babies, hadn't Ruth left Kate with her again so she could go to a hen night, of all frivolous things? What sort of mother was Ruth, anyway, drinking in wine bars and clubs, coming home past midnight? And she'd left Kate with Clara, someone she barely knew, just so that she could hang around on the edge of Nelson's investigations, lapping up vicarious glory. Seconded to the Serious Crimes Unit indeed! Who is she trying to kid? It was all Ruth's fault that Clara had been snowed in with Kate, that Judy had to risk her life driving over the snow-covered marshes. No wonder Judy's hardly spoken to her since. And now she'd done it again. She has obviously deeply insulted Tatjana. And why? Just so that she can go and dig up an old boat, probably just some fishing boat that ran aground in a storm.

By the time her students arrive, standing self-consciously in the open doorway, shuffling their papers, Ruth has decided to go straight home after the tutorial. She'll stop all this ridiculous detective business. It's no business of hers whether the wreck is that of a fire ship, part of Operation Lucifer. It's no business of hers who murdered Archie Whitcliffe, Hugh Anselm or Dieter Eckhart. Her job, as Tatjana pointed out, is being a mother. She'd better get on with it.

It's not one of her best tutorials. Luckily, the students do most of the work themselves, one of them reading a paper, the others discussing it. They are all mature students from China and America and they are scrupulously polite to each other. All Ruth has to do is to steer the conversation in certain directions and to correct some misconceptions about Neanderthal Man. Then they are backing out of her room, the Chinese students literally bowing.

Ruth's phone rings. It's Nelson.

'Ruth, I'm off to Sea's End House. There's a few more questions I need to ask. What are you doing?'

'Well, Craig, one of the field team, rang to say that they'd found a boat on the beach just beyond Broughton. They think it might be a fire ship. You know, part of the coastal defence.'

'Are you going down to have a look at it?'

'I might do.'

'I'll see you there, if so. And Ruth?'

'What?'

'Be careful.'

Ruth turns off the phone but, almost immediately, switches it back on to call Sandra. She'll just have a quick look at the boat. She'll be home by six at the latest.

Nelson had asked if he could speak to Irene on her own, but when he reaches Sea's End House he is told by Stella that her mother-in-law is unwell and can't be disturbed.

'What is it?' Nelson does not return Stella's smile.

'The doctor thinks it may be a small stroke.'

'Jesus.' Nelson is taken aback. A stroke is serious. Why aren't they running about calling ambulances?

'At Mother's age these things are almost inevitable,' says Stella, leading the way into the sitting room. 'There's no point her going into hospital. She might as well stay here, peacefully, in her own bed.'

There is an air of resignation about her which Nelson finds disturbing. In her own bed. People talk about dying 'in their own bed'. He's not going to do that. He's going to die in a speeding car or saving some child from drowning. Peace is overrated, in his opinion.

'How old is Irene?'

'Ninety-three.' Again, that calm smile.

It seems odd not to have Irene fussing about with the tea. There's no sign of Jack or Clara either. But that suits Nelson. Stella has always struck him as the sanest one of the family.

'Jack and Clara have taken the dogs for a long walk,' explains Stella. 'Jack needed to get out of the house. He's been so worried about Irene. And Clara could do with a break too. She's had a bad time of it recently.'

'Was she very upset about Dieter Eckhart's death?'

'Very. I think she really cared about him.'

'Was she in love with him?'

Stella looks slightly reproving. 'They'd only known each other for a few weeks.'

But it happens, Nelson wants to tell her. Didn't he fall in love with Michelle as soon as he saw her, that day in the Blackpool Rock Shop?

'Mrs Hastings,' says Nelson. On Saturday night they had been on first name terms but that seems a long time ago. 'How much do you know about the war years at Sea's End House?'

'Quite a lot,' says Stella placidly. 'More than Jack, I daresay. Irene talked to me a lot. Buster too. I was very interested.'

'Did you know that Irene used to visit Archie Whitcliffe?'

'Yes. She was fond of him. Buster had been almost like a father to him.'

It seems odd to think of the elderly man with the regimental tie having a father, surrogate or otherwise. Nelson remembers what Archie said about Buster Hastings. *Hell of a chap. A real old devil. One of the old school.* Not the most loving of descriptions.

'What about Hugh Anselm? Did she visit him?'

'She went once, a few years ago. She wasn't so close to Hugh. I don't think Buster liked him much, he always referred to him as that damned commie.' She laughs softly.

'Did you ever meet Hugh?'

'Yes. I drove Irene over to see him that time.'

'And Archie?'

'Once or twice.'

It's incredible, reflects Nelson. He had thought that Jack was the key to Sea's End House but all the time it was the quiet woman sitting in front of him. She had known all Irene's wartime stories, she remembers Buster, she had taken Irene to visit both Archie and Hugh.

'Mrs Hastings, did Buster ever talk about Daniel West?'

'Daniel West? No, I don't think so. Who is he?'

'He was a young boy in Buster Hastings' platoon. He killed himself in 1940.'

'Killed himself? How horrible.'

'He killed himself to escape the memory of a war crime committed by Buster Hastings and his men.'

'What do you mean, war crime?'

'Has your husband told you about the film we were watching that day at your house? The day when it snowed?'

'Only that it was some nonsense produced by Hugh.'

'In the film Hugh Anselm accuses Captain Hastings and his sergeant of killing six defenceless German soldiers. The six bodies we found at Broughton Sea's End.'

'That's not true!'

'Your husband believed it.'

'Jack? He can't have.'

'You said yourself that the war was a desperate time. People do desperate things in desperate times.'

She looks at him as if half conceding the point. In the background, a clock ticks.

'Mrs Hastings,' says Nelson. 'Do you know how Hugh Anselm died?'

Stella's brow furrows. 'Some sort of accident, wasn't it?'

'He was found dead in his stairlift.'

'How terrible.'

'We think foul play may have been involved.'

He meant to shock her and he does. Her eyes widen and her hand clenches on the arm of her chair.

'What do you mean?'

'I mean that someone deliberately stopped the stairlift. Someone who knew that Hugh Anselm had a heart condition and that the agitation of trying to free himself would be likely to kill him.'

'What are you suggesting?'

'Archie Whitcliffe was suffocated,' says Nelson brutally. 'I think the same person killed both men.'

'Archie? Suffocated? I don't believe you.'

'A post mortem examination cannot lie,' says Nelson, though they can and do.

There is a silence. Out of the French windows, Nelson can see the sea, brightest blue under a paler blue sky. A white-sailed yacht moves slowly across the horizon.

'Detective Chief Inspector,' Stella is very pale but her voice is perfectly steady, 'am I to understand that you suspect someone in this family of these horrible crimes?'

'I suspect no-one and everyone,' says Nelson portentously.

'What does that mean?'

'Someone killed those men and I think it was to protect the memory of Buster Hastings. Dieter Eckhart too. He was about to uncover the truth. I think someone killed to prevent that happening.'

She stares at him, her hands still clenched on the arms of her chair. An alarm goes off, making them both jump. Stella Hastings looks at her watch.

'Time to check on Mother. Excuse me, Detective Chief Inspector. I won't be long.'

And she goes out. Leaving Nelson to look out of the window, across the bay to the lighthouse. In front of him is a row of plants, one of which, he now realises, is planted in a German officer's helmet.

Ruth is glad that she came. It is a beautiful afternoon, the sea sparkling in the sun. There is no snow left on the beach and it could almost be a summer day, if it were not for the sharp air that makes her catch her breath and wish she'd brought a scarf.

Craig is waiting for her at the foot of the slope. He is warmly dressed in a donkey jacket and black woolly hat.

'Where's Ted?'

'He had to go back. Some domestic crisis. I said I would wait.'

'That was kind of you.'

As Ruth follows Craig across the beach, she wonders about Ted's domestic crisis. As far as she knows, he isn't married or living with anyone. He's a bit of an enigma, Irish Ted. He once told her that his name wasn't even Ted.

Sandra had been happy to look after Kate for an hour longer. 'No problem. Don't worry so much, Ruth.' But Ruth does worry. Tatjana's words have left her feeling bruised and vulnerable. She has tried a couple of times to ring Tatjana back but her phone seems to be switched off. Is Ruth really such a terrible mother? She loves Kate more than her life but maybe this isn't enough. Certainly the whole maternal thing doesn't come easily to her, as it does to women like Michelle. Ruth never knows what to say to Sandra or to other mothers – one excruciating morning at a mother and baby group was enough to show her this. She doesn't know what baby food to buy or which car seat to avoid. She's never read a parenting magazine or watched *Supernanny*. She and Kate are having to make it up as they go along. And she'd thought she was doing all right, until the conversation with Tatjana.

But Tatjana has her own issues. Ruth knows this but she still shies away from talking properly to her friend. She has had her chances over the past weeks, but she has been too

cowardly to take them. Tatjana will go home tomorrow and
Ruth may never see her again.

They have left Broughton now and are crossing the beach
where the barrels were found. The tide is out, rock pools
stretch in front of them and Ruth can see the remains of
the Victorian sea wall, like a green-slimed monster rising
from the water, but something in the air perhaps, or in the
wild calling of the seagulls, tells her that the tide may be
about to turn. They'd better keep an eye on it. There's no
way off this beach and the cliffs are too high to climb.

'How much further?' she asks.

'Just round the next headland.'

They have to climb over rocks, sharp with barnacles and
crusted mussels, then in front of them lies another bay, a
perfect semicircle scooped out of the sandstone cliff. And
there, rearing out of the shallow water, is the unmistake-
able hull of a ship. The water has eaten away at the wood
and Ruth can see the blue sky through its prow but the
shape is still there, a largish boat, about the size of the
launch that took them to the lifeboat. It looks both menacing
and strangely sad.

'Have you any idea how old it is?' asks Ruth, splashing
forwards, despite the fact that she isn't (for once) wearing
her wellingtons. The water is freezing.

'I don't know but I think about sixty or seventy years old
by the shape of it.'

Ruth knows nothing about the shape of boats but this
one looks as if it has been here forever. 'What makes you
think it was a fire ship?' she asks.

'There are barrels inside,' says Craig. 'Take a look.'

'We'd better be quick,' says Ruth, looking out to sea at the waves coming in towards them, shockingly fast.

'Oh, we've got all the time in the world,' says Craig.

Nelson is still staring out of the window when Stella comes back into the room.

'How is she?' he asks.

'As well as can be expected. Peaceful.' That note of resignation again. It casts a shadow on the bright afternoon, a shadow reflected on Stella's face as she joins Nelson by the window.

All that is left of the garden at Sea's End House is a thin strip of land, about a metre across, that runs alongside the house. The back garden has disappeared completely. But someone has taken trouble with the tiny piece of ground that is left. There is a narrow ribbon of lawn and someone has been tending the flowerbeds.

'Strange to see the flowers coming up again after the snow,' says Stella. 'They're hardier than you think, spring flowers.'

'Are you a keen gardener?' asks Nelson. He isn't, though he quite likes mowing the lawn. Michelle loves garden centres; they're her idea of heaven.

'No, but we have someone who comes in. There's not really enough for him to do now but he's always looked after our garden. And his grandfather before him.'

Something stirs in Nelson's brain as he looks at the spindly tulips pushing up out of the chalky soil.

'Wasn't he in the Home Guard? Your old gardener?'

'Yes, Donald Drummond. He was devoted to Buster. And to Irene.'

As clear as if it is being amplified into the air around him, Nelson's hears Hugh Anselm's voice: *Donald said they were only filthy Jerries and would do the same to us.* Donald Drummond, the gardener.

And, like a kaleidoscope spinning before his eyes, so fast that the colours are blurred and the shapes indistinct, Nelson sees himself looking down from Archie Whitcliffe's window. He is watching the gardener mow the lawn. Then, he sees himself at Hugh Anselm's sheltered accommodation, admiring the grounds, so beautifully kept, recently mown, newly planted.

'What's the name of the gardener you have now? Donald's grandson?' he asks, so sharply that Stella steps back.

'Craig. I assumed you'd know him. He's an archaeologist too. One of Ruth's team.'

30

The hull of the ship is so weathered and encrusted that it seems part of the rocks around it. Peering inside, Ruth sees pools of stagnant water, mussels like obscene growths clinging to the wood, a crab scuttling warily across the remains of a bench seat. But the basic structure remains, there is even a rudimentary cabin with the door bolted shut and, in the lowest part of the ship, partly submerged, two sealed barrels. Ruth leans forward and pulls at something trapped under one of the barrels. It looks like cotton wool, stained and discoloured by the water but smelling unmistakably of sulphur – gun cotton.

She looks at Craig who is peering over the side of the boat.

'How come no-one's found this before? It's quite visible at low tide.'

'Oh, people know about it. It's even on the maps. I just don't think that anyone has made the fire ship connection.'

It's possible the boat was already a wreck when Hastings and his men primed it, thinks Ruth. It has probably sat in this lonely bay for years. Hastings would have known about it, she is sure that he knew every inch of this coast. He would have come down here in Syd Austin's boat, probably with Ernst, the clever scientist, and filled the rotting hull with barrels of explosives, stuffed with the lethal cotton. They may even have had a way of setting off the explosion from a distance. The impact would have set the very sea on fire.

'I wonder what's in the cabin,' she says. 'It's still locked.'

'Let me have a look,' says Craig, climbing over the side of the boat.

'Funny,' says Ruth. 'The lock looks new. It's not rusted at all.'

'That's odd.' Craig comes to stand beside her. Even though the boat is lodged tight in the rocks, it still tilts slightly with the two of them aboard. The timbers creak and Ruth wonders if they will hold out.

The bolt slides back easily, too easily. Ruth feels the first, slight, frisson of alarm. She hears the sea thundering towards them and the gulls overhead. The tide has turned.

'Have a look inside,' says Craig.

Ruth turns, suddenly scared. It is a few seconds before she realises that she is looking down the barrel of a gun.

Nelson is ringing Ruth's number. No answer. Leaving Stella looking bemused, he runs out of the house, sprints to the end of the drive and along the cliff path. Ruth's car is in the car park. There is only one other car, a blue Nissan.

Nelson goes to the rail and looks down at the sea. The tide is coming in, crested waves rolling in towards land, smashing against the remains of the Victorian sea wall.

There is no-one on the beach. At the spot where the bodies were found, police tape still flutters in the breeze. He looks at his watch. Five o'clock. A blameless time of day. Michelle will be cutting someone's hair, chatting about holidays. Rebecca will be home from school, eating toast and talking to her mysterious on-line friends. Clough will be asking who's going to the pub after work. Judy will be ignoring him. And Ruth? Ruth should be picking Katie up from the childminder. Instead, her car's here and she's nowhere to be seen. What had she said? *Craig, one of the field team, rang to say that they'd found a boat on the beach just beyond Broughton.*

He walks back to Sea's End House and takes the sloping path down to the beach. The same route taken by Captain Hastings and his men that moonless night. But this is a bright, spring afternoon. Surely Ruth cannot be in danger? He looks up at the house, the Thirties gothic folly, its sombre grey walls rising up out of the cliff. Inside that house, a woman is ill, perhaps dying. He remembers the shadow that he saw on Stella Hastings' face and shivers.

I am going to swim out beyond Sea's End Point. I am going to swim and swim until I can swim no more and then I am going to let the sea take me.

Danny West had swum to his death from this beach. Dieter Eckhart had been killed and his body thrown onto the rocks. Six murdered men were buried in the gap between the cliffs. Hugh Anselm had apparently thought that the beach at Broughton had an unwholesome atmosphere. Hardly surprising, given what he had witnessed there, but Nelson himself had felt something of the sort – though he could hardly have put it into words – the first time that he looked down at the narrow bay, with the cliffs on one side and the tall grey house on the other. This place has known death before.

He walks to the point of the headland and looks out across the next cove. Deserted. This was the place where they found the barrels, he remembers. The cliffs are higher here, streaked yellow and grey. *The beach beyond Broughton*, Ruth said. He rings her number again. No answer. He tries her home and gets the answer phone. He doesn't know who he expects to answer anyway. The cat? Next he rings Judy, she's best at the local stuff.

'Judy? What's the next beach beyond Broughton?'

'Going north or south?' At least Judy never asks unnecessary questions.

'North.'

'Rockham. Beyond that, it's Cromer.'

'Can you get down to the beach from there?'

'Yes. There are some steps.'

'Can you meet me there as soon as possible? Bring Cloughie too.'

'Okay, boss.'

As Nelson clicks off his phone, a wave breaks over his feet. Soon Broughton will be cut off by the sea and Ruth is still on the beach somewhere. There's not a moment to lose.

'What are you playing at?' asks Ruth angrily.

'Get in the cabin, Ruth.' Craig is smiling, that gentle smile that she has always rather liked. He was her favourite of the field team, she remembers, because he never argued with her.

'You must be joking. Put that gun down.'

'If you don't, I'll kill you. Just like I killed Eckhart and the others.'

'*You* killed them?'

'Yes,' says Craig, still in that sweet, reasonable tone. 'I had to. I had to protect my grandfather's memory.'

'Your grandfather?'

'Donald Drummond. My mother's father. He was one of the Home Guard.'

Donald. The gardener, who presumably had the key to the summer house. The one who had wanted to kill the Germans outright.

'He was a fine man,' says Craig. 'He brought me up, you know. My father scarpered when I was a kid, Mum couldn't really cope. But my grandparents, they were always there for me. Constant, steady. It was a different generation. A better generation.'

Ruth remembers Craig telling her that he was brought up by his grandparents. Thanks to them he can make oxtail soup. Is it thanks to them that he is also a murderer?

'Granddad told me all about the war,' Craig says. 'And when I was old enough he told me about killing the Germans. It was them or us, he said. I understood. He was only doing his duty, fighting for his country.'

'They killed them in cold blood!'

Craig turns on her furiously. 'What do you know about it? Where would you be, you and all the bleeding heart liberals, if they hadn't protected you? They stood on this coast line and they defended it. They defended it with their lives.'

'Did you kill Archie and Hugh?'

'I felt bad about Archie,' says Craig. 'He was a good man, but he was going to tell someone the secret. I did the gardening at the home and I saw how friendly he was getting with that carer, Maria. Then, when Nelson visited him, I knew it was time to act. I just popped up to his room after I'd finished in the grounds and sent him to sleep. It only took a few minutes. A merciful release, really. Archie hated getting old. Hated being in the home.'

'What about Hugh? That wasn't a merciful release.'

'Hugh was a filthy communist. Granddad hated him. Anselm should have been a conchie and had done with it, but no, he had to go whingeing on about his conscience. You can't afford a conscience in wartime. But Hugh always thought he was better than the rest of them. He had to go bleating to that German journalist. Telling our wartime secrets to a German! No, Hugh deserved everything he got.'

'You stopped his stairlift?'

'It was easy. I did the gardens there too. Got hold of the master key from that dipso warden and let myself in. Flicked the switch and there you go. I knew Hugh had a weak heart. I knew he'd kill himself trying to get free. Serves him right, in my opinion. Writing all those letters to the papers saying we ought to be friends with the Germans. Friends! He made me sick.'

Craig looks down, smiling complacently. While his attention is momentarily diverted, Ruth presses the mobile phone in her pocket, touching random keys, hoping that she'll get through to someone, anyone. 'Help me,' she says aloud. 'I'm on the beach at Broughton. Craig's trying to kill me.'

'What are you doing?' Craig snaps to attention again, narrowing his eyes.

'Nothing.'

'Give me your phone.'

'I haven't got it.'

Craig comes closer and, pressing the gun against her head, pulls her hand from her pocket. He prises her fingers from the phone and throws it into the sea. Ruth hears it splash and, despite everything, can't resist an involuntary moan. Her phone! Her life is contained in her phone. Now it's at the bottom of the sea with the barnacles and rusting tin cans.

'Don't try anything else, Ruth. I'm a crack shot. My grandfather taught me.'

'Like he taught you gardening.'

'Exactly. My family have always looked after the gardens at Sea's End House. Even now, when there's hardly any garden left, I still tend it. I still care for it.'

Tend, care. Strange words for a murderer to use. Can this softly spoken man, an *archaeologist*, for God's sake, really have killed three people?

'I'm glad I killed that German,' Craig is saying now. 'He just wanted to dig dirt on Captain Hastings and his troop. He wasn't fit to lick their boots. And he was deceiving Clara. He told me that he was married, boasted about it almost, one night in the pub. So I waited for him that night. I had the keys to the garden room, you see. I'd done the garden earlier and I just waited. Eckhart was sitting in his car, sending a text to someone. Probably his wife. I asked for his help. Said my car had broken down. When we got to the car park I stabbed him and threw his body in the water.'

'Clara was devastated. You broke her heart.'

Craig laughs. 'She'll get over it. Can't have a Hastings marrying a German, destroying that fine English bloodline. No, Clara's destined for higher things. I might even marry her myself.'

In your dreams, thinks Ruth. The Hastings family would never let their daughter marry the gardener. To them, Craig, like his grandfather before him, is a servant. They would sooner let Clara marry Dieter Eckhart. Class is a stronger social adhesive than nationality. But Ruth decides not to say any of this to Craig. She has to keep him talking, get him to feel sorry for her.

'Don't kill me, Craig, I've got a baby. She needs me.'

'Your baby! You're never with her. She wouldn't miss you, she never sees you.'

Another tribute to her mothering skills. But Ruth knows that Kate does need her and, for this reason alone, she's not going to let herself be killed. She throws herself to one side, splintering the rotten timbers of the boat. Craig shoots but misses. The bullet lodges itself in one of the barrels. In seconds, the sea is on fire.

Nelson sees the smoke from the cliffs at Rockham. Judy and Clough haven't arrived yet but he doesn't wait. He leaves his car on the grass and makes for the steps, a rickety wooden structure marked by a sign saying, unambiguously, 'Danger! Do not take the steps at High Tide. Danger of Drowning.' Nelson, bounding down the slippery planks, sees a semicircle of shingle beach below. A line of grey rocks separates it from the next cove but the sea still hasn't reached the bottom of the cliff. There may still be a chance to get to Ruth. The smoke spirals high in the air, like a distress flare. What the hell is happening? Is this Ruth's way of attracting his attention? If so, it's working . . .

He runs across the beach, stumbling over the pebbles. Michelle once told him that this was good exercise. Now it feels more like torture, like one of those nightmares where you are running your hardest but get nowhere, where the ground turns into marshmallow and your feet become lead weights. Surely he should have reached the cliff by now. The waves are breaking over the furthest rocks. He'll have to climb to get onto the next beach. Jesus, if only he was fitter. He should never have let his gym membership lapse.

His phone rings. He answers it, still running.

It's Judy.

'We're at Rockham, boss. Where are you?'

'On the beach.'

'There's a ship burning on the next beach. A real inferno. Black smoke everywhere.'

'Any sign of Ruth?'

'No, but we can't get close enough to see.'

'Call the coastguard. And the fire brigade.'

'I already have. The coastguard says the tide's coming in fast. You'd better get back up here.'

'No. I've got to get to the next beach.'

He clicks off the phone. He has finally reached the rocks and sees that they are, in fact, the remains of a man-made wall, huge grey breeze blocks, covered in seaweed. He tries and fails to get a foothold, falling back onto the pebbles. The waves are crashing against the end of the wall. He should go back, wait for the coastguard. It's not going to do either Michelle or Ruth any good if he gets killed. But he launches himself back at the wall, clinging on with his fingertips, hauling himself upwards by sheer willpower. Then, somehow, he's there, standing on the very top of the sea wall. The next cove is filled with black smoke. He can't see anything else at all. He pauses, catching his breath, and is hit in the small of the back by what feels like a tidal wave. He falls heavily, hitting his head on stone.

The force of the explosion sends Ruth flying. She lands on the beach, lying on her back, unable to move. In front of her is a solid sheet of flame. Where is Craig? Surely he must have been killed? Smoke stings her eyes and she can hardly breathe but she knows that she has to get off this beach. If the fire doesn't get her, the tide will. She stands up, staggering slightly and heads towards the cliffs. She may just be able to climb round into the next cove. She falls, scraping her knee against stone and, almost accidentally, finds herself in the sea. She kneels in the water, thankful for the kindly cold, splashing water onto her burning face. The salt stings but even that is welcome; it proves that she is still alive.

Looking back, all she can see is blackness, even the flames have disappeared. The smell is overpowering. It must be the oil burning. Hastings' long-forgotten booby-trap has gone off with a vengeance. And where is Craig, the man who has dedicated himself to preserving Hastings' good name? If there's any justice, he'll have been blown sky high when the barrel first exploded. Killed by the devices planted by his beloved Home Guard. But Ruth doesn't believe in that sort of justice. She struggles on, waist deep in water. If she can only reach the sea wall, she can climb up, call for help. Surely someone will have seen the flames? Maybe the fire boat will save her life?

She's dizzy, disorientated. She doesn't realise that she has reached the wall until she literally walks into the first submerged rocks. She falls again, tasting salt water, but she manages to climb onto the rampart. A wave almost knocks her off her feet but she holds on, hands and knees across the seaweed and pointed barnacles. She's nearly there. Just a few more steps.

'Hallo, Ruth,' says a familiar voice.

31

It's Craig. Somehow he is above her, standing on the highest part of the wall. His face is black with smoke but he seems unhurt. So much for poetic justice. He doesn't seem to have his gun but he is stronger than her and heavier. And he's already killed three people.

Ruth lies on the wet, slippery wall. Waves break over her, icy and relentless. She can see Craig getting closer, his sturdy archaeologist's boots, his combat trousers, soaking wet now, his hands clenching into fists. She can't do anything; she can't even stand because she knows that the waves would knock her down again. Her only chance is to . . . as Craig comes within reach, she grabs his ankle and pulls.

'Bitch!'

He falls almost on top of her. His face is within inches of hers and she claws at him, desperate to dislodge him from the rocks. But he fights back, prising her fingers away and pushing, using all his body weight against her. She finds herself sliding. He's above her now. She can see a demonic white grin in his blackened face.

'Bye-bye, Ruth. I'll give your love to Ted and the others.

Such a sad way to go. I'll tell them how I struggled to save you.'

He stamps heavily on her hand. She lets go, falling backwards into the churning sea. Surely this is it. The long descent into unconsciousness, the waters closing over her head, her life spiralling away from her – Kate, Nelson, her parents, Erik, Peter, everything. Even as she falls, she thinks: who will look after Kate? Please let it be Nelson rather than her parents. But, as she thinks of Kate, suddenly she feels a superhuman surge of strength and she kicks out, fighting against the tide. Her head emerges above the water, coughing and spluttering. She sees Craig, black against the sea wall and another wave crashes over her head. She fights again, striking out for the wall and this time, miraculously, her fingers close around something, a metal loop, probably for tying up a boat. The rusty iron cuts into her hand but she holds on as the waves buffet her against the rocks. Craig can't see her. The air is still full of smoke and he must be sure that she has gone under.

How long she hangs on she doesn't know. Again and again, the tide pulls her away and then throws her back against the wall. She is freezing, almost delirious with cold. She thinks that hypothermia might get her before Craig does. Maybe she should just let go, take her chances against the waves. Then she hears someone calling her. The voice seems to be coming from a long way off but, at the same time, speaking directly in her head.

'Ruth. Take my hand.'

It is Tatjana. Why she is here Ruth doesn't know. It is all mixed with another day, another fire, the flames of a burning town. Tatjana, a gun in her hand, saying, 'I have to do this, Ruth. Don't stop me.'

Now Tatjana too seems possessed of extraordinary strength. She hauls Ruth's waterlogged body above the water while Ruth herself scrabbles against the sheer stone. Then Ruth is lying face down on the sea wall and Tatjana is still pulling at her. 'Come on, we can't stay here.' Why not? All Ruth wants to do is lie down and sleep, even with the whole North Sea bearing down on top of her.

'Come on, Ruth. We need to get moving.'

Nelson is floating. The waters are dark and rather soothing. They speak to him in his mother's Irish voice. 'It's all right, son. You're safe now.' Then he hears another voice which, oddly enough, belongs to Cathbad.

'Don't give up now, Nelson. Fight it.'

Nelson opens his eyes and the sky explodes in front of him.

Another voice.

'Wake up, boss. We've got work to do.'

Jesus, now he's hallucinating about Clough. He shuts his eyes again and surrenders himself to the tide.

Tatjana is wearing a red jacket and Ruth follows it blindly, running back along the wall until they reach the foot of the cliff. Then Tatjana jumps into the next bay.

'Jump, Ruth.'

Ruth jumps. The water only comes to her knees but the tide is strong, making it difficult to move forwards. Ruth fixes her eyes on the red jacket and struggles to put one foot in front of the other. It reminds her of that day with Trace, trying to cross the beach as the waters rose. But, unlike Trace, Tatjana keeps looking back, encouraging, cajoling. 'Come on, Ruth. You can do it. You have to do it. Kate needs you.' And, every time, that name spurs Ruth onwards. You have to do it. Kate needs you. She keeps going, half walking, half swimming. There's no sign of Craig. In the distance she can see Sea's End House, its flag fluttering gaily. If they can just reach that headland, surely they can call for help.

They are almost at the next wall when he appears, as if from nowhere. Maybe he was hiding in one of the caves. He knows this beach well, Ruth remembers. Now, without speaking a word, he powers towards them through the foaming waves. Ruth screams.

He throws himself at her, knocking her back under the water. She struggles, kicking out. Then she feels him being lifted away from her. Tatjana must be helping her. She can hear screams, shouting, and another noise, a great mechanical whirring, directly above them.

'Leave her alone!'

Ruth wrenches herself free and swims towards the noises, the waves suddenly seem incredibly high. Now, other hands are pulling her up onto the sea wall. Tatjana is next to her, putting her arm round her. Craig is still in the water but, as she watches, people are reaching down to him too. A helicopter circles above them, churning the bay into a whirlpool. Now Judy is there, putting handcuffs onto Craig.

'He tried to kill me,' says Ruth.

'I know,' says Judy. 'I saw.'

'You don't know the half of it.'

The police launch appears beside the wall, bobbing in the choppy water. Judy climbs in with Craig, and Tatjana and Ruth follow, falling clumsily into its bows. Now they are heading back across the cove. People wrap foil blankets round them and try to give them hot drinks but Ruth suddenly feels exhilarated, invincible. She starts to laugh. Judy looks at her in concern.

'It's okay, Ruth. You're safe now.'

But Ruth can't stop laughing, it's all mixed up – joy, fear, exhaustion, and an overwhelming sense of relief that she isn't going to die after all. Not this time.

Tatjana puts her hand on Ruth's arm.

'Ruth. I'm sorry about earlier.'

'That's okay. You saved my life.'

'You saved yourself.'

'How did you get here anyhow?'

'You rang me.'

'I just pressed random buttons,' says Ruth, 'you must have been the last number I called.'

'Well, I thought you sounded like you needed help.'

'Thank you.'

'You should have rung the police,' says Judy, slightly reprovingly. She is sitting beside Craig who is huddled in his blanket, staring into space. Hard to imagine that a few minutes ago he seemed inhuman, a monster possessed of terrible powers.

'I'm used to taking the law into my own hands,' says Tatjana.

She looks at Ruth and smiles.

* * *

When Nelson opens his eyes he is being carried in some sort of hammock. The sky unfurls at a tremendous speed, full of seagulls, black against white. Now he is surrounded by people and light, noises like computer games, the sound of an engine, a siren, fading away into the distance.

'Jesus, boss. I thought you were a goner.'

Nelson focuses his eyes on Clough's face. His sergeant is dripping wet, soot-stained and, unaccountably, smiling.

Another face swims into view – kindly, middle-aged, unknown.

'Just lie back, son. Don't overdo it.'

'Where am I?'

'In an ambulance. On the way to hospital. Don't worry, you'll be fine. We just need to check you over.'

'Where's Cathbad? I thought I heard his voice.'

'He's not here, boss,' says Clough. 'It was just me and Johnson. She went for help and I saw you fall into the water. I had a hell of a time getting you out.'

'This young man saved your life,' says the ambulance man. 'He pulled you out of the sea. By the time we got there, he'd already given you the kiss of life.'

Nelson closes his eyes again. 'Just kill me now,' he says.

It was the end of summer. There were crops in some of the fields but no-one to do the harvesting. Some of the volunteers tried to organise teams to cut the hay but no-one really knew what they were doing and, besides, most of the farms had been burnt to the ground.

The hotel became uncomfortable as the weather got colder. At night the wind whistled through the broken glass and

Ruth shivered in her thin sleeping bag. She knew she would have to go home soon; the academic year was starting and, in a way, she wanted to go back, to sleep in a proper bed, to watch television, to eat something other than rice and beans. But a far stronger part of her wanted to stay. How can they leave when there are still bodies piled high, waiting to be identified? Every week brought news of a new mass grave. Erik was everywhere, riding in an open truck like Che Guevara, a scarf over his mouth to keep out the dust, spurring the volunteers on, arguing with the officials, handing out mugs of stolen wine to his weary troops, praising, encouraging, sympathising. He always had a special word for each of them. When he saw Ruth, his ice-blue eyes would soften and he'd say, 'What would I do without my Ruthie?' And Ruth, cold, exhausted, sickened by the suffering that she saw every day, would glow in the warmth of his approval.

Tatjana grew very quiet as summer turned to autumn. Sometimes Ruth thought that she had given up hope of finding Jacob. But she still cried every night and, when people came from the south, she still questioned them. Only now it seemed as if she did not expect to get any answers.

In late September a small group, including Ruth and Tatjana, travelled to a town near Mostar, the capital of the new Herzegovina. There were rumours of a grave near a large refugee camp. Children from the camp had apparently been found playing with human bones.

It was Ruth's first sight of one of these notorious camps, and as their truck moved slowly though the line of tents, children running excitedly after them, she was relieved that it wasn't as awful as she'd feared. There was order, a Red Cross van handing out food, even some attempts at normal life: a group of boys playing football, women hanging out clothes, children playing in a stream.

Next to her, Tatjana was rigid with tension. When one of the children jumped on the side of the truck, she screamed.

'What's the matter?' asked Ruth.

'Nothing.'

On a hillside to the north of the camp they found their first bones. Heavy rainfall had dislodged the earth and human bones were indeed lying in the open and even floating in the stream that bordered the camp. For three days the archaeologists sorted and catalogued and attempted to identify. This was farmland and there were animal bones mixed in with the human, but all the evidence pointed to a massacre – men, women and children, their bodies thrown into a shallow pit.

As the days went by Tatjana became more and more withdrawn. She worked efficiently enough but in the evenings she sat on her own, wrapped in her coat, apparently deep in thought.

Then, on the fourth day, Ivan, their driver, came bursting into their camp with the news that a group of rebel Serbs were in the area. They had apparently burnt the church and were on their way to the refugee camp. As he spoke they watched the smoke rise up above the trees, a dark cloud in the evening sky.

Ruth remembers that she had never felt more frightened

in her life. She had lived for twenty-five years without ever once experiencing physical danger. She wasn't really one for extreme sports; the nearest she had come to death was probably eating a dodgy kebab from Bilal's All Night Burger Stall. And now, a band of deadly ruffians was on its way – people who would not baulk at the murder of civilians. She remembers that she had actually been sick, dry-retching at the back of the tents, while Erik and the others packed their gear into the truck.

Erik had been calmness itself. Even now Ruth feels a twinge of vicarious pride as she remembers how Erik had insisted on going down to the refugee camp. 'Who knows, our presence there may save lives. We are connected to the International Aid Effort, after all. They can hardly kill us all in cold blood.'

Ivan had clutched his arm, his normally ruddy face white with terror.

'You don't understand, Professor Anderssen. It's . . .' And he said a Serbian name which meant nothing to Ruth.

But it obviously meant something to Tatjana. She stepped forward out of the shadows and started questioning Ivan in Bosnian. Ruth remembers that Ivan had grown more and more desperate as he confronted Tatjana. It was as though whatever he had seen in the burning village was not as terrifying as this small, dark-haired woman.

All night they waited at the camp. Erik told them to make a fire. 'Throughout the ages, it's always been the same. Fire comforts us and it warns our enemies. It is both the flame of the hearth and the white heat of battle.' So they had gathered around Erik's bonfire, as close to the flames as they dared. First it was just the archaeologists then, slowly, the refugees began to join them, so that the circles around the fire expanded like ripples on a pond. Everyone, it seemed, wanted to get close to the hearth that night.

Except Tatjana. Early on, Ruth realised that she was missing but she had been scared to leave Erik and the comfort of the fire. Then, as the night drew on, Ruth knew that she had to find her friend. She went back to the archaeologists' tents on the edge of the hillside and found Tatjana getting into the truck, a petrified Ivan beside her and a gun in her hand.

'Tatjana! What are you doing?'

'Stay out of this, Ruth,' said Tatjana, pale but very calm. 'It's nothing to do with you.'

'What are you doing with that gun? What's happening?'

And, eventually, Tatjana had told her. She had recognised the name of the rebel leader. It was the man who had killed Jacob.

'What are you going to do?'

But she knew.

'I'm going to kill him,' Tatjana had said calmly.

There was that look in her eyes again. That burning intensity, painful to witness.

'I have to do this, Ruth. Don't stop me.'

And so Ruth hadn't stopped her. She hadn't known what to say to her friend – had not been able to find the words of reason, of understanding, of comfort. So she had let

Tatjana go. And when she heard in the morning that the rebel leader was dead, shot while he slept, she had known that she had failed.

She still feels that she failed. But now she understands. She understands only too well.

32

May

Kate must be getting heavier, thinks Ruth. It's been quite a strain to hold her throughout the short service and now, at the end, people seem to want to take endless photographs. Her arms ache as she hoists her daughter higher in her arms.

'Hold her up, Ruth. That's it. Just a bit more. Smile, Kate!'

Ruth's face aches too, as she tries to maintain a sunny, maternal expression. She still doesn't know why she let Nelson talk her into this. Ever since Craig's arrest and his own near-drowning, Nelson has been obsessed with the idea that Kate should be christened in a Catholic church.

'But, Nelson,' Ruth had protested, 'I don't believe in any of that stuff. The body and blood, the saints, life after death.'

'You didn't believe in Cathbad's rubbish either but you still went ahead with the naming day. What's the difference?'

Ruth can think of several differences (she couldn't be accused of holding the naming day ceremony just to get

Kate into a pagan primary school, for example) but, in the end, she gave in. Nelson has been uncharacteristically depressed after the events at Broughton Sea's End. Maybe it was the fact that he hadn't been able to save Ruth or maybe it is just the realisation that he owes his life to Clough, but Nelson has been anxious and ill-at-ease. He rings Ruth several times a day to check on Kate and nags her continually about the baby's welfare.

'I'm doing this on my own, Nelson. We agreed. Remember?'

But, in the end, the deciding factor for Ruth was that, if she made Nelson and Michelle godparents, they could have a formal role in Kate's life. When it comes down to it, she is slightly scared of doing the whole thing on her own. Those terrible moments in the water when she saw not her own life, but Kate's, unfold in front of her, made her realise that it was dangerous for Kate's welfare to depend so entirely on one person. She is not particularly scared of dying but she is terrified of leaving Kate on her own. So she agreed to have Kate baptised into the Catholic Church, only making the stipulation that Father Hennessey should come from Sussex to perform the service. She has also made a will, naming Nelson and Michelle as Kate's guardians in the event of her death. She doesn't feel any qualms about leaving Kate in Michelle's care. She's a good mother and, this way, Kate will be able to be brought up with her half-sisters. Far better than a sterile existence with Ruth's parents in South London.

Nelson explained to Michelle that Ruth had been brought up a Catholic and had decided on the christening 'just to be on the safe side, belt and braces job'. Michelle had accepted this without question. She is spectacularly uninterested in religion and has never questioned Nelson's decision to have their children baptised as Catholics. If you have to be something, why not Catholic? That's her view. At least you can dress girls beautifully for their First Holy Communion.

Michelle herself is dressed beautifully today. She is wearing a pink flowered dress and beaded cardigan. Ruth, in dark trousers and a white shirt, feels distinctly outclassed. At least Cathbad, complete with cloak, evens things up a bit. Ruth decided that it would just be too weird to have only Nelson and Michelle as godparents, so she has asked Cathbad and Shona as well. The more the merrier. And, as Father Hennessey pointed out, three of the four are actually baptised Catholics.

'I'm not exactly a practising Catholic,' said Cathbad, with modest understatement.

'Oh you can never get away from the Catholic church,' smiled Father Hennessey. 'You be a devil worshipper if you like, you'll still be a lapsed Catholic to us.'

Tatjana had called Cathbad a devil worshipper, Ruth remembers. She never worked out whether this was a joke or not. She does know, though, that Tatjana has moved a long way from the Catholicism of her childhood. The night after Tatjana came to Ruth's rescue on the beach, appearing on the sea wall like one of the Norse water spirits so beloved of Erik, they had sat up late into the night, talking. Tatjana told Ruth that, in her quest to come to terms with Jacob's death, she had run the gamut of spirituality.

'I've tried them all – past life regression, séances, Buddhism, Zoroastrianism, I even belonged to some made-up church called The Fellowship of The Fisherman. Rick was very good about it. He wanted us to have our own kids but I couldn't bear to. I didn't want a child. I wanted Jacob. If anything happened to Kate, having another child wouldn't make you forget her, would it?'

'No,' said Ruth, touching wood surreptitiously.

'I wanted to get in touch with my little boy again but, of course, it was impossible. Oh, I had all those so-called mediums saying, "I've got a little boy here asking for his mummy." Complete frauds, the lot of them. Not that I wasn't taken in for a while, but Rick helped me to see what charlatans they were. They pick up on your grief and they feed off it, like vampires. No, the only thing that helped was finally finding his grave. Erik was right about that, you know. We need to see the burial place. It's a fundamental human requirement.'

'So you did find it.'

'Yes. I met this wonderful woman, Eva Klonowski, who runs the International Commission on Missing Persons. She's a forensic archaeologist and she's been in Bosnia since the Nineties. She helped me. They're using all sorts of new technologies there, you know – satellite imagery and spectral analysis – and they're still finding bones all the time. We found a grave that looked like it might be in the right place and from the right time. The bodies had been moved several times but Eva helped me get DNA testing done. They don't fund it, you see, except in special circumstances. The tests proved that it was Jacob and my parents. I buried my parents there, on the hillside, but I had Jacob's bones cremated and I brought them home with me. Do you think that's weird?'

'No.'

'I'm glad, because those ashes are my greatest comfort. I keep them in a casket on my bedside table at home and I've even got some in here.' She touched the gold locket around her neck. 'You understand, don't you?'

Yes, Ruth did understand. She now has an insight into the ferocious world of motherhood. She thought that this was the first time she had spoken to Tatjana, really spoken to her, since the day in the pine forest. She was glad to have her friend back, to have salvaged something from the wreckage of Bosnia. But the next day Tatjana had left to go back to America and Ruth does not know if she will ever see her again.

So, Tatjana is not among the small group gathered in the characterless modern church of St Peter and St Paul. Judy isn't there either; she is on her honeymoon. A week ago, Ruth attended her wedding, an elaborate affair in a far grander church. Judy had looked beautiful, her round-faced prettiness transformed into something quite spectacular. Her colleagues had formed a guard of honour outside the church and there had been the obligatory jokes about stop-and-search, truncheons and handcuffs.

Ruth didn't have much chance to talk to Judy. The reception, in a four-star hotel, was packed and she was stuck with Judy's colleagues from the station. Nelson was there, with Michelle, but he was on a more important table. He looked fed up, fiddling with his tie and glowering at the jokes about the police force. Michelle, of course, looked gorgeous in exactly the right kind of hat.

After the meal there was a disco. Ruth dutifully danced

with the policewomen, who had commandeered the dance floor. She even managed an embarrassed shuffle with Clough (Trace having refused to dance). But as 'YMCA' segued into Kylie, she escaped, looking for some air and a chance to take off her shoes. After trying several doors, all of which seemed to open onto conference rooms, she eventually found French windows leading to a terrace. She had sunk down with relief onto a stone seat but, to her surprise, she wasn't alone. Judy was there, looking out over the landscaped grounds, mysterious in the moonlight.

'Congratulations,' Ruth had said. She felt slightly awkward. What do you say to the bride, after all? And it felt wrong to see her there, by herself, in her big white dress. A bride is meant to be in company, isn't that why she has attendants, to ensure that she is never on her own? 'It's a lovely wedding. I'm sure you and Darren will be very happy together.'

Judy had laughed, rather oddly. Her eyes were glittering and her headdress was askew. 'Are you? I'm not.' And she had gathered up her skirts and gone back to join the conga.

What had Judy meant? Ruth doesn't like to guess. She has had enough uncertainty to last her a lifetime. If Judy, marrying her childhood sweetheart, isn't happy, what hope is there for the rest of them?

Certainly Clara isn't happy. Ruth catches a glimpse of her at the back of the church, pale and pretty in a grey shift dress. Ruth invited Clara to the christening because she seems genuinely fond of Kate. Also, Ruth feels rather bad about having suspected her, even briefly, of the murders. She now sees that Clara is just a rather directionless young woman, a child almost, still mourning her first real love. But she has, at least, been on a few archaeological digs and is, apparently, considering going back to university to study forensic archaeology. Ruth hopes that Clara's subsequent career will be less eventful than her own.

Irene Hastings is dead. She died just as Craig attempted another murder to protect the family name and Nelson fought for his life in the water. Nelson still feels slightly uneasy about the expression that he saw on Stella Hastings' face that afternoon. She had known that her mother-in-law was not going to survive. Had she hastened her death? How much did Irene really know about the murders? She had visited Archie Whitcliffe and Hugh Anselm. She had been close to all the members of the Home Guard, including Craig's grandfather who, apparently, was 'devoted' to her. She had known enough, certainly, to plant hardy annuals in a German officer's helmet. Could Irene have colluded with Craig? Who did the gardening scissors really belong to? And who had warned Craig that Hugh Anselm's troublesome conscience was stirring once more?

But Nelson keeps these doubts to himself. The case is closed and Whitcliffe is satisfied. Craig will be charged with the murders of Archibald Whitcliffe, Hugh Patrick Anselm and Dieter Eckhart. He has made a full confession.

Archie was given a proper military funeral, conducted by Father Tom, and is buried in the graveyard at Broughton. There may still be an enquiry into the deaths of the six German soldiers. Hugh's film, so carefully preserved all those years, has been sent to the CPS but there is a feeling that, as all the people concerned are now dead, there is little point in pursuing the case. The German families seem remarkably lacking in desire for vengeance; all they want are their loved ones' bodies back. As Erik knew, there is a powerful comfort in having a grave to visit. Ruth sent the rosary to the family of Manfred Hahn, in whose hand it had been found. Manfred was, presumably, the man who had cried out to God before he was shot, a prayer heard by the young Hugh Anselm. Manfred Hahn's granddaughter sent Ruth a nice letter saying that they would treasure the rosary forever. Ruth hopes that Hugh would approve of this *entente cordiale.*

So the reputation of Buster Hastings, the 'old devil' who 'fought the good fight', may well survive. But the grandchildren of the men in the Home Guard – Clara, Craig and Whitcliffe – they will remember.

Whitcliffe is buying Maria a flat.

'He says it's what his grandfather would have wanted,' Nelson told Ruth.

'Well, he's probably right. He can't be such a bad bloke after all.'

Nelson has his own suspicions. Could Superintendent Whitcliffe be the father of Maria's little boy? Could this be why Archie left the code in her hands, knowing that it would find its way to the police force and, maybe, unite George's parents in the process? Is this the meaning of the cryptic note in Archie's will? *Gerald, I'm so proud of you and I know you'll do the right thing.* Nelson doesn't know and Whitcliffe isn't telling. But, one way or another, he can't quite summon up his old hatred and contempt for his boss. It's a shame really. He misses it.

Sea's End House is being knocked down. The council has declared it unsafe, and though Jack Hastings is threatening to take the matter to the European Court of Human Rights he actually seems resigned to losing his family home. His mother's death hit him hard and, on the few occasions that Ruth has seen him since, he seemed subdued, shrunken even, a small man once more. He no longer talks about an Englishman's home being his castle and has even mentioned the idea of retiring to Spain. Ruth herself feels a pang for the sinister grey house high on the cliff. She can't forget the night she spent there – the snow falling on the beach, Nelson's face in the candle-light, the clock striking midnight. She still has that odd time-slip feeling; the sense that if, during the course of dinner, she had ventured out of the house, she would have seen not the snow-covered cars and the flashing hazard lights on the coast road, but Captain Hastings and his men taking the sloping path to the beach; seen the boat being rowed ashore, heard the shots in the long-vanished summer house, watched as the shallow grave was dug under the cliff. She thinks too of Tony, Jack's elder brother, the child who watched from the turret window. Tony, dead of cancer in his thirties. Was it this death which haunted Irene Hastings or the deaths of the six men, killed on her husband's orders?

Cathbad wants a picture of himself holding Kate. Ruth hands her over thankfully. Her arms have gone numb. Cathbad holds Kate face outwards, like a football trophy. Ruth has noticed that a lot of men do this. Shona takes his photograph, then has one of herself with Cathbad and the baby. They look like a proper nuclear family, if you ignore Cathbad's cloak. Ruth notices Phil looking distinctly put out. Shona, Ruth knows, would love to have a baby but Phil feels that his years of fatherhood are behind him. She wonders if Shona will be able to persuade him. Certainly Phil is still besotted with her, following her round like a puppy, carrying her hot-pink pashmina like a badge of office.

Cathbad hands Kate back to Ruth. 'What about a picture of you with all the godparents?' he says. 'I'll get Harry and Michelle.'

'It's okay, thanks,' says Ruth. All these photographs are too much for her, though Kate seems to be enjoying them no end. Ruth had wanted a quiet service, no pomp and cere-mony, just a few friends and a drink afterwards. But Nelson has arranged for them all to have lunch at The Phoenix. And, though Father Hennessey has obviously tried to keep things low-key – he isn't wearing robes, for example – there is something somehow grandiose about the ceremony itself, even when pared to the bone.

'Do you reject Satan . . . and all his works . . . and all his empty promises?'

Ruth noticed that Cathbad kept rather quiet when this question was addressed to the godparents. Nelson, though, answered in ringing tones. 'I do.' Just like a wedding.

'Do you believe in God, the Father almighty, creator of heaven and earth? Do you believe in Jesus Christ, his only Son, our Lord, who was born of the Virgin Mary, was crucified, died and was buried, rose from the dead, and is now seated at the right hand of the Father?'

Tricky one, Ruth thought. But Nelson answered up again. 'I do.' Beside him, Michelle and Shona murmured supportively and Cathbad looked enigmatic.

Father Hennessey lit a candle – shades of Cathbad's sacred fire – and gave it to Nelson to hold. Then he had taken the holy water and fairly doused Kate's head in it. Ruth had been amazed; she had been expecting a few polite drops. Kate had been too shocked even to cry. Ruth thought of her parents, who believe in Full Immersion for Adults. They are not here today, for them this ceremony would be no better than the pagan naming day. Worse probably. Pagans can be laughed off as harmless eccentrics. The Holy Catholic Church, the communion of saints, the forgiveness of sins – that's serious stuff.

'Kate Scarlet. I baptise you in the name of the Father, and of the Son and of the Holy Spirit.'

Ruth just hopes that all the spirits are satisfied.

Outside the sunshine is warm on their faces and the trees are full of blossom. Summer is almost here. Kate's first summer. Nelson goes off to organise the cars and Ruth finds herself next to Michelle.

'She was so good,' says Michelle. 'She didn't even cry.'

'She likes all the attention.'

'My two were just the same.'

Michelle stretches out a casual finger and strokes Kate's hair, the little whorl that always goes in the same way, stubbornly against the tide.

'Funny,' says Michelle. 'Harry's got a bit of hair that grows just the same way.'

And, all afternoon, through the lunch and the speeches and the general outpouring of goodwill, Ruth sees Michelle's face and its slowly dawning suspicion.

ACKNOWLEDGEMENTS

Broughton Sea's End is an imaginary place. There is, however, a Lincolnshire town called Moulton Sea's End which is lucky enough to be home to my dear friends John and Colin. I have borrowed part of the name but nothing else. Several towns on the east Norfolk coast are genuinely threatened by coastal erosion, Happisburgh in particular.

The invasion story is also totally fictitious. There were numerous invasion scares during the Second World War and for details of these I am indebted to two books by James Hayward: *The Bodies on the Beach* and *Myths and Legends of the Second World War*. Thanks to BBC 2's *Coast* for the listening post and to Dr Matt Pope who first had the idea about the bodies on the beach.

Thanks to Andrew Maxted and Lucy Sibun for their archaeological expertise. However, I have only followed their advice as far as it suits the plot and any resulting mistakes are mine alone. Thanks to Marjorie Scott-Robinson for the Norfolk background and for the stairlift idea. Thanks to Peter Woodman for sharing his knowledge of classic films and to Becki Walker for her eagle-eyed proof-reading.

Thanks, as always, to my editor Jane Wood and all at Quercus. Thanks to Tim Glister and all at Janklow and Nesbit. Special thanks to Tif Loehnis, without whom the Ruth Galloway books would never have been written.

Love and thanks always to my husband Andrew and to our children, Alex and Juliet.

Elly Griffiths, 2010

Read a chapter from the next
Ruth Galloway novel

A ROOM FULL OF BONES

PROLOGUE

31st October 2009

The coffin is definitely a health and safety hazard. It fills the entrance hall, impeding the view of the stuffed Auk, a map of King's Lynn in the 1800s and a rather dirty oil painting of Lord Allenby Smith, the founder of the museum. The coffin's wooden sides are swollen and rotten and look likely to disgorge their contents in a singularly gruesome manner. Any visitors would find its presence unhelpful, not to say distressing. But today, as on most days, there are no visitors to the Smith Museum. The curator, Neil Topham, stands alone at the far end of the hall looking rather helplessly at the ominous-shaped box on the floor. The two policemen who have carried it this far look disinclined to go further. They stand, sweating and mutinous, under the dusty chandelier donated by Lady Caroline Smith (1884–1960).

'You can't leave it here,' says Neil.

'We were told "take it to the Smith Museum",' says the younger of two men, PC Roy 'Rocky' Taylor.

'But you can't just leave it in the hall,' protests Neil. 'I want it in the Local History Room.'

'Is that upstairs?' asks the older man, Sergeant Tom Henty.

'No.'

'Good because we don't do upstairs. Our union won't allow it.'

Neil doesn't know if they are joking or not. Do policemen have unions? But he stands aside as the two men shoulder their burden again and carry it, watched by myriad glass eyes, through the Natural History Room and into a smaller room decorated with a mural of *Norfolk Through the Ages*. There is a trestle table waiting in the centre of the room and, on this, the policemen lower the coffin.

'It's all yours,' says Taylor, breathing heavily.

'But don't open it, mind,' warns Henty. 'Not until the Big Guns get here.'

'I won't,' says Neil, although he looks with fascination, almost hunger, at the box, whose cracked lid offers a coy glimpse of the horrors within.

'Superintendent Whitcliffe's on his way.'

'Is the boss coming?' asks Taylor. Whitcliffe may be the most senior policeman in Norfolk but, for Taylor and others like him, the boss will always be Detective Inspector Harry Nelson.

'Nah,' says Henty. 'Not his type of thing, is it? There'll be journalists, the works. You know how the boss hates journos.'

'Someone's coming from the university,' puts in Neil. 'Doctor Ruth Galloway, head of Forensic Archaeology. She's going to supervise the opening.'

'I've met her,' says Henty. 'She knows her stuff.'

'It's very exciting,' says Neil. Again he gives the coffin a furtive, almost gloating, look.

'I'll take your word for it,' says Henty. 'Come on, Rocky. Back to work. No peace for the wicked.'

1

DOCTOR RUTH GALLOWAY, head of Forensic Archaeology at the University of North Norfolk, is not thinking about coffins or journalists or even about whether
she will encounter DCI Harry Nelson at the Smith Museum. Instead, she is racing through the King's Lynn
branch of Somerfield wondering whether chocolate
fingers count as bad mothering and how much wine
four mothers and assorted partners can be expected
to drink. Tomorrow is Ruth's daughter's first birthday
and, much against Ruth's better judgement, she has
been persuaded to have a party for her. 'But she won't
remember it,' Ruth wailed to her best friend Shona,
herself five months' pregnant and glowing with impending maternity. 'You will though,' said Shona. 'It'll
be a lovely occasion. Kate's first birthday. Having a
cake, opening her presents, playing with all her little
friends.' 'Kate doesn't play with her friends,' Ruth had
protested. 'She hits them over the head with stickle
bricks mostly.' But she had allowed herself to be convinced. And part of her does think that it will be a
lovely occasion, a rare chance for her to sit back and

watch Kate tearing off wrapping paper and shoving E-numbers in her mouth and think: I haven't done such a bad job of being a mother, after all.

As Ruth races past the soft drinks aisle, she becomes aware, for the first time, that the supermarket has been taken over by the forces of darkness. Broomsticks and cauldrons jostle for shelf space with plastic pumpkins and glow-in-the dark vampire fangs. Bats hang from the ceiling and, as Ruth rounds the last bend, she comes face to face with a life-size figure wearing a witch's cloak and hat and a mask based (rather convincingly, it must be said) on Munch's *The Scream*. Ruth stifles her own scream. Of course, it's Halloween. Kate only just escaped being born on the 31st of October, which, when combined with having a Pagan godfather, might have been one augury too far. Instead, Kate was born on November 1st. All Saints Day, according to a Catholic Priest who, to Ruth's surprise, is almost a friend. Ruth doesn't believe in God or the Devil but, she reflects, as she piles her shopping onto the conveyer belt, it's always useful to have a few saints on your side.

Funny how the Day of the Dead is followed by the Day of the Saints. Or maybe not so funny. What are saints, after all, if not dead people? And Ruth knows to her cost that the path between saint and sinner is not always well-defined. She packs her shopping into her trusty, rusty car. Two o'clock. She has to be at the museum at three so there's not enough time to go home first. She hopes the chocolate fingers won't melt in the boot. Still, the day, though mild for October, is not exactly hot. Ruth is wearing black trousers and a black jacket. She winds a long, green scarf round her neck and hopes for the best. She knows there'll be photographers at the museum but, with any luck, she can hide behind Superintendent Whitcliffe. She'd never normally get to go to an event like this. Her boss, Phil, adores the limelight, so is always first in line for anything involving the press. Two years ago, when *Time Team* came to a nearby Roman dig, Phil muscled his way in front of the cameras while Ruth lurked in a trench. 'It's wasn't fair,' said Shona who, despite being in a relationship with Phil, knows his faults. 'You were the expert, not him.' But Ruth hadn't minded. She hates being the centre of attention; she prefers the research, the backroom stuff, the careful sifting of evidence. Besides, the camera is meant to put ten pounds on you, which Ruth, at nearly thirteen stone, can well do without.

But Phil is away at a conference so it's Ruth who is to be present at the grand opening of the coffin. It's the sort of thing she would normally avoid like the plague. She dislikes appearing in public and she feels distinctly queasy about opening a coffin live on Primetime TV (well *Look East* anyhow). 'Beware of disturbing the dead,' that's what Ruth's old mentor, Erik Anderssen, used to say. Of course, disturbing the dead is an occupational hazard for archaeologists but Ruth always makes sure that, however long-dead the bones, she always treats them with respect. She has excavated war graves in Bosnia, where mass-murder was a recent memory, and she has dug up the bones of a girl who died over two thousand years ago, killed as an offering to some long-forgotten, blood-thirsty god. But she never lets herself forget that she is dealing with people who once lived and were once loved. Ruth doesn't believe in an after-life which, in her opinion, is all the more reason to treat human relics with respect. They are all we have left.

The wooden coffin, believed to be that of Bishop Augustine Smith, was discovered when builders began work on a new supermarket in King's Lynn. The site, though for many years derelict industrial land, had once been a church. The church called, rather romantically, Saint Mary outside the Walls, had been bombed in the war and, in the fifties, was levelled to make way for a fish-canning factory. The factory itself fell into disrepair and now a shiny new supermarket is being built on top. But, because of the site's history, the builders were obliged to call in the field archaeologists who, as was only to be expected, discovered the foundations of a medieval church. What was less expected was the discovery, below what was once the high altar, of a coffin containing the remains, it was thought, of Bishop Augustine himself.

The discovery was newsworthy for several reasons. The church was mentioned in the Doomsday Book and Bishop Augustine himself features prominently in a fourteen-century chronicle kept at Norwich Cathedral.

In fact, Augustine, one of the earliest Bishops, was always supposed to have been buried at the cathedral. What was he doing, then, buried under a fairly minor parish church in King's Lynn? But inscriptions on the coffin and dating of the wood pointed definitely to Bishop Augustine. The next step was carbon dating of the body itself and, somewhere along the line, the decision was made to open the coffin in public—watched by the great and the good, including members of the Smith family.

And that's the other reason. The Smith family are still alive and well and living in Norfolk. Lord Danforth Smith, the current title holder, is a racehorse trainer and unwilling local celebrity. His son, Randolph, more relaxed about being in the public eye, is a regular in the gossip columns, usually to be found draped around an American actress or Russian tennis player. Previous Smiths have been rather more serious minded and evidence of their philanthropy is everywhere in Norfolk. As well as the museum there is the Smith Wing in the hospital and the Smith Art Collection at the castle. Ruth's university even has a Smith Professor of Local History, though he hasn't been seen in public for years and Ruth thinks he may well be dead.

Ruth parks her battered car in front of the museum. The car park round the side is empty. She's early; it's only two-fifteen. Still not enough time to get home and back. She might as well go into the museum and look around. Ruth loves museums, which is just as well because, as an archaeologist, she's done more than her share of looking in dusty glass cases. As a child, though, she remembers going to Hornimans Museum in Forest Hill. It was a magical place, full of masks and stuffed birds. There was even an aquarium of eerie phosphorescent fish. Come to think of it, Hornimans was probably the place where she first got interested in archaeology; they had a collection of flint tools, including some from Grimes Graves in Norfolk. She remembers the shock when she realised that these oddly shaped pieces of stone had actually been *held* by someone who had been alive half-a-million years ago. The idea that you could actually go and dig up something that old, something that had been worked and honed by that mysterious creature known as prehistoric man—that idea still sends a shiver down her spine, and has sustained her through many a long and unsuccessful excavation. There is always the thought that under the next clod of earth there is the object—weathered and unrecognisable except to an expert—that is going to change human thought forever. Ruth has made a few lucky discoveries herself. There is even an Iron Age girl, found on the Saltmarsh near her house, who bears her name. But there is always the thought of the one big find, of the glass case with the inscription 'discovered by Doctor Ruth Galloway', of the articles, the book . . . She pushes open the door.

Hornimans is a small museum but impressive in its way, with a clock tower at the front and glass conservatory at the back. The Smith Museum is something else. It's a low building, squashed between two office blocks. Overhanging gables, painted dull red, make it look as if it's wearing a hat pushing down low upon

its head. The entrance hall, dominated by an oil painting of an angry-looking man in a wig, is empty. There's
a stuffed bird in a glass case, a sepia map and some
photocopied sheets labelled, rather hopefully, 'For
Schools' but no sign that a media event is taking place.
No canapés or glasses of wine (Ruth is sure there was
a mention of food), no press packs, not even a poster
announcing the Grand Opening of the Bishop's Coffin.
Ruth walks through the hall, her feet echoing on the
tiled floor. The next room is lined with glass cabinets,
shimmering in the dim afternoon light. Looking more
closely, Ruth sees case after case of animals, arranged
in some taxidermist's vision of reality. Dusty foxes gaze
into brown-painted holes, squirrels are tied onto tree
trunks, badgers look glassily at moth-eaten rabbits, a
three-legged deer is propped against a papier-mâché
rock. The walls are painted blue to resemble the sky,
with white clouds and flocks of v-shaped birds. Ruth
starts to find the sad, stuffed faces rather oppressive.
She walks quickly through the rest of the gallery into
the hall at the end.

There she has a choice of rooms. Local History or Our
Changing Planet. A slight sound, a kind of whispering
or fluttering, makes her plump for Local History. She
hopes there are no more embalmed animals.

Her wish is granted. The room seems to be empty
apart from a coffin on a trestle table and a dead body
lying beside it. A breeze from an open window is ri-
fling through the pages of a guide book lying on the
floor, making a sound like the wings of a trapped bird.